"*The Invisible War* is at the top of ... m-bines world-class writing with compelling characters, a riveting plot, and brilliant observations about what's happening to our country and the Church. Michael Phillips has a long, prolific writing career and a large, loyal readership. This book may be his capstone. Start reading this book only after you have 'cleared the decks' because you won't want to put it down!"

> — LtCol Oliver L. North USMC (Ret.), best-selling author of more than twenty books. His latest: *American Gulags*

"I started writing novels after several nonfictions because I know the power of storytelling. Michael Phillips has set a new standard of excellence for storytelling with a message. *The Invisible War* is the best novel I've read in a long time because of its execution and prescience. Its blending of past, current, and speculative future events tells a fascinating story about the decline of America's society and its church and points the way out. You will want everyone you care about to read this book!"

> — Jim DeMint, former U.S. Senator, best-selling author, and founder of Conservative Partnership Institute

"Michael Phillips's Tribulation Cult series should come with two warnings. First, do not read it before bed, or you will have a difficult time putting it down! Second, do not read it if you are unwilling to be challenged and have some of your religious dogmas blown to bits. The best fiction helps you see reality clearly, and *The Invisible War* will shake you out of your preconceptions and complacency about the dark days ahead for the United States. After forty years of masterful writing with millions of books sold, no one is better suited to tackle the critical topics of the end times and the American Church than Michael Phillips. Read *The Invisible War*, first book of the series, and dare to ask yourself, what should I do if these are the last days of the United States of America?"

> — Aaress Lawless, Houston, Texas—president of DuoParadigms Public Relations & Design, Inc.

"*The Invisible War* by Michael Phillips captures a clear and profound focus on the past and current world stage, balanced with truth and hope. Starting with actual historical influences in America as seen through a telephotographic biblical worldview, this novel starts in the 1970s with the seeds of the Progressive movement. I was alive then, but I didn't see it. Michael Phillips uses his 20/20 hindsight as he draws his characters through history and to the present day pitting the light against the darkness in that dynamic range. I get it now! Invisible forces have been at work to plan America's takeover, but this book offers that depth-of-field hope that I needed. God is at work! I've read nearly all of the books by Michael Phillips, and this Tribulation Cult series is his masterwork of art. I love, love, love this book!"
— Lora Hattendorf, M.F.A., B.A., Wheaton, Illinois,
Wheaton College, class of '79

"Reading Michael Phillips's latest work was an unforgettable experience. I'm not sure I've ever read a novel quite like *The Invisible War*— the book hasn't left me since I finished an early copy months ago. It reads like the best character-driven, multi-generational historical fiction, and I barely noticed when the book continued telling its prescient story years into the future. I cannot wait to see what happens next to these characters. And yet, I hardly know if these are really fictional characters and events, or if Mr. Phillips somehow has a window into the future of our Western Civilization. We need books like this!"
— Joseph Dindinger, Austin, Texas, Publisher,
Wise Path Books

"Do not begin *The Invisible War* unless you have plenty of time! It is engrossing and time slipped away from me unnoticed. It reads like an action thriller but with eerily familiar themes that drew me into the world of its characters. The style is that of the Michael Phillips beloved by so many readers; the content redolent with significance for those bewildered and dismayed by the way Progressivism has hijacked America's Judeo-Christian values and thereby our entire culture."
— Julia Yacoubian, Atlanta, Georgia

"'How could this decline have happened so quickly?' That question is often pondered within circles of friends and family. Books, articles, and podcasts mention contributing factors and name some specific 'bad actors.' Delving deeper to understand 'but why?,' many things ring true, but it has always seemed preposterous and terrifying to believe there has been an intentional and masterfully orchestrated effort to destroy our country. Yet here we are—with inconceivable, concurrent declines in education, churches, government, business, among friends, and within families. Enter Michael Phillips's exceptional book *The Invisible War*. Starting with the first page, Phillips succinctly provides a chronology and factual evidence for what we now know to be true. Yes, the book is a work of fiction; however, it is a fictionalized account of what we have experienced and can see in the rear-view mirror of our lives. It was, and still is, a skillfully invisible war. Much like the Wizard of Oz, Phillips has pulled back the curtain on the 'bad actors.' In his distinctive writing style, Phillips engages the reader with realistic characters, clarity of storyline, and an imperative call to wake up and ask, 'How far are we willing to go?'"

— Angi Bemiss, Atlanta, Georgia, MBA, CFO (retired), CMP, CTHP

"What a book! *The Invisible War* kept me reading. I could not stop because the plot was wonderful. I needed to know what was next. Tells the story of why we are where we are today. Sure does tell us what has happened in our country and the Church. This is a must-read for all Americans. Be sure you have time to read it. You can't put it down."

— Steven Turner, Indianapolis, Indiana, representatives supervisor, World Renewal International

MICHAEL PHILLIPS

THE INVISIBLE WAR

TRIBULATION CULT BOOK 1: A NOVEL

FIDELIS
PUBLISHING

Fidelis Publishing ®
Winchester, VA • Nashville, TN
www.fidelispublishing.com

ISBN: 9781956454321
ISBN: 9781956454338 (ebook)
The Invisible War: A Novel – Tribulation Cult Book 1
Copyright © 2024 Michael Phillips

Author's Note: This is a work of fiction, futuristic and conjectural. The story spans seventy years of great tumult, conflict, debate, controversy, diversity of opinion, and political upheaval in the United States. There is no intent whatever to malign anyone on either side of the political spectrum, but to capture the often rancorous spirit of division which characterizes the times in which we live. When speaking of living political figures, none of the fictional characters in this book represent the full viewpoints of either the author or publisher. They are intended to fictionally portray the divisive differences of opinion that have existed in our country for some time, opinions which span the spectrum from conservative to liberal. This story is entirely fictional, as is the Alliance and its membership.

Order at www.faithfultext.com for a significant discount. Email info@fidelis publishing.com to inquire about bulk purchase discounts.

Scripture references are from (RSV) Revised Standard Version of the Bible, copyright © 1946, 1952, and 1971 the Division of Christian Education of the National Council of the Churches of Christ in the United States of America. Used by permission. All rights reserved. Or the author's paraphrase.

Author photos by Melanie Bogner, DuoParadigms Public Relations & Design
Cover design by Diana Lawrence
Interior layout design and typesetting by Lisa Parnell
Editing by Amanda Varian

Manufactured in the United States of America

10 9 8 7 6 5 4 3 2 1

FIDELIS
PUBLISHING

Contents

Contents

PART 3—WEAPONS OF DIVINE POWER (2014–2032)

PART 4—STAND STRONG IN TRUTH (2031–2034)

Contents

"First we overlook evil.
Then we permit evil.
Then we legalize evil.
Then we promote evil.
Then we celebrate evil…

Then we persecute those who still call it evil."

—FATHER DWIGHT LONGENECKER

> *Be sober, be watchful. Your adversary the devil prowls around like a roaring lion, seeking some one to devour. Resist him, firm in your faith.*
>
> **1 PETER 5:8–9**

PART 1

A SILENT ROARING LION

1973–2014

1

SEEDS OF CHANGE

1973

OVER THE lawn of the campus quad, faint strains of the Beatles' "Revolution" sounded from some distant open dormitory window. Across the central hub of the campus, where anti-war protests disrupted schedules and emptied classrooms a few short years before, a steady stream of university students, some faculty members, a handful of visitors from the community, and several hundred collegians from around the country, walked toward the Humanities building, where tonight's much anticipated address would be held in the university's largest lecture hall.

Though the turbulent decade of the 1960s gave way to a quieter post–Viet Nam and Watergate era on university campuses, this was California after all. Interest in anything with a whiff of counterculture remained keen. There were few activist protests, sit-ins, and stump speeches these days. The revolution birthed in the sixties abandoned the quad for the classroom. Doing so gave it a more respectable air. *Ideas*, not megaphones nor music, would henceforth represent its arsenal.

Mesmerizing ideas. Powerful ideas. Alluring ideas.

Sinister and toxic ideas.

This evening's lecture had been widely publicized. Dr. Tate Robinson's course, The Social Contract in Changing Times, was one of the most popular offerings of the political science department, usually filled two terms in advance. The hands-on work of what was euphemistically termed "community organizing for change" was intrinsic to its appeal. Dr. Robinson practicalized the protests of the sixties by taking students out into the community, identifying needs of the underprivileged, and devising programs to help them. It was an example of classical liberalism and gospel Christianity at its best—the desire to help those in need.

But Viet Nam and the social revolution of the sixties shifted the ethos of liberalism from helping people to overturning what was vaguely called "the system." American liberalism was in the process of rebirth. The "New Left" as it would later be known would leave the gospel of Christ far behind, except when hijacking aspects of that gospel to suit the Left's agenda. The new movement would not exactly leave the poor behind. Helping those in need, however, would fade as a primary goal. It would become instead a *tool* to advance a new objective—power. The New Left would *use* and *manipulate* the disadvantaged toward that end. Whether they actually *cared* about the poor would be a question future historians would heatedly debate.

With power, a more far-reaching ultimate goal would come into focus—overturning American culture, society, and politics, and changing the nation birthed in 1776 into a country unrecognizable from what it had been for two hundred years.

Dr. Robinson taught the mechanics of effecting change at the local level. The birth pangs of the New Left were coming to life. The social revolution birthed by the musicians and protesters of the previous decade was now being carried into the future within the halls of academia. Underlying the attempt to feed, clothe, and house, Robinson placed equal importance on volunteer political involvement in the campaigns—local, state, and national—of Democrat candidates. The purpose was far more than political. Involving students in the politics of the Democrat party nourished seeds of change that would make the protests of the sixties look like child's play. That Dr. Robinson, a handsome and charismatic figure cut in the mold of Sidney Poitier, was descended from slaves, was Martin Luther King's close friend, and was involved with Charles Hamilton and Stokely Carmichael in the writing of *Black Power*, made him one of the most popular men on the faculty and no doubt contributed to the popularity of his subtly activist course

4

offerings. He and those like him were looking toward something more fundamentally influential than food banks.

This evening's address, however, would not be given by Robinson, but by lecturer, businessman, entrepreneur, and financial wizard, reportedly already a multi-millionaire at the age of thirty-four, Viktor Domokos. That Domokos's antecedents were not widely known, even to his friend, accounted for the brevity of Dr. Robinson's introduction.

Robinson opened the lecture to all comers. Advance notice of the event circulated through the university grapevine as far afield as the East Coast. Fully half of the six hundred now squeezing into the hall hoping to find seats were from colleges and universities stretching coast to coast who flew, trained, bussed, or hitchhiked to California. The evening's lecture would never be so widely known as Woodstock. Its impact in the politics of future decades, however, would be even greater. As Dr. Robinson walked to the podium, two future presidents, two future candidates for the nation's highest office, three future vice presidents, four future senators, and no fewer than a dozen future congressmen, sat before him. It was a confluence of individuals and ideas that would lead to unprecedented shifts in the direction of America's cultural and political destiny.

All that lay in the future. Who could predict the myriad seeds of tactics and strategies planted in the minds of these eager young minds on this day, or the directions the country would move as a result?

2

Rule One

"You have come this evening to listen to me," Domokos began in his characteristic Romanian accent after Dr. Robinson's few remarks. "But I am not the guest of honor. Rather I want to lead you in paying tribute to the man who has been a champion in the cause to which we are committed. It is a cause which unites us in a common brotherhood of purpose and vision. It is the primary cause of humanity. It is a cause of duty. It is a cause of destiny. That cause is change—changing this country into what it can and should be, a country at long last defined by freedom and equality, not only for the few and the privileged, but for all."

Though he had only begun, his words quickly resonated among his listeners. The auditorium broke into raucous applause.

"I speak of my friend, though our friendship was all too brief, Saul Alinsky[1] who sadly died just last year. His name will of course be familiar to you. Dr. Robinson has made sure of that. Though you may be familiar with his work as a community organizer in Chicago, his most significant contribution to the future will surely be his final book, published just shortly before his death last year."

Domokos paused, looked down at his notes on the lectern, and shuffled a few papers. The hall had settled and was quiet.

"I am speaking of Saul's book *Rules for Radicals*," Domokos began again. "The title may at first startle you. But make no mistake—you *are* radicals. Saul was known as a community organizer. That really means that he was an agent for change, committed to helping communities organize in order to press demands on landlords, politicians, and business leaders. But his true objective was much greater. It was to change the entire system which, in his view, kept the poor poor and made the rich richer. His goal was to bring the *Have-Nots*—as he called the disadvantaged—together into grassroots coalitions that would gain them social, legal, economic, and political power. To accomplish this, he advocated any means necessary, including intimidation and confrontation—two pillars in the struggle for social justice.

"Saul taught his followers how to successfully run a movement for change—*any* kind of movement. We here today will eventually start our own movements for justice, for equality, enabling the poor to stand alongside the rich and powerful. Our success will be measured by the extent to which we follow the guidelines Saul set forth. Our calling is to expand those guidelines from local to the national, and eventually, I venture to dream, encompassing the entire globe.

"Saul was a radical and revolutionary no less than Karl Marx. New times are coming. We stand at the threshold of what Marx envisioned but which Russia was too backward and autocratic to bring fully to fruition. We can realize that vision—the vision of true equality for mankind. All of us in this hall who aspire to follow in Saul's footsteps are radicals because our cause is a revolutionary one."

Again the room burst into applause. Domokos did nothing to dissuade the outburst. He recognized the power of emotion to galvanize the young.

It was not only young collegiate radicals who were intrigued by the ideas dominating the evening's agenda. Two swarthy men, one gray and of advanced years, were seated toward the rear of the auditorium, listening intently, though calmly and without applause. Dr. Nasim Bahram, professor of chemistry at the university, was accompanied by his aging father, Husain, who immigrated to the United States from Iran in the late 1940s. No one knew it, but father and son were revolutionaries of bold and controversial ideas, though with a much different master plan in mind than Viktor Domokos or any of his youthful followers would have imagined. Seeing them seated sedately in the audience in their expensive business suits, they appeared every bit as American as baseball, hot dogs, and apple pie. Neither man so much as exchanged a glance as they listened. Nothing would betray their secrets. Centuries of history prepared them for these momentous times.

The centuries also taught them patience. Their day was not yet at hand. But as was clear from this evening's lecture, change was on the horizon for America.

"Saul was a political theorist, it is true," Domokos went on as it settled down. "What he does in his book, however, is give shrewd, sometimes cunning, even devious methods for defeating our enemies.

"Do not be afraid of that word 'enemies.' You have heard me use it a number of times. I do so intentionally. Make no mistake—those who resist the change we will bring, those who cling to the past, those intent on preserving the status quo, they *are* our enemies. They must not merely be defeated. Their outmoded values, perspectives, and spiritual myths must be *destroyed*. Even America's revered Christianity will eventually have to go. We are in a war—nothing less. But we must keep it as an *invisible* war. Our adversaries must not know. They will never realize all that is at stake. That is fundamental to our strategy—the invisibility of our objectives, tactics, and methods.

"What I want to do, therefore, is give you Saul's ten rules for radicals. Imbed them in your minds and hearts. Our enemies will be the future Robert McNamaras and Richard Nixons and Barry Goldwaters. Our enemies may even come in the seemingly bland form of men like Gerald Ford. But they are no less our enemies. Saul recognized that those who hold power, and who resist the agenda of social justice for minorities and the downtrodden, must be removed from power. They are the enemies of change. Their power must be taken from them."

Again he looked down at his notes.

"Let me read it to you exactly so there will be no mistaking Saul's words. He wrote: 'The Prince *was written by Machiavelli for the Haves on how to hold power.* Rules for Radicals *is written for the Have-Nots on how to take it away.*'"

He stopped again to allow the words their full impact.

"Did you hear it clearly? Power must be *taken away*. Our calling, *your* calling, is nothing less than to seize power. But we will not do so with guns like the Bolsheviks. Ours is a quiet, subtle, and invisible revolution. Our ultimate victory will come so gradually that by the time our enemies see it for what it is, it will be too late. The country will be ours."

He paused yet again to let his words sink in.

"Rule Number One," Domokos continued, "is simplicity itself. Again, in Saul's own words—listen carefully: *'Power is not only what you have, but what the enemy thinks you have.'*"

He waited a moment before explaining further.

"This is not as innocuous as it may seem. The strategy here underlies everything that follows. Note the strategic deception of Saul's genius. We must conquer the majority with a *minority*. If you have ten followers and the enemy has a hundred, you must make him *think* you have a hundred-ten. That is the secret of forcing him to concede to your demands.

"Let me give you an example," he went on, "with apologies to whatever faculty may be present this evening. Say you want to force your university administration to make a certain change in policy, but you only have the backing of 10 percent of the student body. By circulating petitions and making noise, creating a hubbub, and holding demonstrations, conducting interviews, and in all these ways drawing attention to yourselves, keeping you and your agenda in the spotlight, and with some judicious stretching of the truth, it should not be difficult to convince the administration that you have 65 percent of the student body behind you. You make noise enough for 65 percent. You set the narrative and drive it home at every opportunity.

"In other words, you *pretend* the whole school is behind you. It doesn't matter if that narrative is *true*. What matters is the storyline you want people to believe that will further your objectives. You set your narrative, then you force it upon your opponents by deception. It is cunningly effective.

"By inflating the perception of your power, you make the administration think that to refuse your demands will result in wholesale protests and walk-outs. The enemy—in this case the university admin-istration—is ruled by fear of whatever might upset the status quo."

Some laughter and a general buzz of approval spread through the room. By now everyone was on the edge of their seats.

"Your weapon against the administration is the perception. It is the threat of widespread chaos. It doesn't matter, with only 10 percent of students behind you, that there *won't* be protests and unrest. It's the threat of them that is your potent weapon.

"Notice another factor you have working for you. It is not only the administration in a sense that you are trying to deceive. You will also make use of the gullible and largely apathetic other 90 percent of the student body. By drawing them unknowingly into your deception and convincing them that most of their fellow students are behind you, they *will* actually join in, albeit passively. They will want to be seen as 'in' with what the majority wants. No one wants to be seen as out of step with what is perceived as right, correct, and generally acceptable. So they will go along with you too.

"The groupthink conformity of the masses thus becomes an equally powerful tool. The inflation of your power resulting from the narrative you set works in two directions—it changes the perceptions of those in power *and* the masses. In the end, you may indeed have your 65 percent."

Laughter now accompanied the applause that broke out. Domokos's audience was eating it up.

"The practicality of Rule One is obvious. If you want to gain rights for minorities, you have to turn that minority into a perceived major-ity. Again, *you* control the storyline. You do so based not on actual facts, but what you want people to believe. You have to convince the enemy that the majority is with you. Nixon called his followers the silent majority. He was right. They are silent. So we co-opt their silence for *our* cause. That is precisely what I spoke of before—convincing not only your enemies but the gullible masses that the momentum of your cause in on your side.

"It's the classic high school gambit—people want to be part of the 'in crowd.' So *you* decide what's *in*. You can make anything in if people believe it. You could turn science nerds into the in crowd instead of the athletes and pretty girls. That might take a little doing!" he added laughing. "But with the right strategies, anything is possible. Think of the most outlandish personal behavior you can imagine. Within a generation you could brainwash the public not only into thinking it normal, you could probably turn what is repulsive today into admired behavior thirty years from now.

"You can make people believe *anything*...if they think everyone else is behind it. It is the emperor strategy. It doesn't matter whether or not he's wearing clothes, as long as people are convinced everyone else thinks he is. It becomes 'in' to believe it because everyone else believes it. Remarkable as it seems, if you make people think the majority believes in a complete lie, they will join and endorse the lie.

"I stand here tonight and tell you something you will have a hard time believing. We will elect a black man president of the United States one day. This is how we will do it. By the clever deception of Saul's Rule Number One. Do you see the genius of perception over truth? Power is not only what you have—the truth—but what the enemy *thinks* you have—the perception."

Again, a buzz of astonishment and approval rippled through the hall.

"The applications of this principle are limitless. Our goal is not merely to change the political structure of the country, ours is a social, cultural, and spiritual revolution. To accomplish our goals, many social stigmas and religious myths have to be overturned. Think of the social stigmas pervading our society. Not all stigmas are racial. Some are quite innocuous and are spoken of freely, even joked about. Baldness, for example. Others may be looked at a little askance, like a man with a tattoo, but are not really serious taboos. Still others are serious taboos and are never mentioned—like homosexuality. We have to eliminate not only racial prejudice, but also many other stigmas so that everyone can live productive and happy lives without being judged by society or by the false standards of right and wrong of an outdated Christian worldview.

"Let me give you a foolish example, but one which demonstrates the power of the principle of perception. Let's say for certain reasons we decide to set the narrative that it is not unusual to be left-handed, in fact that half the population is *really* left-handed, and that it is *good* to be left-handed. Rather than it being a minority phenomenon, we set the storyline, that it is 'in' to be left-handed. We encourage everyone to come out in the open and admit their left-handedness freely and with pride. We could up the ante by adding to the narrative that left-handed people are inherently smarter than their right-handed counterparts. Within a generation or two, we would have eliminated the stigma some children feel about being 'different' because they're left-handed. Hundreds of thousands of people would pretend to be left-handed. They would force an untruth upon themselves because they think it's *in*.

"Or another foolish example. What if we set the narrative that baldness is actually cool, and hair loss is a genetic indicator of intelligence. We bring out statistics to support our narrative that prematurely bald men are inherently smarter than those with full heads of hair. The statistics don't matter. People don't check them. You make up your own study, give it a fancy scientific name, and then quote the statistics supporting your narrative. You say, 'science proves it' in many different ways, with experts who document what you tell them to say, until people are convinced that the facts are irrefutable. Remember, people will believe anything if you convince them the majority of people believe it. The result will be that men will start shaving their heads because they think it's cool. They will want people to think they are among the elite, the super-intelligent. They will *want* to be bald rather than trying to hide it.

"We could accomplish the same thing with tattoos or homosexuality or anything. Within a generation we could convince the majority of the country that bald, left-handed, tattooed, homosexual men are the norm, and are smarter than the rest of the population. We turn them into an elite class instead of a minority. We would see people pretending to be bald, left-handed homosexuals, and covering their bodies with tattoos. We would bring in many statistics and studies to validate our narrative. The news media would report our scientific studies as fact. Our conclusions would find their way into schools. Children would be taught to rejoice in their left-handedness. Teachers would be told to teach children whose parents have forced them to be right-handed to listen to their feelings, and to embrace their left-handedness, not suppress it. Before you know it, eighth grade boys would be shaving their heads and getting tattoos and the right-handers among them would be awkwardly trying to throw left-handed. It sounds too silly to believe. But the emperor strategy is powerful. We could easily turn these stigmas into accepted norms. The masses don't ask what is good or right or true, they only look at what everyone else thinks, then go along. Groupthink is a powerful weapon.

"The principle will work with anything. A gullible population can be made to believe that anything is normal and in. It all depends on controlling the storyline you feed the public."

A smile spread over Domokos's face.

"I once said to Saul, 'So you're saying that the ends justify the means?'

"He looked at me seriously, then grinned a sly grin. 'Of course the ends justify the means,' he said. 'If we play by the rules of etiquette, we'll never get anywhere. Ethics are for do-gooders and fools, not radicals. Most Republicans are fairly decent individuals—straightforward and honest. They have ethical scruples. I don't. If it takes duplicity to reach my goals, so be it. Our objectives are what matter, not how we achieve them.'"

Laughter spread through the room.

"I hope the point is not lost on you. We achieve our goals by making the enemy, as well as the masses, think we are more powerful than we really are. We convince them the facts are on our side, science, truth, and majority public support are behind us. We never admit that our narrative is based on a mirage."

"Archimedes famously said, 'Give me a place to stand and I will move the world.' His actual words were, 'Give me a lever long enough and a fulcrum on which to place it, and I shall move the world.' We, too, can move the world. Our lever is the agenda we establish. Our fulcrum is the gullibility of the masses.

"That in essence is Rule One. Think bald, tattooed, left-handed, homosexual men and you will never forget it. People do not think for themselves. They are conformists. These facts are our greatest weapon. Set the narrative, bring out facts and figures in support of it even if you have to make them up, make people believe it whether it is true or not, keep your strategies secret, and you can lead them as easily as if you have rings in their noses.

"Now, for Saul's Rule Number Two . . ."

Domokos continued for an hour and a half. As his summary of Alinsky's methodology wound down, he successfully energized a small army of future progressives who would devote their lives to his cause.

"In conclusion, then," he said, "it is up to us to take Saul's ideas into the future, even the next millennium, and transform, not merely this country but all of Western civilization, and deliver it from the shackles of its white Christian past. The bigoted standards of race, color, creed, social standing, sex, religion, intolerance, and national origin that constituted the long growing tree of white patriarchal privilege must be torn up by the roots and cast into the fire of revolutionary change. Thus, will we make way for a future of liberty and equality, not for some, but for all. *We* are the legacy. The future is in our hands."

The applause that thundered through the auditorium for several minutes at the conclusion of Domokos's inspiring words was deafening.

3

THE INCIDENT

IT WAS after 1:30 a.m. when two youths in their early twenties walked toward their apartment building. Still talking enthusiastically about the lecture, they were too keyed up to sleep. It was good this was Friday night. There were no classes tomorrow.

They rarely allowed themselves to be out together. They usually traveled by city bus and never at the same time. Even in a college town there were some secrets that had to be kept secret.

But they had been unable to tear themselves away earlier. By the time the lecture finally broke up, the buses had stopped running. They had no choice but to walk the mile and a half home. They should have split up and gone separately. But they were too excited about what they heard and set out not thinking of the consequences. The streets were deserted anyway. No one would see them.

Approaching the four-story complex where they shared an apartment, they saw two men, both black, hanging about, obviously older than students. They were just standing. Waiting. It was too late for people to be out. It was obvious they were up to no good.

The boys stopped, glanced at each other, then turned and began slowly retracing their steps, doing their best to remain calm. The worst thing they could do was panic.

But they had been seen.

A deep voice shouted behind them, then came heavy running steps.

They broke into a trot, reached the nearest intersection, and split up.

"Get back here, you queers!" came another shout. "You can't get away—we're not alone! Your kind aren't welcome here!"

The young men sprinted in opposite directions, one toward the university the other toward town. Their pursuers also split and followed.

A minute later gunfire exploded through the stillness of the night. Two shots. Then a third.

By the time sirens came screaming from the city in the direction of the campus, the streets were deserted.

4

You Do Something

POLICE RESPONDING to reports of gunfire near the university at approximately 1:45 on the morning of the 13th found nothing. They crisscrossed and grid-searched every street in both directions in a one-mile radius for the next two hours. Still nothing.

An early morning jogger on the beach, horrified by the sight as he approached the pier, turned and sprinted for the nearest beachfront house, woke up its residents, who called 911. With assistance from the coroner, police were able to reconstruct the most plausible theory of what must have happened.

Both young men, students at the university, had been shot—one in the back, who, according to the coroner, died more or less instantly, the other in the thigh which sent him to the ground and allowed his pursuer to catch him. Both were apparently driven the five miles to the wharf, ropes tied around their necks, and strung up under the pier from its supporting beams. The one was already dead. His wounded friend was left to hang alongside him.

The southern-style lynching exploded throughout the national news and headlined the newscasts of all three networks that evening. Nothing like it had been heard of in years, not since the Civil Rights Act of 1964, and certainly not in liberal California. The country was stunned.

The police had no leads. The FBI was called in. Dried blood was eventually found at the site of the two shootings several blocks apart, matching that of the victims. Still no substantive leads pointed to potential suspects. After four days, the trail was cold.

The university campus and the entire coastal city remained in shock, mourning, and outrage. Many editorials, impromptu lectures, and stump speeches condemned violence, hatred, and prejudice. That the monstrous crime was racially motivated was taken as fact. Gruesome photos were shown alongside old tintypes of blacks and former slaves of a century before. But the pent-up frustration could find no outlet, no suspects, no neo-Nazis or white militia group, no isolated West Coast version of the KKK, upon which to vent its rage.

When it became known that Vestar Carns and Styles Buckley—students in Dr. Robinson's Social Contract course—had attended the lecture prior to their murder, Domokos wrote a lengthy op-ed for the *New York Times*, using the opportunity to rail against the prejudicial ineptitude of the all-white police department in bringing the criminals—assumed white—to justice. His rant continued against all the usual suspects, calling on free-thinking men and women everywhere who believed in equality to rise in protest against a system in which blacks and other minorities could find no justice A few sporadic episodes of violence and looting broke out in L.A. but were quickly extinguished. Several civil rights activists called for nationwide riots. Fortunately, they did not materialize.

Discussions in Dr. Robinson's class were vigorous and intense as time dragged on. Interest in their former community projects evaporated. His students were focused on only one thing—bringing the murderers to justice. Robinson found it a challenge to channel their rage into constructive avenues. Food banks, clothing drives, and petitioning the city for low-cost housing seemed tame. The campus was on edge. People in town were afraid to go out. The hotheads among Robinson's small band of activists wanted blood.

In the middle of a heated class discussion, one of the acknowledged leaders in student causes, university graduate, and law student Slayton Bardolf burst out with the same thought asked a hundred times before, "Why doesn't somebody *do* something!"

The hall fell silent. Everyone shared his frustration.

Dr. Robinson waited a few seconds, then replied.

"Who is somebody?" he said.

"I don't know," replied Bardolf, "—anyone."

"Fair enough, Mr. Bardolf. Then why don't *you* do something?"

"Me?"

"You're somebody, aren't you? You're a law student. You're active in student affairs. You don't like what's being done. Then do something about it."

Again, the hall was quiet. By now all the heads had turned toward young Bardolf.

"Think back for a minute. What is this course about?" Dr. Robinson began again. "Think about what Mr. Domokos said three weeks ago. Think about the legacy of Saul Alinsky."

He waited a few seconds.

"The common thread is that this country is in trouble. It needs changing. White racism is still with us. Our justice system is corrupt. There is no justice for minorities. That is your frustration. I feel it too. Where is the justice for Vestar and Styles?"

Again he paused.

"All right, Mr. Bardolf—put your money where your mouth is. The rest of you too. You want to bring change to this country. You want to end discrimination. You heard what Mr. Domokos said—we are the legacy. The future is up to us. You have all been active in community projects. I am going to suggest we change our focus. We will follow Mr. Bardolf's lead. We will *do* something. Let's go out and knock on doors and ask questions. Let's become radicals for Vestar and Styles."

By now the room was in a tumult of excitement.

"All of you who can, we will meet at the quad on Saturday," said Robinson above the din. "We will start from the apartment building where Vestar and Styles lived. We will ask every person in that complex if they know anything, or even suspect anything. Then we will fan out from there and continue knocking on doors and asking questions. Someone had to have seen something. We need to find them."

The class broke up a few minutes later, everyone in a clamorous rush to take on the world.

5

How Far Are You Willing to Go?

SLAYTON BARDOLF had been thinking about Dr. Robinson's challenge. He didn't want to wait until Saturday.

He had taken detailed notes of the Domokos lecture, and, after typing them up and adding to them, he even astonished himself. Reading over his final copy was like listening to the lecture again word for word.

Within two days, he was so familiar with Domokos's practical summary of Alinsky's strategies, he was eager to try them out. The tactics were extraordinary. What better way to put them to work than to find out who had murdered Vestar Carns and Styles Buckley?

At the meeting of his law study group three nights later, he brought up the idea of getting more directly involved. Two of the three others were also in Dr. Robinson's Social Contract class. The fourth knew Styles Buckley personally. It was not hard to convince them.

"We're going to face these kinds of situations later in our law practices," said Bardolf. "Why don't we take this on as a pro-bono case?"

"How do you mean, take it on?" asked Devon Crawford.

"Investigate it—see if we can find out what happened?"

"More like detectives than lawyers?"

"Maybe. But lawyers investigate too. Vestar and Styles will be our first clients. Let's pin their murder on somebody."

"Don't you mean find out who did it?" said Crawford.

"Maybe you're right," replied Bardolf thoughtfully. "Slip of the tongue. Although . . ."

He paused.

"Remember what Domokos said about perception? We have to pick our target and go after them. We shake the tree and see what falls. Facts are not as important as shaking the tree. Remember what he said—you make up the facts to support your narrative."

"He didn't say exactly that," said another of the group, Miles Garrick.

"Close enough," rejoined Bardolf. "It's what he meant. If we think we've found something, we turn public opinion in the direction we want. That might force the police to take action."

"Dr. Barnum would kill us if he heard us talking like that," said the fourth member of the group, Oscar Silsby. "He'd boot us out of the program. You know what he says about amateurs trying to be lawyers. Especially if our target is the police. He'd call it vigilantism."

"Oscar's right, Slayton," said Crawford. "Dr. Barnum's brother is the police chief. And Dr. Barnum's a bigwig at some church in town. They're not the kind of people we want to antagonize."

"Maybe," nodded Bardolf. "But both Barnums are part of the system we need to bring down."

"We need him to get our degrees before we start talking about bringing any system down," objected Oscar. "I won't do much good as a civil rights attorney if I get my butt kicked out of law school."

"I'm not suggesting jeopardizing our futures. Of course, we'll have to be careful."

"And secretive," added Garrick. "No one can know."

"Are we pledged together on that?" said Bardolf. "What we talk about stays in this room. No one can ever know. It's an invisible war, like Domokos said."

"*Sic me Deus adiuvet*," said Garrick.

"Are you kidding!" laughed Bardolf. "*So help me God!*"

"I only meant it as a figure of speech," said Miles.

"I know. But if we're going to pledge our silence, let's at least pledge loyalty to something we can believe in. I *don't* believe in God. God is part of the problem. *Mors Deo* is more like it."

The other three shuddered.

"Death to God!" exclaimed Oscar. "Dang, Slayton, lighten up!"

"Christians and their myths," Bardolf went on undeterred. "They're the ones who perpetrated slavery in the first place. You of all people ought to know that, Oscar. Christianity is part of the system that needs to be torn down—uprooted and thrown in the fire just like Domokos said. White racism has its roots in Christianity. It's got to be put to death."

"What are you trying to do, get us all sent to hell!"

Bardolf laughed. "Don't be absurd, Oscar. That's too ridiculous for words. Why are you so on edge tonight?"

"I'm not on edge. I just don't wanna mess around talking like that about God."

"There is no God. It's no different than saying Death to Santa Claus."

"Well, I believe in God."

"And Santa Claus too?"

"Give him a break, Slayton," chided Garrick. "Lots of people believe in God. That's hardly the same as Santa Claus."

"And you?"

"What—Santa Claus or God?"

"You know what I mean."

"I might believe in God," replied Garrick. "I don't know—haven't made my mind up yet."

"Come on, man," insisted Bardolf, "none of you can tell me you *really* believe in hell or rising from the dead or walking on water or a virgin getting pregnant. It's all nonsense."

"I don't know about hell," replied Oscar. "But I believe in God and that Jesus rose from the dead. You can't be a Christian if you don't at least believe that."

"America's God is at the root of the problem of our whole culture," Bardolf continued, refusing to let up. "I can't believe you don't see it.

If America is to be transformed, its God has to go, along with bigotry, white privilege, and injustice. God *and* the rich white fat cats running everything. How about *Mors Deo homini albo*—Death to the white man's God. Is that better?"

"Look man," said Oscar, "I'm black and I'm all for social justice and getting back at the man, you know. That's why I'm studying law. But I'm a Baptist. I don't want no part of death to *nobody's* God. That's blasphemy, man."

"We've all got to decide how far we're willing to go. Are we serious or not?"

"Well, I'm not willing to go *that* far. I'm not about to get involved in anything that'll send God or some white racist lunatic after me. We go poking around in Vestar's business or Styles's, they're just as likely to come after me next. I ain't about to get myself lynched! No way, man!"

"What about you, Devon?" asked Slayton.

"I'm Catholic."

"Do you believe all that stuff?"

"No. You ever seen a black pope? You ever seen a poor pope? Heck no—it's all a crock. My folks made me get confirmed is all. But I don't go no more. Just fat rich white cats, like you said—though I suppose that's my dad too. But still I got no use for it."

It was quiet a minute. The mood was broken. Oscar Silsby was shaken by Bardolf's anti-God rant. He said nothing more. He was agitated and anxious to leave. Bardolf realized he may have gone too far.

"Ah well, it's getting late," he said, rising. "We're not going to settle anything tonight."

6

THE PLEDGE

WHEN SLAYTON Bardolf closed the door to his room the next night and turned back inside, he was looking at only Miles Garrick and Devon Crawford.

"Oscar coming?" asked Garrick.

Bardolf shook his head. "I didn't say anything to him. He was obviously uncomfortable last night. He had cold feet. If we're going to do this, there can be no doubts. From now on this is off the books."

"What about study group?"

"Study group will continue like always. We just won't mention anything about this. Secrecy is our motto from here on. It's just the three of us."

He paused and looked at the two others.

"Are you with me?" he added.

Miles and Devon nodded.

"What we do and say will remain between us, and whomever else we may bring in. Agreed?"

"Agreed."

"I'm in."

Bardolf extended his hand. One by one the other two clasped it.

"To justice, to change, to Alinsky's invisible radicalism!" he said.

"Hear, hear!!" said Garrick.

"And justice for Vestar and Styles."

"You know there's someone else I know," said Crawford, "a guy named Roswell—Talon Roswell, a real gung-ho activist sort."

"Scary name!" laughed Miles. "Though I guess he can't help that!"

"He was nearly arrested the night after the hanging."

"For what?"

"Smashing store windows downtown," replied Crawford, "trying to start a riot."

"Sounds like my kind of guy!" laughed Bardolf.

"What happened?" asked Garrick.

"He split when he heard the sirens. He'd love this."

"Sounds like he might be *too* gung-ho," said Miles.

"He's not really like that. We can trust him."

"I don't know him. Is he pre-law?" asked Bardolf.

"No, Poly Sci—a senior. But he's bright. He knows stuff. His dad's in local politics."

"I'm not sure I like the sound of that," said Bardolf. "We don't want anybody who's part of the establishment."

"No, he's okay. His dad's one of the good guys—marched with King in Selma, led anti-war protests at UCLA. He's involved like Alinsky was in Chicago, trying to stir things up—work toward change and all that. The city council puts up with him because they think it's good for their image. That's what Talon says."

"How so?"

"You know, the ex-hippie they pretend to respect. It's a sham, but at least he's got a foot in the door. Even Alinsky had to start somewhere. The Roswell family's loaded too. We might need financial backing for something."

"An ex-hippie with money?"

"Talon's grandfather was some kind of financial tycoon. He's got a big estate in the hills down by Ojai or somewhere. Talon's dad was raised there, went to college, and became a rich hippie protesting the same system that made his family rich."

"An ironic twist!" laughed Garrick.

"Can this Roswell keep his mouth shut?" asked Bardolf.

"I don't know. I think so if we explain the situation. Everybody loves being in on a secret."

"Nobody can know about this," said Bardolf seriously. "If we take on the man, we've got to remember what Domokos said about secrecy. There will be others who will want in on it. Everyone's angry. We'll have to be cautious about that," said Bardolf. "Anyway, bring your pal Roswell tomorrow. We won't give too much away. Let's see how it goes."

"In your room again?"

Bardolf thought a few seconds.

"Now that I think about it, let's wait a couple days. We should meet in some neutral place so there's no connection to us. We need to give the impression we're part of something important, something bigger than just three of us. Rule Number One—the illusion of 65 percent."

The other two nodded.

"I'll find some empty classroom or study hall," Bardolf went on. "I'll bring some candles and we'll keep the lights off. We'll create a spooky atmosphere. We'll say we're part of . . . what . . . a secret group or something . . ."

"A society . . ."

"Society for justice."

"Pretty tame-sounding. It has to feel important."

"A club, society, guild?"

"We could start a new fraternity?"

"Couldn't be official. Frats have to register with the school. This has to be invisible."

"The justice institute, the league for freedom . . ."

"Those are too anti-establishment buzz words. They'd give us away. The Republicans call you a communist when you talk about freedom and justice and rights and the poor. The name has to disguise what we're about."

"Everybody loves a secret club. When I was a kid, the neighbor boys and I called ourselves the Spy Rock Gang," said Garrick.

"Cool name!" laughed Crawford.

"I've got it!" exclaimed Bardolf. "An *alliance*. All that means is a group or a club. Nothing suspicious about that. The Alliance for Progress."

"I like it!" said Crawford.

"We also need a slogan, a motto."

"What about what you said before, Slayton—*Mors Deo homini albo*."

"We don't want to freak anyone else out like we did Oscar. It's not just the white man's God, but the God that has emerged out of white tradition and power—the whiteness God—the God of whiteness—the white God."

He paused, then smiled. "*The white God must die* sums it up nicely," he said. "Christianity and white power, together, are the enemies of change."

"Not everyone will see it that way," said Garrick.

"They can join some other group. If we're serious about changing things, then let's not play games. Though we'd better keep the slogan to ourselves."

Again, Bardolf extended his hand and the other two grasped it.

"To the Alliance," he said.

"The Alliance," said Crawford and Garrick.

"Deus albus est mori," Bardolf added. "The white God must die."

"*Deus albus est mori*," all three repeated together, their voices soft.

With youth's love of the conspiratorial, a secret order was birthed in that moment. None of the three had any inkling of what they had done, how dangerous was such a vow against their Creator, or where it would lead.

But it would grow.

Secret whispered oaths possess seductive allure. The fruit of the tree of the knowledge of good and evil comes in many flavors.

7

THE ALLIANCE

THE FIRST meeting of the unofficial Alliance for Progress, begun in Slayton Bardolf's apartment, was held four days later in a small study room Slayton discovered unlocked while snooping in the science building.

The three charter members snuck in at ten minutes before 3:00 in the morning to set up a few candles and other paraphernalia, including an incense censer to deepen the air of mystery. Between the three, they invited four others—each thoroughly investigated and cleverly questioned to make sure no more cold-footed Oscars were among them. All four had attended the Domokos lecture. The invitations were enigmatic and inscrutable, with heavy injunctions to absolute secrecy. If word leaked, the suspected party would never be granted an invitation again.

Love of intrigue, a hint of danger, and above all a secret shared by a privileged few, turned them all into boys again. Their hearts beat faster as each made his way alone, taking care not to be seen, through the deserted campus. It was the same feeling they might have had sneaking out of a bedroom window to join a few friends breaking into the deserted house of the neighborhood. Boys would be boys.

But these boys were young men. The stakes were higher. They were capable of far more than harmless mischief. Far-reaching consequences would result from what they began on this night.

As the four invited guests arrived one by one, they found their three hosts, though they did not know them as such, seated silently in the candle-lit and incense-heavy darkness in a circle comprised of seven chairs. They could not help their flesh creeping briefly from the eeriness of it. They took chairs in their turn and remained silent.

When all seven were present, they waited another two minutes. At last Slayton Bardolf spoke.

"We have been authorized," he began, "on behalf of others in the movement committed to progress and change, to privately investigate the hangings of our brothers Vestar Carns and Styles Buckley. It is our commission to bring their murderers to justice."

He paused to allow silence to descend again.

"Who are these others, you ask?" he said after a few moments. "What is the movement? It is an alliance for progress. We share a vision for the future of this country of justice, freedom, and the rights of all, not only a privileged few. Our leaders are Saul Alinsky and Viktor Domokos and men like them. With the ideas of such visionaries before us, we are bound in an invisible brotherhood. It is an alliance that will lead the world into a bright future. With our leaders we are committed to the end of rule by our nation's plantation owners in their board-rooms and their *White* House that keep the lower classes in their place. We are committed to end the worship of their all-white God. The traditions and beliefs of this antiquated ruling class are vestiges of a racist history that must be overturned to make way for the future."

He paused once more. The conspiratorial aura deepened.

"To accomplish these ends, we must work as one," he went on. "Together we vow absolute secrecy. Nothing spoken in this room must ever leave it. We are allies in a cause. We must remain allies and never betray our allegiance to one another. Do you so vow?"

"We vow it," said Miles Garrick and Devon Crawford together.

"Do you all vow it?" repeated Bardolf.

"*We vow it!*" all seven chanted in unison.

"Then we are bound in secrecy by the oath of the Alliance. Do you bind yourselves in secrecy?"

"*We bind ourselves in secrecy!*" came seven voices together.

"Then the time has come to pool our resources, our insights, and our collective knowledge," said Bardolf, "to get to the bottom of this crime which the police force and FBI do not want to solve. I think we can agree on why that is."

"It is obvious that the hangings were racially motivated," said Miles Garrick.

"Of course," assented Bardolf. "It explains the police cover-up."

He glanced around the group, trying to convey that, in spite of his mysterious opening remarks, he was now inviting discussion.

"What about Styles, then?" asked one of the newcomers, Tyson Page. "Why him?"

"Because he was Vestar's roommate," replied Miles. "That's how racists think. They hated Styles even though he was white, just for being the friend of a black."

"Who would target Vestar?" asked another, Nab Kerr. "He was as soft spoken a black kid as you could meet."

"A racist white bigot, is who would target him," said Joe Jakes, himself black. "I've been beat up more times than I can remember for no reason. Their kind don't need a reason. They just hate us."

"I still don't see white guys lynching Styles," said Devon's friend Talon Roswell, speaking for the first time.

"You knew Styles, didn't you, Devon?" said Bardolf. "You know anything else that could explain it?"

Crawford looked down at the floor without answering.

"What is it?" asked Bardolf.

"Well, there was talk," said Crawford slowly.

"What kind of talk?"

"That he was, well . . . you know, different."

"I heard it too," said Kerr. "There's guys that say Styles was a homo. I don't know if it's true. I'm just saying I heard a rumor."

"Whoa—I thought he and Vestar were just roommates!" said Page. "I live in that same building. But I've never, you know, seen anything."

"If it was true, that would definitely change things," said Miles. "Black and white homos living together! Whites would hate that."

"They'd be targets not only against us," said Jakes, "you know, blacks like me and Vestar, but, like you say, the other thing. Those kind of racist pigs—they'd want to kill them both."

"And make a public display of it too," added Kerr. "Their kind hate homos as much as blacks."

"That would totally explain it," said Bardolf. "Gentlemen, I think we've found our motive!"

"There's that Christian frat house," continued Nab Kerr. "Alpha Omega, it's called."

"What about it?" asked Roswell.

"I went to a gig there last year. Girl I was going with invited me— Bible study, they called it. They got off on homosexuals and the Bible. They were reading a letter a guy wrote to some city—seems like it might have been Rome."

"What about it?" asked Devon.

"The guy leading the thing read from that letter and then it got really heavy. It was a pretty freaky scene—talking about sin and homos and prostitutes and murderers, and that they would all go to hell if they didn't repent and get saved."

"They think it's a sin?"

"Oh, yeah they do. Homos and murderers—they're all the same to those bigots. I never went back. That place is a bad scene. Long hairs and street people everywhere—whacked-out ex-druggies. They're talking about what they call the Jesus Movement and how they all got saved—but man, it was weird. Too heavy for me."

"And the girl?"

"I was done with her," replied Kerr. "I didn't want nobody shoving their religion down my throat."

"It all makes sense," said Bardolf.

"What makes sense?" asked Miles Crawford.

"What happened and what we've got to do about it."

"Which is?"

"Exactly what Domokos was talking about. It's our duty to stand up for all segments of society that are discriminated against—not just the poor and blacks."

"You're not suggesting fighting for homos?"

"They're people, aren't they?" replied Bardolf. "They have the right to live any way they choose."

"I don't know. I guess, but—"

"Of course we have to fight for their rights too," Bardolf went on. "If we're fighting for justice and civil rights, that's got to include everybody."

Shuffling went around the group. Such an idea was new to most of the others. The stigma against homosexuality was deeply imbedded.

"Come on, men," said Bardolf. "These are new times. Prejudice has to be destroyed. All prejudice. Christians are the most prejudiced of all. I say we go after them."

"Come on, Slayton," said Miles. "They wouldn't kill anyone."

"You must not know your history, Miles," rejoined Bardolf cynically. "The lynchings in the South were done in the name of God. Christians are the worst hypocrites of all."

"Would you say that to Oscar?" asked Joe Jakes.

"Of course not. He's different. He's a black Christian. It's the redneck whites I can't stand—holier than thou, always quoting the Bible. Racists every one. Now I remember that place—big American flag flying in front of the frat house. Haven't they ever heard of Viet Nam and Watergate. I bet they all voted for Nixon. They're exactly the kind that have to be taken down."

The dark room grew silent. It was impossible to know when Slayton Bardolf would go off on one of his religious rants. Yet none of the others could deny that what he said contained a ring of truth. Between the anti-Christian and pro-homosexual sentiment being expressed by the obvious spokesman of the group, however, two or three of those present silently wondered what they had gotten themselves into. But none objected. It was easier to go along with something they had qualms about than take a stand against a forceful personality like Slayton Bardolf. Groupthink ruled no less on liberal campuses as in the Pentagon.[2]

The awkwardness of the moment was forestalled when Talon Roswell spoke up again. "I think my dad may have some connections, or he could find out if there are any wackos involved at the place."

"You can't tell him why you want to know," said Bardolf.

"Don't worry, I'll be careful. I'll divulge nothing about tonight."

"A good place to start, then," nodded Bardolf. "The rest of you find out what you can. Maybe Dr. Robinson's class will turn up something."

He paused and allowed the mood of intrigue to settle again. He sensed the hesitation about defending homosexuals. It would be best not to push things too far. They had to make sure who was with them all the way. He would leave the slogan about death to God for another time.

"We'll leave one at a time," he said at length. "At one-minute intervals. You will be notified when we will meet next."

8

ΛLPHΛ ΟΜΕGΛ

SINCE THE clandestine meeting in the science building, Slayton Bardolf made it his custom to walk to and from classes along University Avenue to see if any fanatic types might be lurking about. Every time he passed the Alpha Omega house, with its American flag flying in front, his annoyance mounted. *What would Jane Fonda or Angela Davis do?* he wondered—*sneak in and take the flag down and burn it?*

Two men were standing on the sidewalk outside talking. As he approached, he recognized Wally Chisholm who he'd been in a study group with for an economics class the year before. Their conversation having come to an end, the other man turned and walked away.

"Hey, Wally," said Bardolf, extending his hand.

"Slayton," replied Chisholm. "Good to see you again. In the law program, I hear. How's that going?"

"Hard work—the candle at both ends."

"That's what everyone says about law school."

"I didn't know you lived here," said Bardolf. "You involved with Alpha Omega?"

"Joined last year. This is my first year in the house."

"Why Alpha Omega—why not three letters like other fraternities?"

"We're a Christian group. We think of ourselves as a brotherhood. Alpha and Omega—you know, what Jesus said—that he was the beginning and the end."

"Ah, okay. Jesus, huh?"

"He's the one we follow."

"Each his own, I suppose. Were you at the Domokos lecture the other night?"

"I wasn't interested. Not with his liberal reputation."

"He had some good things to say."

"About what?"

"Changing the country."

"You want to change the United States?"

"Who doesn't?"

"Good point. Sure, I agree—there are things that need changing."

"I'm talking about a fundamental change from top to bottom. That's what the lecture was about."

"The classic liberal bias," said Chisholm. "His kind can't see that even with its problems, this is the greatest country in history."

"What's so great about slavery, corporate greed, racism, and poverty, not to mention the war machine that runs the government? If you ask me, this country needs a complete overhaul."

"Every country's got problems. Of course, those things need changing. You won't hear me justifying Viet Nam or slavery. I came over from the high school and participated in some of the anti-war stuff back then. I couldn't vote yet, but I got caught up in Eugene McCarthy's campaign in '68 too. Viet Nam was terrible. I had a peace symbol on my binder too. But even with the problems, America's Christian foundations have accomplished more good for the people of the world than any other country in history. You can't throw the baby out with the bathwater."

Bardolf shook his head in disdain. "Listen to yourself, Wally! That's preposterous. Religion is one of the things we need to get rid of. It's Christianity that brought white supremacy and slavery to the South. Christianity worships a fairy tale. And you're flying a flag in front of your house to honor this country?"

"We do honor this country and the values it stands for. We're proud to be Americans."

"Not me. I'd sooner burn the flag than fly it!"

"Strong words. You could get arrested for talk like that."

"Not for long. The country's waking up."

"Waking up to what?"

"To the cancer of the whole American system."

"The *cancer*! Gosh, Slayton! Aren't you proud to be an American?"

"I'm embarrassed to be an American!"

"Where would you rather live—under communism?"

"It's not such a bad system—in theory."

"Then why did your man Domokos immigrate to the West? Did he find freedom under communism? Would he have been able to give an anti-government lecture in Russia?"

"He's Romanian."

"Same difference. In either place—he'd have been sent to a Siberian gulag for talking about taking down the system. There is freedom here. He's the living evidence of it. America embodies the essence of freedom."

"I thought you didn't go to the Domokos lecture?"

"I heard about it."

"All negative, no doubt—from your Christian friends."

"No, not all negative. You can't paint every Christian with the same brush. We come in different shapes and colors. I've got liberal Christian friends as well as conservatives. I think the people I talked to about the lecture gave me a pretty objective summary—both pros and cons."

"All I know is that new times are coming," said Bardolf, "and I want to be part of it."

"Not all change is good. Just because society is moving in a certain direction doesn't make that a good direction. Progress doesn't always bring good. Some old ways are better than what the protestors want to replace them with."

"I will side with forward progress every time. It's a new world. Guys like you are going to be left behind."

"I'll take my chances," smiled Chisholm.

"Who was that you were talking to? I've seen him around."

"The new history prof—Dr. Marshall. He's our faculty sponsor—great guy."

"A Christian, no doubt?"

"He is."

"Remind me never to take a history class from him! That's all we need, some guy loading down his perspectives of history with Christian myths."

"I'm sorry you feel that way, Slayton. I wish you'd give me the chance to explain what Christianity is really about. There is a lot you don't understand."

"Forget it. I'm not interested. This is the twentieth century, man. That's for people stuck in the Dark Ages."

"Do you think I'm stuck in the Dark Ages?"

"If you believe in miracles and that a virgin had a baby and that a dead man came back to life and went flying up to heaven—yeah, that's Dark Ages thinking. Nobody believes all that anymore."

Chisholm shrugged, smiled again, but did not reply.

"By the way," Bardolf went on, "I was talking to a guy who went to a Bible study here last year. He said you guys think homosexuality is a sin. Is that true."

"That's what the Bible teaches."

"That seems pretty judgmental."

"I'm just saying it's what the Bible says."

"Does God judge people just because they're different?"

"God judges sin in everybody—my sin, your sin. He wants us to get rid of sin in our lives, not keep living in it."

"Whose business is it how I live, or how anyone else lives?"

"God's."

"You think it's God's business how you live?"

"I do."

"Yet you talk about loving freedom? Doesn't that mean freedom to do as you please?"

"Very perceptive question, Slayton. In a way, yes. You're right. We *are* free to do whatever we please."

"But we're supposed to obey the Bible, which says we're not supposed to do certain things," said Slayton. "What kind of freedom is that?"

"The ultimate freedom."

"What do you mean?"

"The freedom to choose. By *choosing* to live by God's priorities, *choosing* to live by his commands, *choosing* to live in goodness as he defines it not how you or I might want to define it, by *choosing* to obey what the Bible says, we step into the ultimate freedom of life as his sons."

Bardolf could not help laughing. "Do you have any idea how ridiculous that all sounds!"

Chisholm smiled a little sadly. "To me it is wonderful," he replied quietly. "God gives us the freedom to choose him as our Father. Therein is the ultimate freedom."

Bardolf shook his head. "And whoever doesn't believe the Bible is a sinner?"

"I didn't say that."

"*Do* you believe it?"

"No."

"But whoever doesn't do what the Bible says is a sinner?"

Chisholm thought a moment. "Interesting question, Slayton. You're a very perceptive guy. I'm going to have to think about that. For now I would say that whoever does what the Bible calls a sin is a sinner. I would go further than that and say that *everyone* is a sinner. That's what the Bible teaches—you, me, everybody. That's why we need Jesus."

"But homosexuals are worse sinners, so they need God more than you?"

"Not at all. I need God just as much as Hitler needed him."

"That's a weird comparison!"

"We're all human beings together. So we're all sinners together. What's so hard to understand about that. Why? Do you think you're perfect?"

"Of course not. I've got faults like everyone else. That doesn't make me a sinner."

"Okay, well I've got faults too, and I think it *does* make me a sinner. Which is why I need Jesus—to help me overcome them. That's where the freedom to choose comes back in—God gives us the freedom to choose to deal with the sin in our lives."

"If you say so, Wally!" laughed Bardolf, though he could hardly hide his disdain.

He turned and walked on along the sidewalk before he said something he really regretted. It was all such nonsense! There was no place for such fools in a university where people were supposed to learn how to think. Morons like Wally *were* stuck in the Dark Ages!

Unconsciously Bardolf glanced back briefly at the irritating display of the flag, just as two men walked out of the house. Both were white, big men, older than most students, probably in their late twenties, one with shoulder-length hair, the other bald and with tattoos up and down his arm. With respect to Domokos's analogy, the look of the tattooed man frightened him—not the kind of guy he would want to meet in a dark alley.

He turned away again and continued. As he went, the brief conversation replayed itself in his mind. It made him more and more angry. Especially that Wally was so calm and satisfied with himself in his blissful ignorance. Ignorance was one thing. But chosen ignorance . . . that was something he couldn't stand. There was no excuse for it!

By the time he reached his apartment, Slayton Bardolf was furious. Not at Wally Chisholm personally. He was an okay guy, he supposed. A fool, but not a bad sort. It was what he represented—backward, narrow-minded, conservative thinking.

America-is-great thinking! Fly the flag and pretend everything is hunky-dory! Let prejudice thrive, let people starve, let Christians judge the rest of the world and call everyone sinners, let bigoted whites string up blacks and homosexuals and do nothing about it!

Exactly as Domokos said. They were the enemy. Wally may have been a nice guy. But he was the enemy.

His thoughts returned to the tattooed guy he had seen coming out of the Alpha Omega house. What was a straight arrow like Wally Chisholm doing hanging around with guys like that?

The more he thought about it, the more convinced he became there was more going on in that house than the squeaky-clean image they presented to the world.

9

THE YOUNG PROFESSOR OF HISTORY

1941–1973

STIRLING MARSHALL, born in 1941, grew up in the foothills of southern California above Redlands and was the son of WWII veteran Clark Marshall.

The deep-rooted evangelical faith of his parents took root within him even more strongly than did his love for his Scottish ancestry. Slow growing, those roots sent down strengthening strands and character-building fibers throughout his personhood. When he and Larke Stevens met, almost immediately both knew that in the other they had discovered a spiritual comrade and soulmate.

In contrast to the societal and cultural changes toward the many leftist ideas inaugurated during his collegiate and post-collegiate years during the tumultuous 1960s, Stirling's Christian faith set him on a divergent life's road from most of his future academic colleagues. During an era characterized by Beatlemania, riots, protests, drugs, and civil unrest, he was a young man whose spiritual grounding interpreted the events of his time through a much different lens than most of his contemporaries.

Stirling's relationship with Larke in the two years after their meeting built not only an anchoring foundation of lifetime commitment and shared purpose between the idealistic young man and young woman, they were also solidifying a mutual outlook on faith, spirituality, the world, the church, and the nature of God.

It was a season in their lives when the soil was being tilled. They sensed they were being called to something nebulously higher than what they could yet perceive. In spite of many ups and downs and the inevitable stresses of professional and family life, they would feel the calling of their shared uncommon spiritual vision with increasing clarity over the years.

Stirling Marshall and Larke Stevens were married after Larke's graduation in 1966. Completing his master's degree and accepted into the University of California, Santa Barbara (UCSB) doctoral program, Stirling took a job teaching history at Lompoc High School, fifty miles from Santa Barbara. He and Larke rented an apartment in Gaviota closer to the high school, from which Stirling continued to commute into the city as often as necessary to continue his doctoral studies while working on his thesis. He completed his PhD work and taught at Lompoc for five years.

In 1972, at the age of thirty-one he applied for and, on the basis of his graduate school credentials, his thesis, and that he was a favorite with everyone on the faculty, was offered a position in the history department in the very halls he walked as a student. It was the job he dreamed of, and he eagerly accepted.

During their sojourn in Lompoc in 1970, *The Late Great Planet Earth* hit the bestseller lists. Over the next several years, Stirling became deeply concerned with the prophecy mania sweeping through US evangelicalism. He was convinced it was not only based on erroneous scriptural interpretations and a false prophetic paradigm, but, far more importantly, on an entirely wrong perspective of the character of God and how he works in the world to accomplish his purposes.

About the same time a small, unknown, and privately printed book came into his hands, sent to him from one of his former undergraduate roommates. The unassuming tan, staple-bound copy was the antithesis of *The Late Great Planet Earth* approach in every way, with no attempt to grab headlines with a flashy cover, but simplistically titled *Feast of Tabernacles*.

In the author's words Stirling found meat that fed his hunger for a higher outlook and more lofty perspective from which to view God's eternal purposes, based as it was on a more sweeping and scriptural end times paradigm than the sensationalism offered by *Late Great*. It was from *Feast of Tabernacles* that he first became alerted to the significance of what was called "the remnant" in Scripture.

Though they were at first but faint fragmentary intimations, seeds were being planted within the heart and mind of young history professor Stirling Marshall.

10

RUMORS AND ACCUSATION

WHERE THE story originated was never discovered.

First were vague warnings beginning to circulate around campus that students should not walk at night along University Avenue.

To these were added speculations about the coincidence—or was it?—that the Alpha Omega house was only three blocks from the apartment complex where Vestar and Styles lived.

The rumor about the two being homosexuals, never known for certain, was only whispered. No one wanted to actually *say* it. But the looks and silences whenever the subject of the hangings came up, which, with the university and city still jumpy, was daily, confirmed clearly enough everyone was aware of the gossip. As with most hearsay, the worse the conjecture the more it is believed.

Whether the television station or local newspaper first learned about the two suspicious older men—white, one with long hair, the other bald and sporting numerous tattoos—seen near the campus on the day of the incident, both were soon running the story. No one knew where the anonymous tip came from. Some said a letter was put through the mail slot of the newspaper office, though no further information was forthcoming. If true, presumably the FBI would scour the envelope and letter for fingerprints and other clues. Nothing more about the letter, if there was one, was ever released, leading to the probable conclusion that the letter was a myth. In any event, the rumor about the two men persisted and was soon believed as fact.

Requests for witnesses were made by the police. Many came forward. The two men apparently made no attempt to keep from being seen until the initial reports hit the news. They had not been seen since. Sketches were compiled from the witnesses, which gradually were blended into reasonably accurate composites the witnesses agreed on.

Whether the FBI had other sources, whether additional witnesses came forward, or whether the widening circle of speculation at the university simply reached the ears of its agents and resulted in the events that followed was never known. By whatever means, the Alpha Omega house soon became the primary focus of FBI interest.

Second-year university history professor Dr. Stirling Marshall, faculty advisor to the Alpha Omega fraternity, thus received a visit from the lead FBI investigator on the case. Marshall knew most of what was publicly being circulated about the hangings. However, he paid little attention to the unsubstantiated rumors swirling in recent days.

"Do you recognize these two men?" asked the agent when they were seated in Dr. Marshall's office. He handed Dr. Marshall the two sketches.

"I believe so, yes," he replied as he looked them over. "Obviously these are just drawings, but they resemble two men we had here a week or two ago giving talks at the Alpha Omega house, and for one of the Christian groups on campus."

"They are *Christians*—what were they talking about . . . God?"

Marshall nodded.

"Are they students at the university?"

"No, we brought them up from LA. They're involved in the Jesus Movement there."

"The Jesus Movement?"

"A spiritual revival taking place in southern California. That's what some people call it. Street people and students and former hippies coming to Christ by the thousands. It's actually quite extraordinary."

"And these two are part of it?"

Marshall nodded. "Both have amazing testimonies. One is a former drug addict, the other was a sixties radical who was imprisoned for inciting protests. They've turned their lives around and are speaking to student groups about their experiences and how Jesus has changed their lives."

"They were at the Alpha Omega house?"

"We put them up for a couple of weeks while they were here."

"And those dates?"

"Uh, let me see." Marshall flipped through the pages in his desk calendar. "They arrived on the 10th of this month . . . and, here it is—they spoke on campus on the evening of the 12th at which I was present. They led Bible studies at the house from the 15th to the 20th. I didn't personally see them off, but I believe they left to drive back to LA on the 23rd. Come to think of it, I think they drove back up again for two or three days last week to meet with some of the young men. You could talk to Wally Chisholm at the house. He was in charge of their activities, and more or less acted as their host during their time here."

"We'll do that. And these two men's names?"

"Anders Cranston and Hobart Parke."

"Do you know where we could find them now?"

"Mr. Chisholm would be able to tell you."

"Thank you, Dr. Marshall. You've been very helpful. We may want to talk to you later. Don't leave town."

Finding the agent's last statement more puzzling than disturbing, Dr. Marshall returned to his work. He had no idea what train of events his candid answers would set in motion until the next afternoon when another young man from Alpha Omega burst into his office.

"What is it, Fred?" said Dr. Marshall. "You look like . . . I don't know what—like you're afraid someone's after you."

"I am. You've got to hide me, Dr. Marshall!"

Marshall almost broke out laughing. The smile quickly disappeared from his face. The young man was deadly serious.

"Tell me what's going on, Fred."

"The police came to the house an hour ago—racing up the street with sirens and lights. They ran into the house, knocked the door in, and a dozen of them poured inside. They had guns, Dr. Marshall. Everybody was in a panic. They asked about Anders and Hobart and were questioning everybody. I ran out the back door and hid in the alley until I saw two of the police cars leave. I started to walk back to the house but then Harry ran out.

"'Don't go back in there, man! They're searching all the rooms and dusting for fingerprints. They arrested Wally! They're taking him to jail.' Harry was really freaked out and ran off. That's when I ran here to tell you."

Dr. Marshall sat back in his chair and let out a long breath. The visit from the FBI agent suddenly made sense. His forthrightness had apparently landed his young friend in jail.

"Do you have somewhere to go, Fred?" he asked as he rose from his chair.

"I've got class in an hour, but I'll never be able to concentrate."

"Do your best to stay calm. I'll head down to the police station immediately and find out what's going on. It's obviously a misunderstanding. Don't worry, I'll get Wally out. Everything will be fine."

11

ᴀFTERMᴧTH

1973–1990ꜱ

Everything was not fine. Within hours, many lives were permanently disrupted.

Wallace Chisholm, charged with being an accessory, was forced to spend the night in jail. After Dr. Marshall essentially begged Alan Bridgewater, president of the university, to intercede for him with the D.A. on Marshall's word that he was innocent, young Chisholm was released the next day without bail. The charges against him, however, stood.

In Los Angeles, Anders Cranston and Hobart Parke were found at the communal Christian house where they lived with a number of others with sketchy pasts. Their Christian conversions mattered less to investigators than their rap sheets. Cranston and Parke were arrested on charges of murder, taken north to the Santa Barbara County jail, where they were held without bail.

The arrests rocked the entire community, and again made national news. More rumors mounted about Alpha Omega, that it was a haven for far-right racists and homosexuals. Both accusations could hardly be true. It had to be one or the other. In actual fact according to everyone who knew the young men who lived there, *neither* was true. But the rumors alone, whether true or not, did their damage. Everyone who had ever lived at the Alpha Omega house was branded forever.

A petition began circulating demanding the Alpha Omega house be closed. Some said it began in the university law school but no one really knew. Editorials in the campus paper and near daily demonstrations in the quad convinced the administration that action must be taken to avoid a major incident against the Christian group. Alpha Omega's status as a recognized club was thus withdrawn for the following academic year. As the university owned the property, Alpha and Omega's lease was terminated immediately, and the group shut down.

At the trial, so many witnesses were called who had attended the event on campus on the night of the 12th at which the two accused men spoke, the same night as the Domokos lecture, as to establish their alibis until about 11:30. Most of the residents of Alpha Omega also came forward uniformly telling the same story, of a late card game of Shanghai involving most of the house, Cranston and Parke included along with Wally Chisholm, until finally breaking up when they all headed to bed around 2:00. None heard the gunshots, though all attested to the fact that Shanghai could be a competitive and raucous game when buying extra cards reached a frenzy.

Absent definitive proof, the three were acquitted of the charges. At its outset, news of the fast-tracked trial again was featured on the national news, with film clips of the earlier arrests—Chisholm, Cranston, and Parke all in handcuffs. Their acquittal several weeks later, however, was not mentioned. Most of the country remained convinced that the hangings were a racially motivated crime of hate carried out by a white radical Christian organization.

The ordeal shook Wallace Chisholm. He dropped out of the university and lost his faith for a season. As for Anders Cranston and Hobart Parke, their past lives during their pre-salvation days seasoned them to roll with worse punches than false accusations. But having a murder charge on one's record, especially a hate crime, even if false, tends to dog the heels forever. Speaking invitations dried up. Neither man was able to gain successful long-term employment. Both bounced around for years from one menial job to another.

The case was not solved for more than two decades. With advances in forensic technology, largely due to the persistent efforts of Dr. Bridgewater at the university, the ropes used in the hangings were analyzed again in the early 1990s. DNA matches were discovered identifying two black men then serving life sentences at San Quentin. Interviewed, one of the two unrepentantly confessed to the murders. "I never could stand a gay nigger," he said, though the actual quote was altered slightly in reports for the sake of what then fell under the purview of the term, newly resurfaced after a seventy-year dormancy, "political correctness"—what Viktor Domokos might have defined as the *perception* of what the phantom 65 percent believed *ought* to be considered correct.[3]

The admission from San Quentin came much too late to do Wallace Chisholm, Anders Cranston, Hobart Parke, or the other members of Alpha Omega much good. Neither was it of much interest to the news media. By then the networks were discouraged from airing stories of black on black, or black on white crime.

White crimes against minorities fit more smoothly into the new "politically correct" media narrative. The initial perception of the crime thus remained lodged in the public consciousness.

12

A WIFE'S CHALLENGE

1973–1986

As a young man, green in many ways, and still in the early years of his academic career, Dr. Stirling Marshall was also shaken by the lynchings, the accusations, and arrests of his young friends, and the venom against the Alpha Omega house. Though the anti-Christian rhetoric was short-lived and the influence of the Jesus Movement even resulted in a revival of interest in Christianity on campus for a time, scars were inflicted on many lives which would remain.

He loved the university atmosphere and poured himself into his students and family. Yet the incident and its aftermath brought home with stark reality the realization that as a serious Christian he was on a divergent life path than most of his colleagues. In a fundamental way, he was living in a different world than much of academia. The easy willingness of the administration to cave to public pressure in the matter of the Alpha Omega house, against his most strenuous efforts, put him in his place as an untenured Christian newcomer whose vote did not count for much. For another decade, however, the steadily deviating worldviews of academia and Christianity managed to coexist within him, if not exactly in harmony, in yet an uneasy tolerance of one another.

As the years went by, Stirling discovered academia was not the only world in which he diverged in outlook from many of those around him. He had never considered himself a non-conformist. He did, however, resist going along with anything he was told he was *supposed* to believe, or adopting the majority opinion for no good reason other than that everyone else did.

He had to think for himself, find truth not opinion, and find *God's* truth not man's interpretation of it—even if that interpretation happened to be the majority opinion of many Christians.

As the 1970s gave way to the 1980s, the street and beach witnessing foundations of the Jesus Movement and the emotional experientialism of the 1960s Charismatic Movement merged and morphed into an increasingly wealthy and expanding evangelicalism catering to the middle and upper middle classes. Stirling found himself more and more departing in outlook, not only from his academic colleagues, but also from the throngs clustering in ever greater numbers to their burgeoning, trendy, influential, country-club churches.

He began to question whether, indeed, the future of Christendom would lie, not with the self-satisfied masses of happy scripturally ignorant churchgoers being fed spiritual pablum by pulpit personalities, but with small enclaves of unseen and unrecognized prophets and protectors of truth. Where, how, and when God would raise up such faithful men and women and speak into their hearts the revolutionary truth that they were not of the world, he had no idea.

Such a time surely lay in the future of God's history upon the earth. Just as generations of ancient monastics preserved the knowledge of God through perilous times, remnant disciples of obedience would again be revealed. When that time came, they would somehow be drawn into an unseen community of life. They would face far more subtle perils than had their brothers and sisters of antiquity, and far different dangers also than the "tribulations" foretold in *Late Great's* simplistic version of the future.

Stirling and Larke Marshall raised their five children—Woodrow (1973), Cateline (1974), Graham (1976), Jane (1978), and Timothy (1980)—in Santa Barbara. As Dr. Marshall's standing at UCSB grew, he devoted himself to his professional work, writing articles, eventually reworking his graduate thesis into his first published book which received surprising notoriety in educational circles. *A History of 19th-Century Scottish Writers and Their Influence on the Greater World of Victorian Literature* (1981) was universally praised in scholarly journals and came to be used as a text for numerous college and university courses. Though its appeal was primarily in the academic world, and thus remuneration for its sales modest, the book's publication and ongoing influence lent to the name "Dr. Stirling Marshall" a certain luster in the world of historical academia that was not lost on his peers at UCSB.

His colleagues knew him to be a devoted, though not an especially outspoken Christian since the events of 1973. Yet his reputation and soft-spoken manner ensured he was admired in spite of being immersed in the increasingly liberal environment of academia. Unseen by his colleagues, the spiritual side of his persona continued to grow.

As Stirling and his wife sat with their coffee and tea one morning in the mid-1980s, neither Larke nor her husband could have foreseen how a spontaneous remark would change their lives.

"You're always writing," said Larke. "When I get up in the morning, there you are with your Bible and whichever pen you are using, writing away."

"It's how I make sense of the things you and I talk about," laughed her husband. "I don't feel I've really got hold of an idea until I can express it on paper in exactly the way I'm sensing it in my brain."

"You don't write all your lectures down ahead of time."

"That's different. That's history. Get me going on history and I can talk for hours. But about theology and some of the enigmatic statements in the New Testament—those things take wrestling with. Writing helps me get at the essence, if you know what I mean."

"What you really need to do, then, is write all this down."

"All what?"

"Everything you and I have been talking about since we met— prophecy, *Late Great Planet Earth*, the church, the commands of the Bible you're always talking about, the remnant, mega-church evangelicalism, where God is taking our nation, where he is taking his people, where he is taking us, where he is taking the world! Your view of Scripture is different than anyone else's. You see things. You see *into* things."

Her husband could not help laughing.

"You're prejudiced, Larke!" he said.

"Maybe a little," she replied. "But I'm serious. You understand God like no one else I've ever met. You're a spiritual coin sorter, like I call it. You need to write it all down. Who but a historian with a sense of the past and a knowledge of Scripture and God's history and the world's history could write with insight about the future?"

Stirling took in her words thoughtfully. It was quiet a few moments as they sipped at their cups.

"Hmm . . ." was all he could say, though the deeply thoughtful sound always said to his wife that his brain was actively at work.

"I have to admit," he said reflectively, "that I have felt building within me for some time a foreboding of evil forces intent on rendering Christianity powerless in this country. I have no idea when these things will come to be. But I am convinced that perilous change is coming to the world—and to God's people."

"Which is why you need to write about it."

"Who would listen? I'm a nobody—a history professor."

"That's not your responsibility. Your job is to write what God reveals to you. The rest is up to him."

Larke grew thoughtful. Stirling waited. At length she drew in a deep breath.

"You know what I would like," she said. "I would love for you to coalesce for me, in writing, what is the *essence* of your personal spiritual vision. Do it for *me*. It would mean more to me than I can say. You are the one I look to. You help me make sense of things. Place your ideas into an overarching perspective of what God wants of his people. Even if no one reads it but me, there is nobody who puts the things of God so clearly and practically as you express them."

Stirling drew in a deep breath.

"Your words mean more than I can say," he replied softly. "Imagine the magnitude of setting down the essence of one's faith, the core of what life means, the fundamental beliefs by which one attempts to order his life. The very idea is breathtaking."

"Will you do it?"

"I am still reeling by the enormity of it."

Stirling began to chuckle.

"Can you imagine what my colleagues would think?" he said. "That would be the end of my reputation if I started writing about the Bible!"

"How would they even know? Academia and Christianity don't intersect much these days."

13

Unspoken Commandments

1986

WHEN LARKE arose the next morning and walked into the kitchen, the house was warm and the lights were on in Stirling's study with the door ajar. None of the children were yet up, though six-year-old Timothy and eight-year-old Jane would no doubt be scampering about soon enough. Her husband had always been an early riser. Yet she sensed something different on this day. Even before she swung the door open, she heard the clacking of the keys of his typewriter beating out a furious cadence.

She waited for a moment, relishing the sight of her husband in his element. He sensed her presence. His fingers stilled and he turned to face her, eyes aglow.

"What!" exclaimed Larke. "You look like you've . . . I don't know what!"

"Seen a ghost?" laughed Stirling.

"No, not that. I don't know—like Moses coming down off the mountain. Radiant."

Stirling laughed again.

"I would not draw that comparison!" he said. "But I must admit to a sense of exhilaration. What you said yesterday—challenging me to write a sort of distillation of my personal manifesto of faith, as it were—the essence of what I believe lies at the core of practical, scriptural Christian discipleship . . . it remained with me all night. I could hardly sleep."

"When did you get up?"

"A little after three."

"Goodness!"

"I know. I'll probably nod off during this afternoon's lecture on Burns! But my brain was on fire. I had to make a beginning."

"Are you going to tell me about it?"

"I'm not quite ready. I don't want to dilute my focus by talking about it just yet. I need to keep everything in my head and not let the steam escape the teakettle with overmuch talk, to use MacDonald's brilliant analogy. Rest assured, you will read it when the time is right."

The momentum did not stop, nor did the steam of inspiration escape the teakettle. Stirling Marshall continued to arise in the darkness while the rest of the household slept and wrote like a man possessed. He occasionally worried that he was neglecting his classes at the university because his thoughts were so preoccupied with what he called his "Essence Book." But he could not stop the flow until he completed whatever was slowly taking shape.

His early-morning writing time was infused with new purpose and vision. It wasn't long before Larke was reading his work almost as soon as he wrote it, offering her own input which, in subsequent drafts Stirling worked into his manuscript.

He began dividing the work into chapters. Gradually a more encompassing thematic overview came into focus. What was flowing from his fingers continued to take on an increasing sense of importance.

Six months and three full drafts later, he had a stack of 225 typed pages. Keeping his completion of the project secret, he took it to the local copy center, had it bound, and presented it to Larke a week later on Christmas Eve after the children were in bed.

As they sat in front of the Christmas tree, the floor around them filled with presents for their excited five children, Larke slowly unwrapped the package and opened the thin box. Her eyes fell on the bound 8½ x 11-inch white manuscript, its title reading, *Unspoken Commandments: The Essence of Gospel Living at the Center of God's Purpose* with the words below it, "To my wife, Larke, the inspiration for this book, my muse, and my lifetime love."

Tears flooded her eyes.

"You did it," she said, her voice husky. "Thank you, Stirling. I asked you to write it for me, and you did . . . I will treasure it."

"There is much of you here as well. It has been a joint effort."

Stirling had no plans for his manuscript beyond the present. He had written it for Larke. It was now in her hands.

Larke, however, had not progressed far in her Christmas gift a week later before she was convinced what her husband had produced was desperately needed in the body of Christ. She secretly had several more copies made and, when Stirling was at the university, packaged them and them sent, with a cover letter from her, to several Christian publishers. She was not surprised when she received a letter from the managing editor at Faith House expressing enthusiasm for the book. When she sheepishly showed the letter to her husband, Stirling was shocked.

Stirling Marshall's *Unspoken Commandments* was published in 1987, and unexpectedly became a bestseller in the Christian marketplace. After several more similar titles, and a work of Christian historical fiction—which he tried mostly to see if he was capable of such a thing, set in the region and era of his particular expertise, nineteenth-century Scotland—he found himself with a growing reputation as a Christian novelist.

By the 1990s, Dr. Stirling Marshall had become one of the elder statesmen and, in spite of his religious leanings—which his university colleagues respected him for not making too much of publicly—perhaps the most esteemed professor in UCSB's history department.

He continued to write historical articles and published a second historical work, *The Mystique of Scotland's Failed Heroes*. Stirling's most noteworthy publications, however, were his devotional books and spiritually thematic novels.

14

Geologist's Daughter

1986–1999

AT THIRTY-SIX, Thaddeus Gray, or "Thady" to his friends, was still a relative newcomer to the faculty at New Mexico Institute of Mining and Technology in Socorro when the sudden discovery in the caverns of Lechuguilla Cave were made in 1986.

The discovery ignited a firestorm of excitement throughout the geology world, and nowhere more than among the faculty of NMIMT. Since the cave's entrance lay within the Carlsbad Caverns National Park, the abandoned mining shaft was controlled by the National Park Service. When the NPS began allowing carefully regulated exploration of the new caverns and passageways, geologists from New Mexico's universities were among the first selected for the honor. Thady Gray, one of the state's recognized experts on the geologic structure of the Guadalupe Mountains, was one of the first names added to the list.

The expression on Thady's face when he burst into the house just before dinner that day in May of 1986 was one neither he nor any of the family would forget. His eyes glowed as he held wife Nadine and their two sons and young daughter spellbound. His explanation of the details, and what new worlds of exploration it would open, lasted well past all three children's bedtimes.

"How often in any scientific field is a spectacular and altogether, completely and utterly *new* discovery made!" he exclaimed. "This is one of those. And it's right here—in our own back yard. We'll be part of it!"

Thady Gray's enthusiasm was not only well-founded—if anything he underestimated the significance of the discovery. As explorations began and the mapping of Lechuguilla continued in the following years, reaching deeper and to a far vaster extent than anyone originally dreamed possible, the discovery gave Gray and his colleagues the first opportunity to actually set foot deep enough into the Guadalupe range to study the five separate geologic formations beneath it.

Within a decade Lechuguilla was recognized as one of the most unique and important cave systems of the world, containing stunning gypsum crystal formations and rare speleothems never before seen anywhere. By then it was the eighth-longest cave in the world, fourth-longest in the United States at 168 miles, as well as the deepest known cave in the continental United States. And its exploration was far from over. By the time of the major underground expedition of 2012, during which many new unexplored passages, domes, pits, and enormous rooms were discovered, Thaddeus Gray was recognized as the man who probably knew more about Lechuguilla than anyone.

The cave's discovery sent down roots in many unexpected directions within the daughter of Thaddeus and Nadine Gray, that neither father nor mother, nor the girl, could have foreseen. The light in her father's eyes went deep in her young girl's imagination. The impact of that day changed her life forever. Though she understood little of what her father said that first day as he excitedly told his family about it, four-year-old Jaylene listened with eyes wide and ears taking it all in. Her father's contagious enthusiasm filled her with a sense of mystery for the undiscovered, the ancient, for secrets hidden in the earth awaiting discovery.

In the years that followed, the girl's two older brothers were always smashing rocks and digging in the ground, trained early in their geologist-father's footsteps, hoping that what appeared an ordinary rock might yield a purple thunder egg or other treasure inside. Every birthday and Christmas added more tools to their geology kits and interesting rocks to their ever-expanding collections.

Jaylene's inquisitive nature followed much the same path. Scientific exploration was the meat and drink of the Gray household. Rather than Dr. Seuss and Richard Scary, the three Gray children grew up on pictorial science books and atlases. Their personal Disneyland was Carlsbad Caverns, which all three children visited a dozen times before they were ten.

Thady Gray could not have been more delighted when his two sons declared their intention to study geology and to discover new caves no one had ever seen. Their dreams no longer seemed far-fetched. After Lechuguilla, anything was possible.

His daughter's ambitions were quieter, and in some ways went deeper into the hidden marrow of her being. When her father took the three hiking and climbing and rock hunting, while her rock-hound brothers were eagerly scampering about and whacking with their hammers, she was watching, observing, *thinking*.

What did the rocks and caves and thunder eggs *mean*? Why were they there? Where had they come from?

Her fascination was for more than mere geology. It was the extraordinary *age* of everything.

Antiquity became the great mystery.

Oldness.

How could anything—rocks, caves, the earth, the moon, the sun, stars, animals, trees—how could things be *so old*?

While her father's description of the cave's wonders filled her brothers' imaginations with images of stalactites and stalagmites such as they knew so well from Carlsbad, it was his words of unfathomable *age* that lodged in Jaylene's brain:

"It took millions of years for these formations to grow into their present form," she heard his voice saying excitedly, ". . . millions of years . . . even hundreds of millions of years . . . just think—one drop at a time . . . millions . . . millions . . ."

The very words "millions of years" reverberated in her mind with indescribable awe. They came to represent in her young brain a mystery that could not be explained, the mystery of *everything*—life and the earth, the entire universe—a mystery whose sheer magnitude faded into antiquity.

Lechuguilla ceased to represent the unknown. *Time* was the greatest mystery of all.

As young Jaylene grew from four to six and eight, and as her father began to realize how vast was the extent of his quiet daughter's thoughtful reflections, his teaching widened. Other scientific disciplines expanded the canvas upon which her imagination and intellect dreamed big dreams—not only the geology of her father's profession, but astronomy, physics, anthropology, archaeology, meteorology, geography. She was a sponge with seemingly limitless capacity to absorb whatever he wanted to teach her. When he gave her books to read, she devoured them.

Thaddeus bought a telescope and they took up amateur star gazing. He took Jaylene to the university and schooled her in the use of microscopes—teaching her to look at both the huge and the tiny, to look *up* and to look *inside*. It was while standing in their backyard at midnight watching a meteor shower, looking up at the vast expanse above them, when she first heard her father say that the universe was over thirteen *billion* years old. The immensity of it was beyond her comprehension. Yet the very words deepened the awe within her of what true *antiquity* might mean. To her flurry of questions that night, he went on to explain the Big Bang. She was only eight, and the concept of infinitely compressed matter was unknowable to her. But she would understand it in time, as well as anyone is capable of understanding it.

By the time she reached high school, Jaylene had completed two years of algebra and was ready to start calculus. She read Stephen Hawking and could have held her own in a graduate level discussion ranging from Kepler's laws, to cosmic microwave background, special and general relativity, quantum vs. Newtonian dynamics, black holes, quasars, the cosmological constant, Schrödinger's cat, Heisenberg's uncertainty principle, the laws of thermodynamics, the expansion of the universe, and the still unsolved Riemann hypothesis. She even dreamed that she might one day be the one to solve it.

Undergirding all the scientific disciplines, the development of the complex world of the animal kingdom, and the mystery of life itself, sat the three-sided Rosetta stone of all scientific knowledge—*chance* beginnings, the *spontaneous generation* of matter out of nothing, and *evolution*.

Thaddeus Gray gave his daughter equal exposure, not merely to Darwin's originating thesis, but to the myriad branches and offshoots which, in the century and a quarter following the publication of *On the Origins of Species*, led to the fully developed evolutionary tree upon which modern scientific knowledge was based.

By ten Jaylene knew every Homo sapiens strain and where and when each piece of the sequential human puzzle had been discovered. While her friends were naming their dolls, she was making up her own names, in the tradition of Lucy, for Homo erectus and habilis and Australopithecus robustus and africanus and afarensis, all the way back to anamensis. The beings of the primate and hominid evolutionary tree were as familiar to her as quartz, obsidian, felspar, mica, and calcite to her brothers.

By fifteen her parents had some idea of her intellect though refused to let her IQ be tested. By then, Jaylene's interests and reading were coming into focus. Rocks and caves and the whole world of geology, though her father would disagree, were to her silent, stagnant, and lifeless.

She was interested in *living* things. In life itself.

Even fossils of snails and fish and bones of dinosaurs and unearthed human remains had once been *alive*—she wanted to know their stories. The emergence and development of life, then human life, was her greatest passion of all. She knew every theory of every branch of man's evolutionary tree extending far back, long before Lucy and Ardipithecus ramidus, further back than six million years when gorillas, chimpanzees, apes, and men had a yet unknown common ancestor.

But she wanted to know what Lucy's *life* was like! Was she an animal, or had she begun to *think*?

The sponge of Jaylene's brain did not merely absorb, it retained. She could easily have challenged enough classes to graduate from high school after two years. Her parents, however, judged it best to give her three. She took the SAT at sixteen, scoring a perfect 1600, graduated, and entered Cal Poly in San Luis Obispo in the last year of the second millennium at seventeen on a full scholarship, by then having narrowed her chief field of interest to archaeology. She did, however, declare multiple minors in anthropology, physics, and astronomy.

15

Academia vs. Spirituality

1993

THE ALTERNATE so-called religious side of Stirling Marshall's professional life went mostly unnoticed at the university for the first several years—the worlds of academia and Christian publishing, as Larke noted, intersecting almost not at all. His apologetic for the Christian faith, *Does Truth Matter?*, three devotional books, and two novels, all of which followed in the four years since the publication of *Unspoken Commandments*, flew completely under the radar of California's university system.

That anonymity was shattered suddenly, unbeknownst to either of the Marshalls ahead of time, when Stirling was featured in the magazine *Christianity in Our Time* in 1993 following the unexpected success of his new title, *Phantasms of Unfaith*. The article entitled "Rising New Voices in Christendom" was quoted in a number of newspapers and one scholarly magazine in which Marshall was highlighted. The comparison was drawn to C. S. Lewis as being both a respected academic and popular religious author of equal power in both fiction and non-fiction. The article brought Marshall immediately into the spotlight among his UCSB colleagues, and subsequently, under the scrutiny of the administration. The university president asked to see him.

"It would seem we have a celebrity in our midst," said Bridgewater.

"Hardly that," laughed Marshall.

"I was not aware you published so much religious writing. This article that was passed on to me," Bridgewater added, pointing to the magazine on his desk, "says you have written eight religious titles."

"A mere sidelight, I assure you. I enjoy stretching my thoughts in many directions. But I am certainly no celebrity in that world any more than I am here."

"Be that as it may, I am not sure I like the implications of your public reputation as a religious author and how it reflects on the intellectual integrity of our history program."

"I cannot see there to be a problem," replied Marshall. "I am careful not to bring my beliefs into the classroom, if that's what you mean."

"It's not that so much, but rather the subtle implication, as I say, that history here at UCSB is being interpreted through a conservative religious lens. That could have negative consequences. I would not want you to become a lightning rod for another university controversy."

The oblique reference to the events of 1973 and Marshall's dogged defense of the Alpha Omega house was more pointed than the mere words indicated.

"Even though, as it turned out, I was right in that case."

"Events have, as you say, vindicated you, that is true."

"And let me express again my profound appreciation and admiration for your persistence in getting the case re-opened and the records of all the young men involved completely cleared."

"It was, uh, the least I could do. The blemish of the . . . uh, what turned out to be the wrongful arrests—it was a black mark on the university's record as well. It was my duty to see it corrected if possible."

"Ah, right, of course—the university had to be absolved. Nevertheless, you have my thanks. You did the right thing."

"But back to your, uh, your religious writings. You must understand that the mood of the country, and education in general, is much different than it was twenty years ago."

"In the anti-Christian bias now so notable in academia, you mean?"

"I wouldn't exactly put it in those terms."

"You might if you heard the degrading and hostile rhetoric of some toward Christian students. Their secularism is not a mere difference of opinion, which would be fine, it is harsh, strident, angry, even threatening. The judgmental bias of some progressive students is truly disturbing."

"Of course, but they are entitled to their points of view. But getting back to *your* writings and how they reflect on the university, I simply feel that we must proceed with caution."

"Have you read any of my . . . what you call my religious books?" asked Dr. Marshall.

"I, uh, not specifically—no."

"I doubt many of my colleagues would think of me as a conservative. Dr. Bahram and I are friends. He is a progressive American Muslim, something of an unusual mix, it is true. But I do not think he would consider me ultra conservative. We share a mutual respect. I may be a traditionalist in certain ways, perhaps. But in Christian circles I am considered something of a free thinker.

"Your bringing up Dr. Bahram is a case in point," rejoined Bridgewater. "Nasim is a thoroughly modern man—just as you say. Whatever his religious views, he keeps them to himself. I assume they are in keeping with new trends of thought. Furthermore, his status as an immigrant and man of color—"

"I believe he is a natural born citizen."

"Of course. I only meant his father immigrated to this country. His ethnicity and background *and* his religious views are compatible with the underlying ethos, as it were, of the university. I am only suggesting that Dr. Bahram might serve as a model for a less controversial methodology which you would do well to emulate."

"I try to bring my perspectives as a historian into Christianity, more than my Christianity into the classroom. I'm certain Nasim would say the same of his religious perspectives."

"That may be. But he does not espouse his religious views in a combative and judgmental way, as do most of those holding to fundamental Christianity. He does not espouse them at all, which is why he is a highly respected figure at the university. That being the case, your integrity as a historian, and by implication ours as a university, could be called into question if, for example, it were to get around that your historical perspectives were colored by a creationist foundation."

"As I say, I try to keep such controversies out of the classroom."

"But you do believe in creationism?"

"Of course."

"Well, there you are," rejoined Bridgewater.

"I'm not sure I see the problem if I do not teach it or refer to it."

"The mere suggestion could taint the perception of your objectivity as a historian."

"If you read my book *Does Truth Matter?* I think you would find my articulation of a balanced perspective between what I might call the Christian worldview and the scientific or secular point of view compelling. I think I have managed to marry the two in a way neither side has ever been willing to consider."

"Perhaps. But even the attempt to bring the Christian view into science, you must understand, in the eyes of many, is suspect at the outset."

"That is a flawed presupposition."

"That is neither here nor there. It is generally believed, and we must adapt to that reality. These are transition times in academia, as you well know. Former presuppositions are being reevaluated, especially those containing hints of religious bias. We must walk with great care to preserve our *bona fides* as an institution walking in step with the times."

Marshall sighed inwardly. "What do you want me to do?" he asked softly.

"For now, probably nothing. We will keep an eye on it. I would only ask that you maintain a low profile with respect to your . . . uh, your religious beliefs. And of course, agree to no more interviews in that vein."

"I have done no interviews at all."

"This article about you was written without your participation?"

"It was. I knew nothing about it."

"Ah, I see," said Bridgewater, obviously surprised. "Well, I can hardly hold you responsible. For now, then, as I say, maintain a low profile. I would ask you to publish no more religious material. I think that would be best. We need to focus on your persona as a historian."

"I'm not sure I can agree to that. Surely I am free to write as I choose on my own time."

"Technically, yes. I would simply hope that you would put the interests of the university above your religious convictions."

"I'm not sure I can do that either."

"Well, you have tenure so I cannot prevent you, or dismiss you if you choose to do so. But you would put the university in a difficult position."

"When C. S. Lewis became a best-selling author during the war while a professor at Oxford, it brought not mere notoriety but an enhanced standing to the university. The effect was just the opposite of what you seem concerned about. Lewis became the university's star, their poster boy as we might say. You know me well enough to know that is the last thing I would want. Nor would it ever happen in today's anti-religious climate. I am only saying that my so-called wider reputation might not necessarily be a bad thing."

"As you say, that was a different time. The myths of Christianity were still widely accepted. Modern thought has now debunked all that. Academia must continue to lead the way forward, not be seen as clinging to outmoded religious notions."

"Obviously I disagree with that assessment. But I can assure you that I will be as sensitive to your position as my conscience will allow. I will continue doing my best not to color my teaching with my personal views. However, I do plan to keep writing. I will keep you apprised of any future publications well ahead of time. And tenure notwithstanding, if you should feel my presence ever becomes a detriment to the university, I will voluntarily resign."

16

Expansion and Influence

1970s-2000

Everything begins small. One man's doodles on a scrap of paper may spawn an international empire two generations later. Microsoft, Apple, Google, Facebook, Amazon, not to mention the Beatles, all began with one or two young people, or four, in possession of an idea, a dream—in dormitory rooms, garages, apartments, or business offices. Social movements have similar beginnings.

Secret societies, too, while hidden from view, expand organically on the strength of the ideas of their founders.

It is not surprising, then, that what began as little more than a whim in an apartment at a California university in 1973 with a few vague ideas about changing the world—inspired by charismatic and radical leaders of a counterculture then riding the crest of 1960s energy and vision—should grow and expand to other universities in the coming years.

By the time Talon Roswell graduated from UCSB, he was, with Slayton Bardolf, recognized as one of the primary leaders of the Alliance for Progress. Transferring to UCLA's graduate school in political science, where his activist father was an alumni, it was only natural that young Roswell would export the ideas he imbibed and helped expand as an undergraduate, and thus act as founder for a second chapter of the Alliance. Young Bardolf had also developed a friendship with the university's Dr. Bahram. Sharing some of his ideas with his favorite professor, he found in him an ally to the cause. Dr. Nasim Bahram thus became one of their group's oldest initial members, adding faculty, multi-ethnicity, and pseudo-religion to the expanding mix of individuals and personalities being drawn into the movement.

By then, a Charter of Purpose had been drawn up—written mostly by Bardolf with input from Roswell and Devon Crawford, along with macabre theatrics to deepen the ominous adventure of it—which each new inductee signed with a fountain pen dipped in drops of his own blood. As the years passed, and the early members moved into business, politics, and education, most remained committed to the pledge that held them in unbreakable bonds of common cause during their student days.

The movement continued to spread to other campuses, from friend to friend, from father to son, eventually becoming one of the most secretive and powerful university societies, rivaled only by Skull and Bones, Quill and Dagger, the Cadaver Society, and the Wolf's Head.

By the 1990s there were chapters in more than fifty colleges and universities across the country. Their alumni worked closely with graduate and undergraduate students, bringing in new members and expanding their influence in various ways, but mostly in state and national politics. Alinsky's "community organizing" was coming of age. The objectives of the Alliance were by then national in scope, and envisioned a wholesale remaking of American culture that would in time effectively erase all trace of its Christian foundations.

The youthful student sponges listening to Domokos in 1973 were hungry and eager to absorb the optimism of his utopian political theories. They had been fed in the nursery of the 1960s on the feel-good idealism of Joan Baez, Bob Dylan, Paul Simon, Peter Paul and Mary, and the Beatles.

But they quickly left that nursery behind. John Lennon issued a more strident battle cry than dreams vaguely blowing in the wind with his song "Revolution."

Years later, however, when the words of his song came of age, destruction was precisely what the new generation of revolutionaries clamored for. Hatred of the "establishment," the system, was the unifying fuel that fired the social revolution birthed under the disingenuous guise of peace and love.

By the 1990s, Domokos's and Alinsky's disciples were no longer flower children wanting to strew peace and love on a suffering world. They were bent on a revolution to seize power, and you could count them in. The melodically quixotic dreams of the sixties were twisted into the very thing the flower children claimed to despise. The hypocrisy immortalized in the Beatles' words, "All You Need Is Love," would define the duplicity of the elitist progressivism following half a century later. Intolerance and new forms of disguised intolerance, not love, would fuel the agenda the New Left would seek to impose upon the world.

Their influence expanded rapidly throughout the grassroots of the culture. As Alinsky's protégés became professors in the very institutions their sit-ins once disrupted, the education of an entire new generation into the religion of liberalism deepened throughout academia. With cunning effectiveness, Domokos and his disciples channeled their hatred of white privileged America, corporate capitalism, and traditional Christian values, into a movement to undermine and replace them with a new form of humanist socialism.

In 1917, Russia's working-class proletariat overthrew the privileged bourgeoise in a titanic power shift that changed the world. Alinsky modified the terms but the goal was the same, not to make everyone *equal*, but to bring a new elite to power—to topple the Haves and put a coalition of former Have-Nots in their place. His was the same objective as that of the Bolsheviks—to establish a new favored class that would arise from society's former downtrodden minorities.

The greatest secret of all in this illusive stratagem of the New Left, was that this new favored class would *itself* be ruled by a super-elite of progressives who shrewdly knew how to manipulate the Have-Nots into handing them the power to rule. The super-elite would tell their minions how to think, how to vote, what to believe, and whom it was right to hate.

Thus, in the end, America would be remade in the image of a tiny minority, still skillfully using Alinsky's Rule Number One to deceive an entire gullible nation—ultimately leaving the Have-Nots no better off than they were before.

Chapter memberships in the Alliance, initially seven, were expanded to twelve undergraduates. Alumni and graduate members were welcome at any function. A "Committee of Seven" was established to serve in a leadership capacity over the entire network, the Bardolf and Roswell founders as permanent members, the additional five elected from the pool of graduated chapter presidents to serve for a term of two years.

The Alliance's charter now included a progressive document, or "Compact for Progress," written by Bardolf and Roswell, then in their forties and recognized as the two "Grand Masters" of the Alliance. It was largely based on the teachings of Saul Alinsky and Viktor Domokos, who was often invited to secret biennial meetings of the chapter presidents and leadership committee. These highly secret meetings were held on the Roswell estate in the southern California hills near Mira Monte—inherited by Talon Roswell at the premature death of his father—which served as the unofficial headquarters of the Alliance. At these gatherings the general objectives, increasingly political, were established to be taken back and implemented in individual chapters.

The overall American progressive movement was organic and multi-dimensional. Myriad diverse groups large and small, with tens of thousands of foot soldiers, contributed unique specifics as they worked in concert, though independently, toward commonly held goals. But Alinsky's teachings, and Domokos and his disciples, remained at the vanguard, ever pushing, leading, cajoling, and influencing the American public forward toward the tacit acceptance of their increasingly radical agenda.

As more and more of its members reached positions of power in government, business, education, and the media, the political influence and wealth of the Alliance grew. Its finances remained as closely guarded as its membership rolls. The Alliance's wealth, initially due mostly to huge infusions from Domokos and the Roswell legacy, increased dramatically from the donations of many individuals. It was a significant factor in ensuring the successful campaigns of numerous candidates whose agendas dovetailed with the ideals of the Alliance and its Compact.

Money was funneled into the coffers of liberal candidates by so many circuitous means that many of those who benefited never knew it. Others, however, found themselves on both ends of an unwritten *quid pro quo*, receiving financial backing to get elected. The other half of the "something for something" bargain inevitably came calling later in the form of expected votes or favors to advance the agenda.

What was called the Domokos Corollary of Alinsky's rules for radicals remained at the core of the code, philosophy, purpose, and methodology of the Alliance—*secrecy*. Though their tactics occasionally crossed certain legal lines as based on Alinsky's foundational Rule One—deception—the Corollary ensured that the general public never heard about, nor suspected, the existence of such a network.

Those destined to step into the public spotlight, such as their greatest success story thus far—the former governor of Arkansas—would be the few. Most involved in the Alliance would labor in anonymity for the greater good, rejoicing that, having placed a man in the White House, there was no limit to where they could take the country in the third millennium.

As that bright new era of promise dawned, working with their two sons and the leadership committee, in the year 2000 as the mantle of leadership gradually shifted to a new generation, the group's name was changed to the Palladium Alliance for Progress.

An expanded charter was drawn up to define the group's ambitious agenda for the new century. The new name was never to be spoken aloud. The charter was signed by Slayton Bardolf and his son, Loring; Talon Roswell and his son, Storm; and the Committee of Seven. It was placed in a wall safe in the library of the Mira Monte estate.

17

OF THE WRITING OF FALSE PROPHECIES THERE IS NO END

1995–2004

THOUGH STIRLING Marshall loved his profession and loved the university, as he prayed for guidance over the two years following his discussion with UCSB's president, the sense deepened within him that his spiritual writings were growing in import. They could not be a side-light forever.

Increasingly ostracized by his academic peers for his Christian beliefs and religious writings, and disturbed by the direction being taken by the world of academia, Dr. Marshall took early retirement at the end of the school term in June of 1995 at the age of fifty-four.

As the end of the millennium loomed on the horizon, imbued by a new generation of opportunistic scriptural letter-worshippers, the 1990s produced a spate of reincarnated *Late Great* rehash prophetic scenarios.

Simultaneous with his decision to devote more of his future to writing, the publication of a best-selling series of end-times novels began in 1995, and the subsequent response of the Christian public, acted upon Stirling Marshall like a trumpet blast. In almost a blinding vision, he saw that the church of the future would be radically different than what was being predicted, and that a tribulation of far different solemnity and purpose was coming, one most of Christendom would not recognize.

The prophetic hysteria of the final years of the millennium, in Stirling's opinion, set the Christian church back decades, if not centuries, in its understanding of God's true purposes. The enormity of presumption inherent in the series was revealed by the little-known prediction by its primary author of a specific *date* by which the Lord would return visibly to earth.

Stunned as he read the audacious claim, Stirling closed his eyes, both heartbroken and angry, then breathed a silent prayer to be allowed to live to see the date pass rapture-less, and the foolish evangelical star be exposed as the false prophet he was.

Even as he prayed what he immediately recognized as a rash prayer revealing his own immaturity, he knew that when the predicted year arrived *without* the revelation of the Lord in the clouds, no one, least of all those who promoted the false prophecies as a great work of God, would even notice. There was a time when false prophets were stoned, Stirling thought to himself. In these modern days they were lauded as great men.

As these revelations unfolded within him, the Marshall children were growing up.

Woody, twenty-five, graduated from Cal Poly San Luis Obispo in 1995 and was apprenticing with a developer in the area as he worked on his own contractor's license.

Cateline, now Cateline Watson, was married and living in Marysville north of Sacramento, teaching fourth grade at Marysville Elementary School.

Graham graduated from UCSB in 1998 in computer science. Shortly thereafter, he left for the north with a college friend to seek his fortune in Silicon Valley. As aspiring actors and actresses hoped to be discovered in Hollywood, young techno-nerds dreamed of finding their pots of gold in the Nirvana of San Jose, Sunnyvale, Palo Alto, or Cupertino. Graham Marshall now joined their ranks.

Jane, also at Santa Barbara, majoring in English, would soon be the only one of the five still living at home.

Timothy, the youngest, graduated from Santa Barbara High in 1998 and was enrolled in Cal Poly SLO for the following school year. He would follow in his father's footsteps, pursuing a major in history.

The conviction grew within the father of the five as the new millennium dawned that the modest platform he had been given as a result of *Unspoken Commandments* and his other books, though tiny by comparison, might one day impel him to speak in some way against the falsehoods being foisted upon evangelicalism about the second coming and the tribulation awaiting Christ's church if she did not awaken to her blindness.

It was time for voices to issue the call to a remnant of righteousness that would be *taken*, not taken out of the world, but out of the *church*, even persecuted by it. If he was to be such a voice, and if that was his mission, such a high purpose could not be accomplished either in the world's educational system *or* from within the structure of organized Christendom.

Even if his words were but to the few who were set apart within the vast sea of unthinking Christendom—perhaps to a mere remnant—it would be a summons he hoped to be strong enough to obey when the time came.

18

WHERE DID IT COME FROM?

1999

WHEN THE question first entered the inquisitive child's brain of Thady and Nadine Gray's daughter, neither they nor she ever knew. Jaylene's questions were probing and persistent from beyond memory. But *one* question undergirded all others as the inevitable end point of her obsession with antiquity.

At an early stage in her youthful curiosity, antiquity led in only one direction. The opposite end of the infinity-arrow pointed forward toward an inquiry that yet lay in her future.

For young Jaylene Gray, antiquity led *back* in time. Back . . . back . . . always further back.

Millions of years back . . . tens of millions . . . hundreds of millions . . . billions of years . . . back . . . back . . . to . . .

Beginnings.

Where had everything come from?

It was the great scientific mystery, more unanswerable even than the Riemann hypothesis.

She had begun early in life asking her father about beginnings.

"Daddy, where did I come from?"

"You came from your mother and me."

"Where did you and Mama come from?"

"From our parents."

"Where did they come from?"

"From their ancestors."

"Where did all people come from?"

"From our human ancestors."

"Where did our human ancestors come from?"

"We evolved from apes."

"Where did apes come from?"

"They evolved from primates."

"Where did primates come from?

"They evolved from earlier mammals."

"Where did mammals come from?"

"They evolved from reptiles."

"Where did reptiles come from?"

"They evolved from amphibians."

"Where did amphibians come from?"

"They evolved from fish."

"What about dinosaurs?"

"They're also reptiles, so they also evolved from fish."

"What about birds—where did they come from?"

"They evolved from dinosaurs called theropods."

"So everything evolved from fish?"

"Animals at least. All animals originated in the oceans."

"Where did fish come from?"

"They evolved from earlier forms of sea life."

"Animals?"

"Things like jellyfish and sea anemones and coral."

"Where did they come from?"

"There were things called deuterostomes and protostomes, which later evolved into insects, and small worms. Before them came placozoa and sponges."

"Where did they all come from?"

"They evolved from the first multicellular forms of life."

"Where did they come from?"

"They evolved from bacteria, mitochondria, and protozoa."

"Where did they come from?"

"From photosynthesis acting on single-cell organisms. The photosynthesis stimulated them to divide and merge."

"How did all that happen?"

"By accident."

"Where did photosynthesis come from?"

"From the energy of the sun acting on chemicals in the earth's oceans."

"Where did the chemicals come from?"

"From molecules."

"Where did molecules come from?"

"From atoms."

"Where did atoms come from?"

"From sub-atomic particles and gases and energy."

"Where did they come from?"

"From the Big Bang."

"Where did the Big Bang come from?"

"There was nothing before the Big Bang?"

"How did it start?"

"By itself."

"But how?"

Finally, her father was silenced. All her life her father had been a man who knew everything. He could answer every question. Yet to this one inquiry, the man who knew everything had no answer.

As she grew, Jaylene began to wonder if *anyone* had an answer. The scientific disciplines all traced their specific lineages back to the Big Bang. But none could answer the final question: How did it start? Where did the particles, the matter, the atoms, and the energy come from?

Geology measured everything by time. The layers of the Grand Canyon were all functions of time.

Astronomy measured everything by the Big Bang. The Big Bang was itself defined by *time*—how big was the universe 10^{-1000} of a second after the Big Bang. How far had the universe expanded 10^{-10} of a second after the Big Bang? How big was the universe ten seconds after the Big Bang? How big was the universe now—13.7 billion years after the Big Bang?

Evolution measured everything by time. How *long* did it take for fish to become amphibious and crawl up on land? How *long* did it take for birds to become dinosaurs—then for apes to become men?

All developments of life, even the origins of life, were dictated by the passage of millions and billions of years to allow life on earth to develop.

Time was the great equalizer, the great forward-moving constant of life and the universe.

And she wanted to know how the clocks of the Big Bang and geology and evolution were set in motion in the first place.

Where had time itself originated?

Jaylene entered university having read every book Stephen Hawking wrote, some of them two and three times. Desperately she dug for any clue that might shed light on what he thought about the ultimate question of origins. But whenever his theories began to creep too close toward that unknown unknowable, he sidestepped the dilemma by falling back on the *something-out-of-nothing* third of the scientific Rosetta triad—answering the most important question with no answer at all.

It was a response no intelligent child would be satisfied with. It was not an answer that had satisfied the child Jaylene Gray.

Like all scientists, the great Stephen Hawking always started with something, but never asked where the *something* came from. It seemed to Jaylene a simple enough question. Why did no scientist attempt to answer it? It was the one question by which even Thaddeus Gray and Stephen Hawking were stumped:

Where had it all come from?

To all other scientific inquiries—from black holes to dark matter to extraterrestrial life—science remained uniformly inquisitive, willing to spend millions, even billions to investigate and build the most advanced equipment to delve into the most insignificant questions. But to that *one* question, science remained as deafeningly silent as was Stephen Hawking. Was it because it was a question not accessible from scientific inquiry at all? Was science simply unwilling to admit itself stymied?

As she set out for the university, therefore, lurking behind all the knowledge with which the years and her reading and her father's instruction had filled her, was the great unanswerable for which there seemed to be no credible scientific theory.

Therefore Jaylene Gray did what all good scientists unconsciously do. She put the question of ultimate beginnings away in a box, locked it tight, shoved it down into the deep recesses of her mind where hopefully it would eventually be forgotten altogether...and threw away the key.

19

The Only Theory on the Market

1999

That FORGETFULNESS never came.

Science's non-answer to beginnings was still not satisfactory to university junior Jaylene Gray, by then the darling of Cal Poly's archaeology department. She had successfully kept the question locked away. But stirrings were beginning in the hidden regions of her ever-active brain.

Reading an article in *Time*, suddenly the author's bias jumped out at her.

Using disparaging language at the notion of giving consideration to a religious hypothesis, he wrote: "In the late 1970s, Arkansas and Louisiana required that if evolution be taught, equal time must be given to Genesis . . . masquerading as oxymoronic 'creation science.'"

It was his scarcely disguised embedded use of the word "moron" in his statement that suddenly offended Jaylene as she read. She was insulted by the author's obvious lack of scientific objectivity.

More derogatory and belittling words from the article leapt off the page one after another:

Never-never land . . . absurdity . . . ignorance . . . anti-intellectualism . . .

The entire article smacked of disrespectful elitism toward those who believed in the Genesis account of creation.

She didn't believe in it either. Yet the words set off a chain reaction of new and unexpected questions.

Why was the scientific community so closed-minded?

The opposite side of the coin did not immediately occur to her—why the religious community was equally close-minded? She knew nothing about religion. Her family never talked about such things. She had never been to church. She was knowledgeable enough to know a few of the basic tenets of Islam, Judaism, Christianity, Hinduism, and Buddhism. They were nothing but fairy tales to her. People joined clubs. Other people joined churches and mosques and synagogues and whatever Hindus and Buddhists joined. To her they were one and the same. None were of interest to her. She didn't know whether religious people were open-minded or close-minded, and didn't care. That was their business.

But she *was* an inquisitive scientist. She wanted to know why *scientists* were close-minded.

The dichotomy slammed into her brain with the seismic force of a 10.0 earthquake.

Why did the scientific community not accept the religious theory of beginnings as a recognizable theory?

The creation account had never been disproven. It was believed by many people. By the scientific method, those two facts alone accorded it the status of a "theory."

No scientist had to say it was *true*. Maybe it was true, maybe it wasn't true. Probably neither side of that coin could be *proven* beyond doubt. It was probably like the Riemann hypothesis—unprovable.[4] That's why it was called a *hypothesis*. It was yet to be proven true or false.

Why wasn't the religious "hypothesis" placed on the level of any other valid theory about an unknown which some people believed and others didn't—a hypothesis, possibly true or possibly false? Why did scientists malign and ridicule those who believed it?

This wasn't the flat-earth scenario where a onetime theory had been categorically *disproved* beyond doubt? Neither the existence of God nor a creationary component to beginnings, had been disproved. That meant they were still on the table.

Without *disproof*, any theory remained a theoretical possibility. Why did science maintain a double standard toward religious theories that it would not force upon any other kind of theory?

The hypocrisy of it was suddenly so plain.

Science wanted its theories accepted *prima facie* as legitimate but refused to do the same toward religious theories. It was an especially untenable position given that as far as she understood it—and she admittedly knew nothing about religion—religion proposed a theory in the one area for which science had none of its own to offer—ultimate beginnings, where matter came from, what pushed the button that ignited the explosion that led to the formation of the universe, and to life itself?

Logic would seem to indicate that science would be *eager* to hear what contribution religion might make to advance knowledge into a region of which it knew nothing.

Now that she thought about it—this was an incredible dichotomy!

Truth be told, thought Jaylene, she didn't believe in God. Her family had never given religion a moment's thought.

Yet if science had no theory to propose that would bring raw matter and energy into being out of nothing, here was a theory that did. Religion at least proposed *something*, as incredible as the idea of God might seem at first glance. In that sense, it was already far ahead of science in the matter of ultimate beginnings.

Perhaps it was a preposterous theory. But it was the only theory on the market.

Not only did the scientific community not recognize religion's hypothesis as one to consider, it ridiculed and scorned those who did consider it.

Science went further—it vilified those who dared even *ask* about ultimate beginnings, disparaging and stigmatizing them as unscientific, stupid, and intellectually backward.

Jaylene had asked her father where everything came from. Was *she* stupid and unscientific for wanting to know? Was it backward and intellectually deficient to ask hard questions of science?

Why was *this* one question out of bounds?

Again, she scanned the *Time* article. In speaking of a recent ruling by the Kansas school board to remove evolution from its curriculum, which she agreed was a questionable decision, the author wrote: "In doing so, the board transported its jurisdiction to a never-never land. . . . The major argument advanced by the school board . . . smacks of absurdity and only reveals ignorance. . . . Why get excited over this latest episode in the long sad history of American anti-intellectualism? Let me suggest that . . . we should cringe in embarrassment. . . . no one ignorant of evolution can understand science. . . . The road of the newly adopted Kansas curriculum can only spiral inward toward restriction and ignorance."[5]

It was so biased, close-minded, and unscientific as to be laughable. Yet the author was one of the most highly respected geologists in the country—one of her father's own colleagues. How could a scientist be so prejudiced against a theory that sought to answer a question for which he had no alternative?

He was the small-minded one, just as small-minded as those he denigrated who refused to look objectively at the science behind evolution.

And with that realization, Jaylene Gray dug the locked beginnings-box out of the basement of her mind and began to search for the key.

Though we live in the world
we are not carrying on a worldly war.

2 CORINTHIANS 10:3

We are not contending against flesh and blood,
but against principalities and powers, against the
world rulers of this present darkness, against the
spiritual hosts of wickedness in the heavenly places.

EPHESIANS 6:12

PART 2
NO WORLDLY WAR
2000–2014

20

STRATEGIES

2002-2003

THE ELECTION of 2000 shocked the left-leaning end of the political spectrum. It was a wake-up call. Suddenly they realized that the Clinton years could not make them complacent.

Had the clandestine gathering of business, economic, academic, and political leaders been publicly known, it would have led every broadcast and talk show of *Fox News*, though might have received no mention on CNN, CBS, ABC, or NBC. MSNBC might have mentioned it as a strategy session for defeating George Bush in 2004. As it was, however, neither conservative Bill O'Reilly nor liberal Chris Mathews knew a thing about it.

In truth, the covert agenda of closet visionaries was more far-reaching than the next election cycle. George Bush's hanging-chad victory over Al Gore was an annoyance to be sure. In spite of his ratings home run speech in the ruins of New York's Twin Towers, they would do their best to defeat him next time around. But Bush's moment on the national stage was but a blip on the screen. He was a lightweight who would not seriously impede their ultimate momentum.

They had come together to look far into the future, beyond their own lifetimes, ten election cycles from now if it took that long. Besides being an invisible war, their goals were not those of a short-sighted worldly war. Theirs was a grandiose vision to remake American society, economics, business, education, and religion, to orchestrate the emergence of the ultimate system of governmental and societal inter-course toward which all the nations and governments had ineffectually been striving for thousands of years. Their combined intellects, vision, and financial resources, they had no doubt, were capable of laying out a blueprint beyond what the greatest minds of history were able to envision. Not even Karl Marx could have foreseen it. Now was the appointed time. The hope of mankind was in their hands. Destiny had chosen them to guide humanity into its glorious future.

Why people of means—those who benefited most from the Ameri-can system of government, from its society and culture and traditions—were often the most vocal about tearing down the institutions of the past, will doubtless be one of the great conundrums facing historians of the future. Logic would assume that they would be the *most* capable of perceiving the inherent *goodness* of America in spite of the flaws and growing pains which all nations progress through in their bumpy his-toric advance. Why then were the elite, the wealthy, the powerful, the famous, the privileged—from Hollywood to academia to politics to the media—so determined to divorce America from the very foundations from which they had benefited, and which spawned its unique excep-tionalism in the world? Why did atheistic socialism, with such clear examples of its failure apparent around the globe, so appeal to those who should most clearly see the strengths of democracy, capitalism, and Christianity working in concert?

What births antagonism toward one's roots? Does perhaps an invisible binarism exist in the human psyche, a hidden code embedded deep in some miniscule strand of DNA, which develops in some as an inherent gratefulness for the gift of life, and the capacity to take it as it comes without resentment, while in others, if the binary code is switched in the opposite direction, creates dissatisfaction and inborn anger, marked by the urge to rebel against one's place in life?

To the former, life's circumstances are the soil in which to grow, mature, work hard, focus on their own personal responsibilities rather than what is wrong around them, and make life a good thing. To the latter, what they perceive as wrong in the world obliterates the many "rightnesses" of life.

Are political and social leanings therefore, in fact, genetic rather than cultural, educational, or environmental?

Such questions were not on the minds of those present on this day. They were all of one mind—for whatever reason—in their belief that the foundations of the United States of America, which had given them so much, needed to be discarded and new foundations laid according to their radical social agenda.

Communism, socialism, fascism, democracy, capitalism—all had fallen short. So too had the visions of ancient Greece and Rome. The imperialism of the mighty British Empire had come and gone. Now the American experiment in democracy was floundering because, in their view, its history was corrupt. The inherent greed of American capitalism rewarded the rich, white, and powerful and kept minorities and the poor from participating in the illusion of the American dream.

Even more lethal was the systemic ignorance, bigotry, and racism of American's Christian tradition, which maintained a stranglehold on the hearts and minds of the most backward thinking regions of the country. It was a religious system as fanciful as Santa Claus and the Easter Bunny, fittingly celebrated alongside their two most powerful myths they called the incarnation and the resurrection.

Both the wealthy white privilege of American capitalism and politics, and the fable of Christianity had to be eliminated before the new American dream could be ushered in—a dream which would truly bring a new order to the world. They would heed the words of Alexander and Caesar, Napoleon and Marx and Hitler, as well as Voltaire, Rousseau, Hume, Smith, Jefferson, and Locke. But they would strip them from the inherent racism of their times, bringing a new vision of human freedom and equality to grand fulfillment.

"In light of the fiasco of 2000, which put an illegitimate candidate in the White House," Nevada Senator Henry Rice was saying. "I think we are compelled to ask what measures we might undertake to insure the abolition of the electoral college."

"A worthy objective, Senator. But a permanent solution must be more far reaching." The speaker was fifty-four-year-old Slayton Bardolf, one of the two Grand Masters of the League of Seven of the Palladium

Alliance, to which about half of those present belonged. Though none of the others had an inkling of the group's existence, several owed their present careers and positions of leadership to it. They only knew Bardolf as one of the strategists of Vice President Gore's ill-fated campaign and, in spite of Bush's so-called victory, one of the shrewdest political minds in the country. "It may be time," Bardolf continued, "for us to ask if our current democratic model, which gives equal votes to the ignorant of the Bible Belt, is a workable model for the future."

"What are you suggesting?" asked Congresswoman Nora Penskey.

"That we take steps to keep it from happening again."

"In what way?"

"We must indoctrinate the electorate—slowly and shrewdly, of course—and also *expand* the electorate so that the religious faction loses its identity, and thus its influence. By both these means, we will remove uncertainty from the equation of future elections."

"Uncertainty is built into the democratic model," rejoined Penskey.

"Not always—not if we control the narrative, control how people think. Germany in the 1920s—though it led to, uh, certain unfortunate results—nevertheless is instructive for our purposes. The populace was carefully controlled. They had no idea what was taking place behind the scenes. This is the lesson we must take from it. As I once heard a very wise gentleman say—"

As he spoke Bardolf cast a momentary glance toward financier Viktor Domokos.

"—when you set the narrative you choose, make people believe it, and keep your strategies secret, you can lead the people as easily as if there are rings in their noses."

Light laughter spread through the room. It was clear they approved of the visual image.

"I find myself also intrigued by the current Chinese model," added Bardolf's fellow Palladium Grand Master, Talon Roswell. "They are finding a way to marry communism and capitalism more effectively than the Soviets ever did. Their future bears watching. Of course, there are problems inherent in their system. And for a while longer we have to retain the illusion of democracy, a concern the Chinese do not have.

In time, however, it is my conviction that it may be necessary to move toward a single-party system that maintains control. I see no other way to ensure that the greater good of society is preserved. In that regard, Russia and China have been successful. They have elections, but those elections are no threat to the party's agenda. I foresee something of that nature in our future."

"You must admit that keeping the pretext of discourse alive is useful. Might it perhaps continue to be necessary?" asked California Senator Fenbrooke.

"The recent election has shown that the opposition still wields more power than I am comfortable allowing it. For too long we have allowed them to retain that power in spite of their refusal to acknowledge the trends of the future."

It was silent a moment.

"All these measures take time," now put in the acknowledged elder statesman of the gathering, Viktor Domokos.

In the thirty years since his now legendary address at UCSB in 1973, his Romanian accent was undiminished. Now in his mid-sixties he was a legend, not merely as Saul Alinsky's protégé but as the primary financial donor to causes and candidates which all those present supported—women's rights, abortion, and numerous gay and lesbian groups among them. Though he was not technically a politician, he might well have been the most powerful single individual on the American political landscape. When Viktor Domokos spoke, Democrats listened.

"History is on our side," he went on. "Progressivism will always win out over outmoded ideologies. We must be patient and allow public sentiment to follow slowly. Within ten years there will be a black in the White House, within twenty a woman—perhaps even one who is with us here. Gays and lesbians will not be far behind. History is on our side. These things will come. But the public must be inoculated slowly so they do not recognize where the changes are leading. As Slayton has indicated, there remains superstition and ignorance in certain regions. Our ideology must be injected into the bloodstream of the masses by small doses. We have to feed the idea that homosexuality, for example, is normal. We succeeded with abortion by creating the illusion that killing is *not* killing. The public now believes it. We succeeded with evolution, seducing the public into believing that the science against design was irrefutable, and creationists are fools.

"This we will do with a host of issues. Our friend Mr. Gore has been invaluable in the global warming arena, again convincing the public that the science is irrefutable and that the crisis is entirely man-made. We have even made sure he believes it," he added with the hint of a smile. "It makes him all the more convincing. The point is, we have made enormous strides since the sixties tipped the balance of cultural norms our way. If we are shrewd in setting our narrative, even Christians will accept what we tell them. In time nothing will shock them. Christianity as a system of belief will have been neutralized."

He stopped. As the room quieted, the next to speak was a man whose air of mystery gave his words almost equal weight to those of Bardolf and Domokos. His pedigree as son of a respected post-war Arab immigrant added to the stature in which he was held.

Nasim Bahram, retired academic and philosopher, former UCSB professor and one of Slayton Bardolf's longtime Palladium colleagues, was an anomaly in liberal circles—a culturally progressive Muslim. He had devoted his professional life to science, in which progressive ideas were central. Whatever were his personal religious beliefs he never divulged. They were unknown to anyone in this group, including Slayton Bardolf himself. Both men were skilled in keeping secrets.

"In light of last year's attacks by my terrorist Arab brethren," he began, "you may find what I am about to say hard to believe. I believe that even the September 11 attacks will ultimately work to our advantage in eradicating Christianity as a force in the country. It's so counterintuitive, one scarcely believes that it continues to happen."

He paused. The others waited.

"America has a perverse idea that it must not only forgive its enemies, but that it must demonstrate its goodness by *strengthening* them after defeating them. Who are the most powerful industrial and technological countries in the world alongside the US? Germany and Japan. The US gave them the tools to succeed. Rather than rebuilding Great

Britain after it saved the world from Hitler, the US rebuilt Hitler's Germany and the nation that bombed Pearl Harbor. It's the American way. Forgive your enemies, then give them the strength and tools to undermine your own strength, even, in the extreme, ultimately to destroy you. Now China is joining them. With America's help, China will soon eclipse America on the world stage. America's obsession with empowering its enemies is a perverse form of a death wish.

"In the same way, I predict that very soon American public opinion will shift and actually become *favorable* toward Islam. It's the American way. Because Islamic terrorists sought to cripple the country, we shall forgive them and then enable them to inflict further damage. Mark my words, the attacks of 9/11 will create a *more* favorable climate for Islam to flourish in the US rather than less. Americans will come to view my people as victims of Christian Islamophobia. They will feel sorry for Muslims. The entire equation will turn on its head, until Christians are viewed as evil, judgmental warmongers against Islam's religion of peace.

"Obviously as a Muslim of Iranian descent, this dynamic is of enormous fascination to me. My loyalty, of course, is to America's progressive agenda. Yet I will be watching the long-term impact of the recent attacks with keen interest. I predict that Muslims will become one more favored minority that must be given special advantages. This will translate into Muslims in Congress. We may see a Muslim in the White House in my lifetime. Perhaps my own son!" he added laughing. "But that is unlikely. Sonrab is an academic like me. The point is that this shift in the public mood toward Muslims will be a useful development in the neutralization of Christianity. Yet if we give my countrymen too free a rein, extremists will come in by the thousands. So it will be a tightrope we will have to walk in coming years with great care."

As he spoke, Bahram was himself walking an invisible tightrope, no less perilous than that which he warned about. He was playing a cunning game to bolster his progressive credentials. Neither Slayton Bardolf nor Viktor Domokos suspected his true designs.

Again a brief silence fell.

"Speaking of the upcoming cycles," now said Devon Crawford, the third of the UCSB triumvirate who had launched the Alliance. "I'm not so sure we need to wait ten years to install a black in the Oval Office."

All eyes turned to the outspoken gay man.

"There's a young congressman from Illinois called Barack Obama. I've been following his career." He did not add that on the basis of his recommendation Palladium was secretly funneling money his way and suppressing negative stories about him.

"I know who you mean," said Senator Fenbrooke. "But with his Muslim-sounding name, he wouldn't stand a chance."

"Don't be too sure. We might kill two birds with one stone—a Muslim *and* a black."

"It would never happen," added Senator Penskey. "And he doesn't claim to be a Muslim."

"What are you thinking, Devon . . . 2004?" asked Roswell.

"That's probably too soon. He's a national unknown at this point."

"Speaking of next year," said Bardolf, turning to a man of stately demeanor with a thick graying crop of Kennedyesque hair, "you're still planning to take on Bush, are you not, John?"

"It's early," replied the senator from Massachusetts. "But if Dean and Edwards don't prove too formidable—"

Light laughter interrupted him.

"I think I can state with a high degree of confidence," said a certain former governor of Arkansas, "with the backing of those in this room, that you will have nothing to worry about."

"Adding to the president's observation," Bardolf went on. "That does bring up an interesting possibility. We could use next year's election to move young Obama into the spotlight."

"How so?" asked Kerry.

"He could introduce you at the convention."

"Don't get ahead of yourself, Slayton," laughed the senator.

"You heard what Bill said. You've got nothing to worry about. My point is that such a platform would give the country four years to get used to the Muslim name and his skin color."

"Actually," chuckled Crawford, "I think his being half black would work for him rather than against him."

"It absolutely would," added Domokos. "By controlling the narrative, we would play on white racist guilt. Whites would go for him in droves. They would have to prove that they're *not* racists. It's an ingenious application of Saul's Rule One."

"Reverse discrimination!" laughed Bardolf, "—a ticket to the White House."

"Is he a Muslim?" asked the wife of the former president.

Heads glanced around the room in question.

"I don't know his background as thoroughly as I would like," replied Crawford. "His convictions may lie in that direction, though he's doing the Christianity thing for appearance's sake. There are some pretty sketchy characters around the edges of his entourage. A strident and very racist black minister named Wright would be a problem with evangelicals."

"I know Wright," put in the former president. "He's bombastic in his criticism of America. We would have to massage Obama's image a bit. But my feeling is that he is Teflon—not even Wright would hurt him."

"Spoken by one who ought to know!"

A few chuckles went around the group.

"My Teflon had a few scratches," commented Clinton. "I didn't help myself either," he added, avoiding his wife's eyes.

"But if we could keep Obama's foreign past and Muslim ties, among other things from being looked at," Crawford went on, "I don't think anyone could touch him."

"Could you control him?" asked Domokos.

"Absolutely," replied Crawford. "That's Slayton's specialty! Besides, as a young congressman, he's a pretty face. His speaking ability is like no one's I've ever heard. All we have to do is put the words in his mouth and turn the election into a popularity contest. He's the high school homecoming king, he's the next American Idol."

"What's he done—what's his job history before Congress?" asked Kerry.

"Not much. Community organizing—"

"*Community organizing!*" laughed Bardolf. "You have to be kidding!"

"Really—that's how he describes himself."

"He actually uses the phrase?"

"That's what he calls himself, a community organizer."

Domokos now joined in the laughter. "Trying to channel Saul Alinsky," he said. "Anyone will know what he means—that he's a closet radical. Community organizing is code for 'Overthrow Those in Power.'"

"We'll make sure the Republicans never know," said Bardolf. "We'll have rank-and-file Republicans stumbling over themselves to support him along with Democrats."

"I'm not sure he's actually ever held a job as such," Crawford went on. "Scholarships and grants all the way through. He's had a pretty easy time of it—the perks of being a good-looking, articulate, popular black who rode Affirmative Action to the top."

"Where else but America, right!" added Bardolf, laughing. "I can see the headline now: 'Affirmative Action puts black in White House.'"

Light laughter followed.

"True as it may be," said Domokos turning serious again, "if what you suggest is successful, we don't even joke about such things. Programs like Affirmative Action are the underpinnings of everything we are trying to accomplish—taking away from the whites and giving it to minorities. If anything, we need to broaden Affirmative Action to include the entire homosexual movement, eventually doing away with outmoded preconceptions about marriage and family, even the entire concept of gender. We have many social barriers to overcome. Future offshoots of Affirmative Action will be key to our success."

"Of course," laughed the former president. "But the irony of using racism in the form of race guilt to elect a black man—it's delicious."

"Perhaps. But we can't actually *say* it. Blacks and gays and Hispanics have to think we *mean* what we say about equality. We can't let them realize we are using them."

"Back to the Obama scenario," said Senator Rice. "I am intrigued by what has been said. Yet from what I know of the young man, and from what Devon has said, he can't decide if he's white or black. If we're going to make the racist thing work, we'll have to blacken him up. Maybe get him doing more Ebonics-speak. It's his blackness that will win, not his being half white."

"You're right," added Bardolf. "Racism is a tricky business. It has to be played just right. We've got to make sure whites never recognize themselves as victims of a new and acceptable form of black against white racism."

Nods and thoughtful expressions went around the room.

"What about you, Hillary?" now said the other of their non-political operatives, author and linguist Noam Chomsky. "Everyone has you slated as the first woman president. When are you thinking of making your bid?"

"I'll build my résumé in the Senate until I no longer need Bill's coattails," she replied. "I was thinking '08. I hadn't anticipated someone like this Obama getting in my way. You all seem pretty taken with him."

"Just throwing out possibilities," replied Crawford. "You of course would have the support of everyone here."

"It sounds as if you're already on the Obama bandwagon," rejoined the senator with an edge in her voice.

"Not at all, Hillary," replied Bardolf. "We need to elect a woman, a black, a homosexual, a Muslim, and an illegal Latino who gained citizenship. The order isn't important. Then a ticket of two women, two blacks, a woman and a black. The Latino scenario will be necessary prior to statehood for Cuba. That is down the road. But we can't think too far out until we have undisputed control in all the statehouses to give us the power to push through constitutional amendments."

"I could see that as soon as 2020," said the former president, "as long as no charismatic Republican outsider rides in on a white horse. Barring something unforeseen, Bush should be the last Republican president this country will have to put up with."

"Two-thirds of the statehouses may be more difficult than insuring our hold on the presidency. There remains much ignorance between the coasts. Half the states are run by racists. I'm not sure that will disappear by 2020."

"Unless we flood those states with illegals."

"Again," said Domokos thoughtfully. "I would not advise being in too big a rush. Once the presidency is secure, we'll be able to move the agenda more rapidly. We'll get the Supreme Court safe as well. Then it's just a matter of time. But back to Hillary—have no fear," he said, turning toward the former first lady, "we will back you 100 percent."

"And the congressman?" said Hillary, raising a quizzical eyebrow.

"We'll see what develops," answered Bardolf. "It might not be a bad strategy to run you both in '08. With your name recognition and the woman vote, you will obviously defeat him in the primaries. Then you name him your VP, he rises in the public eye, then succeeds you. That would give us sixteen uninterrupted years. After that, we will be in a position to move ahead even more rapidly."

21

INQUISITIVE SECULARIST

2002

A SENIOR IN Cal Poly's history department, whose biggest decision at the moment was where to enroll a year from now in graduate school, was walking through a grassy area of campus in the Baker Center quad shortly after the start of the fall term when his gaze was drawn to a girl seated on one of the benches reading what appeared to be a Bible. It wasn't a sight one saw often. University campuses were not exactly greenhouses for Christianity.

In no hurry and in a cheerful mood, especially if he might have the good fortune to run into that rarest of endangered species on campus—a fellow Christian—he approached, then paused and greeted her.

"Reading the world's greatest work of literature, I see."

She glanced up and smiled. "I guess that's what they say," she replied.

"Probably not for a class, though."

"No!" she laughed lightly. "I'm not sure I've heard the Bible so much as mentioned in my time here. No, purely personal."

"It looks like, what—Genesis?"

"It is. How did you know?"

"I'm pretty familiar with the Bible."

"And everyone knows Genesis comes first."

"Yeah, but you could probably stick your finger in anyplace and I could guess what book it's in."

"What do you mean, book?"

"The Bible's collection of sixty-six *books* mostly titled by the author's names—the books of the Bible, you know."

"Oh, okay. And you could guess where I opened the Bible?"

"I think I could get close—probably plus or minus one book. Or maybe two if it's one of the shorter ones."

"You mean I could open it anywhere and you would know where I'd opened it?"

"Actually, I don't know," he laughed. "I've never tried it before. But I would be in the neighborhood."

"Then I will test you," she said. "Here, sit down—but no peeking."

He sat down on the other side of the bench while she flipped through the book, then closed it over her index finger, and pointed it in his direction.

"Okay—show me what you've got," she said. "Where's my finger?"

"That's too easy," he replied. "At least give me something hard. Your finger is in the book of Psalms."

A look of surprise spread over her face as if she didn't quite believe it. She opened the book and read the title at the top of the page. "It says right here, Psalm 139."

"One of my favorites."

"That's amazing. Let me try again."

He watched the operation until she was ready.

"Okay, definitely a little harder," he said. "I'm going to say Isaiah."

Again, she opened the book and looked at the page. "I don't believe it! Right again! How did you do that! I'm going to make this one really hard."

She flipped through until she found a few shorter books, picked a page, closed it on her finger, and again pointed the Bible in his direction."

"Oh boy, that is going to be hard. Let me see, I think . . . I'm going to guess Joel."

"I got you—it's, let me look again." Quickly she opened the book. "Ha! It's called Amos!"

"Ah, but I said plus or minus one. I think if you check you will find Joel just ahead of Amos."

She flipped a few pages. "Unbelievable! Right again!"

"I will admit, I got lucky. I could have been off on that one by three or four books. As you probably know, the Minor Prophets are pretty short."

"No, I didn't know. I've never heard of the Minor Prophets. Okay, one more. If you get it, I will concede defeat."

This time she turned toward the back of the book. "Okay, here you are."

"That would be . . . I think . . . Luke."

She shook her head. "I admit both amazement and defeat. I've never seen anything like it. How did you do that?"

"I've been studying the Bible a long time. I know most of its books pretty well."

"Like those, what did you call them, Minor Prophets."

"Right," he laughed. "Them too."

"Seriously, I didn't know young people—I mean, you know, our age—actually read the Bible anymore. Are you a theology student or something?"

"No. History. I'm Timothy, by the way."

"Hi, I'm Jaylene."

"Majoring in?"

"Archaeology."

"That makes us practically colleagues—both engaged in the study of the past."

"I love anything old," said Jaylene. "I was always interested in antiquity. Farther back than anything was the question of beginnings. It was the unanswered mystery. I used to ask my father about it when I was young—where did everything come from. My poor father and my million questions!" she laughed.

"What did he tell you?"

"Not much of anything. You know the stock answer—evolution back to the primordial soup, before that the Big Bang, before that nothing. I could never get a satisfactory answer. Finally, I quit wondering about it. I assumed scientists weren't supposed to ask where everything came from. So I stopped asking—until recently."

She paused thoughtfully.

"That's why I was reading in Genesis," she went on. "We don't get much in the way of that side of things in class any more than I did when I was growing up. I'm minoring in anthropology too. It's 100 percent evolution, as if evolution explains everything. But it explains nothing about beginnings. Real beginnings, I mean. In that way, evolution is a giant hoax. Everyone pretends it explains where things came from. But it does no such thing. It's like, if you asked me where that tree over there came from and I said, 'It just got there.' That's a stupid answer."

Timothy laughed. This girl was not only a thinker—she was a straight shooter!

"Anyone who thinks a supreme being might have had a hand in anything is laughed out of the classroom," she went on "That's why I'm checking out Genesis on my own. You don't dare ask those kinds of questions in an open discussion. And I couldn't be seen carrying a Bible."

"You're a Christian, I take it?" said Timothy.

"Oh no. I'm an atheist."

"But you're reading Genesis."

"Like I said, beginnings fascinate me. But science has no answer to beginnings."

"What about the Big Bang?"

"I mean *ultimate* beginnings. Before the Big Bang. If I'm going to be an objective scientist, I figured I ought to be well versed in all the theories and possibilities."

22

A Mutual Quest

"So HOW is your search for beginnings coming along?" Timothy asked.

Jaylene's face fell. "To tell you the truth, after reading the first few chapters of this, I'm not sure I'm going to get any answers in Genesis either."

"Why not?"

"It sounds like a fairy tale, the beginning of a 'Once upon a time' story. The time problem is so glaring. I mean, the whole universe created in a week! That can't be. No wonder skeptics are dismissive of it. And don't people who believe the Bible say that the universe is 6,000 years old? That's as ridiculous as the universe being created in a week. The whole thing is obviously untrue. The incredible age of everything fascinates me. So this isn't going to be of any help."

"Did you see any reference to years or the age of the universe in what you read?" asked Timothy.

She thought a moment.

"Come to think of it, I guess not. Just days."

"What if *day* doesn't mean twenty-four hours?" asked Timothy.

"What else would it mean?"

"Maybe it's a figurative term. Or looked at another way—what if it's a day in Einstein's world?"

"Relativity, you mean?"

Timothy nodded.

"Wow—that *would* change the meaning!"

"If I understand e = mc² correctly," said Timothy, "at the speed of light, time stretches to infinity, correct?"

"Something like that."

"So in the milliseconds after the Big Bang when matter exploded out at near the speed of light, a 'day' might be the equivalent of billions of years of our time."

"Oh my goodness—you're right! What an incredible thought! The theory of relativity in Genesis."

"And as the expansion after the initial explosion slowed and the matter from the Big Bang gradually coalesced, the subsequent 'days' would have shortened. But they would still be longer than twenty-four hours because the universe was still expanding terrifically fast. I only throw that out as an example of how reading the Genesis *days* as what we think of as twenty-four hours is problematic from the outset. Yet I still think a truer reading is to recognize the word 'day' as a term of *unknown* and *indefinite* length—a million years, a billion years, many billions of years. I prefer to read the 'days' of the creation account as *eons*. Or, revising what I said before about viewing the time of creation in Einstein's world—I would rather say I look at it in *God's* world, in *his* relative frame of reference. How long were the 'days' from God's perspective? Again, obviously not twenty-four hours since God was using the speed of light to create matter, when time, in a sense, was stretched to infinity. That's why reading 'day' as *eon* is more accurate. We can't possibly know what the length of each day was in God's time-reference."

"What a remarkable explanation. And what you say makes perfect sense. That immediately resolves the 6,000-year dichotomy."

"Precisely. It's actually no dichotomy at all. In my opinion, the 6,000-year thing is a complete myth. I'm a Christian. I believe in the truth of Genesis 1 and 2. But I do not believe the universe is 6,000 years old. It's simply based on a tradition that was wrong and that people need to let go of. In my opinion, at least. Not all Christians agree, though I admit, I'm agnostic on the actual age of the universe"

Jaylene laughed. "A Christian agnostic, that's a new one. How old do you think the earth is?"

"I don't know—probably thirteen billion plus as the physicists say. What are their calculations up to now, 13.6 or 13.7 somewhere? I have no evidence to doubt them. They'll probably end up at fourteen billion—it seems to keep increasing incrementally. I also see evolutionary development of the species all through Genesis 1 and 2."

"So you believe in evolution?" asked Jaylene.

"I believe in God. I believe he used many wonderful processes to develop his creation, one of which *could* certainly be evolution. I definitely believe in micro-evolution or in-species adaptations. *Macro*-evolution, however, is something I cannot reconcile with my extensive reading and study of the Bible. Obviously, God is all-powerful and sovereign, he can do anything he wants, but he gave us the Bible to let us in on his mind and plan."

"You're giving me all sorts of new things to think about—relativity and micro-evolution in Genesis, and Christian agnosticism!"

"I would modify that last one and just say I am a Christian who realizes I don't have all the answers and am hungry to keep learning."

"I like that."

"Surely you know of the book *Darwin's Black Box*?"

"I've heard of it. It's not very highly thought of among my professors."

"I can see why—it blows macro-evolution out of the water, and does so scientifically not because of the Bible or anything spiritual. But back to your comment about agnosticism, on the big question, I'm not agnostic at all."

"The big question?"

"The existence of God."

"And you're not offended that I'm an atheist?"

"Oh, goodness—not a bit! You're inquisitive. You're open-minded. You're searching for truth. Who could ask for more than that? I hope I can say the same thing about myself."

"I hope you're right, about what you said about me at least," said Jaylene thoughtfully. "You sound more open to alternate perspectives than I would have expected for a Christian. Most of those you meet around campus want to preach at you and take you to church and get you saved."

"Not my style," laughed Timothy.

"I can see that! But you're right, I *am* looking for reasonable answers. I'm not used to this kind of thing," she said, indicating the Bible in her hand. "Religion, I mean, the Minor Prophets, God creating the world, and all that. I know nothing about it. But I realized that if I am going to be an objective scientist whose life is based on a quest for truth and knowledge, I need to know about it. I can't block out a whole region of inquiry and refuse to look at it. What kind of scientific method is that?"

She paused, then smiled.

"I always wanted to make some huge new scientific discovery," she said, laughing. "Maybe I'll be the one to find a unified field theory between Genesis and the Big Bang!"

"Well, when you do and you get famous for it, remember the guy who could guess the books of the Bible where you stuck your finger."

She laughed, glancing unconsciously at her watch.

"Oh, my! The time got away from me." Hurriedly she gathered up her things and stood. "I'm going to be late for my class. I'd better hide this before I walk in," she added, stuffing the Bible into her bag. "It was nice talking to you."

She took a few steps, then stopped and turned back.

"I don't mean to be forward," she said, "but . . . well, you obviously know more about all this—religion, I mean—than I do. Could we get together . . . I mean, could I talk to you again sometime? I really want to know more about what you said about how Genesis lines up with evolution and the dating of the universe and eons and all that. I'm very interested. As long as you don't mind being seen with an atheist!"

"Are you kidding? I'll take an inquisitive and open-minded atheist any day over a closed-minded Christian whose mind is made up about everything."

"Well, I hope I qualify."

"Sure, I'd love to talk again. As long as *you* don't mind being seen with a Christian!"

"Ditto to what you said. I'd rather talk to an open-minded Christian than a self-satisfied atheist who thinks *he* has all the answers!"

Jaylene took out a pen and scribbled on a scrap of paper.

"Here's my phone number," she said. "I'll try not to pester you with too many questions."

"Oh, please do. Questions are the bedrock of our mutual quest, right?

"Our quest?"

"For truth, what else? It's what we're both after."

"Amen!" exclaimed Jaylene, hardly realizing what she said until she was halfway to her class.

23

THE PROBLEM IS NOT
∧ PROBLEM

THE CAL Poly junior and senior who had encountered one another serendipitously several weeks earlier outside the Baker Center met twice more for coffee at Starbucks in town, though they still knew next to nothing about one another. Continuing to hit it off, by their second visit they were talking and laughing like old friends. In the noisy atmosphere, however, it was difficult to sustain a meaningful conversation. As they walked out on their second coffee visit and turned to go their separate ways, Jaylene paused.

"You are going to think I'm forward like I said that day at school," she said, "but I'd really like to ask some questions where we can talk more easily than in there," she added, nodding back toward the door closing behind them.

"Sure," replied Timothy.

"Somewhere quiet, you know. But away from campus. I don't want to be distracted if someone I know sees me."

Timothy thought a minute.

"You doing anything on Sunday?" he said. "Would you like to drive over to Pismo?"

"Oh, I would love that! I can't get my fill of the ocean. I hardly ever saw it growing up."

"Shall I pick you up? Around 1:00—that okay?"

"Perfect. I'm in the Driftwood apartment complex."

"I know where it is."

"I'll be outside waiting, by the bus stop."

"Great—see you then."

When Timothy approached the apartment complex the following Sunday a few minutes before one, he saw Jaylene standing on the sidewalk. It gave him a chance to take her in from a distance. In their three brief visits, he hadn't learned more than that she was a junior from New Mexico studying archaeology. When he mentioned her to a friend who was working on his masters in biology, however, his friend raised his eyebrows.

"You're seeing Jaylene Gray?" he said.

"I don't know her last name," replied Timothy.

"How many Jaylenes could there be in that department?"

"We're not really *seeing* each other, so to speak. We've just had a couple conversations. Why?"

"If she's *the* Jaylene Gray, she's the star of the whole anthropology department. When the professors are stumped about anything, they ask *her*."

"I had no idea."

"She lectures in the lower division classes all through the department. She might as well be on the faculty."

"She's only a junior."

"Really!" said Timothy's friend. "I thought she was a graduate student. I'm sure she's doing graduate work."

"I don't see how she'd have time. She's also doing three minors."

"She's a brain, man—probably carries twenty or twenty-two units every term. Everybody in the sciences knows her. She's their rock star. They're already talking about making her an offer."

"What kind of offer?"

"To get her on the faculty before she has her masters or PhD. They don't want to lose her to Stanford or MIT or one of the British universities."

"Amazing. I didn't know."

"You're in lofty company, that's all I'll say."

It could hardly be helped, therefore, that Timothy took in his new acquaintance with a heightened level of interest. She had nothing of the appearance or personality of a superstar. Standing 5'6" or maybe 5'7", she was dressed casually for their outing, Birkenstocks on her feet, faded jeans, and a tan sleeveless vest, open in front, over a blue T-shirt highlighted with yellow daisies. With bangs cut across her forehead half an inch above her eyebrows, her light brown hair was straight, combed over her ears and down the back of her neck to about her shoulders. From here he couldn't tell what color her eyes were. He'd try to remember to look. His mom always told him to notice such things. Now that he thought about it, he supposed he would call her pretty. But not the kind of knockout that would turn heads. The overall effect was . . . well, she looked like any other college coed. What did all that matter anyway—she had energy. She was fun to talk to. She was hungry to learn and grow. What could be better than that?

He also noticed that she was holding the Bible that attracted his attention the first time he saw her. He'd also brought a book along. It was in the glove box. He would keep it where it was for now and decide later if it was appropriate.

He pulled up to the sidewalk. Jaylene opened the passenger door and jumped in.

"Hi, Timothy!" she said. "I'm so excited—I haven't been to the beach since last year before I left for the summer on a dig in Montana."

"You do lead an adventurous life!"

"Part of the curriculum—hands on . . . digging for woolly mammoths, you know."

"Sounds interesting."

"It is. I love it!"

"Brought the Bible, I see."

"I have a million questions. With nobody around I'll have you all to myself and can ask anything!"

Timothy laughed. "I just hope I'm up to the challenge. I'm no expert on anything. I wouldn't want to disappoint you."

"You know more about it than me. There is zero chance of your disappointing me."

They arrived at Pismo Beach on the coast about fifteen minutes later. They parked, walked down to the shoreline and along the water's edge.

"Here, hold this," said Jaylene, handing Timothy the Bible. She stooped, slipped off her sandals and tossed them aside, rolled up her jeans two or three inches, then dashed off along the flat expanse of sand at the water line. When she jogged back, her face was aglow.

"I love this!" she exclaimed, retrieving her sandals. "Will you bring me here every day!"

"I don't know about that!" laughed Timothy. "We do have to graduate. I think we might have to attend a few classes for that."

"Every week then?"

Carrying her Birkenstocks, she fell into step beside him. The mood quieted. They walked up the beach from the water, found a dry log of driftwood above the high-water line from the previous high tide, and sat down.

Jaylene set her sandals on the ground and took the Bible from Timothy. She opened it to the first page and scooted to Timothy's side. "Okay—tell me about all this," she said, pointing to the first chapter of Genesis. "I want you to show me where you see evidence of evolution here. Also, the age thing—about the eons, like you said before, time in God's frame of reference. Tell me everything."

"A pretty tall order!" laughed Timothy. "Christians and evolutionists have been arguing about these two chapters for 150 years without either side convincing the other. And you want a guy sitting on a log on Pismo Beach who's not even a college graduate to make sense of it for you?"

"That's what I want!"

"You don't ask much, do you!"

Jaylene shrugged with an innocent yet playful smile.

"All I have to offer is this one guy's opinion," Timothy began. "Many Christians would probably disagree with everything I might tell you—though more might agree than would have fifty years ago. And probably all evolutionists would think I'm nuts, though I do have a good friend in the graduate program in biology. He tolerates my Christian views."

"That's exactly what I want—your opinion. I don't care what anyone else says."

"Fair enough."

Timothy took the Bible from her hand.

"Okay, first off, like I told you before," he said, "the whole 6,000 years thing is based on a mistake of dating that was calculated in the seventeenth century, obviously long before science discovered how old the universe is. But Christians got it into their heads that the universe is only 6,000 years old. They have been so locked into that belief they are unable to look at evolution objectively. Christians are frustratingly hidebound in their reluctance to let go of their sacred cows, even when there is good evidence that those traditions are wrong. That's what's so frustrating about talking to close-minded Christians. It drives me crazy."

"Tell me about it," said Jaylene. "Try talking about anything hinting at a religious perspective with a close-minded scientist. I know exactly what you mean. 'Hidebound' is the perfect term."

"If you want me to explain how that dating mistake occurred, I can," Timothy went on. "But it's a little complicated and we really don't need to go into that now. It's a side issue except to say that the 6,000-year thing is a fallacy, a red herring. A lot of Christians still believe it, but in my opinion they either haven't studied it enough to realize how wrong it is or are too bound to the traditional view to let it go. So, there's my opinion about that."

"I understand."

"So put the dating problem behind you. It's not even a problem at all."

"Got it."

24

EVOLUTION IN GENESIS

"THE NEXT thing to understand," Timothy continued," is that Genesis doesn't claim to be factually detailed history. It was probably written between 2,500 and 3,000 years ago by Jewish historians. Again, there is a difference of opinion among Christians and Jews about that. The traditional view, which is still held by many, is that God literally dictated the first five books of the Bible to Moses nearly word for word. If true, this would make the Genesis account factually and literally true—even though it contains the incorrect order of plant life and formation of the sun, the instantaneous creation of man, a talking snake in the garden, and so on. Many Christians do believe the account to be literal as dictated by God to Moses, which explains why so many on the scientific side scoff at them. It sounds less than absurd to a secularist to be told that a man about 1500 BC sat down on a mountaintop and took dictation from God. And you have to understand their point—it does strain credibility a bit."

"You could say that!" said Jaylene. "It is pretty far-fetched."

"The scientists also maintain that evolution disproves the instantaneous creation of man, and that a six-day literal creation of the universe is disproved by the observable fact of the expansion of the universe and the backward dating of the Big Bang. That in a nutshell defines the great divide between science and religion, or as it is commonly also termed "evolution and creation." Moses on a mountaintop and a six-thousand-year-old universe which renders evolution impossible, versus a thirteen- or fourteen-billion-year-old universe where life began by accident and evolved by chance into its present form. Obviously the two are poles apart."

"And you, I take it, if I know you—which I am beginning to—" smiled Jaylene, "do not subscribe to either view?"

"You are correct," nodded Timothy. "For that reason, if you have occasion to talk to other Christians, you will find many of them disagreeing with my perspective. What you are getting from me would have been called the minority view, so to speak, until a decade or two ago, though many Christian scientists are now coming to adopt the old earth theory, as it is sometimes called."

He paused and glanced toward her.

"Are you sure you want to be asking me about this? I may not represent the typical Christian view of Genesis."

"Yes, I want to ask *you*!"

"All right, then, I *do* believe the Genesis account tells *true* history. It is not a fairy tale, a myth. It is *history*. It explains the beginnings of our planet, of life, and of the universe. You told me the first day we met that you were on a quest to understand beginnings. Your quest ends here. Genesis 1 and 2 tell that story. This is where everything begins. Obviously, then, it is clear I disagree completely with atheism and chance beginnings. I believe that the universe and life were *created*. Created by God. I am a *creationist*."

"Okay," said Jaylene slowly. "But there's more to it, right?"

"Absolutely. I call the history of creation *interpretive* history, not literal-detail history. *True* history, but interpretive history. Truth exists on a higher plane than detailed *fact*. That's a principle most secularists don't understand about the Bible. They point to this error or that historical discrepancy and say, 'Ha—the Bible isn't true.' It's a juvenile response. Truth isn't like that. Truth is higher than facts and details. The Bible's high Truth is not compromised by factual and detail incongruities."

"You're so right. I never thought about that in relation to the Bible. But that principle undergirds science too."

"That principle of truth undergirds everything. A man or woman could be said to be a person *of truth*, meaning they are seeking to live truthfully and honestly, and do what's right. That doesn't make them perfect, it just indicates what direction they are pointing in life. Being *of truth* does not mean every *detail* is perfect."

"That is a very insightful concept."

"The point is, the Bible speaks of high *Truth*, not detailed facts in every verse. Whoever wrote Genesis, that author did not *see* creation. It is of necessity an overview and *interpretive* history of creation. I would also call it an *inspired* history. I believe God breathed inspiration into the mind of the man or men who wrote it, so that we can take it as more than just somebody far back in antiquity spinning a fanciful tale out of his own brain. I believe it is God-breathed, inspired, and therefore accurate, yet still *interpretive* history. Obviously, that last part about inspiration I don't expect you to go along with since God's existence isn't something you would agree to."

"That's okay," said Jaylene letting out a thoughtful sigh. "Everything's on the table for me right now, though I am somewhat overwhelmed," she added quietly. "I've never heard anything like this."

"Have you had enough for one day? Do you want me to stop?"

"Oh no, please no! I love this. I'm just trying to absorb what you're saying."

"There is one aspect of the account that I would go so far as to call factually accurate literal history. Not interpretive history but *literal* historical history."

"What's that?"

"The first ten words: *In the beginning God created the heavens and the earth.*"

"You might say those ten words define the divide, like you called it, between the religious and secular views," suggested Jaylene.

"You're right—and a more accurate description of the true nature of the divide—*naturalism* versus *supernaturalism.* Unfortunately, people have obsessed on the dating brouhaha that has defined the public discourse. It's sad because it's a completely false debate. The true divide is about *supernaturalism*, not dating. The opposite of creation isn't evolution, it is *chance*. Creation and evolution are compatible. Creation and chance beginnings are not. *That* should define the debate, not the six-thousand-year red herring."

Again, Jaylene took his words in thoughtfully.

"You were going to explain how you see evolution in Genesis," she said.

"Sorry, I got a little sidetracked. Okay, after those opening ten words," said Timothy, "the interpretive eons begin with a bang—pun entirely intended. Day One—*let there be light!*

"Can't you just feel the explosive power of that statement? It's the Big Bang! *Ka-boom* goes the creation of the universe! And the eon of Day One perhaps lasts seven billion years—per Einstein!—as matter explodes outward at the speed of light and gradually slows until galaxies begin to form. I say seven billion of *man's* years, but a day, however you want to define that, in *God's* frame of reference, relativity time, Einstein time."

"I love your time and speed of light explanation," said Jaylene.

"Now here's where you have to read Genesis interpretively and with an open mind, with an eye out for high Truth, not detailed facts. If you get too literal, anyone can poke holes in what you say. It's always the big picture I want to find, not factual exactitude. We *can't* achieve factual exactitude. We *have* to seek the larger picture. That's the only way to discover high Truth. The reason I bring this up is because there are obvious sequencing problems here.

"Look—" he said, pointing down to the page.

"Day One has light and darkness being separated into day and night, yet the sun and moon don't appear until Day Four. Before that, in Day Three, there are plants growing *before* the sun was created. Obviously, something is wrong since plants can't grow without sunlight. The skeptic and critic would point to this and say, 'Ah, ha! The Bible has a mistake. Therefore it's all false.' But like I said before, that's a juvenile approach. We're looking for the high Truth of an interpretive overview. Rearranging the order solves many of the discrepancies, and, to my mind brings Genesis 1 right in line with science."

"I can't wait to hear it!" Jaylene began laughing. "I can't believe it," she said. "You're talking about the Bible and I'm on the edge of my seat! Well, the edge of this log!"

"Okay, then," laughed Timothy, "I'll keep you in suspense no longer. By rearranging the order, I make Day Two, the creation of the sun and moon—in other words, our galaxy and solar system, and thousands of other galaxies and systems along with them—lasting three or four billion years.

"Day Three, oceans and land forming, say another one or two billion years.

"Day Four—life beginning in the oceans, a billion years or less.

"Day Five, animal life in the oceans, plant life forming—another half a billion years.

"Day Six—animal life beginning on land, perhaps two to three hundred million years. Then finally we come to the creation of man. For now I'll leave that part of it alone since it is so fraught with disagreement. Obviously, my dating estimates are just overview and interpretive approximations. I am no expert at detailed scientific dating. But this helps me see the big picture."

"What a remarkable way to read Genesis!"

"I don't know how remarkable it is!" laughed Timothy. "I'm majoring in history. I try to read history by the light of common sense. To me this is the most logical and common-sense way to read Genesis. There are six days or 'eons' of creation—eras during which the universe, then the solar system, then earth, the oceans and plants and all life forms, were developing, all combined as exquisitely portrayed in Genesis, interpretively read, as lasting between thirteen and fourteen billion years—harmonizing very nicely with modern dating estimates."

"Amazing!" said Jaylene. "You have fit the Genesis account into the dating scheme of the scientific community. I am impressed."

"It's obviously not exact" said Timothy, realizing almost as he said it that Jaylene might herself be as much an expert as anyone. "'General' might be a better word to what I have proposed."

"I see what you're saying," commented Jaylene. "I still think it is *generally* sound. You have outlined the correct sequence of events: Big

Bang, expansion of the universe, coalescing and cooling of matter, formation of galaxies which include the sun and planets of our solar system, formation of the earth, emergence of water and land, development of plant and animal life and their evolution, leading of course to man which you left out. So now—clever segue, wouldn't you say!—what about evolution in your timeline?"

"Okay, but again, I am being interpretive here. *General*, not specific as to detail. Many would disagree with me. But I see only a few instances, after the first verse, where the account specifically says that God *created* something. The most obvious of these is with man and woman. If you read the account literally as an instantaneous creation from the dust of the ground, that is problematic from an evolutionary standpoint."

"True, that is the sticking point for evolutionists—*instant* species formation rather than their *gradual* evolution and development."

"But what if," Timothy went on, "the words *out of the dust of the ground* are not literal but also *figurative*?"

"How do you mean?"

"What if they are a metaphor, say, a creative way of speaking of the natural processes of the earth? From there to evolution isn't such a great leap."

"Are you saying that it's something like saying, God formed man out of the developmental, or even evolutionary, processes *of the earth*?"

"Exactly that, yes," remarked Timothy. "I have some other ideas, but we can save them for later. In brief, I would just say that I would make a distinction between the *physical* creation of man—which might have taken place slowly—and his *spiritual* being, which might have been implanted differently. It may be that pre-men, hominids, existed for thousands of years, slowing gaining physical abilities, until a time came when God imbued *homo sapiens* with soul. Perhaps that pivotal moment did indeed come approximately 6,000 years ago with a single man and woman. But I am speculating about all that. For now, let's leave the creation of man out of it and back up.

"The account uses the passive form—'Let there be'—for how God brought about life. The term to my mind is an example of the wonderful inspiration of the text. I paraphrase it as, 'God caused there to be . . . God set systems in motion to cause there to be . . .' Do you see the beauty of it? God could easily have used the evolutionary process to 'cause there to be.' There's no dichotomy between evolution and the words 'Let there be.' It's wonderful."

"I'm not totally following you. But go on."

"Look further. Verses 11 and 12: '*The earth put forth vegetation*.' To my mind this is as clear a statement of the God-driven evolution of plant life on the earth. God gave the earth the creative capacity to bring forth vegetation. Then to verse 20: '*Let the waters bring forth swarms of living creatures*.' And verse 24: '*Let the earth bring forth living creatures according to their kinds*.'

"Again, God-driven life being brought forth out of the water and land. It's another way of interpretively reading '*from the dust of the ground*' into these statements—God's using the creative life-energy he placed into his creation. I love Genesis 2:19: '*So out of the ground the* LORD *God formed every beast of the field and every bird of the air and brought them to the man to see what he would call them*.' What is that, interpretively read, other than a writer 3,000 years ago anticipating evolution which would be discovered later?

"That creative life-energy could not have come from nothing," Timothy went on excitedly. "Nothing comes from nothing. I believe this is exactly what the image of God means. The creative life-energy with which the earth is imbued and which spawned evolution and all life forms is nothing short of the fingerprint of God."

Jaylene shook her head at the magnitude of it.

"Many Christians would be scandalized that I read evolution into those verses," said Timothy. "But I observe evolution at work here between the lines. It is as if God inspired the writer, or writers, all those thousands of years ago to write this imaginative account using terms and in ways that would actually be confirmed by and fit in with the scientific discoveries his descendants far in the future would make about the earth's past and mankind's development. To me it is utterly miraculous how wonderfully this ancient account dovetails with science. It is certainly inspired."

He paused and drew in a breath. Jaylene was clearly overwhelmed.

"The main point," Timothy went on after thirty seconds, "is that there is no intrinsic divide between evolution and Genesis unless one attempts to squeeze these chapters into a factual, detailed, literal mold—which I do not think is the most valid way to read it. As I say, this only gives a rapid bird's-eye view. Micro vs. macro evolution and the creation of man and soul and the development of the hominid anthropological tree—these remain enormously difficult questions about which there is much debate. I have no answers, though I have some opinions which I think make a lot of sense."

"Someday I hope to hear them."[6]

"I love thinking of possibilities, and trying to harmonize science and the Bible," Timothy went on. "None of this—the creation, the evolution within the species, or the writing of the Bible—could have happened without God as the life-creating force inspiring it and driving it forward."

He fell silent for a few seconds again.

"Sorry," he laughed. "I'm afraid I gave you quite a monologue!"

"Don't apologize, Timothy," said Jaylene softly. "I was spellbound. I wish I could take you into one of my anthropology classes and let you give this as a lecture," she added.

"They would tar and feather me!" laughed Timothy. "Some Christians would tar and feather me too. Some of my controversial perspectives tend to upset comfort zones. So I mostly keep them to myself. Let's just keep this our little secret."

"Don't you want to tell people what you see in Genesis?"

"Only if they're interested. People have to discover truth on their own timetable. They don't need me interfering with that process."

"Why did you talk to me, then?"

"You embarked on the quest before I came along. I didn't tell you to investigate Genesis. Your quest began long before that day I saw you on that bench with this Bible on your lap."

A long silence fell.

25

How Can I Know?

"WHAT ABOUT the elephant in the room?" Jaylene asked at length.

"Which is?"

"The existence of God," she said. "Doesn't it bother you that I'm an atheist?"

"No."

"Or at least I thought I was until you came along!"

"None of that bothers me in the least."

"You continue to amaze me! Don't you feel compelled to try to make me believe in God?"

"No."

Jaylene laughed. "But why?"

"Because it's none of my business."

"It's mine, you mean?"

"Of course. It's between you and God."

"And if there is no God?"

"Then it's between you and your conscience, your logic, your brain, your intellect, and your heart. It's still got nothing to do with me."

"It's got a *little* to do with you. It's you I'm talking to about God."

"I see your point. I mean in the final analysis when you or I or anyone have to decide what we believe or don't believe. At that point we're alone with our own mind and will."

"But what if you're the one to help me know what I believe, or what I want to believe or should believe?"

"Sure, that happens to everyone. Then we talk and listen to people we trust to have wisdom we need. You and I will continue to talk. You will think things over and maybe ask me questions and we'll talk some more. Maybe you'll talk to other people—get different ideas than mine, so it's not just me telling you what you should believe."

"But you're not doing that. You're not telling me what I should believe, only what you believe."

"Granted, but what I'm saying is that in the end, there's no one deep down in that innermost place of your soul but you. Though I hope we are to the point where we are sharing a little of that space with each other."

"We definitely are," smiled Jaylene. "You have helped me more than you know. And I do want to know what's true, not just what people tell me I ought to believe, whether it's religious people shoving their views down my throat or my atheist professors shoving their views down my throat. I am so grateful you don't do that. You respect me enough to let me think for myself. But it's all so new. All this, you know, God and the Bible and creation. I am depending on you to guide me through it. I feel like a fish out of water."

"I understand. It's hard to grow into new places. I've gone through that too."

It was silent for several long minutes. Jaylene rose and walked down to the water's edge and stood staring out across the infinite expanse of blue. When she turned and walked back to the log where Timothy still sat, an expression was on her face he had not seen before.

She walked straight up to him, then stood and looked deeply into his eyes. She was a brilliant young woman embarking on what had all the signs of being a distinguished professional career. Yet at that moment, the expression on her face was that of a child.

She stood and stared at him for several seconds.

"How can I know, Timothy?" she asked simply and quietly. "How can I *know* if there is a God? How can I know if he is real?"

Timothy smiled. Sensing the child in the woman, he reached up. She took his hand. He pulled her gently down beside him then released her hand.

Again, they sat for a long while in silence. The waves were gently lapping on the shore, moving incrementally closer as the afternoon advanced. At last Timothy spoke.

"There are a hundred ways people would answer your question," he said slowly. "You could ask a hundred Christians and you would get ninety different answers—most of them, in my opinion, pat answers they have learned to say."

"You know by now, Timothy," said Jaylene softly, "that I only want to know what *you* would say. I trust you. I don't know if you're right about everything. I can figure some of that out later. But right now I feel like a hungry little girl asking my father questions. Yours is the only opinion I care about."

Timothy nodded. "I hope I can be worthy of your trust," he said quietly.

He tried to collect his thoughts. He had never been in such a position before. He realized what a responsibility was on his shoulders in that moment. The one thing he could not do was give Christian formulas or shallow responses.

At length he drew in a deep breath.

"I would say first of all," he began, "that you *can't* know absolutely, as a provable certainty. Through the years people have proposed many arguments and so-called God proofs. Christians love them. They think every atheist will be convinced the moment they hear them. But none of them prove it in a scientific sense. We can't *see* God. There's no spiritual test tube. That's the reality.

"That's why all religions emphasize faith. Belief in God is rooted in faith, not absolute knowing. We *think* we know, we *want* to know, we *believe* we know. But no one can know God is real in the same way that we know the ocean in front of us is real. People *say* they know. But what that means is they *believe* God is real.

"If you're looking for *knowing* in the scientific sense, it's not to be had. God didn't set up the universe in such a way as to make that possible. I don't know why. It seems that it would have saved a lot of confusion for him to have made himself more clearly knowable. But he didn't. So we have to try to know him in spite of that apparent difficulty.

"That's the first thing—recognizing that the instant you ask the question, 'Does God exist?' *faith* enters the equation."

He paused and chuckled. "A well-known Christian writer, who wrote a book about how he progressed from atheism to Christianity, once put it more succinctly than anyone I've heard. 'To continue in atheism,' he said. 'I would need to believe that nothing produces everything, non-life produces life, randomness produces fine-tuning, chaos produces information, unconsciousness produces consciousness, and non-reason produces reason. I simply didn't have that much faith.'[7] Kind of amazing when you think about it, that atheism is based on faith no less than belief in God."

"I'd never thought of that. I suppose he's right. That's a book I'd like to read."

"That brings me to the next thing I would suggest," said Timothy. "You asked how to know—as much as we *can* know. I would say there are three ways we can begin the process of knowing. The first is to investigate. Read, search, ask questions, do your due diligence, maybe read some of those arguments people have put forward. Maybe some of them will help stimulate and clarify your own thoughts. Many of the God-proofs you hear are shallow and, in my opinion, nonsensical. But some of them are truly profound.

"The sixteenth-century mathematician Blaise Pascal wrote some incredibly interesting things, almost like mathematical proofs for the existence of God. One of the most insightful modern attempts to give a rational apologetic for God's existence is found in the first two sections of C. S. Lewis's book *Mere Christianity*. He was an atheist who used rationality and logic to arrive at the conclusion that God must exist. It's a brilliant piece of writing. There is another by an obscure author called *Does Christianity Make Sense?* And then there's the book by the man I mentioned who spoke about the faith required by atheism.

"But these kinds of arguments and personal stories can only take you so far. They are useful to spark your brain and imagination into new realms. Eventually, however, you have to go deep within yourself and decide what your heart and brain and logic and conscience tell you. That's the second way truth comes, by assimilating what you have heard and read into your own heart and brain. Nobody can do that for you. No proof or argument can decide it for you. They are only stepping stones along the way. Then you have to get ruthlessly honest with yourself and decide what *you* believe."

Timothy paused.

"There is a profound passage in the New Testament," he went on, "that is as important to the quest as Genesis 1, and closely linked to it. What you and I have talked about in the Bible so far is the first two chapters of Genesis. But let me show you this passage from the New Testament."

He opened the book which was still in his lap.

"It's from the first chapter of a book called Romans. The author, a man named Paul, makes an incredible statement about exactly what you asked—how to *know* if God is real, even how to know about what he is like. Here, I'll read it."

Timothy found the page. "He is talking about those who deny the existence of God. He says they *should* know God exists. Here's what he writes: '*For what can be known about God is plain to them, because God has shown it to them. Ever since the creation of the world his invisible nature, namely, his eternal power and deity, has been clearly perceived in the things that have been made. So they are without excuse.*'

"It's an unbelievable statement. Paul is saying that if we look around at the universe, God's being will reveal itself."

"I see what you mean," said Jaylene. "That's an amazing thing, if it's true. I mean—wow—that is really an incredible statement."

"If you don't mind my injecting a personal aside," said Timothy, "his last words might be directed toward chance-beginning evolutionists—*they are without excuse.* They have the huge new body of wonderful evidence that the last century has produced of how life grew and developed, more evidence than mankind has ever had, to observe the creative hand of God at work in his creation, yet they are so blind to the obvious truth of design and purpose that they maintain that it all came out of nothing and happened by chance. But enough of my editorializing!"

He paused.

"In explaining this passage from Romans," Timothy went on, "my father often says that if someone walked into his office and looked around, and spent enough time looking at the pictures on the walls and the books in his bookshelves, and really took the time to investigate what everything meant, a complete stranger could figure out, not just a few isolated things about him, but could get to know him very well. He says this is exactly the point of these verses. The world is God's office, I can hear my father say. We have to try to figure out the nature and character of who he is by the things he has made. We live in God's home, his world, his office, his workplace. It's up to us to investigate the contents and workings and systems of God's workplace and figure out what they tell us about its owner. It's exactly like my dad inviting people into his office."

"That's profound," said Jaylene. "If that's true, it changes everything. It would give enormous new significance to the world around us—even new significance to evolution."

"This passage is just as important in understanding the creation as is Genesis 1."

Timothy paused and grew serious.

"Remember what I said when you asked how to know—that there are three ways?" he asked.

Jaylene nodded.

"The last and most important of the three is personal. Very personal. Are you sure you want to go there?"

"Of course. I'm not about to stop now."

"Okay then. The final thing I would say in answer to your question is to pray for wisdom, insight, knowledge, and a revelation of the truth."

"I've never prayed in my life," said Jaylene. "I don't even know how to pray."

"There's nothing to it. Just ask God for wisdom, insight, knowledge, and a revelation of the truth. Ask him to reveal himself through the world, through his creation. Ask him to make the world newly alive to you. Ask him to give you eyes to see his fingerprint, and thus his being, in the creation."

"But what if I'm an atheist."

She paused and thought a second or two. "I suppose I should rephrase that," she said. "I don't know whether or not I believe there is a God."

"It doesn't matter," replied Timothy. "What is there to lose? If there is no God, nothing will happen and you've just prayed to an empty universe. On the other hand, if God *is* real and he *does* give you wisdom and insight and knowledge and a revelation that he is real, then you have just been given a major clue."

"What if God *does* exist but I *don't* get any insight?"

"Then for you the verdict is still out. You wait for more evidence, or answers, or faith. Answers to prayer aren't any more instantaneous, if one believes in evolution, than the development of life on the earth. That's another reason I tend to believe in some form of evolution—it is consistent with God's M.O. Most of what God does, he does *slowly*. He is rarely in a hurry. Just look around at the natural order of the world. Everything grows slowly. God's processes in the world are slow. Evolution harmonizes with that."

"Do you not believe in miracles, then?"

"Oh, of course I believe in them. But they are the exception rather than the rule. Certainly, God *can* act rapidly, instantly, miraculously. But mostly he doesn't. Usually, he allows the natural processes to work their miracle of life slowly. God built miracle into every facet of creation. He doesn't often step into the process. Even some miracles take place slowly."

"I've never heard that before."

"Another of my minority views!" laughed Timothy. "The point I was trying to make about prayer is the same. Sometimes answers come *slowly*. You might pray to be given insight and wisdom, and then the answers God wants you to have will seep into you slowly over many weeks or months, even years. That doesn't mean that God isn't answering, or that you should stop praying, only that God is answering you by his normal method—slowly."

"How would I know whether the thoughts and insights that might come are from him or are just my own thoughts?"

"That's a great question. You are very perceptive! You ask the right questions!"

"How would you answer me?"

"I would say that you might not at first. You could pray that too—to be given discernment to know if God is speaking to you."

"Even then—how would I know. How *does* God speak to you?"

"Through your thoughts and feelings and senses."

"But there we are again—how do you know? It would be hard to tell."

"It *is* hard to tell. God sends no special delivery telegrams. The Bible is full of stories of God sending angels with messages. That's the original special delivery telegram! But that isn't the normal way God speaks."

It was quiet a moment. Jaylene was struggling to absorb a whole new perspective completely foreign to all the scientific knowledge she gleaned in a lifetime of learning. Timothy was trying to find the simplest way to explain one of the great mysteries of life which he himself was still learning to understand.

"The Bible calls it a still small voice," he said at length. "God speaks through our thoughts and feelings in a whisper. He does not use a megaphone. Yes, it is hard to know what he is saying. Christianity isn't just a belief system where you say 'I believe in this list of ideas or doctrines.' Actually, for many people it is exactly that. But that's not what *real* Christianity is. Real Christianity is a way of living in constant and daily relation to God. But it's got no auto-pilot feature.

"All I can say is that you pray for insight, wisdom, knowledge, and discernment. Then you have to decide how to interpret and evaluate what happens over time, whether you believe God has spoken to you. It's a slow and very personal process.

"Remember what I said earlier about faith. There come times when *faith* enters the equation of whether you believe God has spoken or not. There will never be *proof* you have heard from God. It's usually hard to know. Sometimes you make mistakes and misinterpret what the whispers of the still small voice are saying. It is especially difficult because it is a slow process. God does not usually rush his revelations. Sometimes they come in a flash. But not usually.

"Right now, I am praying about where I should go to graduate school. There are three possibilities. I am praying, but I am not hearing any loud shouts from God. If I only get accepted into one of them, that will probably be the answer to my prayer right there. But if I get accepted by more than one, I will have to discern what the still small voice is saying. Hearing answers to prayer, and not interpreting them by our own wants and preferences and biases—that's one of the very difficult aspects of the Christian life."

It was silent a long time. Jaylene was thinking hard.

"What should I say?" she asked quietly.

"Whatever you want," replied Timothy. "If God isn't real, it doesn't matter. If he is, then he's your Creator and Father and whatever you say will be fine because he obviously loves you or he wouldn't have made you."

"This is so new to me. I guess I'm nervous, maybe even a little afraid. It's spooky in a way."

Timothy smiled. "Don't do anything if you feel awkward about it."

"But I want to. It's just so new."

"Then just say something like, God, if you are real, I ask you to reveal yourself to me. And help me know it's you, not just my brain playing tricks on me."

"You can really pray like that? Just talking, I mean?"

"Of course. If God is real, he is our Father. He is the Father of the universe because he created it. *If* he is real, he is either a *Father*, or he is nothing. Fathers love their children. Not all earthly fathers show it very well. But our heavenly Father, *God*, if he exists, surely loves his creation. So anything you say will be welcome. He wants nothing more than for his children to talk to him."

Jaylene drew in a deep breath.

"Do I close my eyes?" she asked.

"It doesn't matter. Sometimes it helps to block out distractions. On the other hand, if God is real, then he is everywhere. Look out over the ocean there in front of us and pray with your eyes wide open if you like. If he exists, he made it and he's *there*. If he doesn't, it doesn't matter what you do."

"You make everything seem so simple," said Jaylene.

Again it was quiet. Timothy said no more but stared down at the sand in front of him. Five minutes went by, then ten. The voice he finally heard at his side was so soft as to nearly be inaudible.

"God, if you are real, please show me. Give me wisdom and insight. Help me know if it's you."

After another minute of silence, Timothy felt Jaylene's hand on his. He turned toward her and smiled. There were tears in her eyes.

Slowly she drew in a deep breath, rose, and again walked down to the water's edge. She stood staring out across the sea. She still stood motionless fifteen minutes when the water swirling up over her ankles brought her to herself.

She turned and began walking slowly along the shore, looking down at the sand and tiny shells and pebbles at her feet, then lifting her gaze to the shoreline ahead of her and at the rising dune of sand covered with sea grass, again out to sea, then glancing up at a seagull flying overhead, then beyond it to the white clouds lazily drifting across the vault of blue, and finally to the three-quarter moon hanging suspended in the distant beyond.

When she returned thirty minutes later, Timothy stood and handed her the Birkenstocks. Still carrying the Bible, he led the way as they headed up the beach to his car. Neither said a word all the way back to San Luis Obispo.

They stopped in front of Jaylene's apartment building. Timothy reached for the glove box and pulled out a small book.

"I don't want you to think me being pushy—" he began. Jaylene reached over and touched his arm.

"I would never think that, Timothy," she said. "You are the most gracious and unpushy person I have ever met."

He smiled. "I brought along this book. I thought . . . I don't know . . . that you might find it interesting."

"Thank you. Yes, if you value it, I know I will."

He handed it to her. *Does Truth Matter?* said Jaylene reading its title aloud. She nodded. "It matters to me," she said. "I can't wait to read it. Thank you, Timothy, this means the world to me."

She got out and walked across the lawn to her apartment with many new things to think about. Suddenly she was struck with the fact that, not only had Timothy not asked her out for a date, in the brief time they had known each other their friendship had been so casual she didn't even know his full name.

26

DEEPENING FRIENDSHIP

TIMOTHY DID not see Jaylene for several days. Remembering her perhaps flippant request to take her to the beach every week, though still not wanting to be pushy, he waited until Friday before calling to ask how serious she had been, and if another couple hours at Pismo would fit into her Sunday schedule.

"Oh, yes—I was hoping you'd call!" she said.

On this occasion the conversation did not probe so deeply, though was no less enjoyable for both. They left their shoes in the car. Jaylene did not bring the Bible. Timothy asked no questions.

"I loved the book you lent me," said Jaylene as they walked barefoot along the sand. "I've read it twice."

"In a week?"

"I'm a fast reader! I'll give it back to you when we get back to my place."

"I meant for you to keep it if you'd like it."

"Thank you. Yes—I would like to read it again, more slowly. By the way," she said, "this is, what, I think the fifth time we've seen each other, so like you asked me last week—are you ready for me to get personal?"

"Sure. Fire away."

She smiled playfully. "I realized when I left you last Sunday," she said, then paused for effect, "that you have been keeping something very important from me."

"I don't mean to. What is it?"

"Just that I don't know your last name! That's pretty major, wouldn't you say?"

A sheepish expression came over Timothy's face.

"Yeah, that's on me. But I had a reason."

"Which was?"

"Because of a book I thought I might have occasion to give you, as it turned out, I did."

"You mean the one you did give me?"

"That's the one. My last name's *Marshall*. I'm Timothy Marshall."

"Marshall?" repeated Jaylene. "You're not . . ."

Timothy nodded. "Stirling Marshall's my father."

"Really—though I can't say I'm completely surprised. Some of what I read sounded familiar," laughed Jaylene.

"In what way?"

"Nothing specific, just in general approach and perspective, I suppose. Now that you've told me, I see that you and your father think alike in many ways."

"I take that as a compliment."

"Why didn't you want me to know of the connection?"

"If I gave you the book, I didn't want to bias you in any way because of the name. I wanted you to be able to read it objectively. I didn't know if you might have heard of my dad. He's pretty well known, and UCSB's not that far away. All my profs here know him, though actually he's retired now. He's written quite a few historical articles and a couple of books, besides his spiritual writings."

"Come to think of it, I think have heard one of my professors mention an article by a Dr. Marshall from UCSB I doubt I would have made the connection."

"Well, you know now!"

In the following weeks as autumn progressed, Timothy and Jaylene not only met on most weekends, driving to the ocean when possible, but began seeing each other during the week as well. As the term progressed, Jaylene's rigorous schedule often involved weekend field trips, so their times together had to be sandwiched into both of their upper division course work, especially as Timothy was in his final year and was working on his senior thesis. In spite of her time constraints Jaylene managed to read all the books Timothy recommended. Their conversations, and friendship, steadily deepened.

In late October, on a rainy Friday evening when her two apartment mates were away, Jaylene invited Timothy for supper. She had another serious question to ask him, she said, and didn't want to be interrupted.

She wasted no time after they were seated and were digging into her offerings of raviolis, spinach salad, and parmesan French bread.

"The book you recommended by Lewis was great," she said. "I loved how he started with nothing but a blank slate, and from there only addressed the existence of God to begin with. But the one by Strobel was mostly about Jesus. I got bogged down and haven't finished it yet. Your father's, too, reminded me of Lewis—so straightforward and written with such common sense. So what I want to ask is about Jesus—why is he so important? I'm still dealing with the question of whether or not God exists, and where creation and evolution and all the issues raised by Genesis fit. Adding Jesus is confusing. I'm not sure what difference he makes? I mean, I know what everyone knows—a good man, great teachings, love your neighbor, do unto others, and that he was crucified and supposedly rose from the dead. Other than that, you cannot imagine how ignorant I am. I was never taught anything about Jesus. So what does he have to do with Genesis?"

"There you go again," said Timothy, "asking piercing and important questions! You have a way of zeroing straight to the bull's-eye!"

"What would you tell me then?"

"Mostly to leave all that for now," replied Timothy. "Take it slow. One step at a time. There's no hurry."

"But I want to know. I want the truth. Isn't that what we've been about together, you and me, just like you said the day we met—the mutual quest?"

Timothy smiled.

"You're right. But there's no need to rush the quest. Take it at the pace you're comfortable with."

"You're always so easy-going about my questions. But *if* I wanted to add Jesus to my list of things to ask you or God or anyone else about, what would you say?"

"You couldn't do better than the books you already have. My dad's got other books too. He's written a lot."

"And you've probably read them all."

"Actually no. Some of his stuff is a little beyond me. He's a pretty deep thinker."

"He sounds fascinating. But besides those books."

Jaylene paused, then quickly went on. "Remember that day when you showed me the verse about the universe showing what God is like and told me about your father's office?"

Timothy nodded.

"Maybe I mean something like that. What other places in the Bible are there to learn about Jesus?"

Timothy thought a moment.

"Boy, you ask great questions!" he said.

"My father used to say that!" laughed Jaylene.

"That's as big as asking how to know if God is real."

"And you answered that one. Your answer has helped me think through many things. So now I want to know what to do next."

Again, it was silent a long time.

"Once you start talking about Jesus," Timothy began, "it's like I said before—every Christian will bombard you with different things— getting saved, asking Jesus into your life, hell, the atonement, sin, the cross. Before you can come up for air, you're so deep into a thousand doctrinal quagmires that you're more confused than ever. Honestly, I don't want to go there. If I can be of any help, it will be to give you clarity, not confuse you, and most of what Christians will tell you can get very confusing. If you want me to explain some of those things later, fine. I'm all in. It's not really as complicated as people make it. I can help it make sense. Properly understood, it's all wonderful. But at this point, you're still trying to figure out if God is real. So first things first."

"I appreciate that."

"Then would you like me tell you what places in the Bible I would suggest? It comes with the same proviso as before—these are just my suggestions, one man's opinion. Then you can take it from there."

"Perfect! That's exactly what I want."

"This is your quest, not mine. When you want to talk, ask more questions, you know where to find me."

"Agreed."

"Okay, it will be like someone coming to me and asking, 'What should I read in the Bible to find out about God and Jesus? Give me the bare essentials. No theology or church doctrine. Just the basics.'"

"That is exactly what I am asking."

"Then I would point to Genesis 1 and 2 and Romans 1, as I already did. To understand Jesus, I would add the four Gospels, the first four books of the New Testament. They will tell you all you need to know—who Jesus is, how he and God are connected, and more specifically what being a Christian is all about. And what it means to be his follower. To those I would add the whole book of Proverbs in the Old Testament. It's in the middle right after Psalms. Then in the New Testament, the thirteenth chapter of a book called First Corinthians. It comes after Romans. And that's it. Those are the Cliff's Notes of Christianity."

"That doesn't sound like much. I can handle those."

"True—but you will spend the rest of your life trying to *really* understand the Gospels. They don't only represent the basics; they also comprise the graduate program!"

"Let me see if I've got it. God's creation and existence—Genesis 1–2 and Romans 1. Then Jesus' life and teaching and relation to God—the Gospels. What are their names?"

"Matthew, Mark, Luke, and John."

"Of course. Everybody knows that. And then—what did you call the last group?"

"I don't know that I called it anything, but if I did I would say practical Christian living."

"And what were those?"

"Proverbs and 1 Corinthians 13. We could add Matthew 5–7, what is called the Sermon on the Mount, but that's already included in the Gospels."

"And that's everything?"

"For now. Of course, there's a lot more . . ."

"I remember—like the Minor Prophets!" laughed Jaylene.

"Very good!"

"But what about all those other things you mentioned before—heaven and hell and . . . I don't even remember all of them."

"Those are all doctrinal things. Time for all that later. They're not important when you're just trying to decide whether or not you believe any of it. If you decide you want to pursue this, then sure—other things come into it. Just not at first. Everything builds on the foundation of these few books and passages. I would add one more book to read in conjunction with the four Gospels. That is my father's book *Unspoken Commandments*. It will help you understand Jesus' life in practical, down-to-earth ways."

"This is great, Timothy!" exclaimed Jaylene. "I can't wait to get started. Will you write all those down in the front of my Bible so I don't forget any of them?"

"Sure."

A peculiar expression came over Timothy's face. Jaylene saw it instantly.

"What!" she said.

"I have one more suggestion," said Timothy seriously. "It will probably sound weird—I hope you won't get the wrong idea."

"Okay . . ." said Jaylene slowly. "I'm used to some of the curves you occasionally throw. I don't think I will be *too* shocked."

"You may be by this one."

"Try me."

"All right," said Timothy. He drew in a deep breath. "I would suggest we don't see each other for a while."

Jaylene stared back at him, then began laughing, though with more concern than humor in her expression.

"Are you breaking up with me?" she said, her face now genuinely puzzled.

"No!" laughed Timothy, trying to relieve the sudden strain. "And breaking up . . . what—are we, I mean . . . we're not—"

He looked away.

"It's not like that, Jaylene," he went on hurriedly. "There's nothing I enjoy more than being with you and talking with you. It's a mutual quest, right. You're one of the best friends I've got. It's just that I think it might be best for you to think, and if you're so inclined even to pray, these things through on your own without talking to anyone else about them, even me. The last thing in the world I want is to push or persuade or try to convince you of anything. I want to give you complete freedom to pursue the quest, at least the next step or two of it, on your own. I want there to be no chance of my opinions or bias tipping the scales."

He paused a moment.

"Remember what I said before," he went on seriously, "about a time when we are alone within our own minds and hearts, when we have to face what we believe on our own. I think this is such a time. It's the last thing I *want* to do. I would love to share every bit of it with you. But I think this is something you need to pursue in that quiet place within your own heart."

Jaylene smiled. "I should have known," she said. "You said what you did because you think it's best for *me*, not because of what you want."

"I do think it's best for you. God will lead you to the truth. You will be glad in the end that *he* led you to truth, not me. It's time for me to step back for a time—a few days, a week, a month, a year, though I hope it won't be that long! You will know how long you need."

"I don't know what to say, Timothy. You are always thinking of me, not yourself. I don't want to stop seeing you. But I trust you. I will do it. Maybe in a way it is exciting. What if God does show me some things on my own? That would be pretty amazing! So can you get me that book of your father's?"

"I thought you'd never ask!" smiled Timothy. "I have one out in my car. I drove down to see my folks last weekend. I had my dad sign it for you."

27

CHRISTMAS
IN SANTA BARBARA

DECEMBER 2001

AFTER MORE than six weeks, Timothy stopped leaping for his cell phone every time it chimed. He expected it to be two weeks or more, hoped it would not be a year, but had no idea how many months Jaylene might want. Or even if he would hear from her again. From all he knew about her, as much from her reputation, with which he was now well familiar, as from their friendship, he knew no half-measures would satisfy her. She was an intellectual, a scientist, a *thinker*, and a thoroughly self-honest young lady. She would leave no stone unturned.

His mother had been talking over Christmas plans with his brothers and sisters and spoke with Timothy earlier in the day. He was expecting a return call. When his phone went off that evening, assuming it was his mom, he grabbed it quickly without looking at the number.

"Hey!" he said.

The phone was silent a second or two.

"Timothy . . . hi. It's Jaylene."

"Jaylene!" he exclaimed. "Sorry about that—I thought it was my mom. Wow, it's great to hear your voice!"

He heard nothing for several seconds. When she spoke again, her voice was soft.

"I'm ready," she said.

When the two met briefly the next day between classes, they spontaneously embraced and stood for several long seconds without words.

"I've missed you," said Jaylene softly.

"The feeling is mutual," replied Timothy.

They saw each other every day for the next week, though sometimes for only five or ten minutes at a time. Their conversations entered a new phase, though often had to be cut short by the increased workload with Christmas vacation approaching.

"You're going home to New Mexico for Christmas, I assume?" said Timothy one day as they were walking through the Baker quad.

"Not this year, I'm afraid," replied Jaylene. "I've got a mountain of work in preparation for next term, a paper I'm not going to finish before the break and I have to finish before classes resume. I'm also doing research for Dr. Sarber on some new discoveries at the Neolithic site at Skara Brae. Knowing you has cut into my studies! So I'm going to be hunkered down with my computer and books."

"Then I'll be able to see you!"

"As long as I get my work done!" she laughed.

"Then why don't you come down to Santa Barbara and spend Christmas Day with my family?" said Timothy. "You could meet my folks and have a chance to talk to my dad."

"Really? I guess that would be nice, though I'll probably be intimidated by your father—the famous author and historian."

"He's as down-to-earth as they come. He would love it."

"You'll have to ask your mom of course."

"No need. I'll tell her I've invited you and she will be delighted."

"She won't mind?"

"My parents' home is always open. I can never keep track of all the people coming and going in their lives."

"Well, okay—that would be nice. But talk to your mother before we decide definitely."

"It is decided! It's an hour and forty-five minutes one way, so I'll be driving down Christmas Eve in time for supper and then staying over. I hope you'll join me."

"You mean, what—spend the night."

"Yes."

"But won't that be imposing on your family?"

"You have a lot to learn about my family! For my mom there is no such thing as an imposition. There's plenty of room. It's a big house. We were a family of seven. Only my sister Jane is home right now. My older brother Woody lives here in San Luis but he won't stay over. My sister Cateline lives in northern California and will be celebrating Christmas with her in-laws. Besides Jane and me, only my brother Graham will be coming down from Silicon Valley for the night. He's unmarried. You see—all kinds of spare bedrooms."

☆ ☆ ☆

Feeling nervous as they pulled into the driveway of the Marshall home in Santa Barbara on Christmas Eve two weeks later, Jaylene glanced at Timothy with an uncertain expression. She climbed out of the car and timidly followed him to the door. They walked inside to tumultuous hugs and greetings and exclamations.

"Mom, Dad, meet Jaylene," said Timothy "Jaylene . . . Stirling and Larke Marshall."

"Hello, Mr. and Mrs. Marshall. I'm—" began Jaylene.

"Good heavens, none of that!" said Timothy's mother, sweeping forward and embracing Jaylene. "It's Larke, my dear! No more *Mrs.*"

"And this is the famous Jaylene Gray!" said Stirling, embracing her in turn. "I've heard about you," he added, stepping back. "I have some good friends on the faculty at Cal Poly I keep in touch with. Dr. Sarber speaks highly of you."

Still recovering from the exuberant welcome, Jaylene at last found her voice.

"As embarrassing as it is to say, I suppose I'm what you might call a teacher's pet!" she laughed. "I don't know why, but he has treated me special since I was a freshman."

"Don't let her kid you, Dad," said Timothy. "She's the star of the department."

"So Dr. Sarber tells me!"

The door opened again behind them and Timothy's sister walked in.

"Tim!" she cried, and more hugs followed.

"Hey, Jane—where have you been?"

"Out walking the dogs."

"Jaylene," said Timothy, turning behind him. "This is my sister Jane. We're the babies of the family, right, Mom?"

"Always my babies," laughed Larke. "And nearly grown up—Stirling, you and Timmy go get their things. I'll show Jaylene her room. Come with me, dear," she said, taking Jaylene's hand, "you'll be in Cateline's room. She's Timmy's other sister."

Christmas Eve went by in a happy blur for Jaylene. She had loved Christmas, albeit a secularized version, with her own family growing up. But she had never experienced anything quite like Christmas in the Marshall home, even with two of the children missing. Graham arrived about 7:00 that evening in time for their traditional Christmas Eve supper of blintz pancakes and eggnog. Afterward came a reading of the Christmas story from Luke's Gospel by Stirling, Christmas carols in four-part harmony with Larke at the piano, accompanied by much laughter, reminiscing, and catching up between the three young people.

Jane and Timothy still saw one another regularly, but neither had seen Graham since the previous Easter and were full of questions about how far along he was to his first million in the tech mecca of the north. The rest of the family plied Jaylene with as many questions as they did Graham, eager to know everything about her family, her father's geology work, and her own career plans in archaeology. All the while out of the corner of her eye Jaylene could not help noticing that there were eight stockings hung along the fireplace rather than seven, an extra with her name on it. Everything Timothy said was true—this family made everyone feel included.

Timothy's oldest brother, Woody, now with his own contracting business, with his wife Cheryl and their three-year-old daughter, drove down from San Luis Obispo on Christmas morning and arrived about 9:00 for a late breakfast.

Gift-giving around the Christmas tree was as raucous and lively as if a whole family of youngsters were involved rather than Stirling and Larke's first grandchild. It didn't take long for Stirling to get down on his hands and knees with his three-year-old granddaughter. Boxes and wrapping paper were strewn throughout the living room.

Jaylene sat taking it all in, overwhelmed as if a tornado of happy activity was sweeping through. As she watched, she was holding several of the gifts given her as if she was one of the family—one of Stirling's novels, his *History of 19th-Century Scottish Writers*, a tasteful blue-gray wool sweater, a box of note cards and stationery from Jane, a CD of Christmas music by Craig Duncan, a $50 gift card from Woody and Cheryl, and from Timothy a snow globe with a somewhat garish representation of a Cro-Magnon man standing in front of a cave, which, as she passed it around, brought on more laughter than any other humorous gift of the morning. She gave Timothy a gift, and brought a fruit and nut basket for his parents in appreciation for their hospitality. But she never expected anything like this.

At about 2:00, the nine took their places around the large oak dining room table. Scents of turkey and dressing filled the air.

"We are so happy to have you with us today, Jaylene," said Stirling. "And you as always, Cheryl, as the newest member of our family. Woody, Graham, Jane, Tim—we love you. Our home will always be yours."

He drew in a deep breath, then reached out to his right and left. Around the table everyone joined hands.

"Our loving heavenly Father," Stirling prayed, "we give you thanks for this day from hearts full of deepest gratitude. All the prayers we can think to utter dissolve into the two words we can never say enough— *Thank you!*

"Thank you for this season of giving and remembering, and for your great gift most of all. Thank you for this very precious and special day when you sent to earth your Son so man might know you as he had not known you before, know that most fundamental aspect of your nature that you chose not to reveal fully until that moment—that you are our *Father*! Oh, thank you, God our creator, whom we now know to call by that cherished and wonderful name. Thank you, our Father! Let us dare on this day especially—for Fatherhood is the message of Christmas, as your own Fatherhood is your greatest gift to us—as Jesus told us we should—let us dare approach you in intimacy, and call you, as he did, our *Abba*, our very own daddy."

Stirling paused briefly, then concluded.

"We join hearts in thanking you for all you have given us and all you are constantly doing for us. Thank you for your provision, for this food, for our home, for our family, for friends, for Jaylene's presence here with us. We ask your blessing on her family this day, on Cheryl's family, and our dear Cateline and Clancy. Now let us rejoice with thanksgiving for the rest of this day. Keep us mindful of the presence of your Spirit among us in all we do and think. Increase our humble gratefulness to you every day of our lives. Thank you, Father. Amen."

Amens followed around the table.

Jaylene was quiet as the meal began. She had never heard such a prayer in her life. But the lively conversation around the table swept her into it soon enough.

"I've been meaning to tell you, Dr. Marshall—" she said.

"I'm sorry, Jaylene, but I must ask you to obey my dear wife," he said with fun in his eyes. "There are no formalities at this table. I must insist on *Stirling*."

Jaylene laughed. "I'll try," she said. "But you have to realize how hard it is. People at Cal Poly know you too. You have a reputation in the academic world, not to mention as an author of a lot of books. It's a little intimidating."

"I do understand. But you will find out soon enough that there's nothing pretentious about this family. As for reputation," he added laughing, "I think mine in the academic world has lost its luster."

"What do you mean?" she asked.

"There are those who don't much care for my Christian publications. They think I should be a good secularist historian and a silent Christian. Finally, that became a bridge too far. I retired from teaching several years ago."

"That's what Timothy told me. I had no idea of the reasons."

"It seemed best. My spiritual writings became awkward for the university to deal with."

"I'm sorry to hear that."

"I miss it. But my life is mostly my Christian writings now."

"Well, I for one am glad you didn't bow to the pressure to be silent. I've read two of your books—the one about truth mattering—three times."

"Three times—amazing!" nodded Stirling. "I'm not sure any of my family can match that, except Larke of course, who proofreads everything. What about it, Woody, my boy," he added with a wink.

"Sorry, Dad—couldn't get into it."

"And you, Graham?"

"Once, Dad, after it came out. I probably ought to have another go at it."

"See what I mean, Jaylene!"

"Well speaking only for myself," rejoined Jaylene, "I will tell you, it helped me more than any book I have read for a long time. I'm very appreciative."

"Thank you, my dear. Your words go straight to my heart. I mean that sincerely."

"Speaking of the books and people who read them," now said Larke, "we received a nice Christmas letter two days ago from David Gordon—you all remember him, don't you, from the north of the state? He asked about you all and sends you his best."

"Why, Mom?" said Woody. "We don't even know him?"

"He feels like he knows you. He doesn't have a family of his own, except his mother and father of course. We're like family to him."

Larke turned to Jaylene.

"David's a man who lives up north of Sacramento who wrote to Stirling probably ten years ago. He was a young man at the time who read one of Stirling's books. He wrote to say very nearly the same thing you just did. He also told us quite a bit about himself and asked Stirling several questions. Stirling wrote back and we have been corresponding ever since. Though we have never met him, David has become a dear friend. That sometimes happens with the people who contact us because of the books."

"I never thought of that aspect of writing. It must be very rewarding."

"But it's hard to keep up," laughed Larke. "I answer most of the mail so Stirling doesn't get derailed from his writing. But sometimes I get weeks, even months behind. People have so many questions they want to ask Stirling. I answer as best I can and turn the difficult ones over to him. His writing stirs up their thoughts."

"I can see why. The two books I've read were seriously thought-provoking. But then I'm new to all this."

"I still have that first letter David wrote if you would like to read it," said Larke.

"I would, very much," replied Jaylene. "Thank you."

"Is he still at his parents' ranch, Mom?" asked Timothy.

"He is. Unmarried and living with his folks. It sounds a little old-fashioned, I suppose, but he absolutely loves the ranching life. He says there is nothing else he has ever wanted to do. He hopes to live the rest of his life there."

"Hey, Tim," said Graham, "have you decided on grad school?"

"I'm leaning toward Davis," replied Timothy. "I've been accepted into the programs at UCSB and Cal Poly. But doing graduate work where Dad was on the faculty would be weird, especially after, you know—what Dad just said. I only applied as a back-up option. Too many people know Dad at Cal Poly too. I think I'd be better off further away."

"What do you think, Dad?" asked Jane.

"I'm keeping out of it!" laughed Stirling. "If I had my way, all five of you would stay at home and attend UCSB and never leave Santa Barbara. I'm the wrong one to ask. What about you, Jaylene? Tim says you'll be looking at grad schools next year too. Any plans?"

"My folks are like you," answered Jaylene, "they'd love to see me back in New Mexico. But I like California. I don't know yet. I'll probably apply to Stanford."

"Whoa!" said Graham. "That's impressive."

"I might not get in. If not, I think Dr. Sarber would make sure I was accepted at Cal Poly."

"I'm sure he would!" laughed Stirling. "And probably with inducements. I happen to know he does not want to lose you."

The turkey and dressing, mashed potatoes, sweet potatoes, gravy and onions, and cranberry sauce went around the table a second time, then a third, until chairs were being pushed away with satisfied groans.

"I'm stuffed," said Larke. "Would anyone agree to saving the pie for later?"

"Hear, hear!" assented her husband, with affirmative votes from the rest.

Everyone stood. Jane, Cheryl, Larke, and Jaylene began removing the dinner things to the kitchen. An hour later, Woody and Cheryl were trying to get their daughter down for a nap. Larke was dozing. Graham, Jane, and Timothy were in their father's office perusing the ever-growing contents of his bookshelves and talking amongst themselves. On one side of the living room, Stirling and Jaylene were engaged in conversation.

"Timothy has not told me a great deal," Stirling was saying, "other than that you were thinking through the Christian faith, perhaps from what you might call the beginning."

"That's a good way of putting it," smiled Jaylene. "I didn't have a religious upbringing. I have been pestering him with questions since the day we met. I'm amazed he puts up with me!"

"He's always been a good and patient listener. I can't tell you how valuable the questioning process is," Stirling went on, "for experienced Christians as well as those new to the faith. We need to know our foundations. I have to think my own faith through from time to time right up from the ground floor, from zero degrees Kelvin, so to speak."

"A humorous metaphor. I think I know what you mean. Starting from nothing."

"Exactly—from nothing, from Genesis 1:1, and trying to make sense of everything we believe. I have the greatest respect for what you are doing, thinking out what is true, and hopefully discarding what is not. Many Christians never learn that skill—to think with acuity and depth. It's one of the great missing ingredients of modern Christendom."

"It seems strange to hear a Christian say that."

"It ought to be from the *inside* that one can best perceive the most subtle weaknesses of any belief system. From the outside, the critic is able to attack the easy targets, though often such attacks are more spurious than legitimate. It's like attacking Christianity because of the Crusades—one of the classic red herrings skeptics love to bring up. But from the inside, where you have inside information from years of experience, you have a right to speak to legitimate flaws in your own system needing to be addressed. At least that's how I see it."

"I hope that's maybe a little of what I am doing about the belief system I have taken for granted for too long—the non-religious perspective, I guess you would say. Timothy has encouraged me to thoroughly investigate the world, to ask questions, to read books like yours, to read the Bible, and mostly to think it all out for myself."

"Many never do that," nodded Stirling. "It is imperative that we know what our beliefs are based on, that they have a rational basis. That requires objective thought and asking hard questions."

Stirling stood. "How about some fresh air?" he said. "Let's go for a walk," he added, leading Jaylene to the door. "The dogs will enjoy it too!"

Timothy heard the door close and came back into the living room. Out the front window he saw the two strolling slowly away from the house. His father's head was turned toward Jaylene's and she was listening intently.

No one ever heard, and she did not share with him what she and his father talked about that day. But it was a conversation Jaylene never forgot.

They returned thirty minutes later. Timothy was waiting and went out to meet them as they approached. They smiled and Stirling continued past Timothy into the house.

Timothy turned. Jaylene slipped her hand through his arm. They continued along the sidewalk in the opposite direction from which she had come.

Neither spoke. It was enough that they *knew*.

28

THE GORDON LETTER

1992

LETTERS FROM readers to Stirling Marshall were nothing new. There had probably been half a dozen letters from colleagues in the academic world who expressed appreciation for Stirling's *History of 19th-Century Scottish Writers* in the fifteen years after its publication. But with the release of *Unspoken Commandments* in 1987, in the afterword to which Stirling took the unusual step of inviting response and including their Santa Barbara address, hundreds of letters began pouring in from grateful readers—usually two or three a week, though occasionally that many in a single day. Some of the letters stood out and led to lasting relationships.

Committed to answering every letter personally, and with his writing and class schedule demanding so much of Stirling's time and energy, Larke replied to most of the mail herself between the students who came and went for piano lessons in her music studio. She answered most of the questions from hungry and searching readers in more detail than Stirling would have had time for. He reserved his replies for those deeply spiritual queries which Larke passed on to him with a brief note attached, "A great letter—this is one you need to answer personally." In such cases, though it sometimes took a good amount of time, he gave his responses much prayerful thought and energy, often typing letters of five or more pages which he worked on for days. Second, third, and fourth letters came, addressed equally to Larke and Stirling. Many rich long-distance friendships were thus established between readers and both of the Marshalls.

Including the whole family in his writing, Stirling drew the other six Marshalls into the plotting of his fiction books, everyone brainstorming together. Many of the children's ideas, even when they were young, found their way onto the final pages of his stories. Larke did the same by reading some of the richest of the letters aloud to the family. She wanted their children to hear firsthand and be able to participate in the impact their father's writings were exercising in the lives of people around the world.

Around the supper table one Saturday evening in 1992, when Woody, a sophomore at Cal Poly came down for the day, Larke brought out a letter that arrived the day before and set the envelope beside her plate.

"One of the most extraordinary letters I think we have ever received came in the mail yesterday," she said. "I would like to read it after supper."

"I've got to be getting back, Mom," said nineteen-year-old Woody. "It's an hour and a half drive and I want to make it before dark."

"Please, Woody—it would mean a lot to me if you stayed."

"All right," sighed Woody, "if it doesn't take too long."

"Ten minutes at the most."

"And I've got a paper due tomorrow," said Cateline, a freshman at Santa Barbara City College.

"Why don't I read it right now, then," said Larke, setting down her fork. "I'll read it while you are finishing your dessert."

She opened the envelope and pulled out the four handwritten pages.

Dear Dr. Marshall,

I am writing to express my immeasurable appreciation for your books. Forgive what may be the personal tone of this letter, but I feel as if I do know you personally.

I am twenty-one years old, born and raised just outside Grass Valley near Sacramento. I am the only son of Pelham and Isobel Gordon. We own a large cattle ranch in the foothills. It is a heritage I am proud of. I am a senior at Sacramento State—an hour's drive, but worth it to be able to live at home. I have no career plans other than to take over the ranch from my father one day. I love our ranch and can think of nothing else I would ever want to do.

My parents are wonderful people. They gave me a strong spiritual grounding and I have been a Christian essentially all my life. My father was one of the founders of Foothills Gospel Church in Grass Valley in the 1970s and has remained in its leadership ever since. My earliest memories are of the church and they are pleasant ones. The atmosphere in college is so stridently anti-Christian that it makes me angry at times to see how the academic environment fosters rebellion against the Christian foundations of our country and encourages those who have been raised in the church to reject the heritage of their past. I greatly value the foundation I received in church.

In the late 1980s, during my last years of high school, the church decided to move to Roseville to expand the reach of its ministry.

The move to Roseville accomplished exactly what its leaders and our pastor hoped. Immediately the church began to grow and has continued to grow ever since, which in a roundabout way brings me to the purpose of my letter.

I suppose the college years are always ones of reevaluating one's past and beliefs and refocusing one's directions in life. As I mentioned, I find so many who are engaged in this process take it too far and reject everything from their upbringing. This strikes me as singularly short-sighted, illogical, intellectually unsound, and frankly a stupid response to what should be a healthy process of growth. I want to discover truth, and deeper truth than I was perhaps aware of in my younger years. Where truth has not been represented in my upbringing, of course I want to replace whatever those misconceptions have been with true truth. But where truth has been represented, I want to personalize and deepen my understanding of that truth.

Of course, doubts and questions and reevaluations are part of the growth process. But it makes all the difference for one raised in the Christian tradition whether one's doubts and questions are taking place in or against faith. When a Christian young person, for example, begins to "question" and "doubt," what is the object of that doubt? What are the motives behind it? Is he trying to break away from faith and the church, or deepen his Christian beliefs?

So many young people are dishonest with themselves. They are not seeking truth. They are looking for an excuse to abandon God and the church. The idea of obligation to religion in any form is distasteful to them. Personal freedom and independence is the god worshipped on campus. Most students, and I would say most professors as well, are not seeking truth; they are seeking independence. Whatever lip-service they give to the quest for truth is a lie. They are being completely disingenuous.

My chief quandaries center upon two questions that have come into focus after our church's move and its subsequent rapid growth.

One, I have been struck recently with how much of what I hear from the pulpit sounds like cliché and formula. Our pastor never tells people to search the Bible or to think for themselves. He just dishes out the rote prescriptions of belief I've heard all my life.

To be honest, it seems shallow and superficial. Maybe I am more a doubter than I realize. What if I am in the early stages of backsliding. But something is wrong—either in me, or in the superficial presentation of what ought to be a more, I don't know, a more meaty or intellectually stimulating gospel.

Then secondly, the role of the church itself—what is the role of the church? I always took church for granted, like you do when you're young. But now as I sit bored with the shallow three-point sermons every Sunday, more and more it seems the people around me are more dedicated to the services and activities of church than living as Christians. Being in church every Sunday morning is the all-important gauge of spirituality.

Nobody talks about obedience or what Jesus says, only about church, church, church. One would think the commandments were: Go to church every Sunday. And by the way, love the Lord your God and love your neighbor too, if you're so inclined, but whatever you do you must never miss a worship service.

Am I in danger of committing that most cardinal of all sins—forsaking the assembling of the saints?

My mention of the commandments is not accidental. Your book Unspoken Commandments has had nothing short of a life-changing impact on my spiritual outlook. Reading it sparked within me such a great hunger to be God's man—completely, whole-heartedly. My heart leapt within me as I read about what you call "centered living." Your focus, not on the church, but on the Lord's commands has seemed so right, so foundational, so organic to the essence of what being a Christian can and should mean.

I have now read the book six or seven times and it is well underlined. Curiously, I did not even notice until my third or fourth time through what has become one of the most profound influences the book offers. That is a new and deeper sense and understanding of the good, gracious, loving, forgiving Fatherhood of God. This stole upon me quietly, almost through the back door of my heart.

It was only gradually that I realized you were talking about God as our heavenly Father in an altogether new way from what I always heard in church. The Father you spoke of was the father of the prodigal with a smile on his face, running toward us to receive us with open arms.

I feel so many questions and uncertainties melting away in the light of such a Fatherhood. If such a Fatherhood indeed reigns at the heart of the universe, how many doctrines might have to be re-written, with divine love rather than divine vengeance at the heart of them?

*I have since located and read, I think, all your writings,
including your two novels through which breathes the same
clean and refreshing air of Fatherhood, if I can express it a little
colorfully, as do your devotional books.*

*I tried to talk to our pastor about some of these new ideas
and perspectives after reading your book, but it was as if I was
speaking a foreign language. His only responses were familiar
clichés in which the church was always central. He had heard of
you, of course, but seemed suspicious of your writings.*

*It was a frustrating and confusing interview. It took me
several days, and a few tears I am not embarrassed to admit,
to recover from the exchange. I went back again to your book
and it brought me back, I hope to the "center." In spite of these
questions, even confusions, I feel I am focused on the true North
to which God's compass is pointing, to borrow one of your
analogies. You have given me an anchoring foundation to plant
my feet upon, and I thank you more than I can say.*

With gratitude,
David Gordon,
Bar JG Ranch
Grass Valley, California

It was silent around the table for several long seconds.

"Amazing," was all Stirling could say softly, shaking his head
almost in disbelief as his wife folded the letter. "There is a young man
who will find the heart of God. Blessed are those who hunger to be
righteous, for they shall be satisfied. He is indeed such a one."

It fell silent again, though only for a second or two. Then Woody
pushed back his chair and stood. "I've got to hit the road. Thanks for
supper, Mom."

He walked around the table and bent down and kissed Larke on
the cheek.

"Bye, Dad. Bye all," he added and left through the front door.

"I need to go too," said Cateline, rising also.

29

THE REPLY

WHEN THE door closed behind Woody and Cateline, the remaining five Marshalls sat a few moments longer. Larke and the three young people rose and silently began clearing away the supper things from the table. Stirling sat where he was, speechless as he absorbed the magnitude of the heartfelt letter Larke had just read.

Would any of his own children ever respond to the depth of his own walk with God as much as had this perfect stranger? Woody and Cateline were close to the same age, certainly old enough to begin hearing the Spirit's voice for themselves. They had been taught in the ways of God all their lives, just as the young man Gordon. Yet they had not yet indicated such visible hunger for a deeper walk with God. He didn't think Woody had read a single one of his books.

Stirling drew in a deep breath and exhaled slowly. Maybe he was writing for a different posterity than his earthly offspring, such as this young man who had reached out to them over the miles.

He began a reply that very evening.

Dear David,

How wonderful to hear from you. Thank you for writing, for your openness and honesty, and for your questions. Yours is clearly a heart hungering, as Jesus says, for righteousness. I must say, you express yourself exquisitely. If I didn't know better, I would think you were the author! Are you an English or literature major by any chance? Most of the papers I get even from my graduate students are not so expressive and do not show such an adept command of ideas and skill in communicating them as did your letter.

I hardly know where to begin. My brain is full with the many points you raise. Let me first emphatically say:

No, you are not in danger of backsliding!

Your questions are sincere and honest and reveal a heart hungry for God's truth. Even though you profess some confusion, I can assure you, you are already well on your way toward the very truth you seek. Your questions, even your doubts about spiritual cliché and the undue worship of the church—two great stumbling blocks in Christendom today, and a profound annoyance to me as well—are not the doubts and questions of unbelief, but of deeper and truer belief.

I applaud you for the honesty of your questions, and for the sincerity of your self-examination!

I don't know if you have heard of the Victorian Scotsman George MacDonald. If not, I will send you an introduction to his work and some suggestions for further reading. "Doubts are the messengers," MacDonald says, "to rouse the honest. They are the first knock at our door of things that are not yet, but have to be, understood."

In other words, doubts properly understood, doubts within faith not against it, exactly as you say, doubts prompted by hunger for truth, questions of inquiry to God and seeking his wisdom to resolve them—such doubts are our friends! Such doubts are the doors we must first knock on, then open, and then walk through, to enter new and wider regions of understanding who God is and what faith in him means.

MacDonald calls the wider regions, which the doors of doubt may at first hide from view, the unknown, unexplored, unannexed. To know God fully, we must knock, pass through, then explore, and ultimately annex these wider regions within his heart.

*So you see, far from drifting away from God, you are
actually moving closer and closer to him. You are annexing new
regions of truth . . .*

By the time it was completed and sent off, the letter from Stirling
Marshall to young David Gordon was even longer than the one he had
received from him.

David and Stirling continued to correspond with longer and ever
deepening letters. Stirling found in young David a hungry spirit eager
to absorb all he could give him.

Thus began what would develop into a lifetime friendship.

30

DORADO WOOD

2002-2014

TIMOTHY MARSHALL graduated from Cal Poly in June of 2002 and entered the graduate program at UC Davis that fall.

During Jaylene Gray's senior year at Cal Poly, the letters between Davis and San Luis Obispo were nearly enough to keep the USPS in business for a year.

Jaylene graduated in June of 2003, valedictorian of her class, and entered the masters and doctoral program at Stanford three months later. She and Timothy were still separated, but by less than three hours rather than five, and saw one another at least every other weekend.

When Jane Marshall married that same year and left for Houston with her NASA-employed husband, Wade Durant, Stirling and Larke Marshall found themselves facing a huge house, an empty nest, and reevaluating their future.

With three of their five children in the central population hubs of the state, they sold their seven-bedroom Santa Barbara home and followed Graham, Cateline, and Timothy north. After extensive research into suitable locations where they thought they could make a new home for themselves, they settled on Dorado Wood, a modest town of 10,000 on the fringes of the Sacramento metropolis some thirty miles east where California's central valley gave way to the foothills of that state's fabled gold country, leading eventually to the peaks of the Sierras and Lake Tahoe. After spending their entire married life in Santa Barbara, they made the 415-mile move in 2004.

It was a modest downsizing, from seven bedrooms to four. Their new home in Dorado Wood would still give them ample space to continue their professional lives in a new setting—Stirling's writing in one of the bedrooms converted to a study, and Larke's teaching in another devoted to a new music studio. With the large master bedroom as their own, that left the final bedroom for guests, which they hoped children and grandchildren would make frequent use of.

The huge open great room of the house, spacious with vaulted ceiling and adjoining a modern kitchen area was far larger than they could imagine needing. It would easily hold thirty or more people. They never envisioned it doing so, though perhaps family Christmases might in time fill half of it.

In the meantime, they filled the expansive great room with floor-to-ceiling bookshelves, sideboards, and furniture from their Santa Barbara home, adorning the walls with framed family photographs, paintings, Scottish and other memorabilia, and the shelves and cabinets with the treasured *things* of a lifetime of memories.

Timothy and Jaylene were married a year later in 2005. Jaylene's parents and brothers came out for a week. Somewhat skeptical of the family of religious fanatics their daughter was marrying into, the Grays met the extended Marshall clan for the first time. Thaddeus and Stirling hit it off like two old war horses in the academic world, each recognizing in the other an expert in somewhat related fields of study. Stirling listened in rapt attention as Thady described his first visit to Lechuguilla. The two men and their wives visited as often as time and distance permitted for the rest of their lives.

The newlyweds took up residence in an apartment in Fairfield, from which it was an easy commute for Timothy to Davis. By then much of Jaylene's work was independent of class schedules and could be carried out on computer and with the use of the Davis library. She also gave some undergraduate lectures, and therefore usually spent one or two days a week in Palo Alto, bunking with a friend.

Working and teaching part-time, it took Timothy five years to complete his masters and doctoral degrees. On a full fellowship and not having to worry about finances, Jaylene easily breezed through

Stanford's in three, then took an additional year for a second doctorate in anthropology. Both completed their schooling, with three PhDs between them, in 2007. Eying Roseville as a potential future home, they began attending Foothills Gospel Ministries.

Offers poured in throughout Jaylene's four years at Stanford. By the time two PhDs were attached to her name, she could have written her own ticket almost anywhere in the world. Stanford enticed her with lavish offers in hopes of adding her to their faculty which no other university could hope to match, although many tried. She could also have worked in the field. Offers to join teams, digs, committees, and engage in research and exploration came from some of the most prestigious names in archaeology in Africa, Israel, Turkey, Iran, Iraq, and England.

But everything changed for Jaylene the day Timothy saw her on a bench at Cal Poly trying to make sense of Genesis 1. She was now Jaylene *Marshall*, and she was thoroughly a Marshall—cut from the same cloth as her husband and father-in-law, a *thinker*, and a creation-believing scientist. Her passion was no longer mere *antiquity*, but both ends of the arrow of time—the twin poles of unanswerability extending back *and* forward.

Unifying the *infinity of eternity* with the *infinity of beginnings*, in a connecting circle of wonder with God's being at the center of it, had become Jaylene's personal Riemann hypothesis.

She had no ambition other than to share her story in whatever way God chose for her to do so—the story birthed on that bench in 2002. The best way she could do that now, it seemed, was in the classroom. Her desire was to expand young minds to consider Truth from a higher plane than that taught by the rote indoctrination of secular academia. Research and expeditions would be fascinating and fun—a positive delight! But what would eternally be achieved by them?

She would now be the one trying to detect those curious, hungry, open-minded bench-sitters whom she might point toward some of the right questions to ask, as Timothy helped her. Her mission, like Stirling's in his books, was to encourage people to *think*.

In the back of her mind, she hoped to write a book about her quest one day. But it was much too soon to think of that. She had only been a

Christian six years. She had decades ahead of her before she would be ready to write her story.

In the meantime, shocking her Stanford professors, after Timothy was offered a position at Dorado Community College, Jaylene accepted an offer to head up the newly formed graduate program in archaeology at Sacramento's California State University, which would be attached to the anthropology department.

In spite of being encouraged by Timothy and Jaylene to join them at Foothills Gospel Ministries, nothing could have been further from Stirling and Larke Marshall's thoughts after their move to northern California than to join a large church. Already reevaluating the scriptural basis for the organized church, they mostly stayed home together on Sundays, or occasionally sought out small congregations in the less populated towns scattered in the Sierra foothills.

Their move to northern California led to the richest friendship of their later years. Soon after their arrival in Dorado Wood, a personal meeting with David Gordon was arranged. Many more followed. Eventually the two families were getting together several times a month. Larke and Stirling spent many hours at the Bar JG, named for David's great-great-grandfather "JG," Jackson Gordon.

That a man of sixty-three, as Stirling was at the time of the move, would consider a man exactly thirty years his junior his closest companion in the Spirit other than his wife, may seem remarkable. But to those who know the depth and strength of those bonds, it is the most natural thing in the world. David Gordon, though still in his mid-thirties, was already on his way to becoming a seasoned veteran of faith. He became a spiritual son in the full sense of the word to Stirling and Larke, a friendship they shared in equal measure with David's parents Pelham and Isobel.

Having been involved in the church's origins years before, the explosive growth of Roseville's Foothills Gospel Ministries in the 1990s and early 2000s was not exactly to Pelham Gordon's liking. But he remained a loyal elder statesman for the rest of his life. With the deepening influence of Stirling Marshall's writings, however, more and more elements of Foothills' mega-church atmosphere grew distasteful to Pelham's son David.

In spite of his misgivings, David led an occasional Bible study during the Sunday school hour, though his uncommon views were of some concern to the pastoral staff and church leadership. Though they were well aware of his affection for Timothy's father and mother, and though their paths occasionally crossed, few close bonds formed between Timothy and Jaylene and the three Gordons.

After the death of David's father in 2014, despite the difference in their ages, the friendship between Stirling Marshall and David Gordon, though still technically that of mentor and protégé, assumed more and more a friendship of equals probing together the high purposes of God.

Stirling and Larke often spent the night with David and Isobel in their sprawling ranch house. Larke and Isobel became the closest of friends. Stirling relished the chance to lend David a hand with what work around the Bar JG his now seventy-plus constitution was capable of.

He continued to write prolifically, eventually penning over forty books, evenly split between fiction and devotional writings on the New Testament.

31

HEARTBREAK

2005–2009

TIMOTHY AND Jaylene knew starting a family would be unwise while they were both in graduate school. They began thinking about it more seriously after they secured their PhDs, purchasing a four-bedroom house and moving to Roseville in anticipation of at least two children, perhaps three. They were in no hurry, however, and threw themselves into their new teaching careers at Sacramento State and Dorado Community College. Being in Roseville also expanded their involvement at Foothills Gospel Ministries, where they began teaching one of the Sunday school electives on science and the Bible.

By 2008 they had been married for three years and were taken somewhat by surprise, though joyously, when Jaylene became pregnant. The rejoicing of the whole family, however, was dashed when she miscarried at nine weeks. The family Thanksgiving at Dorado Wood a month later was subdued.

By Christmas Jaylene had regained her optimism, recovering quickly from the trauma of miscarriage. Having their hopes raised, though earlier than they planned, she and Timothy were now excited and ready to try again as soon as their doctor gave them the green light. She was pregnant again by June. All their friends from church, and of course Timothy's parents, were praying for a full-term successful pregnancy. When she passed nine weeks, then eleven, everyone's hopes were high.

Timothy's first indication of trouble at twelve weeks was being jolted awake at three in the morning by a piercing shriek from somewhere in the house. The other side of the bed was empty and the hall light was on. He leapt out of bed and met Jaylene walking out of the bathroom in tears. She fell into his arms.

"I lost the baby!" she said, then broke into convulsive sobs.

The trauma of the loss this time was devastating. Timothy called the department chair at Sac State later that morning to explain that Jaylene's classes for the day would have to be cancelled.

Jaylene remained in bed for a week, scarcely ate, and lost eight pounds. When she finally set about trying to move on with life, she was weak, pale, and listless. Somehow, she managed to resume her classes after ten days. But she was clearly not herself.

It took a year before her smile and cheerful countenance fully returned. In all that time they had not seen their physician.

It was Timothy who finally made an appointment. For Jaylene's sake, and his, they needed to know the prognosis for the future. Timothy planned to investigate the options, but Jaylene insisted on accompanying him.

"I'm okay, Timothy," she said. "I can handle it. I'll be fine."

When they sat down in Dr. Myers's office, Jaylene spoke first. "I need you to be up front with me, Doctor," she said. "I don't want happy talk or beating around the bush. What are my chances of being a mother?"

"It's hard to say without some tests," replied Dr. Myers. "Two miscarriages, though a factor to consider, may be just a fluke. You could go on to have six successful pregnancies. On the other hand, they *may* indicate that your body will continue to have difficulty adapting to the stresses of pregnancy."

"What tests would you suggest?" said Timothy.

"I'd like to do a full workup, if you are both agreed—" she said, glancing back and forth between them. "Blood work, ultrasound, x-rays, maybe even a CT scan or MRI."

"Then let's do whatever you want to start with," said Jaylene. "Timothy?"

"Of course. We want to know."

They found themselves again in Dr. Myers's office three weeks later. Several files and test packets lay on her desk.

"You told me before that you didn't want happy talk," she began when they were seated. "So I will tell you at the outset the prognosis isn't the best."

A brief gasp sounded from Jaylene's lips. Quickly she recovered herself.

"There is no absolute evidence to indicate you could not carry a child to full term," Dr. Myers went on. "But there are signs that miscarriages may continue. There is some uterine damage—it's hard to tell the cause—and fibroids on the uterine wall could be problematic. Nothing is ever set in stone, but these are cautions to take seriously. I can show you the x-rays and scans if you like."

Jaylene was sitting quietly gazing down at her lap. "Maybe later," she said softly. "I know you probably don't do this, but give me the likelihood of future miscarriages."

"I hate to quantify it in such—"

"Please, Dr. Myers, what is your best guess?"

Dr. Myers drew in a deep breath. "Probably 80 percent."

Tears filled Jaylene's eyes.

"What about Jaylene?" now said Timothy. "Would future pregnancies, and future miscarriages, place *her* in danger?"

Dr. Myers hesitated.

"As I said," she began, "there is some uterine damage that could—"

"Please, Doctor," interrupted Jaylene, wiping at her eyes. "Just yes or no."

"All I can say is that it is possible," replied Dr. Myers.

Timothy tried not to show his emotions. He reached over and took Jaylene's hand.

"If you were in my position, what would you do?" said Jaylene. "Would *you* get pregnant again hoping for the 20 percent chance of success?"

The room was silent.

"I only answer you," Dr. Myers replied, "because I am responsible for the health and safety of my patients." She paused briefly, then added, "I consider the likelihood of danger to the mother significant . . . no, I would not."

The drive back to Roseville was somber. The loss of hope was a devastating blow. Within a week Jaylene decided not to try again.

"Do you remember when you wanted us not to see each other until I did more thinking and reading on my own?" she said as she told Timothy of her decision.

"One of the hardest things I've ever done," smiled Timothy.

"I knew it was hard for you. I didn't see it at first, when I thought you were breaking up with me," she added laughing. "But when you explained, I realized you were doing it for me."

She paused thoughtfully.

"I know you want to be a father," she said after a moment, "and I want to be a mother. But now it's my turn. This is a decision I need to make for *you*. I'm not so concerned about my own life, but I can't put myself in danger—for *your* sake. I'm not going to take even a small chance of doing *anything* that would leave you alone. Of course, I want to be a mother. But more than that, I want to spend my life with you. I will do nothing to jeopardize that."

They did not discuss it again. She had made her decision. But the disappointment remained as a pain in her heart. Neither she nor Timothy saw anything to be gained by talking about it.

32

ΛCΛDEMIC INQUISITION

2011–2014

FOR SOME time, Jaylene had contemplated offering an undergraduate course that would increase her opportunity to give subtle, and she hoped inoffensive, voice to her faith, while compromising nothing of her integrity as a science professor. With that in mind, she developed a unique single semester curriculum that emerged largely out of her first conversations with Timothy about Genesis.

She finally summoned the courage to present the syllabus to the chair of the anthropology department realizing she would have to make a compelling case for the course to be accepted. Surprisingly, he agreed to allow her to offer it. Jaylene's reputation generally got her what she wanted. He assumed the course would take the usual academically-correct position on what he also assumed would be its minor religious elements.

The course was offered in the spring term of 2011, titled, Einstein and Genesis: A New Perspective on Beginnings. Surprising everyone, the course was filled within a week of its announcement. A command performance that fall resulted in such a huge waiting list that in 2012 the head of the university's graduate program in archaeology was teaching two undergraduate courses using the Bible's first two chapters as one of its texts. They were among the most popular classes in the university's catalog. Talk began to spread through the state university system that Cal Poly's one-time darling and valedictorian, and one of Stanford's most highly sought-after graduates, had "found religion."

In 2012, Timothy received the offer he had been hoping for from William Jessup University in nearby Rocklin. It would give him the opportunity to teach closer to home and at a far higher level than a junior college could provide. He and Jaylene were at last doing what they dreamed of. By then Timothy was also moving into leadership at Foothills Gospel, eventually being named to the board of elders.

This halcyon period in their early married lives, however, was brief.

The formal request for Dr. Marshall to meet with the university president and an ad hoc committee of administrative and department heads was not entirely unexpected. Knowing her father-in-law had faced a similar request, Jaylene paid a visit to Stirling toward the end of 2013 the week before the scheduled, as she expected, inquisition.

"It isn't so much that I am concerned for my job," she said. "At least I hope I don't need to be. I'm reasonably certain it's only about my Genesis and Einstein course. They're probably going to tell me it's being dropped."

"Is that what you think they will do?" asked Stirling.

"At least that. I doubt they had any idea how popular it would be. I'm sure you faced similar quandaries."

"My position was different," nodded Stirling. "I was already at an age where I had enjoyed a fulfilling career. Nor did my field contain quite so hot-button an issue as mixing Genesis with evolution."

"I suppose I did rather open myself up for controversy!" laughed Jaylene.

"In my case, the thought of retirement was not so bad," rejoined Stirling, "which came not long after I was called on the carpet by our university president. You are just starting out. Your career is ahead of you. You don't want to jeopardize that."

"But neither can I renounce my convictions."

"Discontinuing a single class may not carry that implication."

"I suppose you're right."

"You were happy enough before."

"I was. Yet if I was led to offer this class, and I believe it has made a difference in the lives of some students, should I bow to the pressure?"

"The answer to that may depend on what other restrictions they impose, and whether or not you could comply in good conscience."

"I see what you mean, that the implications may be larger than this one course."

"I would guess they almost surely will be at this point. Offering the course may have let a genie out of a bottle you can't put back."

Her father-in-law paused.

"Do you remember the walk you and I took that first Christmas when you came to our home?" he asked.

"Of course," smiled Jaylene. "I've never forgotten it."

"You were hungry, honest, seeking truth. I knew then that my son had discovered a jewel. And you have grown into a radiant daughter of God. I am proud of you."

"I am honored, Stirling. Thank you. I am proud to be a Marshall."

"Whatever happens, I know you will do the Lord proud too. You will be his representative to the men and women questioning you. Speak your heart in love and courtesy and respect, and you will be in his hands. It may be he has something on your horizon neither you nor I can see. Go into that meeting with hope and good cheer. Then be yourself. Who could resist you!"

Jaylene laughed. "Thank you, Stirling. There may be some who can!"

"Let me read you a couple of passages I noted in a book I am reading," Stirling said after a brief pause. "They do not paint a very encouraging picture. But you should probably know what to expect. It is surprisingly pertinent to your situation."

Stirling picked up the book from the coffee table beside him and flipped through it to find the passages he had marked.

"At universities within the University of California system . . ." he began reading, "teachers who want to apply for tenure-track positions have to affirm their commitment to 'equity, diversity, and inclusion'— and to have demonstrated it, even if it has nothing to do with their field . . .

"'If you step out of line, especially if you're in the area of opinion-forming as a journalist or an academic, then the aim is to prevent your voice from being heard . . . you'll be thrown out of whatever teaching position you have, or . . . made the topic of a completely . . . fabricated interview used to accuse you of . . . thoughtcrimes.'"

"Oh my goodness!" exclaimed Jaylene. "I'm right in the middle of the system he's talking about!"

"There's more. 'An American academic . . .'" Stirling resumed, "'told . . . about being present at the meeting in which his humanities department decided to require from job applicants a formal statement of loyalty to the ideology of diversity . . . putting those already on staff on notice that they will be monitored for deviation from the social-justice party line.'"

"That's unbelievable!" said Jaylene.

"And this is especially chilling," Stirling continued. "The author compares our current culture to Orwell's book. Listen to this.

"'In *Nineteen Eighty-Four* . . . *Newspeak* is the Party's word for the jargon it imposes on society—it controls the categories in which people think. . . .

"'In our time, we do not have an all-powerful state forcing this on us. . . . the media, academia, corporate America, and other institutions are practicing Newspeak and compelling the rest of us to engage in doublethink every day. . . . *The woman standing in front of you is to be called 'he.' Diversity and inclusion means excluding those who object to ideological uniformity. Equity means treating persons unequally . . . to achieve an ideologically correct result. . . .*

"'Many Christians will see through these lies but will choose not to speak up. Their silence will not save them and will instead corrode them.'"[8]

"That's genuinely frightening," said Jaylene. "Do you really think I might face an inquisition like that?"

"You well may. Such is the sad state of academia today," said Stirling. "My so-called inquisition was almost exactly twenty years ago. Even then, however, the momentum had begun against free and open-mindedness in academia. When I was first starting out, the Jesus Movement was at its height. Christian young people were exercising a great influence not only on college campuses, but throughout the whole country. The church was never the same afterward. It was an extraordinary time to be a Christian in college, or in my case, to be a Christian professor."

"But obviously it didn't last."

"No, it didn't. Progressivism in academia eventually began to squelch rather than encourage free speech and the free flow of ideas. Christianity was the first casualty, which resulted in my inquisition."

"And now I am facing mine," said Jaylene. "Progressivism has completely taken over the university environment. To stand up for Christian ideals is now considered hateful, bigoted, and judgmental—the very opposite of what Christianity actually is."

"We are a completely different country now," nodded Stirling. "White is now black, black is white, wrong is right, evil is lauded, and Christianity and America are despised. The Obama years have all but eradicated the moral, ethical, and spiritual fiber of our foundations. You, my dear, are not a mere twenty years but a *century* removed from the pressures I faced as a Christian academic. Our colleges and universities have become the indoctrination arm of the radical Left. I am not a political man, but I fear our nation has twice elected a Trojan Horse, through whom a cancer has been released into America's bloodstream that will ultimately erode the fabric of our nation. A wolf in sheep's clothing has been allowed into the White House. Heartbreaking though it is for a man like me to admit it, the academic world is the vehicle for the spread of that cancer. As you just said, my dear, you are in the middle of it."

Jaylene sighed, though not happily.

"Remember, my dear, we are not fighting a worldly war, nor contending against flesh and blood, but against the principalities and powers of this present darkness. So I would be wary, and in much prayer as you go into this interview. In a very real sense, you may indeed be entering the darkness of this present world. It may not be so much discussion they want, as your scalp. Even so, remember Jesus' words, 'You are the light of the world. . . . Let your light so shine before men.'"

When Jaylene entered the room a week later, the four women and three men seated in a row on one side of a long conference table wore somber expressions. She sat down facing them on the opposite side. A single sheet of paper lay face-down on the table in front of her. The interview began without benefit of smiles, greetings, or formalities.

"You know why you are here, Dr. Marshall," said the chairwoman. "Your course on Einstein and Genesis does not harmonize with the goals and objectives of the university. We would like to request you to voluntarily discontinue it, and make a public statement to the effect that offering the course was a mistake, adding your apology for any confusion that may have resulted from it, or untruths passed along to the students."

"I assumed you would have discretion to discontinue it yourselves," replied Jaylene.

"We do. We would prefer it came from you. It would look better that way, especially with the apology. The university must keep itself distanced from the taint of religion."

"The course has been very popular. Does that weigh nothing in the balance?"

"Not if you are teaching falsehoods."

"I don't believe falsehoods are being taught."

"What about creation?"

"It's not a *proven* falsehood, just a conjectured falsehood."

"Don't split hairs, Dr. Marshall. It is not a scientifically recognized truth."

"I'm sorry. Perhaps I should clarify, then—I *don't* teach creation."

"Isn't that the point of the course?"

"No."

"What is, then?"

"To ask interesting questions about how the theory of relativity, the Big Bang, and certain features of the Genesis account might harmonize. That's all. I propose nothing other than that my students ask questions they perhaps had not considered before. I have always felt such to be the basis of academic inquiry."

The chairwoman shuffled in her seat and glanced around at her colleagues.

"Will you discontinue the course?" she said stiffly.

"If that is your decision, yes, I can abide by that."

"Will you publicly apologize for any falsehoods taught?"

"Absolutely."

"Oh—well, good. I am glad to hear that. So we may expect a statement to that effect, when? Will a day or two give you enough time?"

"I will do so today, once I have the information so that I can be specific in my apology."

"I'm afraid I don't understand you. What information?"

"I would like to be shown from my class syllabus or the taped sessions of my lectures and class discussions, exactly where I have erred. If I can be shown specifically where I have taught falsehoods, I will not only apologize willingly, but eagerly. As I said, I will release a statement today. However, I don't feel it would be appropriate to issue a statement without that information."

"We were thinking more in terms of a general apology."

"I wouldn't want to apologize for something that never happened. That would not be truthful."

"I see you are determined to be unreasonable. Let me ask you this, then. Will you cease and desist mentioning God and creation in any of your lectures?"

"May I ask for a point of clarification?"

The chairwoman sighed in annoyance. "You may."

"Honestly, I mean no disrespect either to any of you or the university. I am just trying to understand. Do the university's policies of diversity and inclusion apply to the ideas of Christianity?"

"I hardly see what that has to do with the matter at hand."

"We are talking about diversity of ideas. I am asking if diversity applies to me. Or does the policy of inclusion not include my ideas?"

"You are splitting hairs again."

"Am I? I apologize again. I am just trying to understand how tolerance, diversity, and inclusion are defined when certain ideas are *not* tolerated and are specifically *excluded*."

"Just answer the question, Dr. Marshall. Will you not mention God or creation in your lectures?"

Jaylene thought several long seconds. The room was deathly quiet.

"If the university determines," she began, "that it is so closed to free thought and alternative viewpoints as to place constrictions of freedom of expression on its faculty, if thinking for oneself has ceased to be a hallmark of this university but only certain pre-determined perspectives are allowed, if questions are no longer welcome, and if censorship is to be placed on one of your professors, then yes, for the present I would agree to teach without mentioning God and creation. I would do so, however, urging you to consider the peril of banishing free and open-minded inquiry from this university."

A few disgruntled comments went around the group.

"You are untenured you know."

"Of course."

"Are you inviting us to fire you?"

"Not at all. Your question invited a thorough response. I'm sorry if I have given offense."

"Please, then, look at the document in front of you. Will you agree to and sign the stipulations we have proposed?"

Jaylene turned over the paper in front of her and read the three sentences twice. Her inquisitors waited.

"That I cannot do," she said. "To do so would be an affront to free and open thought, an affront to diversity, and would place my signature on a document of blatant discriminatory intolerance."

Gasps of disbelief spread up and down the opposite side of the table. In stunned silence the seven could find no words before Jaylene continued.

"If you make my signature a condition of my continuing on your faculty," she went on, "then I will give you my resignation today. If you desire that I continue, pursuant to my agreement not to bring God and creation into my lectures, then I am willing to continue."

She rose and walked out of the room, leaving a hubbub of shocked outrage behind her.

For the next few days, her colleagues were noticeably cool. News of the testy interview spread immediately through the university. Even skeptics and unbelievers admired her moxie to stand up to the administration.

A special delivery letter arrived at their Roseville home a week later, informing Jaylene of her termination from the faculty of Sacramento State University, effective at the end of the current term.

She had expected it and was almost relieved. She immediately arranged for an appointment to meet with the president of William Jessup University.

Two months after Jaylene's inquisition, in early 2014, she began noticing familiar, though altogether unexpected, signs. She waited another month before telling Timothy. They scheduled an appointment with Dr. Myers, who confirmed that Jaylene was again pregnant.

"I'm scared, Timothy," she said when they were alone. "I can't let myself get excited or hopeful."

He took her in his arms. "We have to remember, God created this life, this child, in you. It is his baby, not ours. I have to believe that he has some purpose for him or her, whether in this life or the next. We are the parents, but he is the Father."

Jaylene did her best to keep a stiff upper lip in the midst of her fears. She and Timothy did not talk about it. They only had to wait, and pray.

Nine weeks came and went. Then twelve . . . then sixteen . . . then twenty. There would be no miscarriage, though a stillborn birth remained possible.

At twenty-five weeks, Larke was especially hopeful. Still Jaylene could not let herself yield. She remained stoic until the very end.

With the first pangs, a laugh of pent-up energy burst from her mouth. They quickly gave way to sobs of joy, followed by shouts to Timothy and a hurried drive to the hospital.

At thirty-nine-and-a-half weeks, on November 2, 2014, Heather Thadine Marshall was born, healthy and energetic, at seven pounds two ounces.

Timothy left Jaylene resting with his new daughter in her arms and hurried out to the waiting room to tell his parents the news.

Larke wept. Stirling's eyes were aglow as he exclaimed,

"God surely has something extraordinary awaiting your little girl!"

> *The weapons of our warfare are not worldly*
> *but have divine power to destroy strongholds. . . .*
> *arguments and every proud obstacle to the knowledge*
> *of God, and take every thought captive to obey Christ.*
>
> **2 CORINTHIANS 10:4–5**

PART 3

WEAPONS OF DIVINE POWER

2014–2032

33

PINECROFT BEST FRIENDS

2014-2016

THE BAPTIST camp outside Colfax in the California foothills fifty miles northwest of Sacramento hosted tens of thousands of teens through the decades, though probably none more prominent as the future would note as having attended in the summer of 2014. At the time, however, fourteen-year-olds Jeff Rhodes and Mark Forster were just two among two hundred looking forward that autumn to their final year of junior high school—Forster from nearby Grass Valley, Rhodes from distant Seattle.

The latter's father saw no reason to send his son to a religious camp. Harrison Rhodes was already laying plans for his son to attend elite summer programs this year and next—one titled Politics for Teens held at the Democrat Party resort on the North Carolina coast, and the next on social activism on the campus of Georgetown University in DC and underwritten by Viktor Domokos. They would be followed the next two years by a week at Colorado's exclusive Gateway Canyons Resort at which President Obama spoke every year at the Future of America Conference, and finally a month-long Leadership Training Institute prior to his senior year. These preparatory introductions for the future he had mapped out for his son would culminate in a congressional internship after his graduation from high school, before returning to enter Georgetown where he would major in political science and theory.

Though the father's ambitions for his son had been in place for years, however, Sandra Rhodes was not anxious to turn her son into a clone of her husband just yet. Still a boy in many ways, she wanted him to enjoy the innocence of youth a while longer. There was also the lingering guilt she felt at not giving him more spiritual grounding. She valued her Baptist upbringing and felt the richer for it. Yet hers had been the curse of a beautiful face and slim figure—difficult roadblocks to character for a girl to overcome. Harrison Rhodes, always panning his surroundings for a captivating face, swept the blond Californian off her feet. Sandra Nelson traded her evangelical roots for a life in the spotlight of Washington politics, became Mrs. Harrison Rhodes at twenty-one, and hadn't been inside a church since.

She supposed she still vaguely believed in an abstract way. But whatever faith she had once had—and that probably wasn't much—made no difference in her life. Not that life in the fast lane didn't have its compensations. But alone with her thoughts, she occasionally wondered what her life might have been had she married the boy she met at summer camp and had a brief crush on—she couldn't even remember his name—who was religious even in high school and whom she later heard became a pastor.

She wondered where he was now. But *Pinecroft*! She would never forget the name of the camp. Though she went only twice, accompanied by several others from their Richmond First Baptist youth group, she loved that place. The memories were still vivid—the mess hall, the swimming pool, always freezing in spite of ninety-five-degree days, the walk along the flume to the American River, the nightly trek up the steep hill to vespers…campfires…singing…the cabin camaraderie.

Subconsciously still regretting she hadn't worked a little harder to pass on *something* of her religious upbringing to her son, she couldn't dislodge Pinecroft from her mind. Without planning it, the day after the memories came flooding over her she found herself asking him an unexpected question.

"What would you think of going to summer camp, Jeff?"

"I don't know, sure, I guess. Where?"

"I went to a camp in California when I was about your age."

"Oh, California—you bet. Would there be surfing?"

"Hardly that!" laughed his mother. "It's over a hundred miles from the ocean."

"Oh, well—it'll probably still be fun."

"It's a *church* camp."

"We don't go to church."

"I know, but I thought you'd like it."

"I don't want religion crammed down my throat."

"It's not like that. They pray before meals and sing Christian camp songs. And there would be a few devotional talks. But mostly it's a summer camp—you know, like Hayley Mills in *Parent Trap*—crafts and activities and games and swimming and hikes, bunking in cabins, making friends. You'll have fun."

Sandra arranged things on her own before springing it on her husband.

"A church camp!" exclaimed Harrison Rhodes. "What in the world for?"

"Because I went there when I was Jeff's age. I loved it."

"But I have him signed up for the Politics for Teens camp in North Carolina."

"Don't you think he's young yet to make a politician of him?"

"It's never too young."

"I would prefer you wait a few years. He won't be young much longer. These are years that will never come again."

Rhodes recognized the edge in his wife's voice. He knew she wasn't pleased about his determination to groom their son to follow in his footsteps. He had to move cautiously. Rather than run the risk of turning her openly against his more sweeping plans, he swallowed whatever else he might have said. In the end he gave in and agreed to the summer camp in the California sun.

Who can tell why friendships begin, and why some are destined to last? Mark Forster and Jeff Rhodes were among eight other fourteen-year-olds in Cabin 8, dubbed "Sugar Pine." The two hit it off from the first night, Rhodes in his sleeping bag on the top bunk above young Forster, bending over the edge and whispering long past lights out at 9:30.

The next day they were inseparable, cavorting together in the pool that afternoon and snickering on one of the back wooden benches during vespers that evening.

In spite of his father's ambitions, as his mother saw more clearly than her husband, Jeff was still a rambunctious boy with little thought of his future or his father's position or that he was special in any way. If anything, he looked up to his new friend. The thought never entered his mind that anyone should look up to him.

Mark rose yet higher in his estimation when Jeff learned that he could ride a horse, even had a horse of his own, and that he lived on a ranch of several hundred acres. Jeff had always dreamed of learning to ride. Before the week was out, the two boys were planning and scheming a visit by Jeff to the Forster ranch. Whatever religious instruction the camp intended to pass on to its attendees was lost on young Jeff Rhodes.

It is in the nature of the universe that boys invent words and languages to give color to their antics and mischief. Hearing that young Rhodes was from Seattle, and knowing nothing of the city other than its landmark market Pike Place, one of their counselors that week dubbed Jeff "Pike." Mark immediately took it up. The origins of "Pine" were a little more circuitous. The week contained too many memories of swimming and hikes, crafts and campfires, boyish shenanigans and boring vespers, to trace exactly how the similarity of his last name to "forest" and the label carved above their cabin door morphed into "Pine" or when Jeff first used it for his new friend.

The nicknames stuck. Within days they were no more Jeff and Mark but *Pike* and *Pine*—the two Ps and bosom pals.

At the end of two weeks, they were each calling the other BF, best friends, with promises to write and remain BFs forever.

Unlike many such fleeting friendships, however, they actually did write. The letters flew between Seattle and Grass Valley. Long before Christmas vacation an invitation was extended to the Seattle Rhodes family to visit the Circle F ranch in the California foothills. The two elder Rhodes declined, though Sandra Rhodes would have liked nothing more than to escape the city's round of political Christmas parties.

But their son's begging entreaties were so persistent that her reluctant husband finally agreed, as long as Jeff would be home for Christmas.

Thus, Harrison and Sandra Rhodes put their ninth-grade son on an airplane at Sea-Tac bound for Sacramento in early December of 2014.

The two weeks the boys spent on the Forster ranch, by the end of which Jeff was relatively comfortable in the saddle, cemented the friendship for good.

"You're looking good, Rhodes," said Mark's father, Robert, as the boys cantered toward the stables following an after-breakfast ride. "All we have to do is teach you to rope a calf while in the saddle and we'll make a cowboy of you yet!"

The boys dismounted and tied their mounts to the top rail of the corral.

"Hey, Mark," Robert Forster went on, "I need to ride over to the Gordons in a couple of hours. I'm going to help David string a quarter mile of barbed wire over that rocky hillside on the way up to Rustlers Butte. The fence there is old. He's afraid his cattle will start getting out. You boys want to join me?"

"Sure, Dad. Should we leave the horses saddled?"

"How long were you out?"

"About an hour."

"They could probably use a rest. Why don't you ride Lobo and Whiskers instead. They haven't been out in a few days. They're probably itching for some exercise."

The two Forsters took their novice horseman the long way around to the Bar JG, over Rustlers Butte where snow lay in the shadows. They stopped and dismounted for a few minutes, showing Jeff the two valleys spread out in both directions, toward the Sierras to the east, now well capped with snow, and descending west into California's 450-mile-long central valley. Remounting, they descended the adjacent flank of the western shoulder of the ridge, reaching the Bar JG a little before noon.

"You're just in time for lunch," said their neighbor and longtime friend David Gordon, now, with his mother, co-owner of the ranch since the death two years before of Isobel's husband Pelham. "My mother's got sandwiches and soup waiting. And I think a blackberry cobbler is about to come out of the oven."

"There's always something delicious in Isobel Gordon's legendary kitchen," laughed Robert.

The three dismounted. Without waiting for an introduction, David approached Mark's friend.

"You must be Jeff Rhodes," he said with a smile and outstretched hand. "Mark has told me so much about you I feel I know you. I'm David Gordon."

"I am pleased to meet you, sir," said Jeff.

"So you two met at Pinecroft, I understand. I spent many happy weeks there when I was young."

"What cabin were you in, David?" asked Mark.

"That was a long time ago!" laughed Gordon. "I probably bunked in three or four of the boy's cabins at one time or another." He paused thoughtfully. "But, let me see . . . the number eight somehow comes to my mind."

"Sugar Pine—that's the cabin we were in!" exclaimed Jeff.

"Well maybe that was it indeed!" laughed David. "Come in and have something to eat. You didn't tell me you were bringing a couple of your ranch hands, Bob," he said, leading the way to the house.

"They're anxious to help," replied Forster. "We've got Jeff comfortable on the back of a horse. Now we need to teach him some of the more mundane aspects of ranching life—like mending fences."

"I hope you brought gloves, though I have plenty."

"We did."

When Jeff Rhodes boarded his flight back to Seattle three days later, he was boasting blisters on both hands, three stitches on his left wrist from a nasty gash, a souvenir of his fence-mending apprenticeship, and a bandage on his arm from the resulting tetanus shot. They were badges of honor to him, though the elder Rhodes was far from pleased with his son's enthusiasm for the ranching life.

34

Young Activist

2015–2017

WHEN THE following summer arrived, the two boys were making plans not only to meet again at Pinecroft but for Jeff to stay on an additional two weeks at the Circle F. Harrison Rhodes finally put his foot down. But gently. He was not prepared to alienate his son by forbidding the trip to California altogether.

"I will agree on one condition," he said to his wife as they discussed the matter privately, and somewhat heatedly.

"And what is that?" asked Sandra testily.

"That he also attend the Domokos conference at Georgetown in August."

"He'll be home from California in plenty of time for that," replied Sandra.

So it was arranged, Jeff returning to Seattle in July of 2015, tan and wearing a cowboy hat, which also accompanied him to Georgetown for the week's conference on social activism.

By the following summer, entering their junior year of high school, both boys had grown six inches and spoke with the timbre of men's voices. It was the last camp they would share together at Pinecroft.

They were growing in more ways than physically, spreading their wings in unseen ways, their characters deepening as the roots of very different upbringings extended invisibly into more regions of dawning personhood. Mark participated in personal sharing around the campfire late at night, while Jeff sat doodling with a stick in the dirt, or else remained at their cabin entertaining himself with the cell phone he had smuggled in against camp rules. While Mark listened attentively to the week's devotional talks, Jeff sat bored wondering what his friend found so interesting.

It was during one such talk by a visiting pastor from the San Francisco Bay Area when Mark Forster heard quoted two sentences that would change his life. He was so stunned by what he heard that he found the speaker afterward and asked him to repeat what he said, writing it down word for word in his notebook. He remained thoughtful and subdued through the rest of the day's activities as he tried to absorb the power of the quote.

"What was that all about?" asked Jeff as Mark came toward him where he was waiting, and the two headed to lunch together.

"I wanted to write down what he said at the end of his talk," replied Mark. "It was the most amazing thing I've ever heard."

"I wasn't paying much attention," said Jeff.

When they parted three days later, neither knew that their Pinecroft days were at an end. The summer's highlight for Mark would always be the quote he heard. It remained indelibly imprinted on his mind for the rest of his life. As thoughts of Pinecroft faded, Jeff's singular memory of the summer came a month later. From the Colorado conference on the Future of Progressivism, he would take with him the feel of the hand of President Obama as he shook hands with the select group of young men and women accepted to attend the exclusive gathering.

The following summer prior to their senior year, Mark Forster spent working ten-hour days on the two neighboring ranches, both for his father and his father's friend David Gordon. As they worked side by side that summer at the Bar JG, talking about the life of Christian discipleship and what David called "centered living," Mark's faith took great strides toward the spiritual manhood David could perceive deepening within him.

Jeff Rhodes, meanwhile, put the same summer to use honing his debating skills at a seminar in public speaking arranged by his father, as well as attending the long-planned Leadership Training Institute in Atlanta.

These differences, however, did nothing to dampen the friendship between the two BFs. For two years they talked privately about attending college together. Those plans went on unchanged in spite of their diverging spiritual and political interests.

Harrison Rhodes hit the roof when he learned what his son was hatching with his clodhopper friend.

"It's out of the question!" he exclaimed. "I don't know what you see in that son of a rancher anyway."

"He's my friend, Dad. I love their ranch. His folks treat me like one of the family."

"Fine. But you don't have to go to college with him, and at some hick state school at that."

"I've already applied, Dad."

"Without talking to me?"

"I knew what you'd think."

"What's wrong with U of W?"

"Nothing. But Mark could never afford it. His dad's struggling to make ends meet with his ranch as it is. If we want to attend the same college, it has to be in California."

"But why Humboldt, for God's sake. It's for loggers and bumpkins!"

"Are you an elitist, Dad?" asked Jeff with a smile.

"I'm just thinking of your future."

"It's where I want to go, Dad. It's more diverse than you might think. It's more liberal than Berkeley. I'd think you'd love it."

"You *will* take the congressional internship I've set up for you?"

"Nothing's changed about that."

"And law school?"

"Of course. Just because I want to do my undergraduate work with Mark doesn't change that."

"So you're not still thinking of becoming a cowboy when you grow up?"

"No, Dad," laughed Jeff. "I love the Forsters. That doesn't mean I want to be like them."

"All right, then, I'll think about the Humboldt thing."

35

Neighbor and Mentor

2016

THE CIRCLE F and Bar JG shared a common boundary of several miles, including the ridge of Rustlers Butte. From the peak, their mutual boundary sloped toward the west down into the abundant broad pastureland of a verdant valley, surrounded by less imposing rises and ridges of the northern California foothills, much of which was shared by the two contiguous ranches.

Robert Forster's great-great-grandfather MacGregor Forster and Pelham Gordon's great-grandfather Jackson were among California's first generation of pioneer ranchers in the 1860s. They discovered there was more wealth to be earned in the California hills than from gold. What the two had founded, their sons built into a ranching empire northeast of Sacramento, whose beef fed much of the new state's exploding population. For generations the Forster and Gordon parents dreamed of a union of their two houses. Sons, however, happened to be plentiful in the two houses, a happy thing for ranchers, but daughters few, and no sparks between the Forster and Gordon youth were forthcoming.

The two ranches were the largest in the region, their ranch houses separated by five miles. Robert Forster and David Gordon grew up first playing, then romping about, being inseparable high school friends and varsity stars, riding together throughout the foothills all about Grass Valley until they knew every inch of their respective ranches, which, as they grew into adulthood, they took over from their fathers. The example of fathers and grandfathers of helping one another, trading and sharing equipment and workers when the need arose, continued, though both had sold land and scaled back operations somewhat since the zenith of the cattle business in the 1950s. Robert was the quieter of the two, an honorable but not a deeply spiritual man.

David Gordon, the most recent scion of his proud name, was an only child and unmarried. The future of the Bar JG was therefore uncertain. David's friend Robert Forster and wife, Laura, were blessed with two daughters, with son Mark between them. Their three children grew up considering the Gordon ranch a second home. There David's mother Isobel, kitchen virtuoso, made sure the house always smelled of pies or chocolate chip cookies.

Though both families emerged from America's staunchly religious rootstalk, the natural ebbs and flow of generational spirituality resulted in a sad frustration on David Gordon's part in being unable to communicate meaningfully with his best friend about his deepening walk of faith. Good man and diligent churchman that he was, Robert Forster had not yet awakened to the daily imperative of *living* spirituality. Beliefs were *ideas* to him, containing little intersection with Monday through Saturday life.

He was not antagonistic to David's attempt to arouse his slumbering spiritual self, but he simply wasn't interested. He could sit and listen distractedly to a sermon and sing the hymns he had known since boyhood and put his weekly tithe in the offering plate as well as the next man. But when he went home and put on his work clothes, he did not think about any of it again until the following Sunday when it came time for the ritual to repeat itself.

On Robert's birthday several years before, David had given him a copy of Stirling Marshall's book that had done more for him than any other in opening new windows of understanding in his walk with God. He inscribed it:

To Robert Forster,

The best friend a man could have. You have enriched my life in more ways than I can possibly tell you. From the deepest depths of my heart, I want to introduce you to a man and his writings that have awakened me to much within myself, in the world, and in my Christian life. I pray you may find meat for your soul in these pages, as I have.

Your friend and brother in Christ,
David Gordon

"I sincerely hope you will give it a try, Bob," said David. "I realize it's no Louis L'Amour, but I happen to think it may be more important. If for no other reason, I hope you'll read it as a token of our long friendship, from my heart to yours."

"Thank you, David," replied Robert. "I appreciate that. I'll certainly have a look."

Embarrassed that he would resort to such a thing behind his friend's back, in the Forster home several months later when Robert and his wife Laura were in the kitchen, David's curiosity finally got the better of him. He quietly walked across the large ranch-style living room and removed the slender volume from the bookshelf where he had seen it on several previous occasions. He opened it to his inscription, and quickly flipped through the stiff pages. The book was still brand-new. It had never even been opened.

Saddened, he replaced it. The subject of his heartfelt birthday gift never came up again between the two friends.

Unbeknownst to David, however, the invisible character-seeds of his faith were not falling on fallow ground. From before Mark could remember, through the narrow opening of his bedroom door, he often heard his parents and David talking late into the night, often too late for David to return to his own ranch on horseback. At such times, he spent the night in one of several guestrooms known as "David's Room." Occasionally, too, the snippets of those conversations drifting into his ears as he lay with his door ajar were about God and church. It was David's voice he mostly heard, with now and then an indistinct question or comment from his mother.

Having no idea what was being planted in young Mark's consciousness, when the stresses of his late-teen years threw the younger Forster into a season of depression, self-doubt, and spiritual questioning, early one evening in September of 2016, David heard a knock on his kitchen door.

He went to open it. There stood sixteen-year-old Mark Forster, his horse tied to the rail behind him.

"Mark!" exclaimed David. "What a pleasant surprise. Have you come alone?" he added, glancing behind him as if expecting his friend Robert to appear.

"It's just me," replied Mark. "I wondered if I could talk to you."

"Absolutely—of course. Come in!"

A minute or two later the two were seated around the oval-braided rug in David's living room. Mark was obviously nervous. David waited patiently.

"I know you talk to my parents about God and living as a Christian," Mark began at length, speaking slowly and fumbling for words at first. "I don't know, maybe I should talk to them, but it's hard with my parents, you know. I mean, I love them and everything, but I'm not sure they'd understand what I'm going through."

"You think I will?" said David.

"I guess maybe something like that."

"I can promise I will try."

Again it was silent. Mark stared down at the floor.

"I'm having a hard time with some things," he began again. "I mean, I want to live like a Christian and be a witness at school. And this last summer's camp at Pinecroft helped me see that. There was a speaker who talked about how God is chiseling our characters for eternity, and how sometimes the chisel hammers things away we want but God knows have to be chipped off. But it hurts to have a chisel cutting and whacking away. When I heard him it all sounded so good and it made me happy. But then when the chipping begins, I don't like it and I want it to stop."

He stopped and turned away, suddenly fighting back the tears.

"I'm sorry. I'm just really depressed. Sometimes I can hardly face going to school. I know I'm being a terrible witness—Christians are supposed to be happy and I'm just not. Sometimes I wonder if I'm a Christian at all."

"Why? Because you're not happy all the time?"

"I guess."

"I wasn't happy when my father died two years ago," said David. "Do you think that meant I wasn't a Christian?"

"No, I guess not," said Mark sheepishly. "But it's different for you."

"Why?"

"I don't know—you're a man. You've been a Christian a long time."

"So you think I could get low and unhappy and still be a Christian. But when you get low and unhappy, it means you *aren't* a Christian?"

"Doesn't make much sense, I guess. That's how I feel."

"Why are you unhappy?"

Mark sighed. "It's embarrassing to say. But for years I've been looking forward to high school so I could play football. I've seen those pictures of you and Dad in your football uniforms—even that one of you both that was in the paper after you beat Folsom that's hanging in a frame in our living room. All I've ever wanted was to be a football player too."

David chuckled at the memory but said nothing.

"I know I'm small for my age," Mark went on, "but I'm decently fast and I thought maybe I could make the team as a receiver. But last year, going into my sophomore year I got cut. Since then I've put on several inches and this summer I've been lifting weights every day and ran wind sprints all summer. I even ran up the trail to Rustlers Butte once, though I had to stop several times. And my dad threw me passes and I worked on my cuts and catching. I was sure I would make the team."

"I've seen how hard you've been working."

Mark let out a long sigh. "But when the roster was posted last week, I'd been cut again. I've never been so depressed in my life. All that work, everything I've dreamed of, all for nothing. That night when I lay in bed, I couldn't help it, I cried. I was so dejected and felt so foolish for thinking I had a chance."

The silence that followed this time lasted more than a minute.

"Do you mind if I tell you a story," began David.

"Sure."

"When I was in junior high, I wanted to be a star. But I was small too. I tried out for football and baseball and kept getting cut. Then I discovered a secret. There was one sport where no one got cut."

"What's that?"

"Track. So I went out for track. I wasn't very good, but I got to compete in races and I tried the pole vault too. I got second a few times and I was on the team and wore a uniform."

"But then when you got into high school you *did* play football."

"That's true," smiled David. "I had a huge growth spurt before my sophomore year. Then I got lucky to have your dad come along the next year. But what I was saying is you could learn from what I discovered in junior high."

"You're suggesting I go out for track?"

"Just an idea. You wouldn't get cut."

"Oh, hey . . . what about cross-country! The season's just starting up."

"A great idea. You said yourself, you're already in pretty good shape from the running you've been doing."

"I never thought of cross-country."

"Let me tell you what you might think about doing. You were talking about God chipping away and chiseling you for eternity. So take what has happened as an opportunity to let him do just that."

"That's exactly what the man at the camp said!"

"If that is true, then you can pray to God and thank him for what has happened because he is fashioning you to be his son. Then you can pray for him to show you what he wants you to do if it isn't to play football. Ask him to reveal his will to you?"

"How will I know?"

"It's very subtle and quiet. God speaks in whispers. You have to be quiet yourself, get calm inside. One of my favorite authors calls it centering down. Then try to feel the gentle nudges. It's a quiet sense of being drawn in one direction or another. You will begin to feel you *ought* to do this or that. Continue to pray. Then wait for the quiet Voice.

Then when you sense it, do what God tells you. That's the most important part—obeying what God tells you to do."

"Okay, I'll try. Would you, I mean, if you don't mind—would you pray for me?"

"It would be my privilege. I will pray for you right now."

David rose, walked over, and sat beside Mark, and laid a hand on his shoulder.

"Our dear Father," he prayed, "I thank you for my friend and brother Mark, who is your child and whose heart is pointed toward you. He desires to be your obedient son. I ask you now to answer his heart's prayer. Draw him closer to you and reveal your will to him. Quiet his spirit during the days to come, even during the tumult of school with all its pressures. Teach him the priceless lesson of being able to center down in the midst of life. Then speak to him, Holy Spirit, by the gentle nudges of your Voice. Show him the direction you want him to go. Show him what you want him to do. And give him a thankful heart for the chipping of your chisel as you fashion him into your son. Amen."

Mark was hot and breathing heavily at the profound prayer. His eyes were wet. No one had ever prayed such a prayer for him.

David quietly rose and returned to his chair. Neither spoke for several minutes.

"Thank you," said Mark at length.

David smiled and nodded.

"How is your Seattle friend Jeff?" he asked.

"Good," replied Mark. "His dad's got big plans for him. But we're hoping to go to college together and room together."

"That sounds like it will be fun. What does Mr. Rhodes do that he's got plans for Jeff?"

"He's in politics, I think—a city councilman or maybe district attorney. I'm not sure exactly. Jeff doesn't talk about it much."

"Interesting."

Dusk was settling over the foothills as Mark mounted his horse and cantered back in the direction of the Circle F.

36

SURPRISE ANSWER TO PRAYER

WHEN MARK Forster returned to the Bar JG one Saturday afternoon three weeks later, David was not surprised to see him. Their previous time together having broken the ice, the two quickly settled into comfortable dialogue.

"Guess what?" said Mark. "I prayed just like you said. The next morning I had nearly forgotten about football. I woke up remembering how much I enjoyed running up to Rustlers Butte—sweating and breathing hard and pushing myself till my lungs were ready to burst. It was the challenge of it. But I didn't want to rush into anything so I didn't do anything for a few days. If God was nudging me, like you called it, I wanted to be sure. So I kept praying he would keep nudging me in that direction if it really was his Voice speaking to me, or that he would dampen my enthusiasm if it wasn't him."

"An extremely wise prayer, Mark! You astound me. Many who have been Christians for years never reach that level of maturity in prayer. You have already taken great strides in your understanding. I often add to my prayers when I am considering some course of action, '*Lord, stop me if I am not hearing you correctly. Put roadblocks in my path. Quell my enthusiasm to move in this direction I am considering. Give me a strong check in my spirit that I am not to proceed.*' This is exactly what you were doing. I commend your wisdom."

"Thank you. I hadn't really thought about it like that. But I guess you're right. I was waiting to make sure."

"So what happened?" asked David.

"I kept praying that God would lead me, and I began to get excited about cross-country. So last Saturday, a week ago, I put on my trunks and running shoes and I went out and ran up Rustlers Butte again. I was excited and I ran hard. I nearly killed myself. I had to stop several times."

By now David was laughing as he listened.

"When I reached the top, man I was exhausted. But it felt great! I was excited to have done it. I knew then that God was showing me a new direction, thanks to you. You taught me to pray in a new way. It's so practical. *'God, show me what you want me to do.'* Then you wait for the nudging."

"I couldn't have said it better myself!"

"The next day I went to the gym before first period, found the cross-country coach, told him I'd been cut from football and I knew practice had already started, but if it wasn't too late I'd like to try out for the team. He didn't hesitate. He told me to be back at 3:00 that afternoon for practice. Just like that . . . I was on the cross-country team. Two weeks ago I hardly knew what cross-country was. Now I'm on the team!"

"Good for you, Mark."

"I ran my first race after school yesterday, against two other schools. And guess what—I got 9th. I was 4th on our team."

"That's terrific! Congratulations."

"Granted, there were only twenty-three in the race. But at least I wasn't last. And I guess I'm not going to get cut!" he added laughing. "It was fun too. I think I like it better than football—especially better than sitting on the bench. No one sits on the bench in cross-country. Everybody participates. What a great team sport. And at the end I outsprinted three guys I'd been following for the last mile. Maybe that run up to the Butte paid off. I think I can improve too. Everybody else has been training longer than me. I did some wind sprints last summer. But most of the guys on the team have been running four to six or eight miles every day. I've got a lot of catching up to do."

"I'm proud of you, Mark. Not only because you did well—but because you took a heartbreaking situation, gave it over to the Lord, said 'chisel me according to your purpose, and lead me in a new direction.'"

"I'm not sure I was thinking about it quite like that!"

"Maybe not consciously. But that is what you did. You acted on the principle of the truth you heard last summer at Pinecroft."

"I hope you're right. But I need to get home. Dad and I are repairing that bit of the barn roof that blew off last week. And winter's coming, you know."

"Do you need some help? I'd be glad to come over."

"Dad told me you would ask!" laughed Mark. "But he said he and I could get it done in two or three hours."

"All right—but you tell him to give me a call if he needs an extra hand."

Mark's next visit to his neighbor came three weeks later, on a Friday after school. The moment David saw him he saw a deeper purpose in his eyes. His face was leaner too. The weeks of training showed. His expression was serious.

It was the first week of October and the weather in the foothills was changing. Winter was on the way. They sat down on a bench in front of the house. It remained quiet for a minute.

"I'd like you to pray for me," said Mark at length.

"I do every day," replied David.

"I mean for something specific. We've got a big cross-country meet tomorrow down in Roseville—six schools. I'm really nervous."

"More than usual?"

"Yeah, I'm not sure why. I've been doing pretty good in practice. In last Friday's race—though it was just us against Colfax—I was third. It's funny, the better I do the more nervous I am. And tomorrow we're going to be running against some big schools. I'd just like for you to pray I'll be happy however it turns out, and that I'll do my best."

David turned toward him, his face beaming. Mark waited expectantly.

"I'm going to pray for you to win!" said David.

Mark stared back dumbfounded. It was the craziest thing he ever heard. He never won anything in his life.

All the way as he rode home, he couldn't imagine why David had said what he did.

He returned to the Bar JG the following day sometime after five o'clock after the team returned from Roseville. He drove straight to the Gordon ranch before going home.

Mark heard David in the barn and walked inside. David saw his shadow in the sunlight of the open door. He turned and walked toward him, his face alive.

"How did the race go?" he asked eagerly.

A sheepish smile came over Mark's face. He looked down at the dirt floor of the barn momentarily, then back at David.

"Actually," he said, "I can't quite believe it, but—well, I won."

David's eyes filled with tears.

"We came around the final bend with about two hundred yards to go and onto the flat grass of Roseville High's athletic field. There were six or seven of us together, though I was last of the lead pack. But I felt good and I just imagined myself cresting Rustlers Butte, so I just took off. I passed them all. I couldn't believe it, all the top runners from the other schools, and I just kept going all the way to the finish line. I guess I outkicked them."

David was beaming. He could not reply.

The photo in the *Sacramento Bee* the following day, with the caption, "Grass Valley's Forster Outkicks Competition," was framed and hanging in the Forster living room a week later next to the one of Mark's father and David from twenty-five years earlier.

And thus began Mark Forster's spiritual journey under the gentle tutelage of his father's best friend, a journey over the next two years eventually leading to David's sharing with young Mark some of the same writings that had been influential in his own life. During the final months of his senior year, after Mark had read two of his books, David arranged for Stirling and Larke Marshall to visit him at the ranch so that Mark could meet the author of the books he had given him.

Mark graduated from high school in June of 2018, and prepared to leave home to begin his freshman year on the north coast of the state.

Another pivotal exchange took place during Mark's final visit to David Gordon before his departure.

"I want to share a passage with you," said David. "It is from 1 Timothy and I believe the Lord revealed to me that it is meant for you. It is Paul speaking to his young protégé Timothy. I think Timothy may have been suffering from a feeling of being too young and immature to be of much significance in God's kingdom. As you and I have spent many hours together in the last two years, you occasionally have that same tendency. But I tell you, Mark, God is doing great things in you. He has a purpose for you to accomplish in his plan. I don't know what it is. But if you continue to pray for his guidance, he will reveal it. He is taking you toward something greater than you can see—not in the world, but in his plan and purpose. Keep your eyes on him, always praying for his quiet Voice to lead you. You are a man of God, my young friend. I am proud to know you."

David paused, then opened his Bible to 1 Timothy 4.

"I'm going to read you some portions of what Paul wrote to Timothy," he said. "And, Mark, these are God's words to *you*. You are God's man. Never doubt it."

He found the passage and began to read.

> "*Command and teach these things. Let no one despise your youth, but set the believers an example in speech and conduct, in love, in faith, in purity. Till I come, attend to the public reading of scripture, to preaching, to teaching. Do not neglect the gift you have, which was given you by prophetic utterance . . . Practice these duties, devote yourself to them, so that all may see your progress. Take heed to yourself and to your teaching; hold to that . . .*"

Then he continued from 1 Timothy 6:

> "*But as for you, man of God, shun all this; aim at righteousness, godliness, faith, love, steadfastness, gentleness.*"

Fight the good fight of the faith; take hold of the eternal life to which you were called . . .'"

He gazed earnestly into Mark's eyes. "Stand tall in God, Mark," he said. "Believe in his good work in you. As you launch into your future life—a future neither of us can see at this moment—I am going to continue to pray that you will be strengthened and enabled to step into your calling. I will repeat Paul's charge as *my* charge to you. Whenever in the future a thought of your old friend David passes through your mind, remember me saying, 'As for *you*, Mark Forster, man of God—pursue righteousness, godliness, faith, and love. Fight the good fight of the faith. Take hold of the life to which God is calling you.'"

Packed in Mark's suitcase a week later as his mother and father drove him the 300 miles north to the small college town of Arcata, were three books given him by the man who had become a true spiritual mentor—Henry Drummond's *The Greatest Thing in the World*, the fifteenth-century classic by Thomas à Kempis, *The Imitation of Christ*, and the more recent small volume, *Unspoken Commandments*, signed by the author.

37

Faith in a Hothouse of Secularism

2018

It WAS doubtless only a matter of time before a graduate of Humboldt State University would rise in the ranks of the world's progressivism to the highest echelons of power. The name of California's northernmost state institution was not so well known as Cal Berkeley. Yet its liberalism exceeded even that of its more esteemed cousin 275 miles to the south.

The small town of Arcata adapted its entire character to the college and its quirky ways. Tucked comfortably between the Pacific and the fading remnants of vast redwood forests of unfathomable depth and antiquity, the town had served as hub to a California gold rush all its own. If the era of big lumber was not quite so lucrative, it had certainly been of longer duration than the gold rush of the American River basin east of Sacramento which spawned it. Redwood mills dominated the landscape and economy for a century.

It would be simplistic to say that the Beatles, drugs, and Viet Nam changed all that. No single factor doomed the lumber industry and remade the character of Arcata from a hard-working middle class lumber town into a sanctuary for long-hairs, protesters, street preachers, and misfits. But the transformation, when it came, was dramatic.

Northern California's love affair with liberalism began in the 1960s when the overflow from San Francisco's progeny of flower children migrated north to Humboldt and Mendocino counties. There they slowly transformed the isolated mountainous coastal region into a marijuana mecca fueled by anti-war protests, sit-ins, strikes, and stump speeches. The ensuing culture of drugs, communes, and political radicalism swept through Arcata like a brush fire.

The sounds of the Beatles, Janice Joplin, and the Mamas & the Papas blared from apartments and dormitories and the radios of brightly decorated Volkswagen buses. Revolution was in the wind, and its music filled the air. In less than a generation, Humboldt State, the one-time sleepy teacher's college of a thousand students was known as California's "hippie school."

How could big lumber possibly survive the onslaught? The "causes" that floated north on the wings of *Rubber Soul, Sgt. Pepper,* and *The Magical Mystery Tour* were as diverse, offbeat, and downright weird as their messengers. Bumper stickers plastered to vans and makeshift campers told the story: *Save the Whale, One Planet One People, Free Tibet, One World Peace, McCarthy for President, Food for People Not Profit,* and the ever popular, *War Is Not Healthy for Children and Other Living Things.*

And of course, *Save the Spotted Owl* and *Don't Destroy Our Forests.*

Environmentalism sprouted like a fabled beanstalk and flourished in Arcata's organic soil of liberalism. It could not have been more perfectly suited to the milieu of tie-dye, body-piercings, drugs, sex, and the pungent aroma of patchouli oil. Forestry and Natural Resources, Humboldt's former signature fields of study, were eclipsed by a host of new "Environmentalist" majors. Tree huggers took on the loggers and defeated them. One mill after another was forced into foreclosure or liquidation.

Within two decades, the lumber mills of the north coast were mostly torn down or converted to other uses. Simpson Timber's enormous facility on the flatland known as the Arcata bottoms became an international bulb farm. With fitting irony, big lumber gave way to the reproduction of lilies as Arcata's predominant industry. The new bumper sticker might well have read *Flowers for Profit Not Trees.* Haight-Ashbury lived on.

As Y2K ushered in a new era, long after San Francisco's hippie days were a distant memory, the streets of Arcata remained a repository for balding, pony-tailed, pot-smoking, anti-establishment Peter Pans determined to retain the outer symbols of the sixties long after its idealism had gone blowing in the wind. What few mills still stood were by then silent and empty relics of bygone times, rusting and dilapidated monuments to California's storied past along with the ghost towns, museums, and tourist landmarks of the Sierra foothills that had once teemed with miners dreaming of fortunes pulled from the mother lode.

Leaving the legendary sixties a half century behind, Arcata's liberalism extended its reach in the new millennium and flew in directions often too bizarre to be imagined. That its city council had two dozen resolutions on the books declaring its intent to secede from the nation told the story of the town's political leanings well enough.

Two freshmen entered this greenhouse of eccentric far Left ideas in 2018. Both were born within a few months of one another in the first year of the new millennium—true "millennials" in every sense of the word. Whether the symbolism of that fact carried the prophetic significance certain spiritualists might make of it would be for history to determine.

Lifelong Californians that they were, neither Robert nor Laura Forster had ever driven all the way up the coast on Highway 101 and to the small former lumber town of Arcata until visiting the state's northernmost college the previous spring. Now here they were a second time to say goodbye and launch their son into his future.

All the preliminaries having been arranged, they drove straight to the dormitory which would be Mark's home for the following year. He was soon signed in. With new key in hand, he and his parents took the elevator with his suitcases and several boxes up to the third floor. He didn't need the key. The door to the room stood ajar. Mark walked in. His friend was sprawled out on one of the two beds across the room.

"Hey, Pike—here we are!" shouted Mark, setting down the suitcase in his hand.

"Pine—you rascal, what took you so long?" exclaimed Jeff, leaping to his feet. "I've been here two days. Hello, Mr. Forster—Mrs. Forster," he said, turning to Mark's parents and shaking their hands.

"How are you, Jeff?" said Mark's father. "All set for your college adventure?"

"As long as this son of yours keeps me in line!"

"No wild frat parties?"

"I'll keep Pine on the straight and narrow."

"I don't think it's me he's worried about," laughed Mark.

"Are your folks here, Jeff?" asked Mrs. Forster.

"No, they put me on a plane. The proverbial puddle jumper. It took us an hour to land, waiting for a break in the fog."

"So you came alone?"

"Yeah. My dad's not too happy about my choice of colleges. He had no interest in seeing Humboldt."

"That's too bad. It seems like a nice setting—tall redwoods everywhere."

"My dad's a big city guy. He only agreed to this if I would promise to work for his campaign next summer, and in his office every summer after that if he wins. I think my mom wanted to come, but she didn't feel she should."

"His *campaign*?" said Mr. Forster.

"He's running for mayor of Seattle next year."

"Oh my!" exclaimed Mark's mother. "I knew he was in politics. I didn't realize he was so high up."

"He's got ambition, I'll say that for him," laughed Jeff. "He's deter-mined to make a politician of me too!"

"I'm sure you'll do him proud."

The Forsters returned to Grass Valley the next day. Left alone with four days before the first week of classes, the two friends explored every inch of the campus and the small college town, hiked in the redwood forest behind the school, and delighted in resuming their friendship on their own.

For four years the two were as close as two friends could be whose families lived 800 miles apart. Messages, long and short, by phone and computer, even with the rare occasional actual "letter," were frequent between Sacramento and Seattle—more accurately between the foothills ranch of Mark's parents and the extravagant estate on Bainbridge Island in the middle of Puget Sound where Jeff grew up. Now at last their plans for college had come to fruition.

Two days after Mark's arrival, they paused on their way back to the dorms in front of the bulletin board outside the Campus Activity Center.

"This looks interesting," said Mark, scanning a poster announcing what was called a Dagwood Supper the following evening. "New and returning students, come meet fellow Christians," he read aloud. "Get the year off on the right foot. Sandwiches, chips, and soft drinks provided—everyone welcome. Sponsored by Campus Christian Fellowship."

He jotted down the time and address.

"Why would you want to go to that?" asked Jeff. "Soft drinks—come on, man. We're in college now. I've been invited to a party at the τκε house. I'm sure they will be serving something more substantial than coke!"

"Not for me, thanks. I'm going to this Dagwood thing. A frat house beer bash is the last thing I'd be caught dead at."

"Aw, your folks aren't watching—time to loosen up."

Mark turned and looked at his friend as if the words were spoken by a stranger.

"God is watching, Jeff," he said, still with almost a puzzled expression. "More than that, *I'm* watching."

Now it was Jeff's turn to stare at his friend in confusion. "I have no idea what you mean," he said. "Watching *what*?"

"Watching myself. Being careful what influences I surround myself with. I would rather mix with Christians than beer-drinking partiers."

As it turned out, rather than show up alone at the "Teke" house, Jeff accompanied Mark to the CCF Dagwood Supper. The introductory pitch by one of the leaders of the group for the weekly round of Monday, Friday, and Saturday activities could hardly have been of less interest to him. But the sandwich buffet was superb, and the evening repaid itself many times over by the vision across the room of possibly the most gorgeous face he had ever seen. It took Jeff a while to find an opportunity when she was not talking to someone else. But when the moment came, he seized it quickly.

"Hi," he said, flashing a smile that experience told him he could usually rely on with the fairer sex, "I'm Jeff Rhodes."

"I'm Linda Hutchins," the vision replied, smiling in return.

"New this year?"

"I am—how could you tell?"

"I couldn't. Just making conversation," he said modestly giving his words just the right tone of self-effacement. "Isn't that what you do at these things?"

"I suppose you're right," she said, laughing lightly.

"I'm a freshman too—from Seattle."

"Oh, wow—so am I. Well, sort of."

"Why sort of?"

"Our folks are divorced. Our mom lives here—in Eureka. My brothers and I used to split our time between here and Seattle. My oldest brother loves the city—he's an attorney in Seattle. But I like the small-town atmosphere, and I've got a free place to stay, so here I am. What about you—what's your excuse? Why Humboldt?"

"My best friend's a Californian and was coming here—that's him over there," said Jeff, cocking his head toward Mark who was talking to someone a short distance away. "We wanted to go to college together. So as you say, here I am."

"I guess it's a kind of the same with me. My other brother is here too. He's a year ahead of me. Besides our mother being here, I followed him like you did your friend."

"What a coincidence, right? You're one of the first people I've met, and a fellow Washingtonian—"

"Hey, Sis," said a voice at their side, "and you thought you wouldn't find anyone to talk to."

Jeff turned.

"How's it going?" said the newcomer jovially, extending his hand. "I'm Ward Hutchins."

Jeff cast a glance toward Linda.

"My brother," she said, "a seasoned sophomore, life of the party, and vice-president of CCF."

"Right," nodded Jeff. "I heard you outlining the activities a bit ago."

"I hope you'll be able to join us. Our first Saturday morning Bible study is tomorrow—1 Corinthians 13. Greatest chapter in the New Testament. Bring your Bible. Meet in front of the CAC at eight."

"Ugh—pretty early!"

"Food for the body and the soul—never too early for that! There'll be rides down to my place. I live in an apartment near the business district. My roommates and I will have all the hotcakes and bacon you can eat."

"I'll check my social calendar!" laughed Jeff.

"A comedian too!" said Hutchins.

"Ward, this is Jeff Rhodes. He's from Seattle."

"Really—small world. Not any relation to the city councilman?"

"Actually, he's my father," replied Jeff.

"Whoa, the world just got smaller! I hope you don't share his politics."

"Not now, Ward," said Linda. "No politics."

"You're right, Sis. Sorry—question withdrawn."

"Don't worry about it," laughed Jeff. "But let me introduce you to my friend.—Hey, Mark, come over here a minute."

Mark had been watching them out of the corner of his eye. He sauntered over.

"This is Linda and her brother Ward," said Jeff. "Hutchins, was it?"

Ward nodded.

"He's vice president of the group. This is my friend and roommate, Mark Forster."

"Glad to meet you, Mark," said Ward, shaking his hand enthusiastically. "I was just telling Jeff about tomorrow morning's Bible study at my apartment downtown. We meet for breakfast and Bible study every Saturday."

And thus began a foursome that would remain with them all their lives, one that would take many unexpected twists and detours through the years.

✫ ✫ ✫

Mark walked alone from the dorm at five minutes before eight on the following morning, Bible in hand, to join a cluster of eight or ten others across the street from the library. By the end of the morning, he had made several new friends and realized that in the group called CCF he had found a home. Though he made only one or two brief comments during the discussion following breakfast, Ward Hutchins recognized in Mark Forster a level of insight he was eager to probe more deeply. When the study broke up, he approached his new acquaintance.

"I'm going to walk up to campus instead of driving," said Ward. "Want to join me?"

"Sure," replied Mark. "It's a nice day. You can tell me about the town."

Ward's sister Linda accompanied them. They set out on the mile and a half to the university, Mark walking between brother and sister. After some light conversation, the subject of sports came up.

"You ever do any running?" Ward asked. "I'm on the cross-country team. I'm not very good, usually sixth man on the team. But I love getting out there with the guys every afternoon."

"I do run, actually," said Mark. "I signed up for cross-country too. I ran in high school."

"That's terrific. That means we'll see each other every day."

"I'll look forward to it," rejoined Mark.

Mark found Ward Hutchins almost larger than life—friendly, outgoing and personable, a dedicated and outspoken Christian, an obvious natural leader who, even as a sophomore, seemed more than anyone he had yet encountered to be the driving energy of the CCF group. His sister Linda, though a knock-out by any standard, which ordinarily would produce a level of self-assured confidence among people her own age, was soft-spoken and rarely contributed in group discussions. She seemed vulnerable, a flower not yet fully open, a personality in the process of formation, still trying to discover who she was. In the group, she was comfortable deferring to her brother, and being known as Ward's sister. Unusual in one so attractive, there was no hint of flirtation about her. It was as if she didn't realize how striking she was.

While Jeff saw neither of the Hutchins with quite the same frequency and was never to be seen at the Monday evening prayer meeting, when he learned that Linda never missed a Saturday morning Bible study, which were led by various members of the group, he forced himself out of bed to accompany Mark on most weekends.

If doing the Christian thing, as he called it to himself, was what it took, he could do that. He had picked up enough of the lingo from Mark to be comfortable in that world. From his father he had picked up the knack of fitting into any world. He thus managed to keep himself in Linda's orbit. Hampered at first by not having a car, and with her living eight miles away, he had to satisfy himself with CCF functions and the "accidental" campus encounters, which, as soon as he was in possession of her schedule, he shrewdly made sure occurred with almost daily frequency.

By the time they began formally dating, he was not hesitant about using Linda's car. Within a few months he had a car of his own. By then it was obvious that the tentative feminine flower had begun to blossom under the blandishments of Jeff Rhodes's attentions.

38

Paths in a Yellow Wood

THOUGH JEFF shared neither Mark's nor Ward's spiritual inclinations, the three were nevertheless often together, Mark's friendship
with both being the glue holding the threesome together. Jeff had his
own motives for wanting to appear closer to Ward Hutchins than
would have otherwise been the case, and more involved in the inner
circle of CCF than for reasons of shared spiritual inclinations.

On the way back from a Saturday breakfast Bible study several
months into the year, again held at Ward's downtown apartment, the
four walked back to campus together, Jeff and Linda hand in hand,
Mark and Jeff laughing and telling their two new friends about their
first meeting and their years at Pinecroft.

"We were a couple of goofballs, no doubt about it!" laughed Mark.

"Speak for yourself, Pine!" said Jeff.

"*Pine*, what's that?" asked Linda.

"That's Mark. We had nicknames for each other."

"What's yours?"

"He's *Pike*," answered Mark.

"I get it—Pike Place, right?" said Ward.

"You got it. I was branded with the Seattle imprint from our first
days at camp."

"It sounds like it was fun," said Linda.

"I loved Pinecroft," said Mark. "Though I was raised nearby, it was
like entering another world."

"That's exactly how I felt," added Jeff. "The smell of the pine forest and hundred-degree days—I'd never experienced anything like it. Even now, when I get a whiff of pine needles on a hot day—which isn't often living on the coast, either in Seattle or Arcata—a wave of nostalgia sweeps over me."

"There was a spiritual component too," said Mark, his tone growing more thoughtful. "I was just a kid in so many ways, but the atmosphere of those camps somehow deepened my awareness of God. It was a wholesome environment. We were surrounded by good people, people of character and . . ."

He paused and smiled.

"There were some profound things that stuck with me," he went on. "One day in particular I will never forget. A visiting minister came to the camp for the day and gave a devotional talk late in the morning just before lunch. You remember, Jeff?"

"Can't say I do."

"It was a singular moment for me," continued Mark. "In looking back, I realize some of the spiritual seeds my folks and others planted through the years were sending down roots in my life. The man's name was Rev. Boyce van Osdel. He ended his talk with an anonymous quote from *Streams in the Desert*. I was young but listened stunned by what he said. When his talk was over I went forward, waited a minute until he was through talking with a few others, stepped up, and asked if he would repeat what he had said. He spoke slowly so I could write it down in my notebook as he repeated it. You remember, Jeff—you were standing waiting for me."

"Yeah, now that you mention it."

"The quote has never left me. Just writing it down lodged it so deep into my brain that I never forgot the words. It's not too much to say it changed my life."

"I want to hear it!" said Ward.

"All right," replied Mark. "It goes: '*The present circumstance which presses so hard against you, if surrendered to Jesus, is the best shaped tool in the Master's hand to chisel you for eternity. Trust him then, do not push away the instrument, lest you spoil the work.*'"

It fell silent as they walked. Ward slowly shook his head, seemingly as moved by the words as Mark had been.

"It is almost too much to take in," he said softly. "I mean—if you could really get hold of that truth, take its reality inside, all the time—it would change everything! All life, every situation, would take on new meaning. Thank you for sharing that, Mark. I want you to write it down for me too."

Mark nodded.

"Well, it's all Greek to me!" laughed Jeff. "Can't say as I remember the fellow, though Mark was always more interested in that stuff than me. Hey, Linda and I are going to Clam Beach this afternoon—you guys want to join us?"

Ward drew in a sigh at the abrupt breaking of the mood.

"We have to be at the gym at one o'clock," he said. "We have a cross-country meet at two. We hoped you two would be there to cheer us on."

"No thanks, pal," laughed Jeff. "Cross-country's hardly a spectator sport. You race off into the woods and are out of sight in thirty seconds. Then half an hour later you come sprinting back into view. Then it's over. We see you for a minute tops. It's boring."

"What about you, Sis? You never missed one of my races in high school."

Linda shrugged, glanced at Jeff, then smiled sheepishly but did not reply.

39

CONTENTIOUS ELECTION

2018–2020

WITH WARD'S two roommates graduating in June, he invited Mark and Jeff to join him in his apartment for the 2019–2020 school year. Ward now CCF president, their apartment became a hub of CCF activity. It was even more a second home to Linda between classes and evenings before she returned to Eureka every night than it had been during her first year on campus. The foursome was often together for supper and the evening. On Sundays, Ward and Mark attended the Baptist church near campus. When a new book on biblical prophecy, in the tradition of The *Late Great Planet Earth*, became a best-seller, Ward was caught up in the new round of second coming fervor sweeping through the church. He was soon leading prophecy studies in the CCF group based on the book everyone was talking about, *Rapture in Our Lifetime—Be Ready!*

Despite divergent spiritual and political outlooks, the three apartment mates made their friendship work. When Mark and Ward were together, their discussions usually revolved around running or the Bible. Both improved to 3rd and 4th men on the team behind their top runner Shaun, though occasionally interchanging positions. They always roomed together on cross-country trips with the seven-man traveling squad.

When the three apartment mates were together with Linda, however, running took a back seat. The subject was usually politics. As the election of 2020 heated up, the sophomore and junior from Seattle replayed the Trump-Hillary contest over and over, with many equally spirited Trump vs. Biden debates—Ward on the one side and Jeff on the other.

Though she had never cared about politics, Ward could not help noticing the gradual change taking place in his sister. Jeff's influence was obvious. Some of the comments popping out of her mouth almost shocked him. Though she didn't say much, he took it for granted that she was on the same spiritual track as he was. Yet she seemed oblivious to the game Jeff was playing. Or worse, *was* she aware of it, but didn't care?

The discussions in the apartment, sometimes lasting late into the night, were nearly always split down the middle. Seeing Linda gain confidence in herself was a good thing, but in what direction was that confidence pointed? Sometimes Ward wasn't sure.

One evening Mark and Ward took a break from their homework and were talking casually.

"Maybe you and Linda could come down to my folks' ranch over spring break," Mark was saying.

"That would be great," replied Ward. "Although it may be hard to convince Linda. Jeff will probably want to see her in a bikini on a beach somewhere."

He shook his head and sighed. "The thought of it makes me sick."

"We'll bring Jeff along," said Mark. "He used to love the ranch."

"Good luck. I doubt if you and I are the kind of people he will want to spend spring break with."

"You and I will go then. I'd like you to meet our neighbor David. He's the man who introduced me to Thomas à Kempis."

"I've heard you mention him, but I've never read anything by him."

"I thought I'd shared my *Imitation* with you. I meant to." He reached across his desk and took hold of a small leather volume. "David often talks about the centered life," he said. "That's Kempis—keeping you oriented toward those aspects of character that are central, practical, essential. There's not much theology—just how to live a centered life walking with God. Don't argue over doctrine, maintain unity, listen more than you talk—all very practical."

Mark rose and walked over and handed the book to Ward. "Have a go at it," he said. "You'll be wanting your own copy soon enough!"

"Thanks," said Ward. "I will dive in tomorrow morning in my quiet time."

Mark returned to his desk. "Listen to this," he said pulling out a sheet of paper from the top drawer. "I've written out my own summary of some of Kempis's high points. These are just a few—but even though they were written 500 years ago, they're unbelievably practical. *Keep company with the humble and plain, the devout and virtuous. Do not be too confident in your own opinion. Do not busy yourself with the words and deeds of others. Unlearn evil habits. Become strong by patience and humility. Be patient in bearing with the defects of others. Weigh your neighbor in the same balance with yourself. Be careful to avoid those things in yourself which displease you in others.*"

"Those are just different ways of expressing the golden rule," nodded Ward. "I see what you mean—it's powerfully practical!"

"I know," said Mark. "Kempis is great. *Do not be idle or spend your time in talk. Be grounded in true humility, live in simple obedience, walk in love and patience. Live a life adorned with virtue. Avoid small faults. Turn all things to good. Live peaceably with hard and perverse persons. Make simplicity your intention, purity your affection. Seek nothing but the will of God and the good of your neighbor. Walk in simplicity. Do all things purely. Delight in what is plain and humble. Pray for grace to—*"

Behind them the door opened. Jeff and Linda walked in. Mark and Jeff turned to greet them.

"—so unbelievable . . . what he is thinking. I can hardly believe it!" Jeff was saying heatedly and shaking his head.

"What's up?" asked Ward.

"It's Trump again—we were listening to a speech he gave earlier. He's down at the border and is full of boasting and bravado about his wall. Another 200 miles has been completed. It's so unAmerican."

"What is? Having a secure border?" said Ward. "That's unAmerican?"

"It's the way he's doing it that's unAmerican."

"You don't think we should have a secure border?"

"Not to keep people out who need help."

"What should we do then?" asked Ward.

"I don't know, but not build a wall. They're people too."

"They're not American citizens."

"What does that have to do with it?"

Ward did not reply. The answer seemed too obvious to bother saying it.

"Trump's such an idiot," Jeff went on, "a blowhard, a buffoon. Biden or whoever the Democrats pick will kill him next year. I hope he rots in—"

He caught himself just in time.

"At least he's real," said Ward. "He's no hypocrite."

Jeff laughed in disdain. "How can you say such a thing! He's a bigot and a racist."

"Ward wasn't talking about bigotry or racism," said Mark. "I think you misunderstood his meaning, Jeff."

"Which was?" said Jeff irritably.

"He was using the word 'hypocrite' according to its technical definition. He wasn't saying that Trump was bad or good, a bigot or not a bigot, or anything like that, only that he wasn't a hypocrite."

"What's the difference?"

"The difference is what the word means. Ward is absolutely right—Donald Trump isn't a hypocrite."

"That's ridiculous, Mark."

"Not according to what the word means."

"What do you mean by the word, then?"

"A hypocrite is someone who pretends to be what they're not, who's two-faced, who puts on an appearance of being one thing but inside is another."

"Exactly—you've described Trump perfectly!"

"I think you're wrong," said Mark. "You aren't thinking about this rationally. You detest Trump so much that it blinds you to the illogic of what you're saying. Trump may be immature, bombastic, arrogant, sometimes crude, and lacks self-control. Those are serious character flaws. If he doesn't correct them, you're right—he will probably get beat in November. But none of those things make him a hypocrite. He doesn't hide who he is. What you see is the *real* him—no pretending, no pretense. He doesn't pretend to be a spiritual man—which is the worst kind of hypocrisy of all. That's what Ward meant."

"Of course," nodded Ward.

"Then do you think Biden is a hypocrite?" asked Jeff.

Ward and Mark glanced at each other.

"I would not use that word," replied Mark. "All I will say is that he *does* pretend to be what he's not. He pretends to be a dedicated Christian and Catholic. But what he stands for politically tramples on the precepts of Christianity. It is the same with many progressives. They quote the Bible but see no obligation to follow it politically. Hypocrisy is one of the flaws of liberalism. There is a pretense of Christian belief, when most liberal policies, as I say, trample on the precepts of the Bible."

"How can you say that, Mark?" now said Linda heatedly. "That's so judgmental. Talk about hypocrisy! For you to defend Trump like that—you're the hypocrite, Mark."

Mark glanced away, obviously hurt by her words. It was silent a moment.

"I'm sorry, Mark," said Linda. "But what you said was pretty strong."

Mark smiled sadly. "Was it? I was trying to state what I thought was an objective observation. I have never heard Trump pretend to be a spiritual man. But I *have* heard Hillary and Penskey and Biden do so. Yet all three of them condone same-sex marriage and abortion, not to mention removing Christianity from schools and teaching children about sex. Obviously, the Bible doesn't directly say that public-schools should teach Christianity, though it does command teaching children to obey God's commands. That's only an example revealing their support for anti-Christian policies while pretending to be practicing Christians."

"You actually believe that liberals are more hypocritical than conservatives?"

Mark smiled again. "I'm sort of between a rock and a hard place," he said. "Anything I say is bound to be misunderstood. So I will withhold comment. If what I said was judgmental and hypocritical, then

I was wrong. I will take the matter up with the Lord and pray for him to reveal if that is the case. The person most in need of enlightenment, yet most blind to it, is the hypocrite. Until I subject the matter to prayer about my *own* need of enlightenment, I will say no more about hypocrisy."

"What about you, Ward?" said Linda, her eyes still flashing. "Do *you* think liberals are more hypocritical than conservatives?"

"I think I should take my lead from Mark," replied her brother. "But I do find the pattern Mark suggests to be true. Liberalism, in general, wants to cling to Christian values while promoting anti-Christian policies. I think Mark is right. Abortion is against everything Christianity stands for, yet liberals say all the time, 'I am a Christian, I believe in the Bible, but abortion is okay.' It's hard for me to see the consistency in that. You don't see that with conservatives. They say. 'I am a Christian. The Bible teaches all human life is sacred. Therefore, I believe abortion is a sin.' If someone calls herself a Christian, abortion is a very serious matter. If someone wants to believe abortion is okay, that's their right in our country. I may disagree, but that is still their right. But don't base a pro-abortion stance on the Bible. That's where the hypocrisy comes in—pretending it's 'Christian' to believe in clearly *anti*-Christian policies. It's exactly the same with homosexuality and same-sex marriage. People have a right to believe those practices are okay. I may disagree but they have the right to believe what they want. Just don't call such practices Christian. They're not."

"You sound like a fundamentalist fanatic, Ward," said Linda, shaking her head. "I can hardly believe I'm listening to my own brother sound so homophobic and judgmental."

Ward sighed but did not reply. Did his sister suddenly know him so little?

"There is another point to be made," said Mark, speaking up again. "Let's leave the question of hypocrisy for a minute. That is doing what you say you will do. That is a biblical virtue—letting your yes be yes and your no be no. Trump displays that virtue."

Jeff opened his mouth and was about to slam Mark for his statement, but Mark cut him off.

"Before either of you react emotionally," he said, "please just hear what I said. I did *not* say that he was a man of virtue. I am not so blind to his flaws that I consider him a paragon of virtue. I only say he lives by the principle of this one particular virtue—his yes is yes and his no is no. He does what he says he will do."

"And you don't think liberals are capable of that?" said Jeff.

"Of course they are capable of it. But if you are objective, you have to admit that Democrats tend to say most anything to get elected. I honestly think Trump would rather lose the 2020 election than not be true to himself. He would rather lose than say something he doesn't mean or really believe. Can you say that of Biden?"

"All I know is that when I met President Obama—"

"You've met him?!" exclaimed Linda.

"Well, sort of," said Jeff. "I was at a leadership conference a few years ago and I shook his hand. There was a long row of us moving past him one by one, all shaking his hand. But what I was going to say is that when I looked into his face, I said to myself, 'Here is a man of truth.'"

Mark did not reply.

"You don't agree?"

"No comment."

"I really want to know," pressed Jeff.

Mark sighed. "All right. No, I don't agree," he said.

"Why?"

"His yes isn't yes and his no isn't no. With regard to that one point of character, Trump exhibits higher virtue. I consider the former president, in my opinion, one of the most disingenuous politicians of our generation. You asked, and that is my opinion. I do not believe him to be a man of truth."

40

WARNING IN LOVE

2020

AFTER THE heated exchange, Mark avoided further political discussions with Jeff. As the 2020 election drew closer, however, Jeff continually baited him and did his best to draw him into debate. The antipathy toward the president in Arcata was so irrational, even violent, reaching outright hatred, that Humboldt's student body would likely vote 95 percent for challenger Biden.

Jeff was so convinced that right was on his side he seized every attempt to ridicule Trump and belittle anyone who spoke positively about him. He little realized that in so doing he was attacking the veracity and integrity of a close friend who, in fact, was more capable of objectively evaluating the character and perspectives of the two men than he was.

Mark steadfastly kept his thoughts to himself, confirming to Jeff that his friend was ignorant about politics. Though he would never say it to his face, Jeff considered Mark one of those whom Hillary Clinton would put in her basket of deplorables. Leaping to the common judgments of many in the liberal cocoon of Northern California, Jeff followed Mrs. Clinton's lead to the conclusion that Mark's evangelical ethic made him, by definition, sexist, racist, xenophobic, homophobic, and Islamophobic. For the first time since their meeting, Jeff Rhodes began to look down on his friend.

Mark endured the snide comments and jabs. Though Jeff intended his words to be taken in jest, they contained the unmistakable snobbery of superiority. Mark loved Jeff as a friend. It hurt to realize how little Jeff valued his thoughts, feelings, and perspectives.

More outgoing of personality, not opposed to a vigorous argument, and not so grounded in Kempis, Ward Hutchins had no qualms about mixing it up with Jeff and was able to give it out in equal measure. The two did not exactly come to blows. But it was clear the election changed the tone in the apartment. It finally reached the point where the two rarely spoke to one another except to argue and debate. Mark had his hands full acting as peacemaker between them, not always with success. In private he encouraged Ward to keep his pro-Trump opinions to himself.

"Nothing you say will change Jeff's mind," he said.

"But he's so blind to the truth, Mark. He has to be told."

"Why? There's no Scripture that says people have to be informed of their blind spots. Jesus and Kempis actually say just the opposite. It does no good, Ward. It's wasted energy. Pearls before swine."

"How can you stand by and listen to the lies and say nothing?"

"Sometimes silence is best."

"What about standing up for truth?"

"You are standing up for your political views, Ward. I'm not sure you can equate that with *truth*. Donald Trump is not our standard bearer, Jesus is. Don't mistake the two."

"I see what you mean. But it's so frustrating."

"I agree. But we've got to walk the high road. What Kempis says about doctrine applies equally to politics. *'What will it avail you to argue profoundly of the Trinity, if you are void of humility? Words do not make a man holy and just, but a virtuous life make him dear to God.'*"

"But the future of the country is at stake."

"Which is not as important as a holy and virtuous life. All you have to do is change one word from what I just quoted from Kempis and I believe we will discover God's mind on the matter: What will it avail you to argue profoundly *of the election,* if you are void of humility?"

"Jeff is certainly not humble."

"You're right, he's not. I'm embarrassed for him. That's all the more reason why you and I need to be."

Ward took in Mark's words thoughtfully.

"Your witness to Jeff can't be based on political debate," said Mark, "but on character and love. Argumentation only drives him further from you. There are bigger things at stake than this election."

The more serious result of the widening rift between Jeff and Ward was the inevitable fissure that developed between brother and sister. Like Mark, Linda was caught in the middle. But unlike Mark, she made no attempt to play the peacemaker. They had been as close as any brother and sister could have been. When she made her choice now, however, it was to follow a heart which thought itself in love with Jeff. As she did, she became less timid to speak against the traditional values she and Ward and Sawyer were taught by their mother. The critical tone that was more frequently heard in her voice was completely foreign to the sister Ward had always known.

Mark and Ward were not the only ones to notice the change. It had been Ward's practice never to miss a Sunday dinner with his mother in Eureka. Especially with the tension in the apartment in recent months, it was good to be with Linda and their mother once a week when politics was not mentioned.

"Hi, Mom," Ward called as he walked into his mother's house one Sunday afternoon about three.

"Hi, dear," replied Mrs. Hutchins, coming out of the kitchen wiping her hands on her apron. "I just took the roast out of the oven."

"I can tell—it smells great!"

"Sawyer called an hour ago. He's been promoted to ADA. He said to say hi."

"Good for him. The oldest and continuing to outshine Linda and me!" laughed Ward. "He'll be King County DA before he's thirty."

"How was church this morning?"

"It was great—half the congregation is made up of college kids. It's so unusual having a thriving church right on campus. You ought to come with me sometime, Mom."

"You know me—I like a smaller church. I'm happy where I am."

Mrs. Hutchins lowered her voice. "Linda hasn't been going much recently. Do you think everything's, you know, okay with her?"

"Yeah, I know. I'm planning to talk to her, Mom. She hasn't been going with you either?"

His mother shook her head. "I can't say I'm as taken with the Rhodes boy as she is," she said, lowering her voice even more. "He's nice enough, and always treats me kindly. It's nothing I can put my finger on, but . . ."

Her voice trailed away.

"I know what you mean. He doesn't have much spiritual grounding. I'm praying for him."

"I wish Linda would show more interest in Mark."

"He is a great guy," nodded Ward. "He would be a better influence on her."

"Why doesn't he ask her out?"

"Too late now," laughed Ward. "He's met someone—a sophomore, I think—Grace Thornton. Sweetest girl you can imagine. I'm afraid Mark's out of the running for good."

"I'm happy for him. But why wasn't he interested in Linda before?"

"Mark doesn't put himself forward. He saw how it was. He knew what was on Jeff's mind from the first time we all met. So he remained in the background. He's not the kind of guy girls notice. Jeff is smooth and personable, everybody's best friend, and good-looking to boot. He set his sights on Linda the moment he saw her. She didn't have a chance. Mark would never have tried to get in the middle of that."

"Do you think . . . I mean, how serious are they?"

"I don't know, Mom," answered Ward. "I think Linda may be more serious than she ought to be. Jeff likes having a pretty girl on his arm. But it doesn't stop him looking around. That's what worries me."

"Does Linda know?"

Ward shook his head. "She has no idea what kind of guy he is. She's still naïve in a lot of ways, Mom."

"Talk to her, Ward. Tell her to be careful."

"I will, Mom."

The opportunity Ward hoped for did not come immediately. He judged it best to wait until after the election. He hoped that an end to the volatile political atmosphere might put her in a more receptive frame of mind.

He talked the situation over with Mark, who knew Jeff better than he did. Mark confessed his sadness that their friendship had lost the magic of their high school years. He loved Jeff like a brother but could see well enough the direction Jeff was heading. Mark was aware of it earlier, but now saw a simple disheartening fact—Jeff was in love with himself. He used people to gain his own ends.

The two agreed to talk to Linda together. Their opportunity came on the eve of President-Elect Biden's inauguration in early 2021, just as the Covid pandemic passed the peak of its third wave. At his father's insistence, Jeff flew north to Seattle to be at his father's side for Seattle's inauguration party. As the president-elect's Washington campaign manager, it would be a night of triumph for Harrison Rhodes.

Knowing they would not be interrupted, Ward invited Linda to the apartment for supper. Afterward the three sat down together in the small living room.

"We would like to talk to you about something, Linda," Ward said.

The serious tone of his voice put Linda on edge. She found it equally irksome for Mark to be sitting so calm and quiet at Ward's side. Immediately on the defensive, she felt ganged up on.

"You know I love you, Linda," Ward began. "I know I speak for Mark as well. We both love you as a sister. You are my sister. You have been my best friend. I could not love you more. So please believe that what I have to say comes from nothing but love."

He paused. Linda's eyes were glued onto her lap.

"I'm afraid you may be getting in over your head with Jeff," he went on after a moment.

"And why is that?" said Linda brusquely, eyes still riveted down.

"I just don't think he is all he appears to be."

"He's a hypocrite, is that it?"

"Good heavens, Linda—I didn't say that. I like Jeff. He's our roommate. I just think there may be more going on than he lets people see."

"Which, if I remember, was your definition of a hypocrite."

Suddenly she looked up and turned toward Mark. "Don't think I've forgotten," she said, her face flushing, "that night we were talking and the two of you were fawning over Trump, when you called everyone who disagreed with you a hypocrite. I've never heard anything so judgmental in my life. Talk about hypocrisy—the two of you are the worst. That's when I realized I wanted no more of your kind of religion."

Ward and Mark sat stunned by the outburst.

It was silent a long while. The tension in the air was thick.

"I am so sorry, Linda," said Mark softly. "If I recall that discussion correctly, I believe I said that I would take the matter up with the Lord in prayer, and ask him to show me my own attitudes. Since then I have not spoken with Jeff once about politics—not through the entire election. I hope I do not say that to defend myself, but just to reassure you that I would not call *anyone* a hypocrite without first looking into the mirror to examine my own heart. I think all Ward wanted to say was to encourage you to be careful, to guard your heart."

"Why?"

"Because we love you and want the best for you."

"And you think Jeff isn't right for me?"

"I can't say that. You will have to decide that for yourself."

"But what do *you* think, Mark. Tell me. For once don't be such a coward and hide behind that soft-spoken demeanor. Just tell me what you think."

The words stung. Inwardly Mark drew in a sigh, then smiled a little sadly. "All right," he said. "I have known Jeff a long time, Linda. He has been my best friend. I love him more than I have ever loved a friend. But he is changing. He is headed in some directions that concern me. I agree with Ward, that there is more to Jeff than he lets on. It's possible you may be in over your head. All we're saying is that you need to be careful."

Linda let out an exclamation of disdain. "Ha!" she said. "How transparent can you be, Mark! It's so obvious it's ridiculous. You can't stand seeing me with Jeff. You want me for yourself. You've had a crush on me from the beginning. I've seen it all along. It's laughable. Do you actually think I could ever be interested in a guy like you!"

Mark winced as if he had been struck in the face. His eyes slowly closed and his head sank onto his chest. He rose a few seconds later. The very act of climbing to his feet took all the effort he could muster. Tears in his eyes, he silently left the room. A few seconds later they heard the bedroom door close.

"That was uncalled for, Linda," said Ward.

"He deserved it," she retorted.

"Do you really think that's true?"

"I've seen how he looks at me."

"Don't you know Mark well enough by this time?"

"I thought I did. I thought I knew you too. I didn't dream the two of you would turn against me. Now you're shocked because you had no idea I could think for myself. You still assume I have to agree with you in everything. Well, I've changed. I'm not a little girl anymore, Ward."

She rose and started for the door.

"Just a minute—please, Linda," said Ward. "If I still mean anything to you as your brother, will you allow me to say one more thing? Not a word about Jeff. I promise. This is just you and me, Ward and Linda, brother and sister, like old times."

Linda drew in a breath and sat back down. Whether or not the personal appeal found an entry into her heart could not be discerned from her expression.

"You have changed," said Ward, speaking softly. "You're right—maybe I have been slow to recognize it. I am sorry. I ask your forgiveness if I have played the big brother and have treated you like a little sister when I should have recognized you as a woman and a free thinker and my equal. I mean it—I am very sorry."

Linda nodded in acknowledgment, but said nothing.

"You have changed, I have changed, Mark has changed. I'll be graduating in a year and be off to seminary. You and Mark and Jeff will be seniors. We are all growing. But there are many kinds of change. There is good change and unhealthy change. I just want to leave you with one thought, and this is something I have been seeing for years. If you believe I have any insight at all, please hear me out."

He paused briefly, breathing a silent prayer for wisdom in choosing his words.

"There is within the political agenda of people like Jeff," he went on, "something that subtly, almost insidiously erodes Christian faith. It is endemic to liberalism that the vibrancy of discipleship tends to dry up. What is left is the shell of Christian belief without the pulsating energy of a daily walk with God."

Whether Linda was able to absorb Ward's thoughtful words, or was listening at all by now, was probably doubtful.

"I don't know why it is, but it *happens*," her brother continued. "At their core, cultural liberalism and Christian discipleship are incompatible systems of belief and lifestyle. Liberalism feeds on character flaws that Jesus commands us to put to death. Please . . . change for the *better*, Linda."

Ward tried to catch her eyes, but she refused to look at him.

"Use these years to deepen your commitment to the life Jesus wants us all to live. Do not allow the gods of modernism to eat away the foundations of your—"

"I've heard enough, Ward," interrupted Linda, standing again and walking across the room toward the door. This time Ward did not try to stop her.

41

Λ STAR IS BORN

2021–2022

IT WAS in Humboldt's milieu of weirdly heterogeneous causes, all of Arcata basking in the glowing vindication of Trump's defeat and assured that the radical vision of the Obama years was back on track, that the son of Seattle's mayor fell in love with the public spotlight. It did not take long for him to realize that he could ride his accidental fame, along with his father's backing, just about anywhere he wanted.

The fateful day unwittingly launching Jeff Rhodes's career into the public arena arrived in the spring of their junior year. Covid restrictions were easing. And the new president was engaged in a headlong rush to undo his predecessor's accomplishments.

On a Saturday evening, with nothing to do and with the clock on the last day of the weekend moving through the hours like molasses, Jeff was restless. That he and Mark had grown apart more than either realized was evident in how each spent their Saturdays.

After the InterVarsity sponsored Campus Christian Fellowship breakfast Bible study, Mark attended a filmed lecture that evening with Ward Hutchins by Francis Schaeffer, one of the last filmed presentations before his death.

Jeff, on the other hand, devoted his day to a seminar on "The New Face of World Change in the Third Millennium." Whatever nominal religious roots prompted Sandra Rhodes to send her son to Pinecroft, the political science major had by that time thoroughly soaked up

Arcata's anti-Christian prejudice. He now, though he admitted it openly to no one, especially Linda, considered himself an atheist.

With nothing to do, Jeff accompanied Mark, now vice president of CCF, to one of the other Christian apartments across town where he had some business with the club's president Matt Travis. There they found themselves roped into an hour's tedious conversation, in Jeff's estimation, as Matt and his roommate, computer whiz Morris Fried, huddled about their computers.

"You guys will never believe what Morris is working on," Matt told them, trying to keep them abreast. "He is inventing a program he says will change the entire computer industry."

"Yeah right!" chided Jeff.

"It's true," said Morris, glancing over the top of the screen from where he sat at his desk.

"That's what everyone thinks. But how many really do?"

"Mine will. Nobody's ever thought of this angle before. It's going to be the next Facebook."

Jeff's response was a humorously scornful laugh. "I'll believe it when I see it!" he added. "Besides, Facebook's already on the way out."

"Seriously," Morris persisted. "All I need to launch it is a few hundred bucks—a thousand at most. I'm going to turn this thing into a million-dollar internet sensation. How about it, Rhodes—you can get in on the ground floor. For five hundred, I'll cut you in for a third ownership."

Jeff laughed again. "I have no desire to throw my money away!"

"What about you, Mark?"

"Sorry, Morris," replied Mark. "My budget is strictly hand to mouth."

Jeff stood. "Come on, Mark," he said. "Let's go. I've had enough computer talk for one night. Let's find something to do."

Their business concluded, Mark exchanged a few final words with Matt, then followed Jeff from the house.

"Whew," said Jeff as they walked out into the chilly night. "Man, I had to get out of there. What a couple of geeks! I knew about Fried. But I had no idea Travis was such a weirdo too. Let's go have some fun."

Mark did not reply. An inward pang told him he ought to speak up in Matt's defense. But Jeff was not a guy you crossed. He had been working hard to avoid arguments of any kind. Sometimes it was easier just to keep his mouth shut.

Two hours later, with the evening growing late, they found themselves walking along a side street of Arcata's small business district on the way back to their apartment. They could still hear sounds from the town plaza three or four blocks behind them where students would be hanging out most of the night. Its landmark statue of President McKinley had been removed two years before during the wave of liberal monument topplings that swept the country. As the two walked, however, the streets and sidewalks surrounding them at eleven o'clock were deserted.

From somewhere in the darkness ahead, shattering glass suddenly broke the silence. At the same moment an alarm blared into the night.

Both young men stopped dead in their tracks. The next instant they broke into a run in the direction of the sound.

They rounded the corner of the next block just in time to see a figure climb through the broken glass of the door to Kelly's Jewelers carrying a black duffel bag. He ran off in the opposite direction.

Again, they stopped and took in the scene. A thousand thoughts raced through their brains. Jeff was thinking more of self-preservation than much else. As a natural outgrowth of the drug culture, crime flourished in Humboldt County. One never knew who was lurking in Arcata's dark alleys. He had no intention of putting himself in danger.

More by impulse than forethought, however, almost as if the sound of the thief's footsteps were the starter's pistol before a cross-country race, Mark burst into a sprint. Before he had a chance to think what he was doing, he was after the burglar with all the speed he could muster in street clothes.

"Call the police!" he shouted behind him.

Fumbling in his pocket for his cell phone, his eyes wide at his friend's daring, Jeff watched Mark disappear into the darkness. He punched in 9-1-1, gave his name and explained where he was and what was happening. He stopped to wait in front of the smashed plate glass window, eying what contents the burglar hadn't managed to stuff into his bag.

It didn't take Mark long to overtake his quarry. The thief's legs grew heavy from his sprint, and Mark's gentle shove from behind sent the man sprawling onto the cement. The duffel bag flew from his hands along the sidewalk.

For several seconds he was too surprised and exhausted to move. By the time he began thinking of getting up, Mark was beside him, duffel bag in hand, hauling him to his feet. The short pudgy man in his mid-forties, six inches shorter and obviously not as fit as Mark, knew it would be futile to make a dash for it or try anything of a more violent nature.

"Look kid," he panted, "you got me dead to rights. I'll give you that. I didn't expect to hear footsteps behind me. You're a gutsy kid. What say we just split what's in the bag and go our separate ways?"

"No thanks," replied Mark. "We're going to take it back where it belongs."

Leading the small man back to the store, Mark rejoined his friend as sirens and flashing lights from two police cars came speeding along the street.

"Way to go, Pine!" exclaimed Jeff. "You're the man!

"Just a little extra workout, Pike," laughed Mark.

Seeing the danger passed. Jeff's leadership once again asserted itself. As he resumed the upper hand, Mark retreated into the background. Jeff attached himself to the arm of the thief and shoved him toward the officer climbing out of his car.

"Are you the one who called?" asked the policeman.

"That's me," replied Jeff. "Here's your man. We saw him come out of the store and run off with that duffel bag in his hand."

He pointed with his free hand to the bag sitting on the sidewalk beside Mark a few yards away.

"We chased him down, and here he is."

A second policeman came forward, took charge of the prisoner, handcuffed him, and led him to one of the police cars.

"All right then," said the officer in charge. "I'll need both your names and full statements."

By the time the incident made the next evening's papers, Jeff, as the acknowledged spokesman and obviously feeling more comfortable than his friend in front of microphone and cameras, came off as the hero of the evening. His bravery and quick thinking, according to the reports, saved Mr. Kelly thousands in losses with the recovery of all the stolen merchandise. A television interview followed a few days later.

By then Jeff was in his element and clearly enjoying the celebrity. Mark was not asked to participate, nor did Jeff suggest it. Mark had no interest in sharing the limelight. He laughed it off as one of the qualities everyone liked about Jeff—he was an unabashed ham.

The incident changed Jeff more than it did Mark. By the following year he was a campus celebrity, ran for public office as a senior, and became the youngest member ever to sit on Arcata's decidedly liberal city council at twenty-one.

His rise to fame coincided with the school's elevation to the big time in the California university system. In January of 2022, Humboldt was renamed California State Polytechnic University, Humboldt. Humboldt Honeys were replaced by Humboldt Techies, though the hippie culture was impossible to extinguish, and the 1970s ambiance of Arcata's Co-op remained alive and well. The words *Cal Poly* Humboldt added a luster to Jeff's undergraduate résumé that could not help pleasing his father.

By then, with Ward, now in his fifth year taking two final required classes prior to the completion of his degree, Jeff and Linda were talking openly of their future together. There was no ring, and to neither Ward's nor Mark's knowledge had there been an official proposal. But it was obvious, at least in Linda's mind, that they had an "understanding."

Mrs. Hutchins, not particularly adept at keeping her motherly curiosity to herself, could not help asking.

"Are you and Jeff engaged?" she finally asked.

"Not officially," replied Linda. "Jeff wants to wait until we're in Seattle to make the announcement. His father's an important man, you know—I've told you about him. He will make a big thing of it. It's best that way, Jeff says."

"And next year, after you graduate?"

"I'm going to law school, Mom. I told you that."

"I didn't know you had decided. But how will you—I mean, I will try to help. But I don't think even your father and I together could afford—"

"Not to worry, Mom. Jeff's father is taking care of everything. I've been accepted at U of W thanks to some strings he pulled."

"But what about the cost?"

"I told you—it's all taken care of. I have a full scholarship that will see me all the way to my law degree. It won't cost you a thing."

Jeff resigned from the city council after one year. By then his father's plans for his future took priority.

Jefferson Rhodes entered the University of Washington's School of Law in the fall of 2022, with Linda Hutchins, even more radiant now as a graduate student, following in his wake.

The two were instantly recognized as the school's poster couple—their high-profile notoriety increased even more by the elder Rhodes's close association with the new US president—and were clearly destined for great things.

42

A Litany of Anomalies

2022

WHY A man like Viktor Domokos had risen to become the world's most prominent financier of socialist and culturally radical causes was one of the curious anomalies of America's political landscape. By all logic he should have been as conservative as Ronald Reagan, a man whose billions were given to new generations of conservatives like Donald Trump rather than neo-socialists and anarchist causes. Millions of souls from eastern Europe just like him owed their freedom to Reagan's tough anti-communist bravado. Domokos likewise owed his billions to American capitalism.

Yet in his later years, he was putting those billions to work to destroy the very capitalist underpinnings of America's constitutionalism, and replace it with a kinder and gentler form of the communism he had escaped as a young man. His brand of so-called "enlightened democracy" could not masquerade forever as anything other than the soft-totalitarianism of a sinister new iteration of socialism. Thus far, however, he and his thousands of disciples had deluded their followers into believing the charade.

Nothing about the man made sense. He had suffered under communism. He saw his fellow Jews imprisoned and murdered under Stalin and Khrushchev before immigrating penniless to England and then the United States from his native Romania. It stood to reason that he would view the free societies of the West as saviors from the dictatorships that had always been, and remained, such an allure to the powers of the East. All the more so, it was the capitalist economies of London and Wall Street that had made him one of the world's wealthiest men.

Yet it was now his life's mission to undermine the foundations of Western civilization, politics, and economics, and replace them with a free, open, borderless society, unfettered by the historic flaws of the West. In the new world order of his vision, complete equality was the birthright of every man, woman, and child on the planet. Not merely equal opportunity, but equality of every form—with equal income, equal privileges, equal status. But not, of course, equal *power*. That would be closely held by a new non-European, non-Christian, non-traditional elite.

His vision would spread money equitably and evenly around the world. There would be no Have-Nots. By a variety of means, the Haves would be forced to relinquish their excess, thus balancing the global financial teeter-totter. With the exception of the ruling elite, for whom the rules would be different, the janitor, the plumber, the CEO, the university professor, the investment banker, and the homeless man, would all earn the same—not paid for their work but for their humanity, with minorities given an added racial or "prior prejudice" bonus not available to whites. Immigration would cease to be a problem because everyone would be free to go anywhere. Every individual, no matter his background, education, skin color, or social standing, could demand and expect the full rights and privileges due every human being—which meant having anything they wanted and anything anyone else possessed.

Domokos's goal was the establishment of a world defined no longer by sovereign states, but by a global community whose constituent nations, none more powerful than any other, were based on the principle that everyone shared an equal right to freedom, equality, and prosperity. He gleaned the basis for his views around the idea of the "open society," a term popularized by Austrian Karl Popper in his 1945 work *The Open Society and Its Enemies*. Building on Popper's foundation, Domokos added to it the tactics and strategies of his mentor Saul Alinsky. By the end of the second millennium, he had taken his sweeping and radical agenda to new heights as he envisioned the new world of the twenty-first century. He knew he would not live to see it. But he was raising new generations molded by his vision who would carry it forward.

A globally open and transparent society, in his view, was the only way for humanity to overcome the challenges of climate change and nuclear proliferation, and eradicate the systemic racism, xenophobia, Islamophobia, homophobia, and anti-feminine bias of white male supremacist Anglo-Saxon Western civilization. The mortal enemy of his vision was right-wing, white, Christian nationalism. It was an influence that would persist until it was crushed and destroyed.

His grandiose dream was nothing short of a complete transformation of all national and international politics and society.

The devil, of course, was in the details. What would Domokos say to the Somali pirate who demanded of this new world order that he had a right to the same income as a German industrialist? Or to the Mexican who walked into Arizona and claimed it as his equal right to bring his extended family of twelve in to occupy the house built by the rancher whose family had worked the land for three generations? Or to the Syrian terrorist who decided he had an equal right to occupy the US White House as did the American president?

Equality was a slippery commodity to radical visionaries such as Domokos and his powerful allies within the burgeoning alumni of the Palladium Alliance. It was not productive to look at the details of global equality too closely.

The devil again. How would law and justice, crime, personal accountability, the good of society, and the role of elections, prisons, banks, and police forces be redefined in this new order?

Would there even be police and banks? If criminals had the equal right to freedom as everyone else, would prisons be emptied and shut down?

How would economics actually *function* if the capitalist incentive to work and make money and get ahead were removed because everyone had the right to the same income and benefits from society's global slush fund?

Absent capitalism, who would keep globalist industry, technology, and food production steaming along?

Did Domokos really imagine that uneducated peasants could do as well as Iowa farmers, New York bankers, California businessmen, and Texas ranchers in keeping the interconnected engines of the world actually working?

Then there was the tricky matter of censorship and freedom. If, as Domokos believed, the right-wing media must not merely be marginalized with misinformation but stamped out and destroyed as the enemy of the public good, where did the freedom of conservatives to express *their* beliefs stand in his new calculus of equality? Were certain forms of censorship necessary evils in pursuit of mankind's greater good? Might Hitler and Stalin have reasoned along similar lines?

It didn't do to wonder such things. Domokos was so convinced that progress was on his side, his envisioned ends justified even flagrantly inconsistent means to achieve them.

Domokos was deafeningly quiet about these and many other of the myriad systemic flaws of his socialist utopia. So too was the rising new generation of leaders of Palladium, led by Loring Bardolf, Storm Roswell, and its League of Seven. They were, if possible, even more committed to their cause, and more ruthless in what they were willing to do to achieve its far-reaching objectives, than their fathers who had founded the secret organization.

They had grown up considering abortion, homosexuality, same-sex marriage, unfettered immigration, and militant anti-religious secularism normal practices and perspectives which the populace must be forced to accept by any means necessary. Deviations or alternate views were not open for discussion. They were *wrong* perspectives that must be eradicated for the common good. Alternate perspectives on gender or abortion or immigration had to be rooted out and eliminated along with white systemic racism and the evil corporatocracy.

Many of the secret organization's rising new generation of leaders had cut their political teeth in Antifa and Black Lives Matter. Six of the League of Seven spearheaded the post-election violence in the Capitol on January 6 just prior to Biden's inauguration, and ensured the blame fell on outgoing president Trump and a handful of his followers. The new generation of Palladium—the *Protectorate*—was ruthless and diabolically clever in placing blame where they wanted it and making sure the news media—into which they placed thousands of their alumni at every level—reported everything according to their script. All was done for the world's good, to protect the utopian vision of its future. None of Palladium's membership—now 144 strong—doubted that theirs was a righteous cause.

With Slayton Bardolf gone from a heart attack at sixty-five—replaced among the Seven by his son, Loring—and with Devon Crawford retired for health reasons, aging Talon Roswell was the only one of the three founders still active in the League, and still living at his family's compound in Mira Monte.

One of the largest elephants in the room behind Palladium's closed doors was the future of the Christian church and Judaism. If the two cousin religions were the joint historic authors of white supremacy, homophobia, and masculine authority in the world, they must be eradicated. But there could be no overt move against the worldwide Christian church. As toothless a tiger as that bloated institution had become, even a tiger without teeth has claws that make him, when aroused, a dangerous adversary.

They all agreed that Christendom must not be aroused. The progressive movement had thus far successfully lulled institutional Christianity into the slumber of self-satisfied apathy. It had thus been brought into modernism's fold in a way that its lemming-followers had not perceived by gradually turning the church into a social club.

They must keep it that way. Christianity must continue in its hibernal state until it was dead altogether. Domokos was less concerned about the Judaism of his own ethnic heritage. It had been essentially dead for two thousand years already. The nation of Israel would have to go. But they would leave that to the Arabs.

If there were skeletons in Viktor Domokos's personal closet, he kept them well hidden. Three wives, all now dead, may have had stories to tell, but dead women, no less than men, tell no tales. When a destitute immigrant amasses such wealth in such a short time, how can a few eyebrows not drift upward? Money like his usually flows out of one of two coffers—one legal, one illegal, though both equally secretive and nefarious—international finance, or organized crime.

Whether he had his hands in both tills, no one knew. There were hints that surfaced occasionally indicating more to the story of his past than his public rags-to-riches story let on—shadowy connections to mob interests in regions further east than his native land. Even the far-right media stopped short of using terms like "spy" and "on the take," though the implications pointed at by putting two and two together from the words of their "unnamed sources" were not difficult to ascertain.

Progressive interests, however, were not about to see their golden goose tarnished by such dirt even if the allegations were true. What did it matter as long as the tap remained open and the money continued to flow. It was not difficult, following Saul Alinsky's Rule Five for Radicals, to shoot the messenger with bullets of ridicule, and discredit the allegations as from bigoted, xenophobic, conspiracy kooks.

Political perspectives, hidden motives, financial interests, lust for power, and the alliances they interweave, often work completely outside the bounds of logic. Strange bedfellows that they were, Domokos now sat in secluded conference—with eight or ten members of Palladium who were merely identified as his personal advisors.

With them were two former 1960s radicals, a known Palestinian terrorist, one former US president, two Supreme Court justices—whose presence bordered on the illegal, but no one in this group worried about such things, especially as the US attorney general was one of them—the heads of Meta, Amazon, Google, AI Tech Industries, Apple, and Microsoft, the Speaker of the House, head of the CDC, two other Wall Street billionaires like himself, three senators, half a dozen presidents from the nation's most prestigious universities, and several media moguls whose responsibility it was to ensure that their minions toed the party line and regurgitated the approved narrative day after day.

These latter men and women from the media were responsible for the indoctrination machine feeding the combined agenda of this clandestine consortium to the public.

There were secrets some of those gathered even kept from each other, which might have explained why the only one among them wearing a Covid mask was CDC Director Murdoch Cluney. He explained it, however, for the purpose of protecting the others, not because of what he already suspected to be the inefficacy of the protocols.

All present had been among the first to publicly display their Covid-19 vaccination cards, bolstering the illusion that what was being called a "vaccine" actually prevented infection. More than half, however, were not vaccinated at all, knowing the public vaccination push to be little more than a wishful thinking misinformation campaign.

They were from diverse backgrounds but were equally committed to a multi-dimensional program of interconnected objectives. These included the elimination of white-based power structures—curious given that three-quarters of those present were white—the neutering of Christianity, the destruction of the Republican Party, the outlawing of homophobia and racism as they defined it, consolidation of their control of the media and elimination of dissenting voices within it, permanent Democrat control of all three branches of government in Washington, DC, and the remaking of the United States into a proto-type for a classless, cashless, and borderless society up and down the economic spectrum.

Curiously, neither the current president, whom they had installed as a place-holding figurehead, nor his vice president, were informed of the meeting. Secrecy, of course, would have been impossible to maintain had the Biden-Harris duo been invited. And above all, secrecy was essential. But that was not the reason for their absence; in Palladium's view, they were inconsequential lightweights. Neither were the two Clintons present. They were of the past. It was time to look beyond them. Both would have been furious to know they were excluded. But neither *would* ever know.

Those present who were not members of Palladium so benefited from its money and support that, if not members, they were too deeply in bed with what was the most powerful secret political organization in America to turn back now. The Palladium Alliance had become more influential than whatever remnants remained of the Illuminati, the fading Masonic network, or the Bilderberg Group. Those former institutions had too many white business antecedents to continue in the current climate as powerful as they once were. Their most influential men were slowly being absorbed into the more inclusive and women-friendly, rainbowed coalition of the *Protectorate*. Palladium now invisibly called the shots.

43

CONSPIRATORIAL STRATEGIES

THE FIRST snows of late autumn fell the night before on the Vermont hills surrounding the lodge where they sat. A roaring fire in the huge stone fireplace sent cheerful light into the large room, belying the clandestine purpose of the gathering.

"Though the recent years have been troublesome," eighty-three-year-old Domokos was saying by way of introduction, "the Trump years are at last behind us. While we all mourned Hillary's loss six years ago, I have come to moderate my first reaction. I now believe Trump's buffoonery may actually be the best thing that could have happened to us. We have so successfully convinced the public to think of his supporters as Neanderthals that, in spite of the interruption to our momentum, it will not hurt the cause in the long run. The interlude, in fact, will slingshot us forward even more rapidly in reaction against the Trump years. The effect will be identical to Barack's election after W. Those conservative blips on the screen work to our ultimate advantage. How else could we have placed such a nincompoop—one of the more colorful words in your English vocabulary—as our esteemed vice president so close to the Oval Office. We owe that to Trump. It is time, however, for us to run the table without further such Republican interludes. Our goal of 2050 is closer than ever. Twenty years ago even I could not have dreamed how far we would come in the short eight years with our friend Barack at the helm."

Heads turned toward the object of Domokos's praise, with a few comments of approbation and light applause.

"I would now like to turn the floor over to Loring Bardolf," said Domokos, glancing to his right.

"Twenty years ago," began the scion of Palladium's founder, "my father, and I think Mr. Domokos would agree he felt similarly, considered the homosexual question one of our greatest hurdles to overcome in the public consciousness."

As in all such meetings, the *Alliance* or *Palladium* was never mentioned by name. The vow of secrecy at every member's initiation was inviolate. In the rare instances in which confirmation of identification might be required, though all members supposedly knew one another, the secret code "46" was allowed between them—in reference to the atomic number 46 on the periodic table identifying the metal *Palladium*, rarer than gold or platinum, whose meaning from the Latin was "protectorate"—but only in the most extreme circumstances. Some used it as a private telephone extension, or as a number imbedded in passwords or other secret codes. There were rumors of auto accidents, suicides, and lethal illnesses following unguarded carelessness by members. No matter how powerful one's position, things could happen. The non-members present knew nothing other than that Domokos was surrounded by certain powerful individuals in various fields whom he trusted implicitly.

"Yet it turned out to be no obstacle at all," the middle-aged Bardolf went on. "Even Christians fell into lockstep in favor of same-sex marriage and welcoming gays and lesbians into their churches—even into their pulpits. I must admit I am amazed how effortless it has been to normalize gender issues. The same is true with acceptance of Islam and recognition of systemic white racism. Even with Joe's unfortunate mental state, our southern borders are opening rapidly. The dominos of the agenda are falling more rapidly than my father, were he still among us, would have dreamed possible. We may not even have to wait until 2050. However, we must continue to be shrewd and not overplay our hand. Our ultimate ends must remain out of the public eye."

"Your optimism is admirable," said Speaker of the House Penskey, a veteran of many such enclaves. "And while I agree we could not have foreseen how easy it was to get the public to accept the changes you mention, I'm not sure I am quite so ready to write an obituary on the Republicans just yet. They have a way of resurrecting themselves. I personally had to deal with the idiot Trump during the years of his tenure. It was enough to give a woman a nervous breakdown."

Light laughter spread through the room.

"And he may not be done yet. In any event, I think we need to be very careful and start planning aggressively for 2024. There are Republicans waiting in the wings if Trump's legal problems turn out to be mortal. And with this Covid-inflation spike and runaway gas prices, coupled with Joe's ineptitude and plummeting approval rating, it is not inconceivable that we could lose Congress again, even the White House two years from now. And frankly, legalities notwithstanding, I'm not convinced the world has seen the last of Trump."

Nods went around the room.

"We thought Joe to be a worthy puppet," agreed Supreme Court Justice Frey. "But he has been a nightmare. We have to convince him to step down before that happens."

"If he lives that long," said Penskey, who was in fact older than the president.

"There is that. Or the 25th Amendment," observed Frey's fellow justice Marston. "But with our standing in the Court a minority at present, we don't want to get into any legal battles. The recent *Roe v Wade* reversal demonstrates just what a problem we have in the Court. We have to get it permanently in our control. In any event we have to pray Joe holds it together."

"Not only that," added Attorney General Garland Marks, "Kamala would be a disaster against a strong Republican, even as an incumbent."

"Which is why we have to look to a new generation of leaders, to youth and charisma," added Bardolf.

"Such as California's Newsome," nodded Marks.

"I would think we would be looking more toward one of color than another white male," said Diana Sorrell, the first black president of Google, whose rapid rise through the ranks was orchestrated by Domokos.

"Or a woman," added Kate Blakeley, chairman of the board of Chase Bank, an alum of Palladium's collegiate subsidiary Oraculous, from Yale.

"But *not* Kamala," emphasized Cluney through his mask. "What about you, Kate?"

Blakeley laughed. "I'm happy where I am."

"Newsome may be our best bet for the new future," persisted the attorney general.

"Perhaps. He definitely bears watching. But even if there should be a resurgence of the conservative vote in the future," Bardolf resumed, "the agenda will not be impacted. Election setbacks are mere bumps in the road. Let them elect another Republican. The LBGTQ and social justice agendas are the true benchmarks of our momentum. With those in place changing the culture of American society, everything else will fall in line, no matter how many elections the Republicans win."

"When will Akilah be ready?" asked NBC president Judd Lockwood, former Oraculous chapter president at Columbia, turning toward Domokos.

The political future of Domokos's granddaughter had been increasingly discussed in progressive circles for a decade. It was well known that the timetable for her advancement rested solely on Domokos's shoulders. His own decidedly anti-religious, though supposedly open and tolerant, views were put to the test with her marriage to Muslim Aswad Samara and her personal conversion to Islam. Domokos had adapted himself to the change, something he would never have done had she married a Christian.

"I know many of you have been eyeing her prospects," said Domokos. "But she is far too young yet. Nor is the country ready for an openly avowed Muslim. Give it another several cycles. Besides, I don't think she relishes a tangle with ACH for the nomination. We can be patient."

"I thought she might be here with you."

"It seemed best, knowing her name could arise in discussions, that she not be present. She is an ambitious young lady. I have every confidence in her. But politics is often about waiting for the right time."

"You're not suggesting ACH for '24?" asked Lockwood. "She's not old enough. She'd be more of a dark horse than Newsome."

"She'll be thirty-five before the election," rejoined Penskey. "And she's the most ambitious member of the House. I think she's after my job!"

"What about that fellow in Washington you are high on, Brad?" asked Omar Suadela of Lloyds Bank. "What is his name?"

"Harrison Rhodes, mayor of Seattle," replied Dave Smythe, head of Microsoft. "Good friend of mine—native of Seattle. Jay knows him too. He's tight with Joe."

Amazon CEO Jay Izara, Oraculous alum from UCLA and personal protégé of Talon Roswell, nodded. "He's a good man," he said.

"From any other state he might be a VP possibility. But Washington's a lock for us. The ticket won't need him," said New York Governor Stanton Garrett, another of many whose education had been financed by Palladium and who was now a member of its seventy-two. "But we might talk about your fellow Rhodes, or Pérez for that matter, in '28 or '32."

"By then, no matter what happens in '24," said Penskey, "you can take it from me, ACH will be throwing her weight around. She will be a force to contend with."

"We also have to keep on the alert for future appointments to join us on the Court," said Frey. "It's never too soon."

"Long term," said Domokos, weighing in once more. "I'm not concerned about the presidency. In the larger plan, we have to focus on the statehouses and local judiciary appointments. Getting constitutional amendments through will require the states, not just Congress."

"That's where men like Rhodes will be necessary," said Amazon's Izara.

"But Washington's state houses are secure," rejoined Governor Garrett, "just like ours. The difficulty will be in the south and central states. We have to break the Bible Belt problem once and for all."

"I'm not sure I see the difficulty," now said aging Talon Roswell. "If you normalized same-sex marriage as easily as you did, not to mention transgender athletics, my God, you could push through anything! Constitutional amendments will be child's play after the elimination of gender from human anatomy. Not that I quite understand the reasoning myself. But it's clear the public will accept anything. Can you imagine," he added chuckling, "if the country had been ready for it and if he had had his sexual epiphany sooner, Bruce Jenner could have made a comeback in his thirties and won Olympic gold in the *woman's* pentathlon. Think what a display that would make in his trophy cabinet—a man's *and* woman's gold medal side by side!"

Though laughter went around the room, the three lesbians and two transgenders in the group, not to mention half a dozen gay men, found little humor in it. These included Adair Buttenby, himself a potential presidential hopeful.

"You'll have to forgive my father," said Storm Roswell. "He's from another generation. As a track enthusiast he watched Bruce Jenner's gold medal performance. Knowing what a powerful man he was, he still struggles a bit pretending he is a woman. But—"

"*Pretending?*" interrupted Buttenby pointedly. "*He . . . man . . . woman*—listen to yourself!"

"Oh, right—sorry. I forgot myself. My father still struggles, I should say, with the fact that Caitlyn now is a woman. But I'm working on him, right Dad?" he said, glancing at his father.

"We old dogs just take a little longer to learn new tricks," nodded Talon.

"Mr. Roswell is right about one thing," said Redley Skopes, Meta's guru of public information guiding Facebook's rebranding phase, rescuing the discussion from further awkwardness. "These things won't be a problem. Working with Diana and Jay and Judd, not to mention my humble efforts, we will make sure the public believes exactly what we all want it to."

"As has already been proven," nodded Domokos. "After same-sex marriage and gender neutrality, such things as the banning of Christian literature, open borders, reparations, replacement theory, Cuban and

Puerto Rican statehood, elimination of Social Security for the wealthy, CRT, deepening white guilt, minimum national income—these will all be easy enough. By then we will have completely overhauled the country's educational curriculum to eliminate white bias and reframe our history."

He paused briefly, then smiled.

"We could go so far as to throw out the Constitution and Supreme Court altogether if we wanted to!" he added. "After a ten-year campaign to convince the public the Constitution is a white supremacist, pro-slavery, Christian document, and that the Supreme Court is too subject to the personal whims of conservatives, the people will clamor for them to be tossed on the scrapheap. And we will humbly say, 'We can take care of that, thank you very much.' We could abolish Congress if we wanted! People will believe what we tell the media to tell them to believe."

"Ten years—it would take less than five!" laughed Google's Sorrell.

"Careful, we don't want to go that far!" put in Dr. Sonrab Bahram, son of the late Nasim Bahram.

"His point is well taken, however," said Bardolf. "Even with all our cultural advances, even we might not fully realize how gullible the public is."

"I agree," nodded NBC's Lockwood. "Look how effortlessly we turned the media into our mouthpiece after Walter Cronkite. The eager young people who work in our newsrooms and for our agencies are ambitious pawns. They don't even know the difference between news and propaganda. Our allies in the university journalism departments have made sure of that. They report what is handed to them. Most of them actually believe it," he added, laughing.

A brief silence fell. The next voice to be heard commanded the attention of the room even more forcefully than that of Domokos. He had listened quietly the whole time and was now ready to hold court.

"With the exception of Antifa and Black Lives Matter, which served our purposes at one end of the spectrum," said the former president, "our agenda has managed to remain mostly invisible until we have it securely in place and there's no going back. Yet the sweeping transformations we began during my years, seen in the light of US history, are indeed radical. Though we avoid calling attention to that fact, inoculating the public by normalizing one idea at a time, I think we do well to remember that we are seeking nothing less than a wholesale transformation of everything America has represented, exactly as Viktor has said. Even with public gullibility, pushback and resistance will occasionally be inevitable. The power of white authority will not die easily, nor will the country relinquish its affection for its Christian heritage. Even if we have to continue playing the Christian game for a season, we cannot lose sight of the methods that have brought us so far. Our radicalism may be more soft-spoken than Lenin's, but we cannot forget Alinsky's Rules. We must continue to use them shrewdly, cleverly, and invisibly to slowly and quietly reshape the American myth."

"Do you really think the Ten Rules still apply after all this time?" asked Skopes. "It seems that our control of social media renders them obsolete."

"They work in concert, to be sure. But the Rules still represent our marching orders against racist conservatism and homophobic evangelicalism. Alinsky's tactics *always* work. Attack them by their failure to keep their own rules—imperative with Christians—pretend our numbers are greater than they are, keep them fearful and off balance, seize the initiative and force them onto the defensive, and above all— ridicule, ridicule, ridicule. Trump may have been a blowhard, but he rode Alinsky's Rule 5 all the way to the White House. He was a radical too, in his own way, and a master of ridicule. He utilized more of Saul's methods than I'm sure he realized. Hillary was well-schooled in Alinsky's methods too. Her basket of deplorables was classic ridicule, as was my own guns and religion remark, though I got hammered pretty good by Hillary for it!" he added laughing. "But I learned my lesson. Throughout my presidency we used subtle ridicule in a thousand ways to keep the Republicans on the defensive. It's one of the main reasons we were able to remake societal mores so completely even without laws being passed."

As he listened, Loring Bardolf recalled hearing his father Slayton talk about Viktor Domokos and the 1973 speech that had ignited his vision, and led to the founding of the Alliance. He had heard his father's stories so often that they, and Viktor Domokos, took on the aura of legend. The priorities and dreams of their vision were drilled into him from before he could remember. Unlike his own daughter Amy, who had unaccountably been lured into a fanatical evangelical church, he had absorbed it all. It was good he had kept everything about Palladium from her, thought Loring. But her brother Michael was ready by his mid-teens.

He glanced briefly at his son sitting beside him, content to watch and listen. Mike was now twenty-one, graduated last year from Harvard, twice president of the university's chapter of Oraculous. In time Mike would place his own stamp on the future of the country as his grandfather and father had before him.

This was Mike's first such gathering. Unlike Amy, he had always been a tough kid who would do what was necessary to get ahead. He would rise quickly in this world, thought Loring. Nevertheless, he knew Mike was awed by the personalities in the room around him. He had introduced him to Viktor years ago. The older man took an instant liking to his son. But this was Mike's first meeting with the former president and most of these other major players on the world stage. But Mike was also a bit cocky. Loring would bring him along slowly so he didn't get above himself.

Get used to it, Mike, thought Loring wryly. *Within three decades, half of these men and women will be gone. Those who sit in their places will be looking to you for direction. You may be the one, not me, who presides over the half-millennium when your grandfather's dream will at last be a reality.*

44

GRADUATION AND THE FUTURE

2022–2024

DIVERGING SPIRITUALLY all the more from the sister who had for so long been his closest friend, Ward Hutchins entered Portland Seminary at George Fox University after his graduation from the new Cal Poly Humboldt. In much the same way that eyes were taking note of his former apartment mate in the sphere of Washington politics, Ward's energy and dynamism quickly earmarked him as a young man to watch in the world of evangelicalism.

Mark Forster, meanwhile, the soft-spoken and least ambitious member of the foursome, left California's north coast and returned to the gold country foothills. There he took two years, dividing his time between the Circle F and Bar JG ranches, reflecting and praying about his future as he worked for his father and his father's friend David Gordon.

He tried to keep in touch with his collegiate friends. But their responses to his messages and emails and letters became infrequent and eventually dried up altogether. Within a short time the others were on the fast track to success. Mark was no longer part of their world. His disappearance into obscurity, his seeming lack of drive, and his disinterest in making a name for himself, made it clear that their life roads and his diverged, not in a yellow wood but somewhere in the pine and redwood forests of northern California.

When Mark Forster took his first ride to the Bar JG the day after his return, David beheld him with new eyes. Though they had visited often during the past several years and saw one another every time Mark came home from college, he was suddenly struck with the obvious fact that Mark was a youth no longer. The light of maturity shown in his eyes. David thought of the day he had challenged Mark with the passage from 1 Timothy. Now he saw standing before him the fulfillment of what he had seen in the spirit that day. His young protégé, son of his best friend, was well on the road to spiritual manhood.

Working under the hot California sun, Mark added another combined several inches in height, shoulders, and biceps, enjoyed working side-by-side with his father, and continued to grow rapidly in his Christian faith under David's influence. Though his father was not spiritually expressive like his friend, and thus their influences were different, Mark came to recognize the two as complementary mentors of character, and was all the more grateful for his privilege to have grown up under two such men.

Mark's future came up frequently in conversations with his father and with David. It was more difficult to talk about God's leading with his father. The conversations at home focused on the practicalities of making a living, putting his education to use, where he wanted to live, even the future of the ranch. Mark's mother, of course, who met her on several visits to Arcata and was delighted with the northern California native, was anxious to know where Grace Thornton fit into her son's plans.

To her questions, Mark only smiled and answered cryptically, "We are talking, Mom."

"About marriage?"

"Let's just say about the future. We both want to do what God wants us to do. Grace will finish her degree this year. She is thinking of devoting a year to missions work before we decide anything."

"Missions—where?"

"She's applied for an internship with Missionary Aviation Fellowship in Mexico next year."

"What do you think about it?"

"I want her to do what she feels God is leading her to do," replied Mark. "I would never stand in the way of that. I want us to spend our lives together, but I'm not that interested in the mission field. Those are the kinds of things we have to work out. Maybe God will lead me into missions, or maybe she'll work with MAF for a year and decide he has another direction for her to pursue."

"Such as with you, I hope. If a woman loves a man, that's the only future she ought to think of."

"These are new times, Mom. Young women have plans and dreams and goals of their own. Sure, marriage is part of that, but not the only part. I love that Grace has ambition and wants to use her skills for the Lord and to help people."

When Mark was with David, on the other hand, the conversations usually took a more spiritual direction.

"I don't know, David," Mark was saying one day as they were riding beside one another leading some of David's cattle out to pasture. "I can't help thinking I'm supposed to graduate from college and know what I want in life and set out on a career and never look back."

"Who laid down such an expectation?" replied David. "I know of no such rule."

"Isn't that the way it's done?"

"I'm sure that's true for some."

"It's what my friends are doing."

"Maybe that's not what God has in mind for you. He may lead you differently."

"But how is he leading me?" said Mark in a tone betraying uncertainty. "If only I could get some clear idea of what he wants me to do with my life. Now Grace is down in Mexico flying for MAF."

"She's a pilot?" asked David in surprise.

"I know," chuckled Mark. "Kind of amazing. And I can't help wondering if . . . I don't know . . . maybe I'm supposed to join her."

"Are you drawn to the mission field?"

"Not really—not *foreign* missions, at least. I guess I want to help people here in our own country—help people know God."

"Don't forget one of God's primary methods of accomplishing his purposes—*time*," rejoined David. "He doesn't usually send telegrams. He takes time to make his will known. Being in a rush is one of the most common causes of *mistaking* God's leading, not discerning it. People who are in a hurry do not hear very well from God. Maybe he is getting you ready?"

"Ready for what?"

"Ah—the sixty-four-thousand-dollar question!" smiled David, glancing over from where he sat in the saddle. "Whatever it is, it will be better than you can imagine."

"How can you know that?"

"Because you have committed your way to him. You are seeking what *he* wants for your life. If you were seeking your *own* will, I would not say that. When they graduate from college, most young people are seeking their own will, not God's. It is easier for them. Pursuing one's own will is the easiest thing in the world. But you are not seeking your own will. You have a much more difficult road to walk."

Mark thought about his words.

"You remember my friend Ward," he said. "He visited here over Easter break two years ago?"

"Of course," replied David. "A dedicated young man, enthusiastic for the Lord. How is he doing?"

"Very well, as far as I know, though his emails are sporadic. He's in seminary in Portland. He seems to love it."

"Seminary . . . he's planning on the pastorate?"

"That's his goal. He'll be good at it too. He's personable and excited, outgoing, loves people."

"Assets for a pastor, certainly. Do you feel he is one who has sought God's will in making his plans, or his own?"

"He is the most dedicated Christian I have ever known other than you. He wants to minister to God's people. How can that not be God's will?"

"I sincerely hope it is. But the church draws many who are seeking their own wills just as does business or finance or politics or academia. Wanting to be in what is called 'ministry' is no guarantee that one is in

God's will. Christian ministries are breeding grounds for the flesh no less than any other endeavor in life. The pastorate, especially, is not by its nature the most ideal environment for the crucifixion of the flesh, or, in Kempis's words, the best setting in which to nurture the imitation of Christ."

Mark thought about his words for a minute.

"I know there is a lot wrong with the church," he said slowly as he tried to formulate his thoughts. "You have shared some of your misgivings with me, especially about big mega-churches. I suppose I share those concerns. I'm not sure about Ward. I think he may be drawn to the rock concert atmosphere more than I am. But I know his heart. I know how deeply he loves the Lord and wants to serve him. It seems God needs people like Ward to bring the church back to its foundations, to make a difference in people's lives the right way—not revering the institution but calling people to obedience."

"I couldn't agree more," said David. "Sadly, such influences in the pulpits of Christendom are few and far between. I'm not sure how much those influences can be heard in the midst of the rock concert atmosphere, as you call it."

"Isn't that all the more reason people like Ward, and perhaps I, *should* be such voices in the church—trying to quiet the din and make voices like Kempis's heard?"

"It is a worthy objective. Honestly, Mark, I am not sure it is possible. It may be. Only God knows. But I have my doubts."

David paused and eyed Mark quizzically.

"Are you thinking of following your friend's lead?" he asked.

"I have to admit I am," replied Mark. "I hope you won't be disappointed in me."

"Oh, Mark—never! If God is leading you into the ministry, I will back you 100 percent! Maybe you will be the one to prove me wrong. Maybe you will be the one to show that Kempis can get into the marrow of the church to help quell the spirit of pride and self-satisfaction so endemic in mega-evangelicalism. How thrilled I would be for you to succeed in such a wonderful endeavor."

"Well, I'm not there yet," laughed Mark.

"You obviously must be feeling a leading in that direction."

"A *leaning*, perhaps. I don't know that I would call it a definite *leading* yet. But the idea of making a difference, as I said, of helping people see the true nature of the church and what the priorities of the church should be, introducing them to men like Kempis and Drummond and MacDonald and your friend Marshall—that excites me. People need such influences in the church."

"They do indeed."

"Can MacDonald and Kempis and Marshall penetrate the country club atmosphere of evangelicalism?"

"Again, the sixty-four-thousand-dollar question," replied David seriously. "As I said, I have my doubts. But I would love for you to be the one to prove it can be done."

They rode along some distance in silence. The only sound was the rhythmic clomping of their horses' hooves on the hard-packed dirt of the road beneath them.

"I remember vividly what you shared with me that day from 1 Timothy," said Mark. "I've never forgotten the words as you read them—'*Command and teach these things.*' At first I could hardly imagine that God could say that to me. But they never left me. I now believe it was God speaking that challenge through you. And yes, more and more I am wondering if it is through the ministry he wants me to fulfill it."

David did not reply. In spite of the enthusiasm he had tried to convey, such was not the path he would choose for his young friend. But he could not overlay whatever spiritual counsel he might give with his own predilections, biases, or opinions any more than he already had. Mark might be young, but his heart was pointed toward God's True North. Therefore David could, and would, trust him to be led by that internal compass without interfering in the process with too many of his own thoughts.

Walking back to the farmhouse from the barn after their ride, they saw David's mother running out of the house.

"David, David," she called, "come—hurry!"

He and Mark broke into a run for the house.

"Larke called. Heather's in the hospital. She's in critical condition."

David ran inside and hurried to the phone. Mark and Isobel stood waiting.

"I see . . . we'll be praying, Larke . . . yes, of course—I'm on my way. I'll be there in an hour or less. I'm leaving now."

He hung up. "Sorry, Mark," he said. "We'll have to cut this short. Stirling and Larke's granddaughter is hanging by a thread at Sutter Hospital in Roseville. I've got to go."

"Of course, David. I'll see you next time."

45

FATEFUL RIDE

AUGUST 2023

NINE-YEAR-OLD HEATHER Marshall, daughter of Stirling and Larke Marshall's son Timothy and wife, Jaylene, had always been energetic, rambunctious, and inquisitive. All infants and children are curious. But she came out of the womb as inheritor of her mother's intense, almost paranormal curiosity about everything around her.

As her so-called miracle baby, Jaylene was granted the extra blessing of a daughter who seemed to have fully inherited not only her curiosity but her enormous intellect. Heather was beginning to read by two. Almost simultaneously as she began talking, she seemed to recognize the connection between the sound of spoken words and the look of those same words on a page. Without being pushed to do so, by first grade she was reading hundred-page books and adding multiple rows and columns of numbers. Early IQ tests were out of the question just as Jaylene's was as a girl. Heather's parents were prodded by others to start her into second grade at six, or possibly even third.

They wanted her to enjoy a normal childhood, however, and kept to a normal school schedule. Had it not been for their own efforts, both being teachers themselves, Heather might easily have become bored, and possibly have languished far behind her ability. But they supplemented what the classroom could provide, working closely with Heather's teachers, all of whom recognized her advanced intellect, with plenty to satisfy Heather's enormous hunger to learn. A stranger to the home, listening in on their family discussions, might have assumed the family comprised of three PhDs rather than two.

Heather's curiosity about the natural world, however, differed from her mother's in being almost entirely focused within the animal kingdom in general and horses in particular. It was no surprise that those first books she read were stories about people and horses. All girls go through horse stages. But Heather was born with an almost abnormal passion for horses.

Though living in Roseville on the fringes of Sacramento's sprawling and ever-expanding metropolis, Timothy and Jaylene sought to give her what opportunities were available among the dozens of ranches and stables scattered through the foothills east of the city. Their favorite, owned by Pearl and Dewitt West from their church, was located a few miles south of Auburn east of the Folsom-Auburn road, where the flat California valley rose through rolling hills into the gradually more rugged Sierra foothills.

Heather was comfortable in a saddle by five, and by seven was riding and jumping like a seasoned horsewoman. Her connection to almost every horse she climbed on was uncanny. The moment an animal felt Heather on its back and heard her voice, they seemed to move as one. Pearl was already discussing with her parents how far they wanted to pursue Heather's dream, confident that she had a future in gymkhana, dressage, and a variety of competitive events.

The presentation of a horse of her own—a six-month-old chestnut mare with which she established a special bond at the West ranch from the day of its birth—on her eighth birthday was one Heather looked back on as the most supremely happy day of her life. Pearl had asked her to name the newborn filly, which Heather dubbed Nutmeg.

Now Nutmeg was her very own.

It was a ride along the trails of the West ranch a little over a year later that changed Heather's life, and that of her family, forever.

Neither Timothy nor Jaylene were fond of riding. Sometimes they took Heather to the Wests and left her for the day, which delighted Pearl. On other occasions one or both of her parents waited at the house for her to enjoy a ride of an hour or two. She was still a little young to be sent out alone into the hill trails east of the stables. But both Pearl and Dewitt were confident enough in her ability to turn her loose in the expansive pastures surrounding the house and stables.

One day in the autumn of 2023, Dewitt West was slated to lead a group of four college young people from Sacramento for an afternoon's trail ride. Heather was helping about the place for the day. She eagerly jumped at the chance to go along.

"I'll lead," Dewitt told Heather as they saddled their mounts. "You bring up the rear. These aren't experienced riders. So keep an eye out. Shout to me if we need to stop or slow down or if any of them seem nervous."

They set out from the stables forty minutes later. Dewitt led northward through the pasture, then over gentle hills which gradually took them into a lightly forested region where the trail climbed to about eight hundred feet before making a wide, curving semi-circle through the trees back down the ridge, crossing two streams where they tumbled toward the north fork of the American River, then returned to the ranch from the east. At a leisurely pace suitable for beginners, it was a ride of about an hour and a half.

It was a hot day, easily ninety-five degrees as they entered the shade of the trees. The shadows and sunlight played tricks on the eyes as they left the open pastureland. Dewitt saw no danger below his horse's hooves as he passed, and the rider following also continued without incident.

The third horse in line, however, saw a movement on the ground out of the corner of its eye. In sudden fright, it leapt ahead. A cry of alarm escaped its rider as she clutched the saddle horn. Somehow, she managed to keep her seat. Her two companions behind her saw what happened. They grabbed on for dear life as their horses also lurched over the huge rattlesnake now stretched six feet across the trail.

Bringing up the rear, however, and startled by the sudden panic of the other horses, Nutmeg shrieked in terror and reared dangerously straight up on her hind legs.

Heather had no time to brace herself. She fell straight back out of the saddle and toppled to the ground. Nutmeg leapt high over the instantly coiled rattler just as Heather hit the hard packed dirt on top of it.

The terrified cries from horses and riders already had Dewitt spinning around and jumping to the ground. He was by Heather's side in seconds.

He yanked her back and drew the pistol he always carried on such rides for exactly this reason.

Six explosions echoed through the forest as he emptied every chamber, kicked the dead rattler off the trail, and knelt at Heather's side.

She was moaning though barely conscious. Whether she had injured her back, he couldn't tell. But the tear in her Wranglers three inches above her left knee told him all he needed to know.

He threw the gun aside, grabbed the knife from his belt and frantically ripped at Heather's jeans. The two puncture marks were unmistakable. There was no stream or cold water nearby. He would have to do this the old-fashioned way.

"Courage, dear—this is going to hurt!"

Wincing himself, he sliced two deep slits at cross angles over the wound. Heather screamed as Dewitt bent down, put his mouth over the wound, and sucked hard, then spit out the blood mingled with yellow venom, did so again—and again, until what came was mostly red.

"Get off your horses!" he yelled to the four watching in obvious shock. "Hang onto your reins!"

Dewitt ripped off his shirt, made a cut with his knife, tore it into three lengths, wrapped one tightly over the bleeding wound and tied it tight around Heather's leg, then did the same with the other two in a tight tourniquet above the wound.

"Come over here, you two!" Dewitt shouted to the two boys. "You girls—take their reins."

The boys came forward more timidly than Dewitt liked.

"I'm going to mount," said Dewitt. "You two lift her up behind me."

He bent down to Heather.

"Heather, you've got to get on your feet," he said. He took hold of her lifeless hands and pulled her up. "We've got to get back to the ranch."

"Grab hold of her!" he said to the boys, then mounted.

"Okay, here we go—lift her up."

The boys struggled with Heather's limp form. Barely conscious, she weakly lifted her leg over the horse's back and stretched her arms around Dewitt's waist. Her two small white hands disappeared inside the grasp of his huge brown left hand.

"I've got to leave you!" he said to the four. "Call 911 on your cells. Tell them the DeWitt ranch south of Auburn!"

He grabbed his reins in his right hand and wheeled around. "Walk your horses back the way we came. Don't try to mount. If you don't know which way to go, stop and wait. I'll send someone for you."

He turned and dug in his heels. "Git-up!" he shouted. "Go, Amber—git, git!"

Wide-eyed and still stunned, the four would-be cowboys who had come to the stables for a leisurely ride watched as the horse and its two riders flew through the trees, clods flying up behind the receding hooves, and disappeared from sight.

Not knowing how long she would be gone, Timothy had only a few minutes earlier driven up the long driveway to the stables. He and Pearl were talking outside the house when they saw a single rider galloping toward them. There was no sign of the others.

Dewitt did not slow. "Timothy!" he shouted as he came on. "Come—now!"

Timothy ran forward as Dewitt reined in. At last, he saw Heather's small form behind him.

"Take her," said Dewitt, loosening his hold on Heather's hands.

The moment Heather's limp form was hanging in Timothy's arms, Dewitt leapt to the ground.

"Snake bite, Timothy," he said. "It's bad! Even if the kids got through, the ambulance will never get her in time. You'll have to take her. Get her to Sutter."

They ran toward Timothy's waiting car. Dewitt opened the back door. Timothy laid her on the seat. The two men did the best they could to strap her in with the seat belts.

"Sutter—off Roseville Parkway where Sunrise ends. They had a snakebite earlier in the week. They should have serum on hand. Drive like the wind, Timothy!"

Timothy climbed in. A second later the car revved to life.

"I'll call them—they'll be waiting for you!" said Dewitt. He slammed the door and jumped back.

Timothy ground down on the accelerator, skidding the car in a half circle throwing up gravel behind it, then sped back down the driveway as Pearl and Dewitt raced for the house.

Driving as recklessly as he dared on the winding road from the ranch to Newcastle, Timothy scarcely slowed when he reached the interstate, turned left up the ramp and was passing eighty in twenty seconds, flying south toward Roseville. Three minutes later a siren came screaming behind him. He glanced in the rearview mirror and saw the flashing lights bearing down on him.

What was best to do! The hospital was still too far. He could never make it all the way without a serious incident.

He began to slow, rolling down his window, and tried to motion the CHP car alongside. Still the sirens and lights followed.

"Pull over! Pull over now!" came a voice over the police bullhorn.

He had no choice. Timothy slammed on his brakes, and half-skidded to a stop on the shoulder of the highway. Trying to stay calm, he jumped out of the car, hands raised, and walked quickly back toward the police car as it came to a stop behind him.

"Stay where you are!" came the order on the bullhorn.

Slowly the door opened. A highway patrolman stepped out, his hand on the butt of his pistol.

"I'm on my way to Sutter!" called Timothy. "I have my daughter—she's been bit by a rattler!"

The patrolman ran forward, took one look at Heather unconscious in the back seat, a bloody bandage around her leg, then raced back to his own vehicle.

"Follow me," he said as he ran by Timothy. "We'll get you there in one piece."

By the time Timothy was again behind the wheel, the police car tore past him, siren blaring and lights flashing. It was all Timothy could do to keep up as his speedometer went past ninety and approached a hundred.

They pulled up in front of Sutter's emergency room eleven minutes later. A gurney and hospital staff were outside waiting.

46

∧FTERNOON
WITH ∧ LEGEND

SPRING 2024

D AVID GORDON continued to pray for clarity, for himself and for Mark. As he did, the face of Stirling Marshall rose before his mind's eye. He needed to bring together again the aging man of God and his young neighbor who was just embarking on his kingdom journey. It could prove a divine appointment of eternal significance.

The two had met previously during one of Mark's frequent visits to the Bar JG years before. They had not crossed paths since Mark's departure for Humboldt with an autographed copy of Stirling's *Unspoken Commandments* in his suitcase.

With Stirling and Larke Marshall over eighty years old, most visits with David now took place at their Dorado Wood home. David managed to prevail on them, however, to make the drive into the foothills again for another weekend at the ranch. He hoped for the opportunity, he said, for them to visit again with his friend and neighbor Mark Forster.

Mark was excited at the prospect of the visit. Having read several of Stirling Marshall's books, supplied by David during his college years, he would be better able, he hoped, to glean from the aging author's wisdom. Knowing that the two Marshalls were being driven up to David's on Friday evening by one of their sons, Mark rode over to the ranch on Saturday morning, planning, at David's urging, to spend the day and night with him.

David heard Mark ride up. He went outside and the two unsaddled Mark's horse.

"It is wonderful to see you again, Mark," said Stirling, standing on the porch as David walked back from the paddock.

The two shook hands.

"You have put on a few inches since I saw you last. That must have been, what . . . five or six years."

"Something like that," replied Mark. "You are looking well."

"Thank you—you are probably being kind, but at my age, I'll take it!" said Stirling, laughing lightly.

"What's your father up to today, Mark?" asked David as he led them inside.

"He's still trying to break that stubborn young mare," answered Mark.

"He's getting too old for that kind of thing. He ought to let you do it."

"Don't let him hear you say that? As I recall, you were in the saddle just last weekend doing exactly the same. You're hardly one to talk."

David laughed. "You have me there!"

"Besides," added Mark, "I could never match my dad in the saddle. I may be younger, but that mare would put me on the ground in three seconds."

They walked into the house where the smell of blackberry cobbler filled the kitchen.

"Hello, Isobel," said Mark, greeting David's mother. "—Hello, Mrs. Marshall," he added, turning to the stately lady beside her.

"How nice to see you, Mark. And please, Larke will suit me fine. We're not much on formality."

"How is your granddaughter?" asked Mark.

"We have several," replied Larke. "Which one?"

"The girl who was bit by the rattler last year?"

"That's Heather—she's doing better. But there will probably be permanent damage. The doctor says her leg may never fully heal. It may also affect her growth. Do you know Heather?"

"No, but I was here last fall when you telephoned and then David rushed off to the hospital."

"That was a terrible day. It was three days before we knew whether or not she would live. Her poor mother, our daughter-in-law, felt like she was Sarah having been given a child when she never thought she would have one, then to have it taken away. Oh, it tried her faith! But she tried to be a faithful Sarah herself, and God answered her prayers. But even though Heather did recover, she missed several months of school."

"But she is all right now?"

"An amazing girl. She's got such a good attitude about it all—and is begging her father and mother every day to let her get back on her horse!"

"Isn't that what they say—when you fall, get back on."

"The rest of you go on into the living room and have a chat," said Isobel. "I'll bring coffee and tea and then keep working on dinner."

"I don't know if David told you, Mr. Marshall—" began Mark as the four walked into the adjoining room.

"*Stirling*," interrupted Stirling. "You should pay attention to my wife."

"Sorry," laughed Mark. "I'll try to remember. What I was going to say is that besides your book on the commandments which I took with me to college, David sent me the *Phantasms* book a year or two later— what an amazing concept. I've wanted to tell you how much I enjoyed them both. Not just enjoyed them—that's a bland way of saying it. I've also read *Does Truth Matter?* And David gave me Drummond and Kempis. They all had a profound impact on my walk with God. They sat beside my bed all four years when I was away. I read in your commandments book and the *Imitation* every night and every morning."

"I am honored to be in such company."

"It will take me a lifetime to absorb all you said about the commands, the centered life, and the illusions of Christianity that produce unfaith not true faith."

"I am still trying to absorb those truths myself," rejoined Stirling. "They are lifetime truths. It is your friend Drummond—whom I call a friend in the Spirit as well—who said, 'The world is not a playground; it is a schoolroom. Life is not a holiday, but an education.'"

"I remember that passage."

"I look upon my book as an elementary school primer helping students in the ways of God to prepare for the upper division curriculum of Kempis and MacDonald."

"I would place yours with them, if you don't mind my saying so," said Mark. "At least so it has been for me. I know I will be reading them all for the rest of my life."

"I am humbled and grateful," replied Stirling softly.

Just then Isobel Gordon entered with a tray containing a coffee carafe and pot of tea. The four rose and poured out their preferences.

"Mark and I have been talking and praying together, Stirling," said David when they were seated again, "about his future. His heart's desire is to serve the Lord, but he has received no clear leading as yet. I thought you might have some words of counsel for a young man with his life ahead of him."

"It is a path we all must walk for ourselves," said Stirling. "God's leading is entirely individual. There are no templates."

"I don't know if David shared with you," said Mark, "but I am seriously praying about the ministry. One of my best friends in college is in seminary now. He and I were roommates and often talked about our futures."

"Do you feel led in that direction?" asked Stirling.

"I don't know. A nudge is about all it amounts to at this point."

"Then give the Lord time. My advice to young people is always the same—be in no hurry, pray for direction, and diligently do the work before you. At any given moment, where you are at present *is* God's will for you. God's will can rarely be discovered by focusing too much on the future. God's will dwells in the present—in the eternal *now*. If you are a student, work diligently at your studies. If you are a ranch hand, be the most diligent ranch hand you can be."

"That's me!" laughed Mark.

"And all the while be listening and attentive to the divine Whispers."

"Then how do you move into his will for your future?"

"One step at a time. By taking the next step in the eternal now . . . then the next . . . and the next. Listening steps. Obedience steps. Out of the succession of *next* steps, taken in response to the still small Voice, the future will open before you."

Mark sat absorbing the old man's words.

"Out of diligence, prayer, and patience, God makes his will known," said Stirling after a few moments. "Above all things, beware of the greener pastures syndrome—thinking that God's will must be somewhere *other* than where you presently find yourself. The present diligence and prayer mustn't be rooted in dissatisfaction. You may be exactly where God wants you for the moment. That is the glory of the eternal now. More will be revealed in time. But God's more does not emerge out of dissatisfaction but grows in the soil of diligence."

"Did you ever consider the pastorate?" asked Mark.

"No," replied Stirling. "I always wanted to teach history. It's all I ever wanted to do. I would never have made a good pastor. Two of our children are teachers as well. I think teaching is in the Marshall blood."

"I wish you could have met our son Timothy," said Larke. "He drove us up yesterday. He's a history professor just like his dad. He teaches at Jessup."

"Do you not drive?" asked Mark.

"Stirling still drives around town," said Larke. "But out on the interstate, we don't feel we should—the traffic is terrible and everyone drives much too fast. Timothy made us promise to call him when we need to go any distance. He calls himself our personal taxi service."

"A devoted son indeed," said David. "I need to get together with Timothy again too. I rarely see him at church anymore. I don't get down to services as often as I used to."

Mark turned again to Stirling. "Did any of your students ever seek your counsel about the ministry?" he asked.

"About their future, yes—the ministry no. I can't think of any, can you, dear?"

"I don't think so," answered Larke. "After Stirling retired from teaching, of course we had many letters from young people often asking advice about one thing or another."

"Mostly on points of doctrine, though, wouldn't you say?"

"Probably," nodded Larke.

"If someone had written—someone like me," said Mark, "asking your thoughts on pursuing a career in the pastorate, what would you have said?"

"I would not have been able to say anything specific—not knowing the young man personally."

He paused and thought a moment.

"I suppose I would say, follow God's leading. Only he can tell any individual what he should or should not do. Because I do know you somewhat, though not well, I would add this word of caution—beware of letting an institution make you its slave. When that happens, the ministry becomes more about the church than the commands of Jesus. Much of what is taught in seminary, probably *most* of what is taught, is church-centric rather than Christ-centric. If seminary is the necessary path you must walk to get where God is taking you, do not let it steal from you the heart of why you want to serve God's people in the first place."

Mark took in his words thoughtfully. "I need to pass that along to my friend," he said. "Actually," he added, taking a folded piece of paper and pen out of his pocket, "if you don't mind, could you repeat what you just said. I want to write it down."

Stirling did so.

When Mark finished the brief transcription, Stirling chuckled to himself. "Being forced to say those words again," he said, "as close as I recall to what I actually said the first time, sent my brain off in several directions. You asked if any of my students ever asked me about seminary. I just remembered one young man, a student of mine who paid me a visit at the university several years later. He had just completed seminary and was embarking on his first pastorate, though I had no idea he was moving in that direction when he was an under-graduate. There was a terrible incident when he was a student and I had just joined the faculty. It nearly destroyed his faith for a time. So I was heartened to see him again and delighted with his walk with God. Because of our past together, he wanted to share his story with me. We had him over for dinner, remember, Larke."

"I do—yes," replied his wife. "He was full of vision and enthusiasm to serve God and bring life and vibrancy to the churches where God led him to serve. I've forgotten his name."

"Wallace Chisholm—a very energetic young man," laughed Stir-ling. "I was tired by the end of the evening from just listening to all his ideas and plans."

"And was he successful?" asked David.

A poignant expression came over Stirling's face. "The church nearly destroyed him. I have never seen him again but have managed to follow the threads of his career. He is in the Midwest as far as I know. He served in several churches, but the system, the organization, the power brokers which every church has, the Ally, I call them, all combined to thwart everything he tried to do. The Ally within organized Christen-dom, as I heard it called years ago,[9] is committed to preserving its hold on power at all costs. When a visionary minister does not bow to the system, that system will find devious ways to exact its revenge."

"What became of him?" asked Mark.

"As far as I have been able to discover, there were questions about the orthodoxy of his beliefs at the last church where he served. Rumors and gossip circulated, most of it untrue. His poor wife nearly had a nervous breakdown at being shunned by the respectable and import-ant women of the church. Wallace eventually resigned and now has a counseling practice."

"Church people can be unbelievably cruel," said Isobel. "We have seen it in Foothills Gospel. Though my husband and I helped start the church many years ago, we have been disturbed by some of the direc-tions the church later took. Pelham never lost faith in the ministry of Foothills, but there were things he felt diverged from the original vision we and the others who were with us had in the beginning."

"All the more reason, Mark," said Stirling, "that you are prayerfully sober-minded as you count the cost of what you are considering. Many well-meaning and optimistic men get sucked into the spiritual black hole of organizational Christendom without realizing it until it is too late. If God is calling you into the ministry, it is a high calling. But also a perilous one. It is difficult to keep life at the center as your focus when you are dependent on the organized church for your livelihood. You must recognize that most within the organized church will not share your focus. Your most determined efforts will be powerless to change that fact. Your ministry will be to the 25 percent. If you succeed in bringing life at the center to that 25 percent, yours will be a wildly successful ministry that will bring rejoicing in the kingdom. Once you start preaching the commands, however, and *obedience* to the commands, there will be repercussions from the 75 percent. The challenge to obedience always brings opposition."

The room fell silent as they pondered Stirling's words.

47

THE MANDATE
OF THE COMMANDS

IT WAS a quiet, peaceful afternoon at the ranch. The lawns, gardens, pastures, and fields—all interlinked by wide footpaths suitable for walking or riding—was such that one could wander for an hour and encounter no one. Each of the five was able to relish in the peaceful solitude, enjoying the others' presence, yet in no hurry to fill the silence with words.

A while later Larke and Isobel were seen in their favorite chairs on the wide porch outside the kitchen chatting away as they watched a newborn colt with its mother in the corral by the barn. Their conversation paused as they glanced in the distance, a look of quiet pleasure on their faces to see the three men—of three generations yet each of the three regulated by the same inner spiritual compass, their backs turned but obviously deep in conversation, walking slowly toward the woods in the distance.

After a sumptuous afternoon dinner followed by Isobel's cobbler topped with scratch-made vanilla pudding, a few eyelids grew heavy and gave way to quiet dozing in the living room. Sometime later Stirling confessed his interest in seeing if he could still ride. The men went out to the stables and saddled three horses and set out.

The day advanced, gave way to dusk, and again they found themselves seated in the living room, weary yet full from the richness of the day. A light snack, in which the cobbler figured prominently, was set on the kitchen table. With the appetite of a young man, Mark warmed Isobel's heart by returning for a second portion. Conversations waned as darkness fell.

As they were about to break for the night and head to their rooms, Mark asked the elder statesman of the group a question which, had it been earlier in the day, could well have resulted in another two hours of fascinating discussion.

"Will you be going to church tomorrow?" Mark asked.

Stirling smiled. "We don't go in for church much these days," he said. "Our son Timothy is active in Foothills Gospel—he's an elder now. And our daughter Cateline lives in Marysville, an hour from us, and thinks we ought to be more active. But we've got our hands full trying to *be* the Church. We do not find *attending* church particularly helpful to the process."

"I'm sorry," said Mark, "I'm not sure I follow you."

Stirling smiled. Across the room, David's eyes shown. This is exactly what he had hoped for. He knew young Mark Forster would never forget this day.

"Upper and lower case," said Stirling.

"Of course," rejoined Mark. "How could I be so dense! I remember the contrast from your book—the local organization with its weekly activities, and the invisible worldwide community of living stones being built into God's eternal temple."

"Right you are!" exclaimed Stirling. "I could not have said it better myself, though I suppose I did say *something* along those lines in the book."

"You did, and very powerfully. But as I recall, you spoke at some length about the functions of each within the body of Christ, saying that the activities and ministries of the lowercase church build and contribute to the development of God's eternal Church."

"I did say that, yes."

"Unless I misunderstood you, just now it seemed you were implying the local church is *not* helpful toward the advancement of the eternal Church. Did I misunderstand?"

"No, you understood me perfectly," replied Stirling. "And you are right in that what you read in the book appears to contradict such a view. That was written some thirty-five years ago. I have continued to grow, asking God's Spirit for further enlightenment on the matter. As that process has progressed, I have come to feel somewhat differently. I should make clear that I *continue* to pray for wisdom. I am well over eighty and I hope I will be able to make that statement until the day I die. The man whose ideas and perspectives, doctrines and viewpoints, are set in concrete is an inert dead spiritual being. Unless new and deeper thoughts and ideas and higher revelations of truth, are constantly infusing God's men and women with the energy of becoming, they are not growing disciples in the full sense of the word. All that to say, I am far less sanguine now that the organizational church does contribute in a significant way to the development and *becoming* and revelation of the eternal Church that is and will be the body of Christ."

"You seemed to imply a minute ago that you actually think it hinders it."

"I do believe church, lowercase, often hinders the development of the Church, uppercase. Not always, but often. I find one loses sight of the individual mandate when part of a large group, even a group calling itself a church."

"The mandate?"

"The mandate of the commands."

The words were so stark, so unyielding, so impervious to being misunderstood, so powerful in their simplicity, they hung in the air as if reverberating in the silence. After several long seconds, Stirling spoke again.

"Christianity is not corporate," he said. "It is individual. All the Lord's commands are individual. Those commands represent our mandate. That the local church may play a role in individual men and women recognizing their role in the eternal Church I do not doubt. But the church of man too often turns the church into a corporate entity which is itself powerless to accomplish God's high work, and indeed often impedes it.

"That work is carried out by God's Spirit within the hearts of *individuals*. I repeat, there is no corporate mandate. In my opinion the high work in God's heart to accomplish would perhaps proceed more rapidly upon the earth without the church of man at all. I do not say without God's Church, but without the church of man. But as I say, I continue to pray for enlightenment. Please, do not take my thoughts on the matter as anything but that—*my* thoughts. Seek God's wisdom, young Forster. He will guide you into the truth he has for you."

After two years with his parents, much prayer both alone and with his father's friend, Mark Forster reached the decision that God was indeed leading him to follow in Ward's footsteps. He applied and was accepted into Portland Seminary for the fall, and made plans to join Ward, who would then be in his final year, in Oregon.

Mark had not seen Grace during the whole of the second of those years. After she graduated, she spent most of the year in Mexico. They wrote furiously, and as her commitment to MAF drew to a close, Grace knew that her future was with Mark, not flying into jungles.

His proposal by mail was made official with the presentation of a ring on the day of her return in April of 2024.

Mark Forster and Grace Thornton were married in Eureka in July, with all four of their parents and many friends in attendance, then made preparations for the move to Oregon and the beginning of their life together.

David Gordon kept his own counsel, but could not help feeling Mark's spiritual depth and level of scriptural understanding would contribute more to the kingdom elsewhere than in the pulpit.

Laura Forster, however, was thrilled at the prospect of having a pastor for a son.

48

HOW SHOULD CHRISTIANS RESPOND TO THE TIMES?

LATE 2020s

STIRLING MARSHALL neither feared death nor courted it. He knew he and Larke were at an age when anything might happen. They were healthy, vital signs and cholesterol good, heart and lungs in acceptable working order. Except for occasionally painful back and knees if they walked too far or spent too much time in the garden, they had no complaints. Stirling was writing as much as ever. And though Larke kept contact with some of her former students, now and then taking on one or two young pianists to get them started, mostly the music floating out of her studio these days was her own.

Yet they believed in preparedness. They spoke frequently about the advance of the years and the plans they needed to make, and what ought to be their contingency plan should one of them need extensive medical care. Mostly they discussed such things so they would not suffer the added trauma of not being ready to face it should death come suddenly. They were always aware of the Kempis injunction, "Lead your life that death may never take you unprepared."

Thus, along with wanting to be emotionally prepared for the inevitable parting with one another, their cemetery plots and headstone were paid for. They felt it incumbent upon them to make as many arrangements as possible ahead of time to keep the burden of those decisions from their children.

In no sense were they waiting for death. They were enjoying life to the full, delighting in one another after sixty years of marriage more than they had after ten. They saw Timothy and Cateline and their families frequently, though visits with Woody, Graham, and Jane—scattered across the state and, in Jane's case, the country—were rare. Both were secretly praying that the other would be taken first—and from the most selfless of motives, not wanting the other to be left alone, each hoping they would be the one to bear that final burden.

Stirling and Larke had been reevaluating the scriptural basis for the organized church for more than three decades, from even before their move north from Santa Barbara. As a result, as Stirling had intimated to Mark Forster, they did not have what would be termed an active church life. Truth be told, they had almost no church life at all in the way the words were commonly understood. Whenever they visited small and unassuming congregations, the entreaties to return and become more "involved" were well-meaning and sincere. But they were not in search of a "church home," but rather humble brethren of a far higher community than made by the hands of man. Such was the road they chose to walk, not from dissatisfaction with any particular church or denomination, nor because they were in search of some elusive ecclesiastical Eden, but because they felt that distancing themselves from all organizational attempts to represent Christ's eternal body was the right thing to do. From their study of Scripture, they had arrived at the belief that the lowercase church of man's design was never Christ's intended vehicle for the spreading of the gospel at all. They had slowly withdrawn from that world, therefore, not out of protest, but out of conviction.

As the years went by, Stirling and Larke remained in many ways more spiritually connected to David Gordon than to any of their own children other than Timothy and Jaylene. Under their influence during his twenties, thirties, and forties, David's understanding of God and his ways deepened until the expansive spiritual vision articulated in Stirling's corpus of writings could not be separated from his own. By the age of fifty, David Gordon had completely absorbed the legacy, priorities, and worldview of his spiritual mentor.

Living in Roseville, Timothy and Jaylene continued to be active in Foothills Gospel Ministries—where the Gordon name was still revered as among the founders of one of the area's leading evangelical megachurches. For his mother's sake, David remained passively connected with the affairs of the church. Timothy, Jaylene, and David encountered one another on occasion. Their respect was mutual, though their friendship could not yet be characterized as an intimate one.

After the weekend at the Bar JG, rekindling their affectionate friendship with David in the setting of his ranch, which they loved as a second home, the youthful dedication of young Mark Forster turned Stirling's thoughts reflectively toward his own future. Mark was hungry for input and counsel. Now Stirling found himself turning the advice he had given Mark upon himself.

"What do you want me to do, Lord?" became an even more constant prayer within Stirling's heart than before. "What are you stirring within me?"

Humbly recognizing the impact he had been privileged to exercise in David's life—witnessing that legacy expanding into yet another generation as David poured his spiritual vision into young Mark Forster—Stirling's prayers gathered ever more seriously about the question of what should characterize his final writings.

New generations would continue to arise. Young Mark Forster would grow and mentor young people in the ways of God. If the pastorate was indeed his calling, even if only to the 25 percent, Mark would be in a position to turn hearts to the divine Fatherhood for decades to come. The Deuteronomy vision of passing on God's truths and commands would continue, generation after generation, to a thousand generations of those who love God and keep his commandments.

Stirling was more keenly aware with every passing year how perilous the times had become. What might God want him to say before the curtain closed on his earthly days—to this present generation, to Mark Forster's generation, and to the following generations . . . to his granddaughter Heather and her generation and his other grandchildren and *their* children and grandchildren?

Might the end times actually be approaching? he wondered. *Silently, invisibly, in ways none of evangelicalism's prophetic gurus were capable of apprehending?*

His discussions with Larke and David, and even occasionally with Timothy, took on increasing import. Never one to link politics with faith, he came to recognize that perhaps they could no longer be viewed as distinct entities. As the church of man was increasingly lured into the deviancy of the times, was it even possible to address the future of the church without taking a stand against the degeneracy of the culture that the church had allowed to corrupt it?

With increasing urgency, he found himself wrestling with the fundamental question: What should be the dedicated Christian's response to the accelerating ungodliness of the times and the decline of the country he loved and the church of Christ into a pit of wantonness?

Could the two responses—to the world and to the church—be separated?

His concern for God's people—not recognizing how fatally the world was sweeping the church into oblivion—brought tears to his eyes. Organizational Christendom across its denominational spectrum had no idea of the cancer of worldliness eating away at its foundations.

He realized that David knew his heart more intimately than anyone but Larke, though he sensed Timothy and Jaylene were being drawn into that same deep fellowship of understanding. They were reading his books more regularly and asking about them, when they were written and what prompted them. More and more, too, their conversations focused on the high purposes of God. He rejoiced to see signs that Timothy understood his heart on a more profound level than before. Their youngest son was growing into readiness to carry on their legacy. He could only pray the other four would follow. If God pleased to give him a final message, Stirling now knew—and with the realization came profound thankfulness—that it would be delivered through David and Timothy together.

"Something is stirring within me," he said during one of David's visits to Dorado Wood when he asked Timothy to drive over from Roseville and join them for the evening. "I don't know what it is, but I sense it is coming . . . coming . . . a great good is coming . . . good is always coming, as the man said," he added with a smile.

"The Scotsman's influence betrays you, Dad," said Timothy.

"Very shrewd, Timothy, my boy," smiled Stirling. "Not many would pick up on the reference. I think you may know the Scotsman's words better than I do."

"I doubt that, Dad. But I do know that if you keep writing for much longer, you will have written more books than he did."

Stirling laughed. "I'm going to be ninety soon, Timothy," he said. "By then I will have outlived him by ten years. I'm not sure I have enough time left to catch up."

"Then David and Mom and Jaylene and I will do our best to keep you healthy and at your computer. Won't we, David?"

"We will, indeed! We need all the wisdom you can impart to us, Stirling," David added. "I'm praying for you to live to a hundred and write many more books."

Again Stirling laughed. "That is in the Lord's hands, as is whatever else he gives me to write."

"Perhaps your memoirs?" suggested David hopefully. "An autobiography?"

"I am giving something along those lines serious thought," nodded Stirling. "Though as I said, something else is bubbling around inside this brain of mine that may preempt it. As I said, I feel it coming, but it is not clarified yet."

In the meantime, until more clarity came, Stirling did as he mentioned and set to work on his memoirs, trying to tie his personal reminiscences of life with Larke into the story of their parents' lives. He told Timothy a little more of what he was attempting, explaining where the materials were located so that he—if he was so inclined—could continue the project if he was unable to.

49

NEW PASTORS

2024–2030

STARTING OUT their married life, Mark and Grace Forster did not anticipated the intensity of the Masters of Divinity program on which Mark had embarked. Nor the expense. Grace was fortunate to find a job as a teacher's aide for twenty-five hours a week—as close to full-time as could be expected. Mark had hoped to work part time as well, but with the heavy school load that proved impossible. They found a cheap one-bedroom apartment in Gladstone, scrimped and lived simply, and with a modest scholarship from the school, financial assistance from both sets of parents, and a small student loan, managed to meet their expenses for the first year.

Ward, of course, took Mark under his wing. The close association of the two friends ensured that Mark would be noticed. It was not long before everyone at George Fox knew Mark Forster as Ward Hutchins' friend. Now in his final year, Ward was gaining experience assistant pastoring in Oregon City. By the end of his first year, Mark was exploring similar options for himself.

He and Grace returned to California where they spent the summer at the Circle F. Grace had the time of her life learning to ride and generally becoming familiar with all the workings of a California cattle ranch. Mark and Grace visited often with David Gordon and volunteered as counselors for the junior high and the high school camps at Pinecroft, then returned to Portland in August, refreshed and enthusiastic for Mark's second year of divinity studies. By then Ward was gone and recommended Mark to take his place in Oregon City.

The following summer they remained in the Portland area for the summer, Mark working at the church full time, gaining valuable experience in the pulpit during the pastor's vacation. Even before his third and final year was complete, he was being contacted by churches throughout Oregon. The offers, however, were all for part-time or youth ministry positions none of which would pay enough for him and Grace to live on.

Meanwhile, Ward's star was on the rise. He was hired immediately out of seminary to pastor a modest-sized but growing independent congregation in Olympia, Washington. Still not yet thirty, Ward's dynamism quickly earned him a reputation in the state capital. It was not long before several notables in political circles were attending his church and became outspoken fans of the youthful evangelical firebrand. Though his forte was biblical exposition and prophecy rather than evangelism, some were comparing his pulpit style to the young Billy Graham who likewise began moving crowds with his oratory when still in his twenties.

Mark continued to explore his options. As the school year wound down, he was offered the pastorate of a forty-member church in North Bend, in the south of the state on the fabled Oregon coast. Though a small church, and though Grace would have to teach—and would earn more than him doing so—it was an actual pastoral position, the objective for which he had gone to seminary in the first place. He accepted the job.

Mark and Grace moved to North Bend immediately after his June graduation with a Master of Divinity degree, and began looking for a house to rent. They were there four years. Daughter Ginger was born their second year in North Bend in 2028, and son Craig followed two years later.

While Ward and Mark were pursuing their pastoral careers, the other two members of their Humboldt foursome were on the fast track to bigger and better things in the world of Washington law and politics. Both Jeff and Linda graduated from the University of Washington

School of Law the same year Ward graduated from seminary, passed the bar, and were soon on their way. Their family connections served them well.

Ward and Linda's brother, Sawyer, arranged for Linda to be hired as an assistant in the King County DA's office. She quickly rose in the ranks.

After two terms as mayor, Jeff's father was now president of Seattle's City Council and remained one of the most powerful men in the county. He easily arranged for Jeff to be hired in the legal department of Seattle's mayoral staff. By the time Jeff was thirty, with his father's connections to the former president and Jeff's obvious good looks and charisma, behind the scenes his father was quietly grooming him for the national spotlight.

An Offer

2031

GRACE FORSTER answered the phone in their North Bend home one evening in 2031. When she handed it to Mark a few seconds later, the voice at on the other end was the last he expected to hear.

"Hey, Mark, how's it going?"

"Ward!" he exclaimed. "It's great to hear from you—it's going well."

"You're happy?"

"Absolutely—Grace and I love it here. Small church, but fantastic people."

"Have you two started a family?"

"Daughter and son, three and one. What about you? Still in Olympia?"

"Not exactly—in transition actually. I'm headed about an hour north."

"That would mean Seattle."

"That's it. Things are happening fast up here. I can hardly keep up. I could use some help."

"Sure. I've loaded enough U-Hauls in my time. Grace and I have moved twice since we got here. Just let me know when, and we'll come up for the weekend. Grace has moved her share of furniture too."

"You missed my point," laughed Ward. "I'm taking over the pastorate of a big Seattle church—Puget Sound Vine Ministries."

"I've heard of it. That's the big time, Ward."

"You're right. It's a cushy pulpit, paid staff, expense account, the works. We're in the transition now. They can't wait for me to get started!" he added, laughing.

"Very perceptive folks—you're a dynamo, my friend!"

"You're biased! Just you don't tell them any secrets from our college days!"

"I doubt there's a single skeleton in your closet. In any case—congratulations."

"Thank you, Mark. You're a good friend."

"I'm proud of you."

"Yeah, I guess you could say things are falling into place for me. Thing is, when the pastor resigned and they offered me the job, his assistant decided it was time to hang it up too. So I've got an assistant pastor's position I need to fill. That's why I'm calling. How'd you like to join me?"

The line went silent for a second or two.

"Uh, what exactly are you asking?" said Mark.

"I'm offering you the job, man."

"Wow—thanks, Ward. I'm honored."

"So what do you say?"

"I don't know. This is completely out of the blue. I'll have to think about it."

"Two-hundred-twenty-five grand a year."

Mark let out a whistle. "Goodness—that's a lot!"

"Hey, we've gotta pay off those seminary loans, right?"

"I'm a little stunned. This is the last thing I expected. I'd love to work with you, of course. But Grace and I will have to pray about it."

"Well, don't pray too long. I need a decision in a week."

"Okay," said Mark letting out a long sigh. "But while we're on the phone, what's the news with your sister and Jeff? I've heard nothing since we were in seminary and you filled me in briefly. Did they ever patch it up and tie the knot?"

"Are you kidding? I thought you knew. Mortal enemies is more like it. A woman scorned, you know. Linda hates him."

"What happened?"

"I think I told you—Jeff rode the coattails of Linda's good looks for their first year in law school, making promises, leading her on, almost proposing but never quite going through with it. He was fooling around with other girls, and when Linda found out she hit the roof. She never got over it. She finally saw what you and I tried to tell her. Sawyer warned her too. But she bounced back and graduated in the top ten of their class!"

"And Jeff?"

"Probably the bottom ten!" laughed Ward. "Linda was pretty proud of that."

"Did she ever marry?"

"She did—a nice guy. Cameron Trent, a lawyer."

"So, she's Linda Trent now."

"And an ADA. Sawyer, our brother, is planning to run for district attorney when the time is right."

"Think he'll win?"

"He may. He's a pretty shrewd guy. And our dad has some clout in Seattle. Not like Jeff's. But the Hutchins name is definitely an asset."

"How's Linda doing—you know, spiritually."

"Fallen off the train—drunk the Kool-Aid, as they used to say. She's as liberal as they come, which serves her well politically in Seattle, but isn't going to serve her well in the next life. It's really sad. Years ago I told her that liberalism erodes the personal vibrancy of faith and plugs the spiritual ears. But she couldn't hear any of it. Truth has a hard time getting through. We don't talk much anymore. She thinks I'm prejudiced and narrow-minded—all the usual talking points used to denigrate Christians."

"I'm sorry to hear that, Ward. I will pray for her with more urgency now. I admit that I've been lax in praying for her and Jeff. I haven't known what to pray."

"It is hard with people like that. They are so swept up in the world's values, yet they consider themselves enlightened and us, who take our Christianity seriously, Neanderthals. How do you pray for them?"

"I guess for the light to break through. In any case, tell Linda hello for me when you see her. I love her like a sister. Give her my best."

"I will, Mark."

"What about Jeff?"

"He's got the fire of ambition in his eyes, in the spotlight whenever he gets the chance."

"Did he marry?"

"He did—divorced within a year. Now he's on number two. A trophy wife. But they seem to be making a go of it. They have a son, so hopefully that'll help the marriage last."

"Do you ever see him—in person, I mean?"

"No—he would never even admit to knowing me. We used to be close—or so I thought. Weren't we? He went to Bible studies and all the rest with us. But again—liberalism's disease is fatal to growing faith. He's further gone in the deception of modernism even than Linda. You should hear how he talks about Christians. He thinks we're the scum of the earth."

"He's been on my mind. I was actually thinking of writing him and trying to reestablish some kind of contact."

"I wouldn't just now, Mark. Not unless you're prepared for a verbal onslaught from a former best friend that, if I know you, you still love as you do Linda."

"Of course I do."

"Let me recommend you wait, then. You will be shocked by the change. Right now, I don't think it's in his best interest to spew his poison at dunces like us."

"You're probably right. I'll trust your wisdom."

"By the way," Ward added, "he's no longer Jeff. He now goes by *Jefferson F. Rhodes*."

51

An End and a Beginning

2031–2032

As the decade of the 2020s came to an end. Closing in on ninety, Stirling Marshall was aware that the stirrings he had been feeling were gradually coming into focus

Along with the sense that something was at hand, however, he could also sadly tell that the life-spirit of his best friend was growing calm and quiet. A stillness enveloped her as of approaching rest. The curtain had begun its descent.

From that time on, he and his beloved spent every waking minute together. When they celebrated their sixty-fifth anniversary in June of 2031, both knew that it would be their last such earthly celebration.

Larke died quietly and serenely in early November of the same year, as the oranges and reds of the California foothills were at their most resplendent. In the midst of a dozing sleep on the couch of their living room between three and four in the afternoon, as Stirling read in his chair a few feet away, she drifted peacefully away. Nothing had been said for half an hour.

At length Stirling glanced over. He knew she was no longer asleep, but gone.

He mourned but did not grieve. They had enjoyed a full life together. His heart overflowed with gratitude to be allowed to outlive her so she would not be alone. She was still with him, though daily he longed to talk to her and glean from her perspectives.

Larke's death brought with it the undeniable realization that his own time was short. He might live another ten years and reach the century mark. But the odds were against it. He sensed that the Lord was keeping him alive long enough to get his final message written, and time was of the essence.

Filled with urgency, his eyes began to glow with the knowledge that the Spirit was at last bringing to the surface what had been fermenting in his brain and heart for years.

He went to bed one evening in early February of the new year with an almost feverish sense of expectancy. In spite of being keyed up, almost the moment he turned out his light, he sunk into a deep, dreamless, restful sleep.

He awoke suddenly. It seemed that Larke called his name. It was pitch black.

Wide awake in an instant, he reached for the clock on his nightstand. It read 3:47. Almost the exact time, though in the afternoon, Larke had left the world three months before.

Something was at hand. He had not felt such an impulsion, given impetus by Larke's exhortation, since the morning he began what eventually became *Unspoken Commandments*.

Was another such inspiration at hand?

Almost quivering in anticipation, Stirling rose from bed, stepped into the shower and let the cold water flow over him for thirty seconds to make sure his senses were keen and awake, then dressed and put on the kettle for tea.

Whatever God might have to reveal on this morning, his unfinished book of family reminiscences would have to wait. The story of his life could be found all around him. Perhaps that was enough.

Thirty minutes later he was seated comfortably, tea beside him, pen in hand. He drew in a deep breath, with no plan of what he was about to say, simply letting come what came.

Silently he prayed:

What do you have for me, Lord? What do you have for me to communicate from your heart to your people? May I be a conduit to speak out of your heart into the hearts of your men and women whose heart's desire is to hear what you would speak into their lives.

His mind and heart grew still.

Then he began to write.

> *Most of what goes by the name of "Christianity" is not true Christianity,* flowed the ink onto the page. *The majority of those calling themselves "Christians" do so because they hold certain beliefs, not because they have dedicated their lives to obeying what Jesus said to do. They can thus be called "believers" in those beliefs. However, that is not the same thing as being a Christian. A Christian is a follower, a disciple of Jesus.*

The words continued to pour out effortlessly beneath his fingers. He did not feel he was writing at all. His brain, then his hand, found themselves responding to an impulse from beyond him.

> *The diverse worldwide multitude of what are called churches, and their related organizations, groups, ministries, and denominations gathered under the broad heading of Christendom is thus comprised of a majority of believers, but a small minority of true "Christians."*
>
> *True Christianity is an internal, personal, and individual spiritual orientation and lifestyle. By definition, discipleship to Jesus Christ can have no corporate, organizational, administrative, clerical, or structural component. It is a lifestyle, not an organization. That lifestyle can only be lived individually and personally. It is out of this discipleship-lifestyle that the true Church of Jesus Christ, his living breathing body upon the earth, emerges. It is a Church not made with hands. It is a Church invisible to the world, whose intrinsic power is passed on through the commands of the Master, and, by the living of those commands, spreads the salt, light, and leaven of God's kingdom-life invisibly throughout his creation.*

After an hour, Stirling's pen stilled. He leaned back, closed his eyes, and breathed in deeply.

Lord, Lord, he silently prayed, *what do you want for your people? What is your Church? How would you have your people confront these evil times in which we live? How is your Church to regain the power and life that changed the world 2,000 years ago?*

Immediately he thought of Paul's words in 2 Corinthians 10. He turned to it and read the fourth and fifth verses:

> *The weapons of our warfare are not worldly but have divine power to destroy strongholds . . . arguments and every proud obstacle to the knowledge of God, and take every thought captive to obey Christ.*

In whatever ways God led his people to address the falsehoods of the world, it would not be with the world's methods or weapons. Only his invisible weapons had the divine power to destroy the strongholds of the world's evil.

For the rest of the day he wrote and jotted down notes and ideas. The hours passed with many starts and stops . . . pauses and surges . . . unanswered questions . . . fragments . . . occasional sentences and paragraphs . . . more notes . . . walks around the house . . . renewed efforts . . . and much inarticulate prayer.

As the day progressed, it was borne upon him that there was an important historical component to what he was struggling to put into words. To understand the present and the future, as he had told his students hundreds of times, one had to build upon a foundation of understanding the past. He must look back as well as ahead.

By day's end he was surrounded with many volumes of church and world history. He had to set God's revelations to the people of the future into the context of what had come before. To confront the godlessness of the present age and the false priorities of a church mired in the its worldliness, he had to learn from those who had boldly confronted the godlessness of the times in which they had lived, including the godlessness of the churches of those times.

He fell asleep that night reading an account of St. Benedict of Nursia, and the establishment of Catholicism's Benedictine order. The order had emerged out of the urgent necessity borne upon Benedict's heart to preserve the truths of Christianity at a time the Roman Empire was crumbling in chaos.

He and Benedict shared the same fear. Theirs was a vision to preserve the future of Christ's Church, his *true* Church, during a season of mortal peril.

52

THE COMMON LIFE

STIRLING MARSHALL'S research continued. Two days after reading about Saint Benedict, he came upon an account of fourteenth-century Dutchman Geert Groote and the Catholic order which emerged nine hundred years after Benedict out of Groote's vision of Christian community and world separation.

Stirling was especially intrigued by the name of Groote's order, the *Brethren of the Common Life.*

More fascinating still was the connection of Thomas à Kempis to the order. What had this man—whose wisdom and insights into Christlike discipleship, were, in Stirling's opinion, the most important ever written outside the New Testament—found among these "brethren of the common life" that kept him devoted to Groote's order his entire life?

What a riveting phrase, pregnant with layer upon layer of deepening import:

The common life.

What more might God have intended by the words than even Groote and Kempis—seeing with the limited vision of their times—were able to fully apprehend.

Was Kempis's articulation of the Christ-life, in fact, a sweeping portrait of something so fundamental to God's purpose in his creation, as to be called the "*common* life" by which man was intended to live?

It was a mesmerizingly prophetic phrase. As Stirling reflected and prayed and turned them over in his mind, the spellbinding allure of the words filled him with the conviction that God was preparing a coming generation of men, women, and even children to be raised into a new era of understanding, able at last to practically *live* the life that Jesus had intended his disciples to example to the world—a life meant to be *common*, daily, practical, and universally lived by and among his people.

God was calling his people, not to form a new separatist "order" within the organized church as Benedict and Groote had done. Rather, he was calling *all* his people to live in *the common life of the kingdom,* remaining in the world while internally living as a people fundamentally disconnected—in motive, priorities, outlook, lifestyle, values, attitudes, worldview, and entire spiritual orientation—from the world. It was a spiritual order that could, by definition, have nothing to do with the church of man, nor with organizations of any kind.

Its life came from *within*, not without.

That evening Stirling again took up his pen and began scribbling in haste. Thoughts and ideas tumbled over themselves so rapidly that he struggled seemingly in vain to give them written expression as quickly as they came.

> *As post-Christian intolerance of Christian values increases its domination of contemporary culture, and as organized Christendom continues its leniency toward these trends and its tacit acceptance of progressivism's God-denying perspectives and tolerance of sin, and as the churches of man and their professional clergy continue their alliance with the world's values, ethics, and morals, the true Church, the invisible worldwide body of Christ, will find itself increasingly required to disengage from the kingdom of man and its systems.*
>
> *The Church will thus confront a crossroads moment in its history. It will be forced to recognize a painful truth—man's church has become the ally of the world. To continue the mission commanded of it by Jesus, perhaps even to survive, the Church will of necessity have to withdraw from the church.*

Again, the flow of his pen gave way to prayer.

53

THE BENEDICT BRIEF

His RESEARCH and readings in the following days gradually coalesced around those eras in history when certain individuals such as Benedict, Groote, and Kempis—some known, some who remained in obscurity—recognized the imperative distinction between man's church and the eternal Church of Ephesians and 1 Peter.

Theirs were voices God raised to speak to their times to call Christ's faithful disciples to a life of obedience and disjunction from the world.

Their challenge was to an *uncommon* life meant to be mankind's *common* life, which had been intended since the days of the Garden. Those who heeded the voices through history were brothers and sisters of a universal and eternal community, defined not by groups and buildings, organizations or memberships, services and schedules, but by the common commitment to the life of Christlikeness.

As he went over his notes and scribblings, slowly Stirling began to place his thoughts into a historical framework, highlighting the continually increasing revelation given through the years to God's listening hearts.

Upon this historical foundation, he then began to weave the perspectives that he believed God was giving him for the Christians of the third millennium, the brethren of a new invisible, eternal community.

A little over a month later, in early April 2032, a hundred pages of handwritten notes and ideas, reflections and challenges, sat on Stirling Marshall's desk.

It was time to bring order to the random flow of ideas and thoughts and notes. He must now type it into a cohesive document he could pass on as a final testimony or witness to what God had given him.

He opened a new file on his computer, thought a moment, then typed the words:

The Benedict Brief.

His fingers stilled. He closed his eyes, drew in a breath, and quietly breathed a few words of inaudible prayer.

He waited. Two minutes passed.

When his fingers again sought the keyboard, the words appearing on the screen were not what he expected. Yet he knew they came from the Spirit of Truth.

By an Anonymous Christian of a New Community of the Spiritual Order of the Common Life.

He was not sure he knew all that the words signified. But if God had given them, their meaning would be revealed in time.

Slowly he began to write:

Two truths stand at the pinnacle of what it means to be a follower of Jesus, to live in the world but not of the world.

He paused and re-read the words. Again he prayed silently for insight and guidance.

"Many through the years have tried to apprehend the full depth and meaning of these truths—to live their principles in practical ways," he resumed, now writing slowly, thoughtfully, deliberately. The feverish, hurried, almost random flow of words and ideas that had characterized the previous month had accomplished its work.

His spirit was now calm, his heart and brain focused. There was no need to rush. God would speak. He must listen.

"Most of man's attempts, however, fall short," he continued.

The words now came steadily and cogently. He did not stop to think about them, but simply allowed them to flow through his hands.

The deep truths underlying their attempts remain interpretively indistinct, and thus always in some measure misunderstood.

Many have been the attempts to discover kingdom living apart from the world. But they fall short because of man's love of externals, rules, lists, and legalistic interpretations of high truth. Men have withdrawn into monasteries and cloisters and remote hideaways, thinking that separation from the world means literal separation—secluding themselves away, seeking isolated sanctuaries where the world cannot encroach.

But it means something far deeper and more personal than can be achieved in such ways. These attempts may point toward separation, but they do not embody the essence of what Jesus meant. Thus, in the end they achieve an outward form of what appears to be "separation" but which in fact is not what Jesus meant at all.

Along with whatever good they may do, such efforts thus also lead to false assumptions and untrue teachings. Upon those untrue teachings have been built many systematic organizations of counterfeit separation—monastic, denominational, church, and community structures which become perpetuated as institutions unto themselves. In time these become empty shells devoid of gospel reality.

All the while, the heart and essence of the teaching—"My kingdom is not of this world"—remains unapprehended and unfulfilled by God's people.

There have been a few men and women, however, whose incomplete efforts through the years have indeed pointed in a true direction toward the kingdom Jesus said was not of this world but would conquer the world . . .

54

FINAL PRAYER

TWO MONTHS later Stirling Marshall completed the final writings of his earthly hands.

What was he now to do with what he had written?

It could obviously not be made public. It would too easily be misunderstood, and thus become a tool in Satan's hands for truth to be *ridiculed* rather than a tool for God's truth to be *revealed*.

He had spoken boldly, forcefully, controversially. The document would be not only scorned by most calling themselves Christians, it would be banned in the political realm. In the wrong hands it would be inflammatory and misconstrued. In the hands for whom God intended it, it could only result in one thing—prayer for guidance and courage.

He must take care that it get into those right hands, and *only* those hands.

It must not be used frivolously or without the leading of God's Spirit. It must never cause division. It must accomplish the purpose for which God had given it.

How could he *prevent* its circulation among those who could not understand, and would use it to mock truth rather than fall on their knees praying, *"God, what would you have me do?"*

He must especially ensure that *God's* Voice be heard through what he had written, not his own.

Over the coming days the certitude grew upon him that he must do nothing to spread the *Brief* or make it public. He must do exactly the opposite. For now it had to remain a private document, known to no one but himself.

He would print two copies, hide them, then leave their future in God's hands. They would either be found or, if such was the Lord's will, lost to history.

At peace with his resolution, he spent the next several days writing, rewriting, and modifying a letter addressed jointly to Timothy and David about what he intended to do, and why, and what were his hopes and intentions if they felt led and prompted to follow them.

In the midst of its writing, thoughts of his children and this final communication brought to the surface many reflections about the life he had lived. Memories of people he had known flooded through him from almost ninety years, stretching back into the indistinct regions of childhood. For years he had done his best to keep his relational slate clean. Yet the sense that these were his final days brought fresh urgency to the conviction that he must leave no unfinished earthly business behind.

"Oh, Lord," he prayed, "make right the hurts I have inflicted through the years. In a miraculous way I cannot fathom, undo my myriad unkindnesses. Soothe and heal and bring eternal good from the insensitivities of my responses and words."

His spirit grew quiet. He was alone with the God he had walked with for nine decades, from even before he was aware of a guiding Presence holding his hand. He was descending deep into the peaceful solitude of readiness, making the last preparations for his final earthly journey.

Years ago, God had revealed to him a great truth. It was possible to send prayer-arrows up into God's heart, then wait in peace knowing that in the fullness of time, at the *right* time—perhaps years later—God would send the answering beams of light down into the very heart that his prayer had lifted into the Father's presence. Those divine arrows of light would be launched from on high at the *perfect* time and in the *perfect* circumstances to accomplish the Father's intent—purposes higher than he could have known, or might ever know.

If time was of no account in the answering of prayer, if God could indeed raise man's small prayers to accomplish greater purposes than the eyes of man could see, why could the mighty truth of forgiveness not likewise be miraculously endowed with the timelessness of eternity? How might repentance and forgiveness be unbound and unfettered from earthly events, transcending even death? How might God's Spirit produce in individual hearts an infinity of small forgivenesses that would each contribute to the great reconciliation of God's universe into his eternal heart of Love?

If God's infinite Mind held within it, as an eternal present, all the universe and its history, its people, its circumstances and events, every life, every human exchange, every word spoken, every thought—if time as we know it was meaningless in that world of God's being—surely prayer also dwelt in that timeless aeonian realm.

The thought of forgiveness transcending earthly limitations—vigorously working in God's eternal timelessness unto the universal reconciliation of all things—overwhelmed him with joyous possibility!

It was his heart's desire to use his final days and hours to appropriate God's eternally mysterious "all things are possible," and through that promise to make himself right with all those hearts his life had touched in less than Christlike ways.

He could set the great work of repentance and forgiveness flowing in all directions, set in motion not merely his half of the reconciliation equation, but taking his share of the obligation of love due every man, in an inexplicable eternal way also stimulate the full flowering healing in all directions with every individual his path of life had ever crossed.

He would begin now! He would pray for God to take up his myriad needful repentances, accountabilities, and forgivenesses, whether he remembered the specifics or not, into his infinite eternal right-making heart.

"Oh, God, eternal Father," Stirling's heart cried out, *"by the infinite miracle of your timelessness, I ask you to take into your heart my desire to repent of every insensitivity, rudeness,*

selfishness, and unkindness—every tiniest lapse of attentiveness. In your heart I ask forgiveness from every person to whom I was less than I should have been. Let me take account for the thousands of such moments I cannot remember. Transform every one of them, every word. Accomplish the work that in my forgetful humanity I cannot. Make whole those moments that my fleshly self spoiled by pride, unkind thoughts, critical responses, judgmental attitudes, insensitive words, and self-absorption. In the eternal Now of your being, may every word I have spoken, every thought, every attitude, be purified and glorified that you may use them to accomplish your purpose.

"Oh, Father, such is my heart's cry! Go back in time— transcend time! Make the prayer of St. Francis a reality in every human exchange I ever had. Bring to life my heart's prayer to be an instrument of your peace in every life however briefly I may have touched it. Convey my sorrow into the hearts where it is needful and glorify it into the blossoming of forgiveness and wholeness. Where I have sown unkindness, replace it with love. Where I have sown injury, impart repentance. If I have received hurt, convey forgiveness. Where I have sown darkness, bathe hearts in your light. Where I have sown sadness, saturate the wounded with joy. Convey your love in place of my insensitivity. Miraculously imbue every heart with what I would now give if I could. Though the earthly possibility for such things may be long past, raise my longing for healing and reconciliation, and transform it into reality.

"Oh Father, work wholeness beyond my capacity to apprehend it. In the timelessness of your great love, take the events and relationships of my life into your eternal being. Convey healing into every heart, wherever they be, whether alive in the flesh or alive in your presence. Implant into them your love through my love. May we be made one in your eternal heart beyond what was possible in our humanity. Bring brotherhood alive. In the imperfection of my prayer, accomplish the finished

result of the reconciliation that is in your heart to set flowing within and between every man and woman of your universal human family."

Stirling's heart stilled. The magnitude of what he was asking God to do was more than he could take in. Yet if he could *think* it . . . *imagine* it . . . *pray* for God to receive the incompleteness of his heart's desire as the perfection of the final result, why could God not miraculously accomplish even *beyond* what he could ask, or even think. Surely God's potentialities stretched infinitely beyond his imaginings.

Satisfied with his letter to David and Timothy a few days later, he returned his attention to his personal family memoirs for a few weeks before the Lord's *"Well done"* came.

Stirling fell asleep for the final time in his chair, as he often said he hoped he would, his pen falling to the floor as the "great waking" came. His memoirs would not be completed, yet he had faithfully written the final message God had for him to deliver.

Then it was time to go.

55

A Legacy Lives On

TIMOTHY FOUND his father that August day. He called Cateline in Marysville, then Jane, Graham, and Woody. His next call was to David Gordon, whom he asked, with the consent of the other four, to deliver a eulogy for his father.

One of David's first letters after hearing the news was to write Mark and Grace Forster—still using the old-fashioned medium of an actual *letter*. Their correspondence had grown so sporadic on Mark's side, however, David had not yet been apprised of their move to Seattle. David's letter thus went to the former North Bend address where, in a world predominated by electronic communication, it was misplaced, and did not catch up with Mark and Grace until some time later.

After the graveside service in Dorado Wood a week after Stirling's death, the five Marshall children planned to gather again at their parents' Dorado Wood home for Thanksgiving.

It was through the grapevine at the Seattle church that Mark finally learned of the passing of the renowned Christian author from the previous century whom he had been privileged to know.

A brief pang went through him as he fondly recalled his conversations with Marshall, and his autographed copy of Stirling's *Unspoken Commandments*, now somewhere among his things—though he wasn't sure where. Sadly, the memories were fleeting.

Not only Stirling Marshall, but David Gordon would have been disheartened to know how far the sober warnings about the pastorate had receded into the recesses of Mark's memory. Puget Sound Vine Ministries was growing rapidly and showed no sign of slowing down. Though its two pastors were young, the duo was beginning to attract attention in wider evangelical circles. Ward remained the acknowledged leader of the Hutchins-Forster team—his book on church growth was due out early the following year and already boasted advance sales in cloth of 150,000. But there were many who had by now also earmarked his second-in-command as a young man to watch.

On the Wednesday prior to Thanksgiving, three months after his father's death, Timothy Marshall left Jaylene and Heather at home and drove the fifteen miles to the familiar Dorado Wood house where his parents had lived for twenty-eight years. Neither would the families of his siblings be present.

According to the wishes of their mother in the funeral instructions, this was a Thanksgiving the five Marshall sons and daughters would share amongst themselves.

> *Be strong in the Lord and in the strength*
> *of his might. Put on the whole armor of God . . .*
> *that you may be able to withstand in the evil day,*
> *and having done all, to stand. Stand therefore,*
> *having girded your loins with truth.*
>
> **EPHESIANS 6:10-11, 13-14**

PART 4

STAND STRONG
IN TRUTH

2031-2034

56

A Pivotal Election Looms

2031

THE CAMPAIGN of 2032, for a variety of reasons, seemed to carry heightened significance.

Not only was it the first presidential election of a new decade, for the first time the Republicans gave every appearance of being resigned to the fact that the presidency was permanently out of their reach. They hardly pretended to put up a fight.

On the other side, however, almost immediately after the dust settled from 2028, a new crop of Democrat hopefuls began positioning themselves as the party's rising young stars. Though a vocal draft-Michelle contingent was making some noise, the old guard of Clintons, Obamas, Biden and Harris, was mostly gone from the scene. By the early months of 2030, half a dozen new faces had distinguished themselves sufficiently to turn their attacks on each other.

None was successful, however, at reaching the level of Adriana Carmella Hunt, still known nationally simply as ACH. She was no longer as young as many of her challengers. But except for the Michelle loyalists, ACH was the darling of the extreme Left. Still a mere forty-one years of age at the turn of the decade, she had been front and center in American politics so long—chomping at the bit to be president before she was legally old enough to run—that she now considered it "her turn." She was not about to let anyone stand in her way—not Chelsea, not Michelle . . . no one.

Ms. Hunt made her mark overnight more than fifteen years earlier, announcing her run for the House the year after her mandatory twenty-fifth birthday from one of the most liberal districts in Vermont. She hit DC like a tornado, immediately making a name for herself with highly visible speeches and proposing outrageously unworkable schemes guaranteed to keep her face in newspapers around the country and featured on most nightly newscasts. She was in love with the spotlight almost as much as she was in love with herself. Being the center of attention was her comfort zone. Of all the character qualities that might be attributed to her, even her closest friends would never think to mention humility as one of them.

It was obvious by the time she was mounting her first reelection campaign two years later that nothing less than the presidency would satisfy her insatiable ambition. She privately chaffed at not being tapped the instant she was legally old enough. When it became obvious that was not going to happen, after her own reelection she ran for Speaker of the House instead. By then the only question was whether she would make a move during the next cycle or bide her time until 2032.

Enjoying the power of the Speaker's gavel, she opted for the latter. Though she did not run officially in '28, however, she secretly hoped to be selected for the second spot, and was infuriated when she was passed over by Senator Fry in spite of his alleged mob ties.

So ACH waited, throwing her hundred thirty pounds around in Congress like she owned the place, as she essentially did. Her nomination in 2032 was such a certainty that she did not even enter the early fray with the crowded field of hopefuls. The only individual who might have stopped her nomination was the scandal-ridden vice president. Preventing what might have become an ugly brawl, however, the one-term VP and former senator professed no interest in a campaign that would undoubtedly bring more to light in his past than he wanted known, and might well have landed him in prison.

By the end of 2031, Ms. Hunt's lead in the polls was virtually unassailable. ACH no longer spoke like a candidate. She was talking like the next president.

The powers of Palladium, however, were concerned. She was not of their circle, and therefore unpredictable. Palladium did not like what it could not control.

57

∧ REQUEST

EARLY 2032

JEFFERSON FITZSIMMONS, a.k.a. "Jeff," Rhodes was not one to rest on his laurels. His solid 2.31 GPA from Cal Poly Humboldt, and graduation from the University of Washington School of Law 151st in a class of 167, might have put him in good stead had private pro bono practice been his career goal. That his sights were set considerably higher required perhaps neither resting nor depending on those academic laurels. He had three advantages neither GPA nor class standing could provide—devilish good looks complete with a self-effacing John Kennedy smile, wit and charisma to match, and a rich, well-known father who had been in the Oval Office at least a dozen times.

Even before leaving Humboldt and returning to Seattle, the up-and-coming scion of the Rhodes legacy in the Evergreen State knew that he and Mark Forster could never again be friends. It was with embarrassment that he looked back on his years at that camp and their ridiculously infantile friendship. How could he not have seen Mark for the country cowpoke he was? The idiotic nicknames, pretending to be interested in all that religious talk at the camp, the Bible studies at that group at Humboldt, whatever it was called—the mere thought of his onetime best friend was mortifying to his pride. Yet he could only blame himself for being so naïve to be drawn to someone so inane.

And then, for God's sake—Mark's deciding on a career in the ministry! Unbelievable! Jeff should have listened to his father. Humboldt was a mistake. Although on second thought, that's where he'd met Linda. She was doing pretty well for herself. Who could tell how she might still be useful?

So might her two brothers. He liked Sawyer. He could prove an able ally in the coming years. But Ward—*God, he was worse than Mark!* The two deserved each other. Fanatical narrow-minded crusaders. They were the kind who wanted to return the country to the Dark Ages. Yet no one could deny that Ward Hutchins was stirring things up. Old Truman Hutchins had produced a talented brood. *What had gone wrong with Ward? How had he ended up so conservative?* The middle child gone wrong, perhaps, though Truman's ex-wife was apparently a religious freak as well. You couldn't depend on mothers. Even his own mother occasionally got nostalgic and religious, like the whole summer camp thing.

Yet Ward Hutchins wasn't a man to make an enemy of either. Even he might be useful if he could somehow be coerced, if not into giving his support outright—that was probably impossible—at least persuaded not to speak against him. Even in liberal Washington, the fewer contrary voices the better. If his father had taught him anything, it was to take nothing for granted. You had to play every constituency like a violin. And on their own terms. If he had to do that with the evangelicals, he would. He knew how to play the game. Living with Mark and Ward had given him this advantage—he learned the lingo.

As for Mark, he was an insignificant pawn. His opinion would matter nothing. But even pawns could be kingmakers if they were in the right place at the right time. And recent events had shaped up—with almost exquisite irony given how far apart they had grown—to place Mark Forster in precisely that position.

He would extend an olive branch, thought Jeff. Mark would not be able to refuse.

When Mark Forster opened the envelope from the Office of Information, Mayor's Office, 600 4th Ave, Seattle, early in 2032, he had no idea what it could be about. He was so shocked by the brief handwritten note that he read it twice.

Hey, Pine old friend!

I've been keeping track of our old buddy Ward since he came to Seattle. But when I read that you had been hired as his assistant, I thought—How great is this, the three amigos back together again!

I'd love to see you. I know you only arrived a few months ago and are probably busy, and I'm swamped as usual. But I hope you might be able to drop by my office next Tuesday and we could catch up. I've got some news, and I can't wait to hear about you and Grace. I've got a pretty clear afternoon—anytime between 2:00 and 4:00 would be great.

Looking forward to it!
Jeff

☆ ☆ ☆

When Mark walked up to the 7th floor of the Seattle city offices, the gold leaf on the door was impressive, and no less than what Ward led him to expect: *Jefferson F. Rhodes, Assistant to the Mayor.*

He walked inside and introduced himself to the secretary at the desk. Seconds later, Jeff bounded out of the inner office, hand outstretched and a great smile on his face.

"Pine, you rascal!" he exclaimed. "I'm glad to see you."

"And I you, Jeff," rejoined Mark as the two shook hands. "You have obviously come far," he added glancing about the expansive outer office.

"Just the trappings of the job—no big deal. Sally—" he said, to his secretary, "this is my best friend from the old days and college roommate, Mark Forster."

She smiled as Mark reached down and shook her hand.

"Come into my office," said Jeff. "We've got years to make up!"

Mark followed him through the door.

"An impressive office," said Mark glancing about. "View of the skyline and Puget Sound."

"Yeah, it's a cushy job, but somebody's got to do it, right!" laughed Jeff. "Come over here—if you look that direction," he added, pointing across the Sound, "you can almost see my folks' place. That's Bainbridge Island where I was raised. Had to take the ferry in to school every day."

"You couldn't drive—no buses?"

"There's a long way around—takes about two hours. There were buses to the peninsula schools, but I was in private schools in the city. The ferry was faster."

They turned back into the office and sat down.

"So how's the pastor's life—you like it?" asked Jeff.

"I do," answered Mark. "Though it's all going to change now, working under Ward in a larger church than I'm used to."

"Where were you before?"

"Grace and I were down in Oregon. I pastored a small church—only fifty or sixty members, but it was nice for us. How we'll cope with the big city and a church of a thousand, that remains to be seen."

"A thousand and growing fast, from what I hear."

"Ward's got the people fired up all right. A natural born leader, just like he was in CCF. I'm not sure I'm equipped to be his second-in-command."

"You'll do great. By the time Ward left school, you were pretty much running the Humboldt group as I recall. A quieter style, a little more personal I would say. But don't sell yourself short—you're a leader too, Mark."

"We'll see," smiled Mark. "You're right about one thing—I'm not quite so given to rousing the emotions as Ward is. But I think what I have to contribute, as you say, is to the quieter places in people's lives. I hope it makes a difference."

"I know it does. I'm sure God is using you."

"So what's your news?" asked Mark.

"Ah, yes, my news." Jeff paused for dramatic effect. "It's not public yet," he went on, "but I wanted you to be one of the first to know. Next week I'm announcing my candidacy for Congress."

"That *is* big news, Jeff. Congratulations!"

"Thank you, Mark."

"But hasn't Representative Thompson been Seattle's congressman forever? How would you unseat him in a primary? He's not retiring?"

"No, nothing like that."

"Unless . . . you're not going to run as a Republican?"

"Not hardly!" laughed Jeff. "No, I'll be running for the sixth district seat, not Seattle's."

"Where's that?"

"The islands and peninsula, north and west."

"I thought you lived in Seattle."

"I do, sort of. But my dad's had his eye on the sixth district seat for a while. He thinks it's vulnerable to a primary challenge. So we've kept my residence listed as my folks place on Bainbridge. The boundary between the districts runs right through the Sound. Officially I am a resident of the sixth district."

"Is the sixth district as liberal as the rest of the state?"

"Not so much. More working class. So even if I win the primary, the general won't be a shoe-in. But it's either go up against Thompson in the primary in Seattle, or take my chances in what might be a tight contest in the sixth. My dad thinks challenging Thompson would be a dangerous move. So we decided on the sixth."

"Looks like you've thought of everything. Good luck."

"Thanks, Mark."

"I would like to think I can count on your support," said Jeff.

"Actually, Jeff, given my position, I try to avoid getting involved in politics."

"You could make an exception in my case, for old times' sake."

"That is a precedent I would be reluctant to begin. Nor am I sure our political positions would be compatible. I am a Republican, Jeff. Surely that doesn't surprise you."

"I won't hold it against you!" laughed Jeff.

"The issues are serious, Jeff. Most of the liberal agenda is contrary to everything I believe as a Christian and opposite to the founding principles of our country. Especially with Adriana Hunt looking like the next president. She is so far beyond the pale, and you will obviously be linked with her."

"I'm not asking you to endorse everything in the Democrat agenda, Mark, or ACH. I know you couldn't do that. You're right—she can be a loose cannon at times. But to support me as a friend, a former room-mate, and camp bunkmate—you know, a character witness. Just tell people you know me and I'm a good guy."

Mark laughed lightly. "I will definitely pray about it," he said. "It will obviously come out that you and I and Ward roomed together in college. With you and Ward both so high profile in Seattle circles, that cannot be helped. As far as that goes, I will be happy if you say that you and I have been friends for years. If asked, I will say the same. Beyond that, I will have to pray about it."

"I appreciate it. What about Ward? He doesn't avoid politics. Do you think he would meet with me and talk about a possible endorsement?"

"You must know how doubtful that is with ACH at the top of your party's ticket, Jeff. He's more conservative politically than I am. His list of what he considers outrageous policies is longer than mine. Really, Jeff, in evangelical circles, I'm actually a fairly tolerant and liberally minded guy. But I believe in absolute not relative truth, in the veracity of the Bible, in God's creation of man and woman as distinct represen-tations of different aspects of his nature, and in the founding principles of the country—which are biblical and Christian principles. My list of convictions crossing over into the political realm is a relatively short one. I'm no political fanatic. But Ward's is a much longer list. If what he says about your views is true, you have become decidedly more liberal. How could you expect him to support you?"

"Honestly, Mark, I'm not Ward's enemy. I just want what's best for the people of Washington. I have to represent them fairly, and Wash-ington is a liberal state. Like you, I'm not really all that political either. I'm a people person—you know me. I'm not running as a politician, but to try to help people."

"You said that the sixth district was less liberal than the rest of the state. Would you be representing the working-class people of your dis-trict who might not be as liberal as you, or would you fall in with the views that dominate Washington as a whole?"

The question took Jeff by surprise. It bit a little too close for comfort. "A congressman . . . of course . . . he has to do both," he managed to answer without betraying his irritation. "He, uh . . . represents both his district *and* his state."

"I'm not sure that's how the Founders intended it."

"Times change, Mark. The Constitution has to be interpreted to reflect that."

"To a degree, of course. But does that justify new interpretations *contradicting* the intent of the Founders?"

"Now you're splitting hairs, Mark," rejoined Jeff, an edge creeping into his tone.

"I don't think so. I think that is precisely the point that liberals don't look at with intellectual honesty. They see themselves as more important constitutionalists than Franklin, Washington, Hamilton, and Adams. They do not see it as their duty to represent those men. They believe *their* perspectives should override those of the Founders."

"What does any of that have to do with my representation of the sixth district?"

"I was only curious what you would envision as your primary responsibility, Jeff—the people or your personal views—the Constitution or the agenda of the Democrat party?"

"I would emphasize both."

"What if they're in conflict?"

"I don't think they are."

"I've read some of your comments and positions, Jeff—abortion up to a week after birth, the right for children to sue parents for damages, slavery reparations, stringent new taxation on churches. Those are political positions, Jeff. Those are *liberal* political positions. Who do they help? Not the people of the sixth district as a whole. I'm passing no judgment, only saying that Ward is going to have a real problem with those kinds of positions."

Inwardly fuming to be lectured by one who knew nothing about politics, Jeff managed to keep his cool.

"Then let's forget Ward for now," he said. "What about you, Mark? Can I count on *your* endorsement?"

"I told you, I am happy to acknowledge our friendship. To the extent that constitutes a character endorsement, then you have it. I doubt I will feel comfortable going further than that. But I promise you, I will pray seriously."

"Maybe you might at least persuade Ward not to openly oppose me."

"Why don't you ask him yourself?"

"You told me, you doubted Ward would meet with me. If we did meet, he would only argue back his talking points at me."

"Would you listen to his perspectives without rebutting them with *your* talking points?"

"Of course."

"You weren't very good at it when we roomed together. Whenever you and he got into it about Trump, he listened more objectively than you did. You were the judgmental one, Jeff, not Ward."

"That's hardly fair, Mark."

"Isn't it? How much public tolerance have you expressed toward evangelical Christians and conservative traditionalists, Jeff? If you could replay some of those conversations we had back then, you would hear yourself being completely intolerant of Ward and his views with a condescension that wasn't worthy of you."

"I hope I've grown since then."

"Hopefully we all have."

"At least tell me you will talk to Ward about toning down the rhetoric against me after I announce."

"I *can* promise you that," said Mark. "I will talk to him."

"That's all I can ask," nodded Jeff, trying to sound upbeat. Inwardly, however, he was more contemptuous of Mark than before, incredulous that his onetime friend could have become, in his eyes, such a backward-thinking fool.

The two made some additional attempts at light conversation. But the undercurrent of awkwardness was obvious to both. Thankfully the visit soon came to an end.

Jeff closed the door to his office, walked to the window, and gazed out at the city. This present circumstance which was before him, he thought to himself, if grabbed with both hands, would land him in DC by year's end.

His lip curled into the hint of a sneer. *I'll get there, with or without your help, Mark,* he said under his breath. *I never did need you, and I don't now!*

Hmm . . . *the present circumstance.*

He turned back to his desk, wondering why such an odd phrase had popped into his mind.

58

SON AND DAUGHTER ONCE MORE

NOVEMBER 2032

TIMOTHY MARSHALL, now fifty-two, pulled out a key, slipped it into the lock, opened the door, and walked almost reverently into the chilly somber home—so familiar yet now eerily changed. Though not the eldest, he arrived first simply because he lived closest to his parents.

Though he was graying himself, he was of this home's younger generation. With his brothers and sisters, he now stood at the vanguard of the family legacy represented by the tomblike silence surrounding him. Moving into the big room, he sat down on one of the two leather couches in the open living area adjoining the kitchen. The dusky quiet was heavy with images of the past—the two easy chairs where his parents sat together every evening, the high wall of bookshelves, paintings and memorabilia adorning walls and sideboards. Abundant framed family photographs—every one flooding him with mingled happy and bittersweet nostalgia—hung on every available niche of wall space.

Darkness was closing in on the late November afternoon. He sat for some time in the dim light, absorbing the silence. The place had always been so full of life and activity. "Exuberance" was the only word to describe his father. That energetic life and boisterous voice…and that high-spirited laugh. They were all now stilled. Henceforth they would live only in his memory.

An hour later, lights on and the chill taken off most of the rooms, he had soup simmering on the stove and a salad in the fridge. The place was beginning to feel like home again. Except he was in the kitchen getting ready for guests rather than his mother.

He was sitting in his father's recliner when the door opened a few minutes after eight. The sound startled him. His head shot around as his sister Cateline, six years older, walked in.

"Tim," she laughed, "you look like you've seen a ghost!"

"Sorry!" he said, laughing to shake off the remnants of his reverie. "I was deeper in thought than I realized!" he added, laying aside the book in his hand and standing. "You hungry, Cat?"

"Starving," his sister replied. She set her small suitcase on the floor and closed the door.

"I waited for you. I've got soup and salad and oatcakes."

"Just like what Mom would have waiting. Did you make the oatcakes?"

"I did. Before I left Jaylene and Heather at home. We couldn't reminisce about Mom and Dad without a good supply—Dad's favorite food."

"Along with rice pudding!"

"How could I forget!" laughed Timothy. "An odd combination, but that was Dad. You know where to find your room."

"Of course. Let me put my things away. I'll join you in a minute."

Sitting around the kitchen table twenty minutes later, brother and sister were chatting freely.

"How are Clancy and Robyn?"

"Good," replied Cateline. "Though they're wondering why they're celebrating Thanksgiving without me. Robyn was hoping to see Heather."

Timothy laughed. "I think all our families are wondering that. But I understand why Mom wanted it this way."

"By the way—I meant to tell you, congrats on your book. Thanks for sending it."

"Thanks. Publish or perish, you know."

"I love that you're following in Dad's footsteps."

"I can hardly keep up with Jaylene. She puts out a new article every two or three months."

"The family business! And you two are carrying it on. And you're the expert on Dad's writings. But honestly, Tim, I wasn't that interested in most of it. With apologies to you and Dad, the two historians of the family, history was never my strong suit. And all his preaching every other page—sorry, it wasn't my thing. Mom and Dad were a little too spiritual for my taste."

"I've never heard you say that before. I thought you were active in church. You haven't . . . I mean, left—"

"Left the church? No, nothing like that. I'm still as involved as ever. But they took it so seriously. I mean, *everything* with them was the Bible this and the Lord said that. It seemed over the top. Church on Sunday is one thing. But trying to bring the Bible into every little thing—it's not for me. I sometimes wanted to say, *'Come on, Mom and Dad, get a life! Get out and enjoy yourselves.'*"

Timothy took in her words with a thoughtful expression.

"Do you remember Dad's laugh?" he asked.

"Who could forget it—one of his trademarks."

"You don't think he enjoyed life?"

"I suppose he did. Actually, Mom and Dad probably enjoyed life more than most people you meet, especially old people. They seemed to enjoy themselves more in their eighties than when we were young. But you can't live by the Bible *all* the time—you know what I mean."

This time Timothy did not reply. He *did* know what his sister meant. But he disagreed as much as he knew their parents would. That was their entire reason for being—to try to live by the Bible all the time.

"Well, all I can say is that Dad's writing is food and drink to my soul. It may be a peculiar thing to say of one's father, but he is my favorite author, my life's mentor. He was my best friend."

"That is an amazing thing to say. I'm not sure I knew that, Tim. I mean I loved Dad. I consider him a great man. He was the best father a girl could have. But I just wasn't cut out to be as spiritual about everything as he and Mom. I remember when they gave me that old book by the Kempis fellow—a monk, I think. I couldn't make a thing of it. It was like reading a foreign language."

Timothy smiled but said nothing. Alongside his father's books, his personal copy of *The Imitation*, a gift from his parents at the same time as Cateline's, was the most underlined and thumb-stained book in his possession—one of his lost-on-a-desert-island books.

"And he was still writing right up to the end," said Timothy after a moment as a fond, sad smile spread over his face. "When I came over that morning and saw him comfortable in his chair in the office, I thought he was dozing. But one of his pens was on the floor beside him, its cap off, a few sheets of paper strewn about. That's when I realized he was gone."

"What was it he was writing when you found him. I was almost late getting here, you remember. I went straight to the funeral home."

"It was a letter to Mom," replied Timothy.

"But she'd been gone for almost a year."

"He wrote her every day. He used to laugh and tell me he was sending them to her by telepathy."

"Was he still writing books?" asked Cateline.

"I'm not actually sure. Dad hadn't published anything in years. But he never stopped writing about the ideas he was thinking about. *Ideas* were his meat and drink. He said every day that he was on a quest to discover an idea, a thought, a possibility, an imaginative mental phantom no one had thought before, and then put it down on paper in such a way that it perfectly captured the image that had formed in his brain."

"That sounds exactly like Dad!"

"He often said that writers *have* to write. I'm sure he hoped some of it would be read, even if just by us. But that wasn't *why* he wrote. He wrote for himself, because he *had* to. Expressing himself, even to himself, was who he was—getting to the bottom of ideas, life's significances, spiritual truths and principles. It was a personal search for the meaning of life, I guess you would say. Dad was driven like no one I've ever met to really *understand* . . . life, the world, history, people, God, the Bible. And himself most of all."

"It sounds like you consider Dad more philosopher than novelist."

"That's it exactly. I mean, he was a great storyteller too, and he loved that aspect of it. But it wasn't the stories that drove him. It was the ideas undergirding the stories. The stories were the outer clothing, the garb he gave to make the ideas more interesting. The characters he developed were but the means he used to weave those ideas and meanings into the practical reality of life. Anything he didn't understand lay like a burr under his saddle, or a thorn in the flesh to use Paul's image. He had to investigate, ferret out, think through, and examine it from every angle.

"Understanding was a compulsion. He *had* to understand. I doubt he imagined everything he wrote would ever be read. But if he could go to his grave understanding—not everything of course, but understanding everything that had come to his mind to investigate and explore and think about, then he would die a happy man."

"And did he?"

Timothy thought a moment and smiled.

"The last time I talked with him, just the day before his death, he said he was on the verge of finally getting to the bottom of the atonement. His voice was animated and excited. The challenge of discovering some new facet of truth drove him no less than it had all his life."

Timothy paused and smiled again.

"He was always trying to figure things out," he said chuckling lightly. "What I just said about the atonement reminded me of another time, years ago—I think I had just started at Cal Poly—when he excitedly said to me, 'I just figured out the rebuttal to the non-closed-system argument why the second law of thermodynamics does not preclude order arising out of chaos.'"

"And what in the world did he mean by that!" laughed Cateline.

"I had no idea what he was talking about at the time," replied Timothy.

"Do you now?"

"I do."

"Probably scientific and complicated?"

"Somewhat, yes. But the point is that he was so excited. Ideas were his life. So yes—he died a happy man, still engaged in the quest that was about to send him into whole new realms."

"What you said—it seems almost prophetic, just on the verge of it, as if he was getting ready to walk through the final door of understanding!"

"You're more spiritual than you let on, Cat!" laughed Timothy. "A wonderful image."

Timothy paused a moment.

"Several months before that," he began again thoughtfully, "he was deep into some new project he said might well be his life's work—what he was put on earth to figure out and then pass on, if he could understand what the Spirit was trying to show him."

"What was it he was writing?"

"I'm not sure exactly—it was still at that nebulous stage where he was reluctant to talk about it. I know he felt severely limited by not having Mom to flesh out the ideas with him. So he was struggling with it—something to do with the end times, I think, and how Christians should live in a culture and political environment that was in such confusion of right and wrong. Once he said his hope was nearly gone, that the country was falling into the abyss and it was too late to stop it. The future, prophecy, end times—I have no idea what the central idea of it was. But whatever he was writing I think it was somehow meant to address how Christians should live in a post-Christian world?"

"An ambitious undertaking. It reminds me of Schaeffer's book."

"You've read Schaeffer?" said Timothy in surprise. "I thought you didn't go in for such heavy spiritual stuff."

"I haven't really read much. I just know about the book. Everybody's heard of it."

"You're probably right. But nearly half a century has gone by since Schaeffer's time. Dad said the question posed in *How Should We Then Live?* had become a completely different dilemma than it was for Schaeffer—an entirely new approach to Christianity was needed."

"But you don't know what that approach was?"

"It's what Dad was trying to hear from the Lord."

"Did you read any of it?"

"No. He said it wasn't ready. He said that he had to get it into a form people could understand. Otherwise, it would just confuse them."

"Even you?"

Timothy nodded. "Sometimes he didn't even let Mom read what he was working on when it was something he felt he had to get into shape on his own."

"So where is this thing he was working on?"

"That's what I've been trying to figure out ever since he died. I can't find it."

Brother and sister fell silent. The house grew quiet. Both felt the spirit of their mother and father around them.

"In his later years," Timothy went on after a minute or two, "I think the main audience he was thinking of when he wrote—besides himself—was the five of us. He hoped we would want to know his heart more deeply after he was gone. He said to me a few years ago that if I was the only one who read what he was working on, his effort would be rewarded."

He paused and laughed lightly. "It would seem even that purpose was foiled," he said. "I can't find his final work!"

Then he grew serious again.

"He was also writing reminiscences of some kind. About when he was a boy during the war and just afterward, I think. Mom's death put him in a reflective mood—trying to put life into perspective, you know."

"That would be a treasure. Even I might be interested in reading that! Where is it?"

"I don't know. He never mentioned it again. I haven't located it either. I'm not sure if he got very far on it."

Again, Timothy became pensive. "I asked him a few times," he said slowly. "Once when we were sitting here in the living room, I brought it up and the strangest look came into his eyes," replied Timothy with a smile. "He didn't say anything at first. He just began looking around. His eyes roved through the whole room, up and down the wall of bookshelves—he loved that wall with all his favorite little mini-libraries, his history and biblical reference books and books about Scotland, his Bible collection, books on Bible translation. Then I saw him gazing at the photographs and paintings on the walls—mostly family pictures. Then he rose from his chair and began wandering about. He was obviously deep in thought. He was walking slowly, like he was gazing at every book, every photograph, flooded with memories. Finally, he drew in a deep breath and let out a long sigh. He smiled a far-off, peaceful, contented smile."

"'My autobiography is *here*, Timothy,' he said at last. 'It's all around you. I don't need to write it. It's here. We're surrounded by it.'"

Timothy paused, then smiled again. "I wonder," he said, "if that's why he and mom wanted us to meet here for Thanksgiving, and to keep the house as it is for a while. Maybe that's what they wanted us to discover—what this house has to tell us about their lives, about who they were."

"You really knew Dad, Tim," said Cateline pensively. "I envy you. I could just never connect with that spiritual side of him."

"It's not too late, Cat."

"What do you mean? He's dead."

"It's never too late. Remember what Jesus said, that it was best for his disciples that he went away so that they would come to know even more of the truth he came to teach them. I plan to get to know Mom and Dad better and better for the rest of my life."

"You ought to write a biography of Dad, Tim. No one else could. You knew him better than any of us."

59

THE MARSHALL FIVE

TWO DAYS later the five sons and daughters of Stirling and Larke Marshall—Woodrow, otherwise known as "Woody," fifty-nine, Cateline fifty-eight, Graham fifty-six, Jane fifty-four, and Timothy, the baby of the family, at fifty-two—were seated around the family dining room table for Thanksgiving dinner. The mood was thoughtful though not sad. They had mourned their parents' passing the previous August. This was a day for nostalgically pleasant memories.

"I wonder why Mom and Dad put in their last instructions that we share Thanksgiving like this," said Woody, "and needed to wait until now to read the addendum to their trust. And why just the five of us, without our families, and that we stay in the house. What's that all about?"

"Don't you know?" asked Jane.

"Seems peculiar to me—like Dad's reaching out from the grave, still trying to control our lives."

"Come on, Woody—that's ridiculous. Dad was the least controlling man you could imagine."

"Are you kidding? He was completely controlling."

"Not toward me."

"Sure—you're younger. You had it easy. I'm five years older than you."

"And you never let me forget it," sighed Jane, frustration obvious in her tone. "I can't believe you'd say that after all he and Mom did

359

for us. I call it loving us and wanting the best for us. You've had an attitude about Dad ever since I can remember. That's on you, Woody, not him. Wanting us to be together like this is a nice thing, a good thing, the kind of thing a loving parent does. It baffles me you can't see it."

"Let's don't argue," said Cateline. "Whatever she had in mind, that's one thing Mom *didn't* want when we got together. I think the answer to your question is obvious, Woody. They wanted us to be together as a family, just the five of us. They wanted us to feel their presence in a different way than we could when they were alive."

"Kind of spooky, Cat," said Graham.

"Why spooky?" said Timothy. "I agree with Jane. Don't you feel a pleasant nostalgia, Graham—not exactly that they're here watching, but a peaceful sense of being a family again like when we were young. I think it's nice."

"So do I," said Jane. "I mean, look around. Everything meant something to them—even the little things. Have you looked at the tiny figurines and shells in the bathroom Mom called hers—she collected those all her life. And those steins we got when we were in Germany as kids, Mom's jar of colored glass from Scotland, that marble plant stand—it's a century-and-a-half old from our great-great-grandparents, or maybe further back. And the books! My goodness—books everywhere!"

"And the bookends," added Cateline. "Dad loved bookends! I love that set with the wizened old man sitting on a stool reading a book."

"Everything I look at in every room is like that," added Jane, "— telling a different story about Mom and Dad. Every inch of the house is full of who they were and the lives they lived."

"Tim said the same thing when he and I were talking before the rest of you got here," said Cateline.

"What?" asked Graham.

"That everything in the house is like a biography of their lives they wanted us to read."

"I didn't exactly say that!" laughed Timothy. "But that is a great insight, Cat. They wanted us to read their lives and understand what they meant."

"I don't care what anyone else says, I love being here," added Jane. "They obviously wanted us to drink in memories that were important to them, hoping they would mean something to us as well."

"Everything is a treasure," nodded Timothy. "They wanted their lives and this house to be meaningful to our children, their grandchildren, too."

It fell silent around the table.

"I'd rather sell the place and be done with it," said Woody. "I don't want to keep coming back. There are no happy memories for me here any more than in the Santa Barbara house."

"Gosh, Woody—what are you saying?" said Cateline. "No happy memories?"

"Not for me."

"Come on, Woody—that's an unbelievable thing to say," added Timothy. "Especially since you hardly visited Mom and Dad here more than a half dozen times after they moved."

"Don't you care about Mom and Dad's legacy?" asked Jane.

"Honestly, no," replied Woody.

The others were silent. Jane was angry. Timothy merely sighed. How could two brothers who grew up under the same roof have such completely opposite memories of their childhood years?

"I'm really sorry to hear you say that, Woody," he said after a few moments. "But if that is how you feel, I'll buy your share of the house. I don't want to change a thing—for a while at least. There are some writings of Dad's I need to find too, something about the future he mentioned to me—prophecy or something else, I have no idea. But I have to find it."

"What's that?" asked Jane.

"I'm not sure," replied Timothy. "He was working on something he said had to do with the church of the future."

"What do you mean—like end times, the second coming, the antichrist and all that?"

"Honestly, I have no idea."

"Whatever it is, you can leave me out of that one!" said Woody with clear sarcasm.

Later in the day four of the five were quietly absorbed in their own thoughts throughout the house. Woody had gone out for a drive. The others were perusing the shelves, losing themselves for long stretches in the many family picture albums, laughing and commenting about trips and memories from long ago.

The casual talk drifted toward politics, as was inevitable in an election year, especially with President-Elect Hunt's easy victory so fresh in their minds.

"You know, I'm glad Mom and Dad aren't going to have to live through an ACH presidency," said Graham almost absently as he was perusing a book by Rod Dreher he picked up in his father's study. "The direction of the country was breaking their hearts for long enough as it was, without having to endure that woman's hypocrisy for eight years."

"I take it you're not a fan!" laughed Jane.

"I'm surprised to hear you say such a thing, Graham," put in Cateline. "I thought all you Silicon Valley types were liberals."

"Just like all you teachers?" rejoined her brother.

"I suppose most of us are at that."

"Well, it's true what you say about tech types. I'm not sure why. What is it about some professions that seems uniformly to make them liberals—high tech, teaching, filmmaking, the news media. Seems odd to me. Why wouldn't people from the entire spectrum of viewpoints be represented in all professions? But given that it's the way it is, I keep my opinions to myself."

"Speaking of your teaching," said Jane, "what do you do when you're told you have to teach gender neutrality and that changing sex is perfectly normal?"

"This is liberal California. I teach it," replied Cateline. "It's my job."

"Gosh, Cat—are you kidding!"

"That's all ancient history, Jane. It's not even an issue anymore. It's part of the curriculum. If you're not comfortable with it, you quit."

"Are you comfortable with it?"

"You get used to it. Things change."

"How do you get used to sin?"

"Like being judgmental?"

"Come on, Cat. You know what I meant."

"Not everybody sees getting used to societal change as sin. If I don't go along, I'll lose my job."

"What about your conscience—filling students' minds with lies."

"I made my peace with that a long time ago. I can't think about it. You have to go along."

"Well people *ought* to think about it. Mom would die if she knew you teach such things."

"That's why I never told her."

"Why aren't you saying anything, Tim?" asked Jane, turning to the youngest of the five. "Come to my rescue here. Surely you don't support ACH."

"You're right, I don't."

"Why?" asked Cateline.

"Because she's a chameleon," replied Timothy quietly.

"A hypocrite, like Graham said, is more like it."

"It's her policies I'm worried about," added Graham. "Post-birth abortion up to six months after evaluation for birth defects? It's murder plain and simple. As a Christian how can you possibly support her, Cat? How can a Christian just *get used to* things like that, as you say?"

A tense silence fell.

"Honestly," said Timothy at length, "I know we're all grown-up adults, but for really thorny and complex dilemmas like this—spiritual, cultural, whatever—I always ask myself what Dad would think. I try to conjecture what he would say if he were here and I asked him about the current political and cultural climate."

"Why do you do that?" asked Cateline.

"Because I valued his perspectives, his opinions, his objectivity, and because he spent his life dedicated to finding and communicating truth. He was a wise man—wiser than me. If for no other reason than that his life experience and truth-seeking quest was longer than mine. If there was a conflict between the two, I would trust his perspective, his wisdom, over my own."

"That seems a little weird, Tim. Aren't we supposed to think for ourselves?"

"Of course. But I'd be foolish not to avail myself of whatever wisdom I can glean in the process of thinking for myself."

Again it was silent.

"So what do you think he would say about ACH?" asked Jane.

"Not much," smiled Timothy. "He would probably say she needs the Lord, she needs to repent, she needs to become God's daughter. He would say that about everyone. But he didn't get into the politics of personality. I do know that he was deeply concerned about the progressivity of the country, and especially the tolerance of liberal ideas infiltrating the church."

"Did he ever write about it?" asked Graham.

"Not that I know of," replied Timothy.

☆ ☆ ☆

"We need to go over to Mom and Dad's storage unit," said Timothy at breakfast the next morning. "All of us together. There are boxes of family things we need to decide what to do with."

"Well, I don't want anything," said Woody. "I'm not a sentimentalist. The rest of you can do what you want with it all. I don't want anything. I'm leaving for home this afternoon anyway."

"Mom wanted us to spend the weekend together," said Cateline. "I don't know how sentimental I am either. But I care enough to honor their wishes."

"Well Dad's not here to scold me. So I'm leaving."

The other four were silent.

"I suppose I'm with Woody," said Graham at length. "I doubt there's anything I want."

In obvious exasperation with her brothers, Jane rose and left the room. The outside door opened and closed a minute later.

Gradually the others wandered away.

Woody left after lunch to return to San Luis Obispo. His departure somewhat dispelled the cloud that had oppressed the others most of the morning, though not entirely. A pall remained, added to by the increase of stormy weather threatening to worsen by nightfall. At about 2:00 p.m. they piled into Timothy's Prius and drove the mile to their parents' storage unit.

Walking inside the ten-by-twenty sheet-metal cubicle did not quite bring with it the nostalgia of being in the house, though the handwritten labels on the boxes in their mother's and father's hand contributed to the melancholy of seeing the lives of past generations relegated to a few boxes stacked in a warehouse.

They wandered about silently gazing up and down and along the rows and stacks of boxes. Cateline and Jane slowly gravitated to those containing linens and dishes and other homey heirlooms, taking down one at a time and starting the process of sorting through them. Graham was soon engrossed in three or four boxes of LPs dating back to the 1940s. Meanwhile, Timothy was at the far end on top of the ladder his father kept on hand.

"Graham, give me a hand, would you?" he said. "There are several unlabeled boxes here on the top shelf. Let me hand them down to you. I want to see what's inside."

"Sure," answered his brother.

He reached up and took the first box from Timothy.

Another came down, then a third.

"This box has your name on it, Tim," he said. "It's called genealogy files."

"I didn't see that. I'll get it home and peruse it later."

They shut the storage unit fifteen minutes later with various boxes they each wanted to look through and headed back to the house. They arrived just in time to avoid a downpour from the predicted storm.

As much as the other four loved Woody, they realized that he did not share the deep honor in which they held their mother and father. Whatever his issues were had been a mystery to them all their lives. His absence freed them to gradually begin sharing their own memories more openly. By suppertime the four were reminiscing fondly, laughing, though shedding a few tears as well, and feeling closer as brothers and sisters than they ever had in their lives.

60

FATHER TO SON

IT WAS after ten before the memory-rich conversation between Cateline, Graham, Jane, and Timothy stilled. Suddenly they realized how tired they were. It had been an emotionally draining day.

Alone in his parents' bedroom—which Timothy used whenever he came for a visit after their passing—he gazed about for some minutes, drinking in the surroundings of their private inner sanctum. The box with his name on it sat on the floor next to the bed. At length he sat and lifted the lid.

Laying on top were five white legal envelopes. His name was written on the top one in his father's familiar hand.

He opened it and removed the two folded computer-printed sheets:

Dear Timothy,

*If you are reading this, it will mean you found the box where I placed it in the storage unit. I was pretty sure you would. The letters to your brothers and sisters are personal to each of them. But to you I am giving a special charge, which, for the present, is **only** for you. More will be made clear in time. But for now, this letter is between you and me alone.*

I know the house contains probably far more books than you will ever want or need. I must simply leave them with you and your brothers and sisters to use, keep, or give away as you consider appropriate. Books are the greatest repository of wisdom in the world, and also the great repository of secrets. The world's greatest mysteries are hidden in books. They may be in plain sight, but only those with eyes to see will be able to discern the meaning of the mysteries. "The greatest secrets are always hidden in the most unlikely places." I hope you will discern the deeper meaning in what I have just said about mysteries hidden in books.

It was always my hope and intent to write a family biography. Of particular interest to me were the authors our parents read and admired. Some of them have much to tell us today about the key to life, which is the task set before us all—to find the key. Discern my meaning, Timothy: Find the key. St. Benedict, Geert Groote, and other ancient brethren of what they called the "common life," for example, have great wisdom to impart about community. Kempis, by the way, one of my favorites, also lived at Groote's community in the Netherlands where he wrote **The Imitation**. *Thomas Erskine much later used another phrase I have recently been taken with that reminds me of the common life. Erskine calls it "the spiritual order" by which God intends man to live.*

To tell my own life was never the purpose for which I began my genealogical research, but to tell the stories and influences of those men and women who came before.

Influences such as that of the Quaker Thomas Kelly, who wrote: "Deep within us all there is an amazing inner sanctuary of the soul, a holy place, a Divine Center, a speaking Voice, to which we may continuously return."

I am wondering if you remember our occasional discussions about the mathematician Blaise Pascal. I was reading him again recently and ran across this brief statement—a prescription for life, wouldn't you say. He said, "One must know oneself. If this does not serve to discover truth, it at least serves as a rule of life, and there is nothing better." He also succinctly stated the quandary between science and deism such as first drew you and your lovely wife together. One of his particularly pithy statements was simply this: "All things proceed from the Nothing, and are borne toward the Infinite. Who will follow these marvelous processes? The Author of these wonders understands them. None other can do so."

Yet another example of bookends in God's creation—from Nothing to the Infinite. I do love bookends—I'm sure you remember.

You five are my chief audience now. I love you and Woodrow, Cateline, Graham, and Jane with all my heart!

I give you this final charge, Timothy my son. The Lord has impressed upon me in recent months a final message, not merely to you, but to his people, his Church, perhaps it may even be, to his "remnant" of true disciples for whom perilous times of tribulation are surely approaching. It is a message which I leave to you to shepherd as God leads you.

*In that regard, my thinking during that process has been profoundly impacted by Harold Wright's insight into the true nature of the enemy, which masquerades as an ally. I urge you to seek him out, to discover his deeper meaning, and mine, for **the key to everything is the books**. Wright wrote: "And because the town of this story is what it is, there came to dwell in it a Spirit—a strange, mysterious power—playful, vicious, deadly; a Something to be at once feared and courted; to be denied—yet confessed in the denial; a deadly enemy, a welcome friend, and an all-powerful Ally." To this I would only make one change— I would reword "the town of this story," to "the nation and church of the future."*

*In all you do, in all you read, in whatever avenues our Father leads you to follow in my footsteps, do not forget, do not ignore, and be ever vigilant against the Ally. Wright wrote no mere novel, but gave prophetic insight into a future time that will birth the remnant. The Ally is insidious, it is everywhere, ubiquitous in all walks of life, in the people around you. **Come out and be separate**, says the Lord. **Come out**—do not be allied with the Ally, the spirit of the age, the spirit of the enemy.*

*The Scotsman's classic passage from **The Hope of the Gospel*** *is a description, in a sense, of the **doctrinal** Ally which proceeds out of the **church** Ally so insightfully illuminated by Wright. Both are cousins of the **political** Ally of soft totalitarianism unmasked by Dreher. You will recognize the Scotsman's words: "Men would understand: they do not care to **obey**. . . . They would search into the work of the Lord instead of doing their part in it. . . . They will not accept, that is, act upon, their highest privilege, that of obeying the Son of God. It is on them that do his will, that the day dawns; to them the day-star arises in their hearts. Obedience is the soul of knowledge."*

*These authors I mention have helped make me the man I am. In some ways, perhaps, I might go so far as to say **they hold the key to my legacy**. As you know, Timothy my boy, books have been my life, and as the Scriptures say, "Of making many books there is no end." Find the books and you will find it.*

*And don't forget Benjamin Franklin's, sage advice, "Three may keep a secret, if two of them are dead." Mine is a secret I want three to keep, but when you read this, only I will be dead, and I am not one of them. Like Orwell said in **1984**, "If you want to keep a secret, you must also hide it from yourself," though I am hiding it from you, until you find it.*

I thus leave my final work in your hands. Look to him to guide you to it. Be strong in the Lord, my son, and in the strength of his might. Stand strong in truth.

With much affection, the deepest love of a father's heart, and in great anticipation of seeing you again soon,

Dad

His eyes swimming in liquid and his cheeks wet, Timothy turned the final sheet over to see if his father had written anything further to illuminate or give him further instructions about his enigmatic reference to a final message.

But there was nothing.

At length he replaced the lid on the box and readied himself for bed. Sleep, however eluded him for several more hours. He could find no satisfactory explanation for his father's curious words about some kind of so-called final message.

It wasn't like his father to overlook such an important detail. Had he simply forgotten? Or had he planned to tell him more, but death had overtaken him before he could do so?

Perhaps he would find something in the box. He would look in the morning.

When Timothy awoke four or five hours later, the house was still dark and quiet. Silently he left the room, made himself a cup of coffee, then returned, and again opened the lid of the box containing the four envelopes to his brothers and sisters, as well as his father's files, photographs, genealogical research, and other papers and writings.

But still there was no sign of a final document he had seemed to be alluding to.

61

NEW ERA IN THE MASTERPLAN

DECEMBER 2032

THE GROUNDS of the lavish estate in the hills outside Mira Monte, fifteen miles inland from the coast of California's Santa Barbara Channel, belied the secretive—some would say sinister, not even its innermost circle would deny deceptive—enclave for which a highly select group of attendees had been arriving for three days. The expensively appointed lounge in which the meeting would be held could seat eighty and had seen many auspicious gatherings during the last forty years, though few so momentous as that which would soon be underway.

The residents of Mira Monte called it the Roswell estate, though the patriarch of the family who built it from a fortune amassed in lucrative though somewhat dubious investment products—as anything slightly shady was enigmatically called in the world of high finance—had passed years ago. The estate, with its two hundred acres of vineyards, had been in the hands of his son Talon since shortly after his graduation from college. Now eighty-two, Talon had effectively turned its management over to his son, Storm, forty-nine, whose own son, Anson, twenty-two, was now also on his own way up in the organization whose agenda had long ago surpassed mere banking and winemaking.

The most important function of the Roswell compound these days was as clandestine headquarters for Palladium and its select and secretive membership.

The locals knew that high-level meetings took place at the estate, assuming them connected with the family's ongoing business interests. The limousines occasionally creeping through town, through the highly guarded gates and extensive security system, thence along the winding tree-lined drive, always had tinted windows. There was no point in being too curious. Nor had anyone forgotten old Orville Shults's disappearance fifteen years ago after spreading it about town that through a two-inch crack in one of the rear windows of a long black limo, he saw the unmistakable face of a certain former president peering out at the countryside. A month later Orville went missing and was never seen again, nor his body recovered.

There were rumors, the gist of which boiled down to: keep your thoughts about the Roswells to yourself. Wine trucks and restaurant vans and other delivery vehicles came and went in full view, keeping the illusion alive that nothing other than winemaking was going on. There was no tasting room. Tours were not given.

Most visitors no longer arrived by limousine. A private paved road now wound from the back of the house through the vineyards and into the canyons at the base of the forbidding white ledge cliffs of the Matilija Wilderness at the eastern extremity of the Santa Ynez Mountains. It was an extremely remote and unfriendly part of the country's most populous state. Deep in one of the canyons, a helipad and several buildings were hidden from even the most adventurous of prying eyes.

The proximity of the estate's boundary to the southeastern extremity of the Los Padres National Forest facilitated the easy circulation through the region of the report that the Bureau of Land Management had installed a post nearby which kept helicopters arriving and taking off with some frequency. The sight of choppers in the distance north of Mira Monte thus aroused only mild curiosity. That the new post was installed by the BLM was true enough, though it was nothing but an expensive empty building serving no purpose other than to shield Palladium's comings and goings.

The approval of the shell facility had been easy to get through Congress. When Palladium wanted anything, permission was the least of its concerns. Its principles neither asked permission *nor* forgiveness.

They made the rules. The captains of industry, finance, and politics asked *their* permission, which was usually forthcoming since the *generals* of industry, finance, and politics were themselves members. Palladium's backing meant success. Without it in most fields, you were dead. And not always, if you tried too vigorously to oppose the secret cartel, figuratively.

As the guests on this occasion arrived by private helicopter, they were driven up to the estate the back way through the vineyards by one of Palladium's full-time staff who lived on the premises. Each guest had his or her private quarters among the seventy-two luxurious three-room suites permanently assigned to Palladium's voting members. When in residence they were waited on as only the elite are. Many of the seventy-two came regularly. The facilities were superior to any Four Seasons hotel, and absolute secrecy was assured.

Though all were well known in their fields, extensive precautions were taken to guarantee the secrecy of those arriving for this meeting, as was the case for all Palladium functions. In conjunction with bogus news reports of their whereabouts, transportation was arranged from Van Nuys' small airport, where all had arrived by private jet. None of the sixty-five who were present on this occasion were thought to be anywhere within miles of Mira Monte. Half were reportedly overseas, most of the rest, except for the California residents, on the East Coast. All were distinguished in their fields, three dozen had or still occupied positions at the highest levels of government, others likewise in their own domains of finance, academia, law, industry, even ten religious leaders—five Christian, three Muslim, two Jewish. All knew one another and had gathered on numerous occasions. This meeting, however, carried more import than most.

The one who would be addressing them was held in higher esteem than any of the seventy-two. He was not technically a *member* of Palladium. Some might have considered him the founder, though he was not that either. He was the inspirational figurehead, guide, visionary, and spiritual heart of the whole, if such a term could be applied to a man who hated religion with every fiber of his being. His far-reaching vision, and his secretively cunning means of achieving it, had given

birth to a cartel with far more extensive reach in a globalized technological world than the Illuminati could ever have dreamed. Palladium
flowed out of his sweeping view of the world of the future. He was Palladium's Moses, its Almighty God.

In the beginning was Viktor Domokos. He declared, "Let there be
a new world order!" And the genesis of Palladium was born.

The brainchild of Slayton Bardolf, with his fellow disciples of that
new order, Talon Roswell and Derek Crawford, the organization had
grown, first as a secretive campus society, then into something far
more, in no small measure because of Domokos's support. Now the
Bardolf and Roswell names were legendary, and the scions of a third
successive generation were on the verge of making their own presence
felt, as had their fathers and grandfathers before them.

Palladium's subsidiaries and affiliates were developed through the
years as the need arose in various fields of endeavor to develop a farm
system, as it were, to evaluate potential new members before bringing
them all the way into the top echelons of leadership. With the secrets,
wealth, and power to shape finance, education, media, arts, entertain-
ment, and culture, and to direct governments to carry out their stealthy
agenda, Palladium's membership was ruthlessly guarded.

Its affiliates carried out its marching orders at the grass-roots level,
its followers never suspecting to what extent their thoughts, actions,
perspectives, worldview, and the agendas of their various professional
guilds were not only being subtly shaped and directed, but also monitored, by Palladium's oversight, with one powerful member of the
seventy-two acting as president or chairperson for each. Their rank
and file knew no more than that they joined associations dedicated to
progressive policies within their specific spheres. They paid their dues,
read their materials, and did their part to further an ingeniously invisible program of worldwide indoctrination. Palladium's vision was thus
spread through the culture by the media and technological tentacles
of a shrewdly crafted con—a stratagem of darkness masquerading as
light, discrimination masquerading as justice, exclusivity masquerading as diversity, and prejudice masquerading as tolerance.

Educators for Inclusion, Diversity, and Equity functioned with the blessing and under the auspices of the National Teacher's Association.

The *Society for Financial Equity* functioned with the blessing and under the auspices of the Association for Financial Professionals.

The *Progressive Journalism Guild* functioned with the blessing and under the auspices of the Society of Professional Journalists.

The *Institute for Social Justice* functioned with the blessing and under the auspices of the American Bar Association.

Republicans for Change functioned with the blessing and under the auspices of the Republican National Committee.

Democrats for Change functioned with the blessing and under the auspices of the Democratic National Committee.

The *Institute for Progress in Religion* functioned with the blessing and under the auspices of the National Council of Churches.

Evangelicals for Biblical Diversity functioned with the blessing and under the auspices of the National Association of Evangelicals.

One of the most important of Palladium's subsidiaries was the fraternal organization that gave birth to the entire movement in the 1970s under the leadership of Slayton Bardolf and Talon Roswell. Most of its members came up through its ranks from university beginnings. It was originally called the Alliance for Progress. As Palladium burgeoned into higher spheres of power, the secretive university fraternal society was spun off into a separate subsidiary known simply as *Oraculous*.

Though none of the thousands of members of the subsidiary federations knew it existed, Palladium yet kept a full-time staff of three whose sole responsibility was to maintain extensive dossiers on every member of these affiliates and follow their activities. Their objective was twofold. They were on the lookout for new leadership. But they were similarly watching for leaks, suspicious activity, loose tongues, ambiguous loyalties, or wavering commitment that might spell trouble. Any such loose ends that could compromise Palladium's ultimate goals were dealt with in a variety of ways. Discrediting reputations was usually enough and resulted in loss of position and status and removal from professional organizations. Failing gentler methods, the means of dealing with more stubborn or problematic influences could be unpleasant, if not fatal.

The series of highly confidential memoranda announcing the meeting to be held on this particular occasion, identifying the special guest who would address the group, perhaps for the final time, stressed the imperative of the full voting membership's attendance. The only absences were due to health concerns of several of the oldest members.

In its early years, the organization grew with no thought to what it might evolve into. In the year 2000, the name was changed to the Palladium Alliance for Progress and a new Charter of Purpose drawn up by then Grand Masters Slayton Bardolf and Talon Roswell, and their fellow members of the oversight committee, or the League of Seven. The new charter set a limit to the voting membership at seventy-two. To these were added an additional seventy-two auxiliary memberships, all of whom were accorded use of the estate facilities and had equal rights and privileges other than voting on matters of policy. All 144 were invited to participate in meetings and gatherings, though the logistics of lodging the non-voting membership occasionally became cumbersome. This was just such an occasion.

No one retired from Palladium, though the toll of age gradually forced its members to become less involved, or to step back altogether from active participation, as in the case of Devon Crawford. Additions to either level of membership occurred only at death. Vacancies to the voting membership were filled by secret ballot of the remaining seventy-one out of the non-voting membership. Vacancies of the non-voting membership were filled, also by secret ballot by the top seventy-two, from a list of prospective members drawn from a pool of names, to which any voting member could add at any time, and which was constantly monitored by the League of Seven. New memberships were evaluated in such a manner as to keep the fields of endeavor and expertise generally balanced, with heaviest weight given to top leaders in politics, academia, and the media.

The son of the evening's host, Mike Bardolf, thirty-one, was several years older than Anson Roswell. Both third-generation scions were now members of the non-voting seventy-two and were present on this occasion. Also present was second-term congresswoman Akilah Samara, thirty-nine, curiously, given her pedigree, also still a non-voting member of the 144 like the younger Bardolf and Roswell. She was the guest of honor's granddaughter, and a rising political star in her own right.

"You are all here," began Loring Bardolf, chairman of the League of Seven, "to participate in the great privilege of hearing from our mentor, guide, and inspiration, Viktor Domokos."

Applause filled the room.

"None of you need be told," the elder Bardolf went on, "for you have heard the story many times, how my father was inspired listening to Viktor during his college years, along with Talon," he added, glancing toward his father's aging friend sitting at the front of the room with the rest of the Seven.

Again, the room filled with applause for the last remaining member of their founding trio.

"I do not want to take any more time from Viktor," Bardolf went on. "He has important things to say to us. So, Viktor—" he said, turning to their distinguished guest, "the floor is yours."

Domokos rose and walked forward, somewhat unsteadily, showing his nine-plus decades, helped by Bardolf up the three steps of the raised dais. He turned to face the room, filled again with applause lasting for several minutes. After thirty seconds he sat down on the chair provided him, and waited for the applause to die away.

"Thank you," began Domokos in his distinctive Romanian accent. His voice was soft though the microphone in front of him made him easily heard. "You are most kind. It is my hope that each of you, in your own positions of influence, will dedicate yourselves from this night on, even more than you have in the past, to the third millennial remaking of the nation which has been known as the United States of America. We gathered here have been engaged in this historic enterprise for much of our lives. Enormous strides have been taken to bring this land out of the Dark Ages of its Western European and racist founders. Yet there remains much to be done to complete the vision to which I have given my life. I believe that the complete transformation out of a white

Christian past into a future where all are free to live without prejudice, fear, or hatred is closer to its realization than ever before."

His voice was somewhat shaky. Yet the power of his influence and reputation remained undiminished. The room was silent. Everyone knew this might be the last time they saw the great man, and they listened attentively.

"You have all been working in this cause for many years," he went on. "We have come far. The nation's government is almost entirely in our control. We have successfully turned the educational system into a well-oiled machine for the transmission of our ideas. The Republican party is but a memory. We have so bolstered the electorate with tens of millions of immigrants that even should some new populist conservative arise, he could never hope to win. The presidency, Congress, and a majority of the statehouses are ours far into the conceivable future."

He paused. His thick gray eyebrows knit together thoughtfully.

"I confess, however," he went on, "to concern about our new president-elect. She may be difficult to manage. I had hoped we would be able to prevent her election. It may be that we have become lazy. We are suddenly reminded that the mere Democrat label itself is no guarantee of our success. It is a potential problem we have not encountered before—one who shares many of our objectives but is outside our influence. I reached out to her office when her presidential run became apparent. I thought if I could sit down with her face-to-face, I might gain a clear sense of whether or not I could work with her. But I was never contacted. I tried a second time, then received a curt reply from one of her underlings saying that the Speaker would have no time available for an interview.

"The situation bears watching. I would far rather we had one of our own people preparing to move into the White House. We are only fortunate that we were able to sway events behind the scenes resulting in her choosing Xavier as her VP."

All eyes turned toward the vice-president-elect, a long-time member in good standing of Palladium.

"The challenge," Domokos resumed, "will be to find means to guide and shape her decisions. I am not altogether optimistic, however, that Xavier's position will weigh much with her. Her militant feminism is unlikely to yield to a man's influence. She was known to have wanted a woman with her on the ticket and only bowed to party pressure begrudgingly. It has been suggested that we bring her all the way into the fold—for you to offer her membership, even relax some of your requirements and initiation procedures. But I consider that extremely dangerous. She would not be one I would trust to keep your existence secret. She is far too independent. She will never be one of us. We must try to find ways for Xavier to mitigate the problem. The most advantageous outcome would be to remove her altogether. But finding an impeachable offense given her popularity would be difficult."

Where he sat toward the rear of the expansive room listening intently, the ears of the grandson of Palladium's founder perked up at the potential implications of the elder Romanian's words.

Domokos reached to the low table at his side and took a few sips of water, then continued. "But presidents come and go. Palladium will live on and will outlast us all . . . and is soon to outlast me," he added with a gravelly chuckle. "I have fought the good fight, as they say, but I must now pass on the legacy to you."

Again he paused.

"I am ninety-three," he said. "Probably no one should live so long. However, the end is at last approaching. I have inoperable cancer, and—"

Low exclamations rippled through the room.

"Not to worry," he said, raising his hand against whatever protests might begin. "It is slow growing. I have two or three years left. Perhaps my years will take me before the cancer does. However, I have made plans to ensure that my legacy lives on. Those plans involve you."

Another pause. The others waited.

"I have made provision to leave a substantial portion of my fortune to Palladium to be used as the organization deems appropriate to carry out our agenda. All the necessary legalities of my will and trust are in place, filed, finalized, and the funds designated for Palladium diverted so circuitously through numerous of my own charities as to be untraceable. My granddaughter Akilah," he added, glancing to where she sat in the front row, "has been designated executor of my will. I have not yet chosen a trustee to oversee the provisions of my trust, who may come from Palladium's membership to ensure all is done according to my wishes.

"It goes without saying that the existence of Palladium and its activities must remain entirely secretive. That imperative convinces me that a closer approach to the president is inadvisable. She may remain an unfortunate disruption to our momentum. Thus far you have managed to remain more unknown than Skull and Bones, even the Illuminati. Though I will soon be gone, however, I sense that threats to your anonymity may be on the horizon. Therefore, I urge wariness and renewed diligence."

The silence which followed this time was broken by a well-known voice.

"If I may . . ."

"Of course, Mr. President," said Domokos.

"I'm certain I speak for us all when I say we are deeply honored at the trust you would place in us, and equally grieved to hear of your illness—"

Domokos waved the comment aside. "Unimportant. I've lived a long life. We'll hear no more about that. You must all take the vision forward."

"Then of course we are at your service," rejoined the former president.

"For some years I have been at work on a personal manifesto," Domokos went on, "call it my final prophetic message, if you will—a summary of my life's vision for world transformation. I hope you will consider it worthy of being placed with the founding documents and the Palladium Charter. You will find nothing so unfamiliar in it. In brief, however, let me give an overview précis of what I have embodied in it in more detail.

"The ultimate objective is the complete eradication in the United States of xenophobia, homophobia, Islamophobia, and Christianity. This must include all publications and institutions—schools, clubs, churches, and privately funded organizations—that further these nefarious priorities in any way."

Domokos spoke for another fifteen or twenty minutes, seeming to gather strength from the articulation of one after another point in his grandiose vision. Most of its specifics were not new to his listeners. But never had they heard him so concisely lay out the whole in such a unified way.

"Obviously these are sweeping reforms that cannot be accomplished overnight," he said as he concluded. "We must engage the public slowly, invisibly, methodically. The work has been underway for decades. Most of the groundwork has been laid for the acceptance of the measures I have outlined. The progress toward the elimination of gender and the nuclear family has advanced so far from what we could have imagined just thirty years ago. History is on our side. Those two aspects of the masterplan have wedged a toe into the door from which all the rest is now possible.

"Yet we must continue to exercise caution and institute these changes slowly and imperceptibly. Their enormity must never be recognized for what it is. Our goal is to normalize what former generations would have considered unimaginable one step at a time. We began speaking of individual freedom, then individual rights, and thirty years later we had successfully normalized murder by calling it a woman's right to make her own medical choices. Abortion is no longer considered killing, it is a *right*.

"In the same way, sexual freedom has led to what would have been unthinkable, marriage between those of the same gender, men competing in women's sports, and operations to change one's biological gender. By using ingeniously inclusive terms, we have successfully normalized all these things. We will soon be in a position to dictate all aspects of what has formerly been called 'family,' eliminating patriarchy altogether.

"We will continue doing so by invisibly educating the public to accept our mandate for the ultimate good of mankind. The changes we have already seen proceeded so effortlessly that I confess that, as pleased as I am, it is almost shocking how easy it has been. When I gave that talk almost sixty years ago now, when Loring's father was present, I could not have dreamed how rapidly we would overturn the mores of the past.

"Christianity must likewise be eradicated by the drip-drip-drip strategy, invisibly emphasizing the truth through every avenue possible—over and over, year after year—that its core beliefs are myth, that the man Jesus was a common criminal, and that its fundamental ideas are inherently racist and bigoted. As you know, because a number of you are involved in the project, we have had a committee of scholars working on a new version of the Bible which is being subtly edited with appropriate terminology to bolster precisely these conclusions. It is near completion. Steps are already underway to spread it through the churches of Christendom as the most accurate translation ever produced. Over a hundred Catholic, Protestant, and evangelical priests, pastors, and leaders have endorsed it. They have all promised, having been given sufficient financial incentives, to replace those editions presently in use in their churches and denominations. It will be published with an appendix of the best selections from the Koran. We are now working to arrive at a name that will appeal to everyone, even the unreligious—something like the *God's Love Bible* or the *Universal Bible*, though nothing has been decided yet."

Domokos paused thoughtfully. The others waited.

"And yet," he began again, "though much of the culture is in our control, with the exception of the presidency at the moment, in recent months I have sensed sinister forces at work. Within my spirit I perceive tremors of an awakening, far stronger than anything we have known, that could undermine all our progress if we allow it to gain a foothold. My premonition is of no new political movement, no new Trump figure on the horizon. Nor is it connected to the cautions I feel about our soon-to-be new president. It is deeper, more widespread, hidden. *Something* is alive, I cannot tell where.

"Whatever this new force is, its invisibility makes it more dangerous than a mere final flicker from the conservative right. It originates from somewhere else entirely. I hold no store by such things, as you know, but it feels like a birthing—the inception of a psychic movement of strange power.

"I cannot be more specific than to caution you to renewed vigilance in our cause. Even this year's date may be significant. I would be curious to know the significance of the year '32' or '33' in previous centuries, even previous millennia. What took place in 1532 or 1032? We must beware of extrasensory awakenings from the past.

"I am unable to describe it other than a sense of foreboding. An unseen evil is afoot. I urge you to take heed. Be watchful and alert. Our victory is not yet assured. Something powerful is stirring. As I leave the future in your hands, therefore, I exhort you to press forward with our agenda without delay."

Where he sat listening, Sonrab Bahram regretted that his son Hamad was not with him. Domokos was speaking of *them*!

62

CLEVER CLUES TO THE KEY

EARLY 2033

TIMOTHY MARSHALL was deeply moved by the letter his father left him.

Perplexed—but moved.

He was equally torn between loyalty to and an almost physical ache of love for the dear man who was as close a friend as any human father could be, and the unsettled awkwardness, even perhaps an unrequited familial pain, of being the only one of his father's sons and daughters to be given such a final charge. That he, as the youngest, should be singled out filled him with a multitude of emotions he could not identify.

Yet what exactly was that charge?

His father's ambiguous words carried a tone of undefined import. He sensed some high purpose behind the vague, almost random, inferences and allusions in the letter. However, it was unclear what exactly his father expected.

The burden of responsibility to discover the answer to that question was with him night and day. He longed to share his quandary, first with Jaylene of course who might see what he could not in the letter and help him discern his father's intent, then with his siblings.

Meanwhile, Timothy did his best to decipher his father's somewhat peculiar letter, and its oddly interspersed quotes and references to various authors. Their inclusion in the midst of thoughts about his memoirs and his parents' lives didn't seem to fit.

What was the "final message" he felt God had given him? And what did he mean when he said he was leaving it in his hands?

Whatever it was, the greater question remained—*Where was it?*

He knew toward the end that people sometimes became incoherent. But he could not escape the sense that the peculiar construction of the letter, with its odd quotes and asides was intentional, and contained hints his father wanted him to find. But their meaning eluded him. And *why* had his father resorted to such a circuitous means of communication? Why not just say what he had to say? And why hide the letter in a box in the storage unit?

Weeks, then months went by. He prayed for light, for guidance, as he pored over his father's words. Slowly one, now another word or phrase from the letter stole into his brain with gradual new meaning. Every reference had to do with books. Clearly books were the key to whatever message his father intended.

He glanced down the letter again, though by now it was nearly memorized.

> *. . . as you know, Timothy my boy, books have been my life, and as the Scriptures say, "Of the writing of books there is no end." Find the books and you will find it.*

Obviously, whatever his father was trying to tell him was somehow embedded in books. Or in a book. Possibly one of his Bibles. But flipping through all the Bibles on his father's desk, hoping another letter or note might fall out from between the pages and answer everything, yielded nothing.

Had his father perhaps not meant the Bible, but the books he had written? On the other hand, it was just as likely that he was referring to his library of books in the house, as he mentioned in the second paragraph of the letter.

His eyes strayed again to the conclusion of the letter.

> *And don't forget Benjamin Franklin's sage advice, "Three may keep a secret, if two of them are dead." Mine is a secret*

*that I want three to keep, but when you read this, only I will be dead, and I am not one of them. Like Orwell said in **1984**, "If you want to keep a secret, you must also hide it from yourself," though I am hiding it from you, until you find it.*

What strange quotes to string together, all the more cryptic with his father's additions!

Two weeks later Timothy was at it again. By now convinced that whatever his father wanted him to find was located in Dorado Wood, he drove to his parents' home on a Saturday afternoon when he would have plenty of time.

He sat down in his father's favorite chair, then again read his father's letter.

Every time he did so, something new drew his attention. Each time he followed wherever it might lead. On this day he particularly noticed the paragraph:

Books are the greatest repository of wisdom in the world, and also the great repository of secrets. The world's greatest mysteries are hidden in books. They may be in plain sight, but only he with eyes to see will be able to discern the meaning of the mysteries.

Then came the additional words in quotation marks:
"The greatest secrets are always hidden in the most unlikely places," with the yet more tantalizing, *"I hope you will discern the deeper meaning in what I have just said."*

If the next to last sentence was a direct quote, why had he not thought before to go to the source of the quote?

Timothy picked up his laptop from the table beside him. A brief online search revealed the quote as from British novelist and children's author Roald Dahl. He had never heard his father mention Dahl. To his knowledge none of Dahl's books were anywhere in the house.

Now that he thought about it, however, he did recall a volume titled *Nineteenth and Twentieth Century Authors.*

He jumped up and went to the wall of bookshelves. It took him some time to locate it, though once having done so he saw that it was in plain sight, spine out along with eight or ten other volumes between two of his father's favorite bookends, oddly sitting next to a copy of *Unspoken Commandments* and his father's favorite Bible, a red cloth 1952 first edition RSV that had belonged to his parents and had been patched and repatched many times. Quickly he pulled out the *Authors Encyclopedia* and flipped to the entry on Roald Dahl.

There in the margin in his father's hand were the words:

God's secrets are waiting for everyone to find who wants to find them—go to HBW.

That was his father all right! An obvious clue.

But why did he write the words here, next to an entry on Dahl, an atheist whose writings were dark, even macabre? His father must have known that *eventually* the quote in the letter would lead him here.

And it did!

Okay, Dad, thought Timothy. *I'm finally on the trail you left. What next!*

So what did HBW mean? Another author's initials perhaps?

Go to HBW . . .

He turned and hurried back to his father's letter where he had set it down and quickly scanned it for the names of the authors he mentioned.

Kelly . . . Kempis . . . Groote . . . Erskine . . . *Harold Wright!*

HW!

Timothy tossed the letter onto the table and ran back to the *Authors Encyclopedia*, flipped through it hurriedly to the Ws. There was the entry:

Harold Bell Wright (May 4, 1872–May 24, 1944) was a best-selling American writer of fiction, essays, and nonfiction. Although mostly forgotten or ignored after the middle of the 20th century, he had a very successful career; he is said to have been the first American writer to sell a million copies of a novel.

Scanning down further to a listing of his books, Timothy saw one title underlined:

The Calling of Dan Matthews.

He thought a moment, his eyes gazing straight ahead. Suddenly they shot wide. There was the book right in front of him! And sitting on the same shelf between his father's favorite bookends, next to *Unspoken Commandments.*

His father placed it where he knew he would eventually see it!

Hurriedly, he replaced the *Authors Encyclopedia* on the other side of *Unspoken Commandments*, pulled out the Wright volume, and flipped through the front matter. There on the first page of chapter 1 was the exact quote his father emphasized in his letter:

*And because the town of this story is what it is, there came
to dwell in it a Spirit—a strange, mysterious power—playful,
vicious, deadly; a Something to be at once feared and courted;
to be denied—yet confessed in the denial; a deadly enemy, a
welcome friend, and an all-powerful Ally.*

There were no marginal notes this time to lead him to another clue. Slowly he replaced the book and returned to his father's chair. He had obviously picked up the trail. But nothing else came to him on this day.

Two weeks later, Timothy was again alone in the house in Dorado Wood, this time on a Tuesday afternoon when he had no classes and had decided to take the afternoon off. He went through the same routine as always, quieting himself hoping to sense something he had not noticed before, as if inviting the walls, his parents' photographs, and the books everywhere around him, to speak.

Two quotes from the letter had led him to books on the shelf in front of him. He knew the letter would lead him further. He just had to pick up the trail again.

After praying and sitting several minutes in silence, again he pulled out his father's letter—nearly ragged from repeated readings—unfolded it, scanned it slowly. For at least the twentieth time he read again the words, "'*Of making many books there is no end.*' Find the books and you will find it."

Suddenly the most obvious thought slammed into his brain. How could he have been so dense not to look up the reference and read the quote in the original!

He knew it well—Ecclesiastes 12:12!

Excitedly he walked to the wall of bookshelves. The obvious place to start was the red RSV. There it still sat where he had seen it so many times between the two bookends along with the handful of other volumes, including the two in which he had already found clues!

He pulled it out and opened it to the twelfth chapter of Ecclesiastes. Glancing down the page, he saw that throughout the chapter his father had underlined a few phrases in pencil. Oddly, however, the *of making many books* line was not one of them.

> *Remember also your Creator in the days of your youth, before the evil days come, and the years draw nigh, when you will say, "I have no pleasure in them"; before the sun and the light and the moon and the stars are darkened and the clouds return after the rain; in the day when the keepers of the house tremble, and the strong men are bent, and the grinders cease . . . they are afraid also of what is high, and terrors are in the way; the almond tree blossoms, the grasshopper drags itself along and desire fails. . . . Vanity of vanities, says the Preacher; all is vanity. Besides being wise, the Preacher also taught the people knowledge, weighing and studying and arranging proverbs with great care. The Preacher sought to find pleasing words, and uprightly he wrote words of truth. The sayings of the wise are like goads, and like nails firmly fixed are the collected sayings which are given by one Shepherd. My son, beware of anything beyond these. Of making many books there is no end, and much study is a weariness of the flesh. The end of the matter; all has been heard. Fear God, and keep his commandments; for this is the whole duty of man. For God will bring every deed into judgment, with every secret thing, whether good or evil.*

What did the underlined message mean?

Remember before the evil days come, in the day when the keepers of the house tremble and strong men are afraid. The Preacher taught the people knowledge, and uprightly he wrote words of truth. The sayings of the wise are given by one Shepherd. My son, fear God, and keep his commandments.

In the margin next to the word "commandments" was the tiny notation, *#23*.

The *commandments* . . .

Might this be a reference to his father's own book? And there sat a copy next to the Bible! All the clues were here together!

He set the Bible aside and pulled out the copy of *Unspoken Commandments*. Quickly he turned to the twenty-third entry: *Rejoice in All Circumstances*.

The words of the first paragraph were underlined:

The formula for unlocking Genesis 1 is the same as that needed to penetrate the mysteries of Revelation 22 . . . and everything between. That powerful key . . .

The 22 in the text was lightly crossed through, with the tiny numbers sandwiched between the lines, 20–21.

Was his father directing him to Revelation 20 and 21?

In the margin was written in his father's hand: *Rev. 20:1, 12; 21:6.*

Again, he read over the phrase from the *Commandments* book. His father knew how pivotal Genesis 1 was in Jaylene's introduction to Christianity. He heard the two of them replay their discussions about it many times. Unlocking Genesis 1 had indeed helped her penetrate many of God's mysteries.

Was his father now pointing to the second of the two biblical bookends, as he had often heard him call Genesis and Revelation.

Was the formula for unlocking that mystery to be found in these three verses?

He smiled at the thought of the Genesis and Revelation connection. His father loved to talk about bookends. The bookends of the Bible . . . youth and old age as the bookends of life . . . creation and eternity as the bookends of God's eternal purposes.

His father *loved* unique bookends, thought Timothy, glancing about the wall of bookshelves. At least a half dozen special sets enclosed some of his favorite mini collections of books as he called them. Several petrified wood bookends were gifts from Thady Gray.

Timothy opened the Bible to Revelation and read the three verses. Again, his father's underlining pointed to the clue. This time only three words were noted.

> *Then I saw an angel coming down from heaven, holding in his hand the <u>key</u> of the bottomless pit and a great chain.*
>
> *And I saw the dead, great and small, standing before the throne, and books were opened. Also another <u>book</u> was opened, which is the book of life. And the dead were judged by what was written in the books, by what they had done.*
>
> *And he said to me, "It is done! I am the Alpha and the Omega, the beginning and the <u>end</u>. To the thirsty I will give from the fountain of the water of life without payment.*

Key . . . book . . . end.

What could they mean? What was the connection? Was the clue found in their order or perhaps a different order—book—key—end.

Or *book—end—key.*

Timothy stood in the middle of the room staring at the wall of books.

What book, Dad? What key . . . what end . . . what book and end?

Suddenly a chill swept through him as his eyes shot open.

Bookends!

He stared straight in front of him. There sat the bookends depicting the Scotsman sitting on a stepstool in front of a bookshelf of books, bent down poring over the volume in his lap. His mother had given his father these antique bookends as a Christmas gift years ago.

Between them stood all the books in which he had found clues so far—*Dan Matthews, Unspoken Commandments, Nineteenth Century Authors*, and his father's favorite Bible.

He picked up the bookend next to the red RSV. A faint metallic clink sounded.

He turned it upside down. A rectangular two by three-inch panel was inset into the heavy slab of the base. He pushed at it with one finger. Feeling slight movement, he shoved a little harder. The panel swiveled in a quarter turn around the screw holding it in place, revealing a hidden recess carved out of the underside of the figure of the Scotsman. A brass key fell out and clattered to the floor.

Book. End. Key.

The next instant Timothy had its twin in his hand, swung the panel back, and dug out a small slip of paper. Unfolding it, he saw the numbers in his father's hand, *179.*

His eyes now scanned the other books enclosed by the two bookends besides the ones he already used: *A Testament of Devotion, The Imitation of Christ, The Spiritual Order, Catholic Separatists from Benedict to Groote, The Brethren of the Common Life, The Benedict Option, Pascal's Thoughts*, and *The Hope of the Gospel*.

Unbelievable!

Here in plain sight, in front of him the whole time, were the books of the authors he had mentioned in his letter, except for Franklin and Orwell! Twelve titles in all. The perfect number to symbolize the signposts his father had left to lead him to the truth he had for him to find. Twelve signs leading to "a powerful key."

He could have made the connection to this mini-collection of books months ago! His father had not just left him *one* trail of bread crumbs. He had left him *numerous* clues! He should have been able to spot these books and the bookends immediately!

Within five minutes he was on the way to the bank where his parents kept their accounts. In mounting anticipation, he asked to see the manager who knew them.

"Did my folks have a safety deposit box here?" he asked when they were seated together.

"Yes, they did," replied the manager. "I wondered when you were going to have it transferred to your name."

"Number 179?"

"Let me look it up," he said. He typed briefly on his computer, waited, then again. He stared at the screen a moment.

"Hmm, that's odd," he said. "No, it's our smallest size box. Number 73. Do you have the key?"

"I think so," said Timothy. He pulled out the key he had found and handed it across the desk.

"That looks like one of ours all right. We already have the death certificate on file you provided. I'll have the box transferred to your name."

Somewhat puzzled, Timothy followed him from his office. Ten minutes later, documents signed and a new signature card on file under his name, he followed one of the tellers downstairs into the safety deposit room. Once the two keys were inserted into box number 73, he was left alone.

Wondering what mystery his father had left for him, obscured by all the clues leading to it, he pulled out the box. It was empty except for one item. Another single brass key.

It did not match the key he had found in the bookend.

He removed the new key and left the bank, bewildered anew. It must be to a second deposit box, and in all likelihood one numbered 179.

But where?

What other bank did his parents do business with? He racked his brain, trying to remember anything that—

Of course! Years ago, his father had asked him to sign a signature card for a new account he and his mother wanted to open—a joint account that would include his name so that if something were to happen to them, he would have access to it.

He had forgotten all about it. Hearing nothing more, and his parents' normal banking continuing with the bank he had just left, he assumed nothing came of it.

He hurried to his car. The next minute he was on his way to Dorado Wood Community Bank.

Carrying the second key, he walked inside and to the safety deposit window.

"Hello," he said, setting the key on the counter. "Is this key for one of your safety deposit boxes?"

"I believe it is," replied the teller. "What is the number?"

"One-seventy-nine."

"I'll just look that up . . . here it is. You are, uh . . . Mr. Marshall?"

"I believe it's in my father's name, Stirling Marshall. He has passed away. I am his son, Timothy Marshall."

"I am sorry to hear about your father, Mr. Marshall," said the teller. "But you are on the signature card with him. Would you like to access the box?"

"Yes, I would—thank you."

Two minutes later, Timothy pulled out a larger document-size box. Inside lay a thick sealed manila envelope, on top of which sat a sealed white business envelope on which were written the words, *Timothy— Open first.*

He removed them, closed the box, and left the bank. He opened neither envelope until he returned to his parents' house. It was the only place he could read whatever his father had to say to him.

Ten minutes later Timothy was again seated in his father's chair, gazing across the room. There were the bookends with the twelve books between them, in plain view just as they had always been.

His father was a wily one!

He sat down and tried to calm himself, feeling a sense of exhilaration yet also a sense of solemn responsibility. He knew that whatever he was about to read might well be the most important thing his father had ever written.

Slowly he slit the smaller envelope and removed the letter of several pages.

Give me wisdom, Lord, he whispered. *Give me understanding into my father's heart.*

He unfolded the pages and began to read.

63

LETTER AND EXHORTATION

July 2032

Dear Timothy and David,

*If you are reading this, you have obviously found the letter and the packet included with it, which represents my final earthly writing. I am delighted, of course, yet I had to take precautions to make certain the Lord was leading you. I'm sure you are curious about all my cloak and dagger instructions and stratagems, and hiding what I actually **hoped** you would find. Perhaps it was nothing more than an exercise in futility. But I felt I had to do what was in my power to prevent my promoting this message that I think and hope and pray is from God. The only way I knew to do that was to give the Lord the chance to **keep** it from being found, to somehow **prevent** the two of you finding it without his help,*

*Most men assume, and women too, that to have a thought or idea represents a commission to tell that thought or idea to everyone they meet. This blindness is one of humanity's and Christendom's great Achilles' heels that leads to untold foolishness, and many **false** ideas being circulated by foolish and immature tongues. It is one of Satan's primary tools for preventing the truths of God from thoroughly spreading through the human race. It never occurs to people that most of the thoughts and ideas in their minds are self-motivated, and that therefore they should do their utmost to **keep quiet** about* them rather than share them. Most of the world's thoughts and ideas emerge and expand out of the entirely worthless vanity of personal opinion.

Most doctrines take wing in the church out of this same soil. Christians seek to promote their opinions and perspectives, assuming them true. Exactly like the people of the world, it never occurs to most Christians that many of the ideas in their minds are self-motivated, wrong, and false, and that therefore they should do their utmost to keep them to themselves and ask God for more truth. The wisdom to keep quiet, to lay down personal opinion, and to seek truth with the objectivity of open-mindedness, represents a level of maturity almost unknown in the church.

I am only human, so of course I succumb to this tendency like everyone. Yet having observed this cancer in man's church for most of my life, I have a healthy terror of lapsing into the same fatal error of opinion-promulgation myself. Therefore, I have chosen to handle this missive, this document, this "brief," differently.

Many would instantly publish and distribute it. If they have an idea, they are **compelled** to pass it on, to broadcast it, to share it with the world. In my case, if I have a thought, I realize that it may not be true and I must not share it. If and when God confirms it and opens avenues for its dissemination without my pushing it forward on my own, then I will stand back and watch him do what he wants to do with it.

You have found the packet. So we must assume you were meant to. To you I entrust it—not necessarily to share or publish or spread it, but rather to seek what is God's purpose for it now, after I am gone. It is not **automatically** to be shared with others. I may have written it only for you. I do not know what should come next. I can say no more than I wrote what I felt compelled to write. God did not show me the next step.

I can only counsel and urge you to go slow and be in no haste. Show it to no one until you are sure. Jaylene, it goes *without saying, I include with you. You two and Jaylene will be a threefold cord. Beyond you three, nothing should be done until you all agree God is leading.*

*I hope in time that you will be able to share it with my dear Woodrow, Cateline, Graham, and Jane. Unfortunately, as of this moment they are not in a position to understand or receive and evaluate it objectively as full disciple-walking men and women of God. I love them with all my heart, but it is simply a fact of their life-journeys that they have not yet arrived at that imperative which we attempted to build into the root system of our family. I hope that will change. However, this is not a **family** legacy I leave, but a **spiritual** one. It must be handled and prayerfully evaluated on that basis.*

*Neither must it be passed on or shared because you think someone "might be interested." **For it to be read prematurely or by those not capable of receiving its truths in exactly the same way I am sharing it with you, understanding the ongoing need for confidentiality just as I am exhorting it upon you, will only work division, misunderstanding, and disunity.***

This you must seek to prevent with great diligent caution and circumspection.

*Please read this letter first, maybe a time or two, prayerfully. Then pray for guidance and perhaps discuss it with one another before opening the packet. You must be certain you are being led to read it. You may not be led to read it. But if you are so led, whenever that time comes, pray to be given understanding and wisdom in what to do with it, and how and when—and **if**—you are to share it.*

*You may **never** share the contents of the packet with another soul. I don't know. God must be the prime mover and initiator in what comes next.*

With these cautions, let me set down some parameters I feel strongly about. I would rather you burn both copies of the thing than that it fall into the wrong hands for Satan to work his disuniting mischief among God's immature people who would misunderstand and then rush out to completely *misapply* every principle I set forth.

1) **Be in no haste.**

2) **Tell no one about the Brief.** *Knowledge of it must proceed only by the Lord's specific leading, and then individually and personally.*

3) **Make no copies yet.** *If and when you are led to share the Brief, do so* **individually**—*allowing another to read one of your copies. The Brief should not be distributed unless whatever copies you make are returned to you. If that time comes when you do make copies, proceed with extreme caution, taking care that those to whom they are given understand the seriousness of these priorities.*

4) **Share only with the spiritually hungry who understand my vision of life with God.** *When and if the time comes for wider dissemination, that process must expand among those, in a sense, who are already to some degree living by the principles outlined in the Brief.*

5) **Curiosity or vague interest is no reason to share the Brief.**

6) **The Brief should never be used evangelistically or apologetically.** *It must never be used as a persuasional tool. This would only lead to debate. It must only be shared with men and women who have independently, led by the Spirit of God, already begun to move in the directions outlined in it. It may become a confirming word, but never a persuasional document.*

7) **Intimate familiarity with my books and spiritual vision must come first.** *The Brief should not be a means to introduce my spiritual vision and outlook and perspectives, or yours, to one not already familiar with them. The Brief is the culmination of my life. It comes as the final chapter of all that has come before. That order must be observed. It is not a starting point. It is the consummation, the finale.*

8) **Beware of feigned interest and openness.** *Jesus reduced everything in life to basic core principles, to life's lowest common*

denominators. His **Don't cast pearls before swine** *graphically captures the essence of the principle that those not ready, receptive, and open to truth will not only misunderstand and fail to receive new truth, they will trample on that truth, argue against it, attempt to discredit it, and attack those who speak it. Feigned interest may be nothing more than disguised hypocrisy.* **You must protect the Brief by sharing it only with those capable of and hungry to understand it because it is their desire to live by its principles not critique it.**

Finally, this added caution. Illogical self-satisfied people cannot be convinced. The best policy is to keep quiet. Closed-mindedness is incapable of perceiving itself. We must follow Jesus' example to withdraw with his disciples and discuss these things privately. These are mysteries not for the world, nor for the Christian "world," which is the Ally, but for those whose hearts desire to probe and live by God's high and hidden truths.

Jesus did not primarily try to change the world, but to change the hearts of those capable of hearing and understanding. That began with a mere handful. He protected and safeguarded his message. He spoke his hidden truths to the twelve, not the five thousand. The church of man has badly missed the mark with its blaring public evangelisms without the follow-up imperative of discipleship. That was never the Lord's way. The five thousand and the four thousand are anomalies in the Gospels. Usually, Jesus taught apart from the crowds.

Likewise, what I entrust to you is for the few not the many. It is not for the church of organized Christendom, it is for the invisible Church of discipleship obedience. That Church will be revealed in ones and twos. Out of the seeds planted in the good soil of the few, the hungry, the receptive, and the growing will God's purposes be accomplished. Thus, will his remnant be birthed in preparation for the tribulations ahead.

The Brief will have nothing to say to the doctrine satisfied, church worshipping masses of unchristian "Christians." When the time comes when you feel the Brief is to be spread judiciously

*into other hands, let these principles be your guide. Find the
men and women for whom it is intended.*

*I love you both, my actual son and my spiritual son. You are
brothers of my heart. And, Timothy, of course, when they are
ready, I hope the right time will come to share this with your two
brothers and two sisters, hoping they will understand my heart
in passing it on to you and David first.*

Stand strong in truth.

The letter was signed in a hand still strong.

Stirling, your dad and friend.

Timothy's eyes were wet as he set down the pages. He sat a long
while in silence. Poignant as it was to read his father's words knowing
that he was gone from his earthly sight, they were also astonishing. He
had never heard his father speak so forcefully.

Timothy picked up the sealed packet which was the subject of the
letter he had just read, held it in his hands, and closed his eyes.

Lord, he prayed silently, *give me your wisdom and guidance. Show
me what you want me to do. Give David your guidance as well. Whatever
this packet contains, it is from you. Give us both your mind and heart.*

An hour later he was on his way back down into the valley, then
through town and northeast toward Grass Valley.

64

MAKING A MARK

SPRING 2033

MIKE BARDOLF had listened to his grandfather Slayton and his father Loring lionize Viktor Domokos all his life. First meeting him at ten, he saw him with some frequency through his teen years. Domokos always spoke kindly, almost as if sharing a special bond with the lad. By his mid-twenties, starting out on his own career in the various family enterprises as befitted its future CEO, young Mike Bardolf revered Domokos as nothing short of a god. His sister Amy was repulsed by the man. But he himself would have walked through fire for Viktor Domokos, or do anything to further the great man's goals.

Though young by Palladium standards, Mike was ambitious enough for two dozen of his elders. After listening to Viktor Domokos lament the election of Adriana Carmella Hunt, he had so personalized the great man's angst, though never having seen ACH in person, that he now hated her as if she were his own personal arch enemy.

With the idealism of youth, now at thirty-two, the illogic of his passion did not enter his thoughts. In reality, he and the new president might be spiritual twins. He was as ruthless and single-minded as she, and committed to many of the same political objectives. But if Viktor Domokos desired her influence on the national stage to be eradicated, Mike Bardolf was determined to take action. He would find a way to grant the man his final wish. His smoldering obsession was fueled all the more that she had snubbed Viktor's effort to find common ground. She deserved what came to her.

He had been watching . . . listening . . . absorbing. Even before Viktor's memorable challenge the previous December, Mike was well aware of the prevailing thinking among the organization's elite. His father loathed the woman, as did most of his circle.

Adriana Hunt was the proverbial loose cannon—more menace than ally. She was the progressive version of Donald Trump, disdained by disgruntled purists of her own party because she "wasn't one of them." Even as Speaker of the House, she had many detractors and had amassed enemies in her own Party. With her in the Oval Office, Palladium would no longer dictate events, set policy, or sway public opinion as effortlessly as before. Their overwhelming majorities in both houses of Congress had enabled them to have things their own way during her tenure as Speaker without her suspecting a thing. The presidency was different. Policies were not enough. Palladium must *control* the flow of power. Control was as fundamental to its *raison d'être* as the objectives it sought to implement.

They had—both directly and indirectly—overseen and orchestrated the direction of American politics and the nation's culture for decades through the multitudinous diverse tentacles of their influence. In ACH they perceived the possibility of that control fragmenting. She had not come up through their sanctioned ranks. If she wielded the reins of government for eight years, building her own power base and sphere of influence, theirs would inevitably be weakened. It was true that many of their people would manage to find their way into her circle. But they could not be assured how much clout they would wield.

The youngest of the Bardolf clan had been listening to the discussion about Ms. Hunt's presidential ambitions for two years. She was the mirror image, though mirror opposite of Trump. A bombastic blowhard. But a powerful one. Unpredictable.

Palladium didn't like surprises.

Nevertheless, her early momentum had been impossible to stop. The Palladium higher-ups, including his father and old Storm Roswell, were stymied.

After the shock of his election has subsided, however, they hadn't worried about Trump. He was an anomaly, an outsider, not one capable of building a permanent power base. To have taken drastic action against him would only have made him a martyr-hero. Dead heroes galvanized public opinion. John Kennedy did more to further the liberal agenda dead than he would ever have done alive.

With Trump, therefore, they had resigned themselves to wait and ride out the storm until the progressive ship was back on course. The culture was moving in their direction and nothing could stop it. But with ACH they were concerned at a more fundamental level that a damaging split in the progressive movement could result.

Though various "final option" scenarios were occasionally heard behind closed doors, they were mostly tongue-in-cheek. Such was not Palladium's style. They had never yet resorted to extreme measures at such a high level. At lower levels it was sometimes necessary. But not a sitting president.

All the while Mike Bardolf was paying keen attention. Nor did he share their qualms about decisive methods. He was looking for a way to make his mark, put his own stamp on the name *Bardolf*. He had been hidden away in his father's and grandfather's shadows long enough. Even in their business enterprises, he was given meaningless assignments with ridiculous titles.

Vice President of Company Morale, for God's sake! He knew his father did not consider him worthy to follow in his footsteps. Perhaps Palladium's ACH quandary provided him the opportunity he needed.

He would have to devise a plan to get close enough without arousing suspicion. And invisibly. Palladium had numerous contacts in the FBI. The director was one of the seventy-two.

He would make a few subtle inquiries.

65

NEW BROTHERHOOD

WHEN DAVID Gordon opened his door and saw Timothy standing before him, he smiled.

"I've been expecting you," he said.

"You found it, I take it," said Timothy.

"Two days ago."

"It would seem we are on the same wavelength. Or, I would prefer to think, being led by the same guiding Hand."

"I would say so. Let's go for a walk," David added, closing the door behind him and leading the way toward his stables. "My mother still has preternaturally keen hearing even at eighty-three."

They walked past the corral where several horses were nibbling on what grass they could find, and a frisky colt scampered about exploring his new world.

"How did you find it?" asked Timothy.

David laughed. "Your father sent me on the most fascinating but puzzling scavenger hunt—more truly a *treasure* hunt! I despaired of ever solving the series of riddles he set for me!"

"As did I!" laughed Timothy. "Were your clues embedded in books?"

"A few," replied David. "But mostly he hid clues in my barn—can you believe that!" he added, laughing again. "The final clue was a safety deposit key behind a small panel in the barn. I have no idea when he planted the clues or placed the key there. What about yours?"

"Mine were all in books in my parents' house. I was completely fogged for a long time, until I gradually began to make sense of the clues he had placed in the letter he left me. They also led to a key—two safety deposit keys, actually."

"How remarkable that we both solved our respective riddles at almost the same time. I would love to hear about your search, and the clues he left you."

"We will definitely have to compare notes!"

It fell silent as they walked along side by side.

"Any thoughts?" asked Timothy at length.

"I've read the letter three times," replied David. "Obviously I've done nothing with the packet, which is still sealed."

Timothy nodded. "As is mine."

"It would seem that we are, as you say, of one mind, as I'm sure your father hoped and probably knew we would be. My only thought at this point, to answer your question, is that I take your father's cautions about privacy with the utmost seriousness."

"I confess I was almost surprised by that aspect of it. I understand what he was saying. Yet it goes against everything the church teaches about spreading the gospel. I see Dad's point. But I have never heard him speak so strongly."

"He knew that important things would be at stake in the coming years," said David. "The enemy will constantly seek to undermine, twist, distort, and misrepresent God's truths. Even *truth*, in the wrong hands, can damage and impede the impact of that truth when misrepresented by those who do not understand it. As your father so strongly emphasized, Jesus' words about casting pearls before swine is in some respects a hard word, but is filled with a grave warning. Many Christians think that simply broadcasting the words of the gospel out into the world, shouting it from the housetops, as it were, will bring people into the kingdom. They are oblivious to the Lord's warning about pearls and swine."

"I see that," nodded Timothy.

"Not all people are capable of discerning truth. There are people who are *of* the truth, and there are people who are not of the truth. To discern deep truth, one must be of the truth."

Timothy smiled. "I said almost that very thing once to Jaylene before we were married."

"It is timeless principle. Your father was simply urging us to make sure his writings were spread only among people who are of the truth."

"In other words—truth is too important to waste on people who cannot understand it."

"Something like that," laughed David. "Your father was wise to caution us, even to prevent you and me reading what he has written before *we* are ready. We have to read *ourselves* into the pearls before swine warning too. As I read his letter, I was struck yet again by the wisdom God gave him. If the document he has entrusted to us is anything like what I think it is, then we will probably spend the rest of our lives attempting to faithfully carry out his instructions."

"In all honesty, I feel ill-equipped for the assignment," said Timothy. "I'm sure you know my father's writings better than I do. I will depend on you as we try to sense the Spirit's leading."

"You are your father's son," said David. "That counts for a great deal. It may be that his death, as is often the case, will imbue you with a level of understanding that may not have been possible while he lived. Often it is death that allows the mantle to be passed—as in the case of Elijah and Elisha, not to mention the impact of the Lord's death in the lives of his disciples."

"I hope you are right. I want to understand his heart all the more now that he is gone," said Timothy. "But I wonder about my brothers and sisters. I feel funny being singled out."

"Do you think any of them understand your father's heart and writings as well as you do?"

"Probably not."

"Who is the oldest?"

"My brother Woody."

"Does he read your father's work?"

No. He actually thinks a lot of it is nonsense, though he probably would not be so crass about it as that. My folks' spiritual training, I guess you would say, didn't really take root in him."

"Is he a Christian?"

"I think he considers himself one. But it's not part of his life—at least visibly. Maybe there are things I am unable to see—that's just how it looks to me."

"And the others?"

"I don't know what Graham thinks. He's hard to read. My two sisters, Cateline and Jane, I think read Dad's novels. But like Woody, they're not really big on his spiritual writings. I don't know what they've read."

"It sounds to me like your father knew exactly what he was doing."

"Maybe. But being the youngest, I'm sure you understand what I mean."

David nodded thoughtfully.

"The apostle John was the youngest of the disciples," he said after a moment. "Yet God knew him to be the one who would in time be capable of understanding his Son's heart in ways none of the others could, and who would be able to communicate that understanding to the world. It may be that God has a similar role for you to play in furthering your father's life message. He will give you the wisdom to don that mantle. Yet we will also pray for your siblings to be drawn into it as well."

"And Jaylene, of course," said Timothy. "She knows his heart as well as I do."

David nodded. "Your father obviously intended that she should read the letter he left us and would be one with us in praying for guidance."

66

SELECTIVE BANQUET

SEPTEMBER 2033

WHEN TWENTY-YEAR-OLD incoming UCLA junior Todd Stewart walked into the dimly lit room, the first sensations to assault him were the incongruously mingled aromas of incense, strong cologne, the smoke of an extinguished match, and baked ham. A glance to his right explained the match—a candle had just been lit in the center of the table nearest him, and the waiter in charge of the operation now moved to the next. Bustle and some clatter of dishes from the kitchen at the far end of the banquet hall explained the ham. The incense seemed to be emanating from a table in the center of the room where he saw a small statue or two, several candles already burning brightly, and other odd-looking paraphernalia he could not make out clearly. The cologne, however, remained a mystery.

"Ah, Mr. Stewart," said one of the upper classmen Todd recognized as among the secret organization's leaders as he approached with outstretched hand. "Welcome. Your table is right over here. I'm Anson Roswell—I've placed you with me."

He led the way and Todd followed to one of a half-dozen circular tables, each seating six. "You'll be here," said Todd's apparent host and sponsor who had arranged for the evening's invitation, though Todd did not know it. "But first, come over and have a drink. I'll introduce you to some of the others."

Somewhat awed by the lavish surroundings and mysterious décor, Todd followed. Everything he was told about the exclusive campus organization was vague—from cult worship to the sacrifice of live animals to various escapades of low-level criminal activity on campus. Mostly the group's reputation was as a club for the sons of rich politicians and businessmen whose chief interest in university life was extracurricular not academic.

Money was said to lubricate its activities, including the ten-thousand-dollar cost of an invitation to join. Even that did not guarantee acceptance. The admittance rules were highly selective and secretive. The first level was an invitation to the annual banquet, though presumably no one was invited who didn't have the wherewithal to move to the next level of an actual invitation to join. *He* certainly did not have ten thousand dollars to join a club, thought Todd. He didn't have *ten* extra dollars. Yet he had received an invitation to the banquet early in the new school year without an idea if he would even be able to afford to complete his third year.

His folks took out a second mortgage on their home to help him for the first two years. But their resources were gone. His part-time job would hardly cover UCLA's stiff tuition, much less his living expenses. But he had decided to attend the banquet. On his budget, a free meal was a free meal.

As he reached the bar alongside the affable Roswell, the heads of six or eight gathered men and women turned, each with beer and glasses of Scotch in their hands. About half seemed to be of student age, but several as old as their thirties, and one graying man at least fifty.

"Look who I have here, gentlepeople," said Roswell, "—the esteemed Todd Stewart, our campus journalist extraordinaire."

"Good to see you, Stewart."

"Glad to have you aboard."

"This is our chapter president Rob Aiken," added Roswell.

"How are you, Stewart—happy to meet you," said Aiken, shaking Todd's hand. "Hope we'll be seeing more of you."

More comments of approbation and welcome circulated as he shook hands as introductions were made.

"And this esteemed gentleman here is our patron and sponsor," young Roswell went on, turning to the gray-haired man, standing beside a younger man who appeared to be in his early thirties. "Meet my father, Storm Roswell . . . and with him . . . this is Mike Bardolf."

Both men offered their hands.

"Stewart," said the latter crisply, though without benefit of a smile. "Brilliant review of the Woodstein book. The guy's gone off the rails and you nailed it."

"Thank you, Mr. Bardolf."

"Anson showed me your piece in the campus paper on that Christian club that's been forbidden from holding meetings on campus," now said the elder Roswell. "Good piece of writing. Shrewd use of the separation of church and state angle to dismantle the freedom of speech argument. Cleverly done."

"I appreciate that, sir."

A few glances and winks went around the group.

"With a little help toward that end by unnamed informants," said one, laughing.

Bardolf shot him a keen glance.

"I think you've had enough to drink, Theo," he said.

"Get him out of here, Anson," added Anson's father. "Take him outside and cool him off. Remind him what happens to loose tongues."

Todd watched as Roswell led the suddenly disgraced young man away.

"You're majoring in journalism?" asked Bardolf, turning again toward Todd.

"That's right."

"What are your plans after graduation?"

"Obviously I would like to get on with one of the major news organizations," answered Todd. "Right now," he added with a light laugh, "I'm just trying to make sure I graduate at all."

"Why is that?" asked the elder Roswell. "Grade problems?"

"No, nothing like that. I've got a three-five. It's finances. My folks are strapped and I'm not inclined to take out three hundred grand in student loans."

"I see. Well, we'll talk about that."

A little more conversation followed as more of the invited underclassmen arrived, to a number of twelve or fifteen, along with another half dozen older men and women.

"It looks like they are about to start serving," said Anson, returning alone. "Come with me, Todd. Let's go sit down."

A moment after they were seated, a wind of oversweet cologne blew toward Todd nearly overpowering him. He turned toward it as another young man, a student like himself, sat down beside him and introduced himself.

Mike Bardolf continued unobtrusively to eye the young would-be journalist for the rest of the evening. He liked the fellow. He might be just the sort he could take under his wing and develop, as it were, for the cause. If his father was determined to keep him out of Palladium's leadership, Mike thought, he needed to begin creating his own network.

Young Stewart and the fellow Aiken might be just the place to begin.

67

OF THE OLD SCHOOL

SEPTEMBER 2033

COURT MASTERS was a cop of the old school, a dying breed in these new times. No nonsense. An old-fashioned law-and-order guy, member of the NRA whose gun collection would have aroused the ire of his wife's liberal friends. He had risen through the ranks, walking a beat in Baltimore, transferred to the capital when Stella was offered a promotion by her tech employer to head up a new DC branch, and gradually worked his way up to lieutenant.

At forty-three, he already had a combined twenty years in and was still a young man. Three more and he'd have the minimum twenty under his belt in DC. Not that he was thinking of retiring. He loved being a cop, even in these days when the police were so hamstrung by liberal courts that they were mostly just window dressing. Fighting a losing battle against liberalism, the thought often flitted through his mind of trying something else—open a bar and grill, write a book, teach at the academy. He had considered doing a book about the futility of the policeman's role in the new permissive culture—especially in the nation's capital. An up close and personal account of some of the people he had been assigned to protect might be interesting too.

Not that he had ever been close enough to any of them to possess much juicy gossip, though he shook Trump's hand once and was on his detail a few times. A great guy, he always thought. But he and the former president had done nothing but exchange pleasantries. Nothing juicy there. And the country was still in no mood to hear nice things about Trump. Years later he was still a national lightning rod.

A book was probably a pipe dream. He didn't know the first thing about writing. The truth was, his was an unremarkable career. He'd never killed anyone, and was glad of it, though he had exchanged gunfire a few times, took down a few perps, and had a slight hitch in his walk from a bullet to his left calf one of those perps gave him. Now he walked with a permanent limp. In the meantime, the shooter was slapped on the wrist with a misdemeanor, six months' probation, and Court still saw him on the streets occasionally, free as a bird.

But that was the reality of the Biden-Harris Criminal Rights Act. He supposed it was all in a day's work, or so he said to Stella, who worried every day when he walked out the door that another bullet might be waiting for him. When *he* left the house every morning, it wasn't another bullet *he* was thinking about. He was wondering how the country could have turned right and wrong so completely upside-down. And no one seemed to care.

It went deeper than right and wrong. It was a *spiritual* divide. The country was fracturing, and the fault line was spiritual. It was more important than ever for Christians to take a stand. Paul's words came to him more often these days—*Be strong in the Lord, put on the armor of God, stand strong for truth.* Yet how was one to stand strong for truth, when it seemed no one was listening. No one even cared about truth anymore.

It wasn't the kind of thing he could talk to his buddies about, even those few on the force who shared his convictions. They were *political* conservatives, not conservatives because of their *spiritual* convictions. He used to consider the two synonymous. But in recent years he came to see how different they really were. *Why* someone held conservative perspectives was more important than their viewpoints. He believed what he did about the country and the culture because of truths he found in the Bible, not Washington, DC. He never said it to anyone, but he held the view that God was a conservative—though he would not be a Republican any more than he would be a Democrat!

He certainly couldn't talk to Stella about his spiritual and political convictions. She was too brainwashed by progressivism that a logical and rational discussion about cultural issues was out of the question. Even as a Christian, she had so bought into the relativism of the times that right and wrong meant something entirely different to her than they did to him. Once politics or abortion or the gay agenda or immigration or same-sex marriage entered the discussion, common sense was gone with the wind.

That was what puzzled him most about their relationship. They went to church together, listened to the same sermons, read the same devotional book on the commands of the Bible together, and yet they saw the world through completely opposite prisms. What went through his prism into *his* mind as light, went through *hers* as black. Likewise, her light was black to him.

How could that be? How could Christians see the world so differently when they were reading the same Bible, reading the same verses about marriage, about male and female, about sin and obedience and accountability and truth and absolutes and right and wrong?

It was a mystery he could not resolve. Why did Christians not present a united perspective of biblical truth to the world?

Not watered down . . . not a version of truth mixed with worldliness . . . not a permissive version of truth that refused to call anything sin. But *biblical* truth.

He walked into the squad room in September of 2033, his mind still occupied with an entry from that morning's commands devotional he and Stella read. It had been his turn to read aloud. He could still hear his voice as Stella sat silent across from him: *What are we to say of the moral relativism, genderlessness, abortion, promiscuity, same-sex marriage, and the normalization of LGBTQ practices, all of which in most eras were nothing less than sin? Nothing is sin anymore. Tolerance is the god of our age. What do we who take the commands of the Bible seriously say?*

He had continued reading the blunt passage on purity. But they hadn't talked about it. They never did. He didn't dare ask Stella how she would explain away the author's words to fit the progressive agenda. No doubt the same way she rationalized Roman 1 as no longer applying to modern times.

It broke his heart. He and Stella used to talk about everything. And see things through the same lens. What had happened? How had progressivism become such a snare to her that it had pulled her away from the Bible—and away from him?

Midway through the morning, his captain, called him into his office. "The new president's doing an open-air speech in Baltimore next month," Nick said. "The Secret Service will handle the security of course, but they've asked a few of our boys to tag along to beef up the uniform presence. That's your old stomping ground. I'd like you to head up our detail."

"Sure, but I left there years ago," replied Court.

"You know the lay of the land. I'm sure you know Patterson Park."

"Like the back of my hand. I proposed to Stella there."

"See what I mean! You probably still have connections. You'll report to Secret Service Director Erin Parva."

68

Λ THREEFOLD CORD

FALL 2033

SIX MONTHS passed since Timothy and David had independently discovered the letter and packet left them by Timothy's father. Jaylene read the letter later the same day when Timothy returned from Grass Valley.

The three had been meeting weekly for prayer in the former Marshall home in Dorado Wood ever since. Being surrounded by, in a sense immersed in, the earthly sanctuary in which Larke and Stirling had lived the final quarter century of their lives, aided in the prayerful attempt to feel Stirling's heart. Thus far neither of the two thick manila packets had been opened.

Timothy had been at what was now simply called Jessup University over twenty years and was now chair of the history department. After Heather's birth, Jaylene did not returned to teaching for five years. When their daughter was enrolled in the church's school, she revisited the standing offer Jessup's president made her following her dismissal from Sacramento State. Though her tenure was not of such duration as Timothy's, her credentials and reputation gave such prestige to the university that the school's administrators made her chair of the science department after only ten years.

Both published regularly. Jaylene contributed numerous articles to various scientific journals. Timothy had two books to his credit, both following his father's interests. The first was an American's guide, so to speak, to the often-confusing English Civil War, the second a similar book on the Reformation, originally written for his own three-term comprehensive upper division course on the subject.

Their two professed life works were incomplete but in process. Jaylene envisioned hers as a personal account of her journey out of secularist atheism into Christianity, in which would be incorporated the substance of her course *Einstein and Genesis: A New Perspective on Beginnings*, always one of Jessup's most popular offerings. Timothy's was probably more ambitious—a biography of his parents.

With Heather also now attending Jessup, majoring in English, father, mother, and daughter were able to enjoy each other, in a sense, professionally as a family, often driving to or from school together, schedules permitting, and at least a day or two a week sharing lunch together on campus. It was a delightful time for all three.

Once again David, Jaylene, and Timothy were seated in the familiar home surrounded by the invisible presence of Timothy's parents. All three had recently begun to sense a change.

"I believe the time may be near when we are to read what my father left us," said Timothy after they had been sitting thirty or forty minutes. "Naturally, I am curious about the contents. But I think these months of waiting have purged mere curiosity from my motives. Rather than curiosity for myself, the sense has been growing upon me of its *importance*."

Again, silence descended.

"I concur," said David softly after five minutes. He nodded his head slowly, as if still thinking, but said nothing more.

"As do I," added Jaylene. "It has been deepening within me for several weeks. I said nothing because I did not want to influence the two of you. I thought it should come from you."

"Exactly as it has been for me," rejoined David. "It began two weeks ago. I had just read that the executive committee of the National Evangelical Alliance unanimously voted to openly encourage same-sex marriage, even, so to speak, to advertise that fact in order to bring practicing homosexual couples and transgenders into their memberships. Immediately something snapped inside me. There was not a single dissenting vote to their decision. Tears came to my eyes. A righteous indignation rose within me that the leaders of God's church in the world could have fallen so deep into the worldliness of the times.

"This has been happening in liberal denominations for years. But now it seems that the evangelical church has become joined at the hip with the world no less than Catholicism, progressive Episcopalianism, and the Unitarians. Immediately I thought of Stirling's Brief. I don't know if it's the kind of thing he addresses or not. But the thought exploded to life within me like a light bulb switched on—if God gave Stirling something to say to an evangelical church losing its way, then perhaps it is time for it to be heard."

Jaylene and David glanced at Timothy.

"I hesitated to speak up," Jaylene went on, "for fear my natural woman's curiosity may be prompting what I felt. I am curious, of course. And my honor of Stirling is so great that I hunger to read anything he wrote, especially his final writings which obviously came from the depths of his heart. But curiosity is a dangerous snare. What you just said, Timothy, relieves my mind. I too have felt my fleshly curiosity giving way to what I hope is also a sense of the timeliness of what Stirling wrote. Still, I feel you two must decide what is to be done."

Timothy smiled. "You, my dear," he said, "are the most objective woman I have ever known. I often trust your judgment over my own. Your objectivity would easily trump whatever curiosity you may feel."

"Nevertheless, in this case," said Jaylene, "to be entirely old-fashioned and traditional about it, the men must take the lead."

Again, the three lapsed into thought.

"There's something else," said Timothy at length. "I've been thinking about this for some time."

He paused and glanced toward David.

"I believe, David, that you knew my father's heart and writings more intimately than any other, indeed, even than his own children—probably including me. I can only hope and pray," he went on, "that God has some purpose in this belated opening of the eyes of my sonship that he will be able to use to expand the reach of my father's vision."

"That is assuredly true," nodded David. "Time is not so important to God as where we get in the end. The progression you have followed may be intrinsic to how God intends to use you now as your father's spokesman and as the heir to his legacy—or one of them, I should say. Hopefully that mantle will eventually come to rest on your brothers and sisters as well."

"Thank you," smiled Timothy, though with a wistful expression of nostalgic melancholy as he glanced about the room which was still so evocative of his parents. "I hope you are right. But I will always wonder if I might have seen it sooner. Or was God preparing me for this time perhaps in different ways than he was you? It will remain a mystery to me. However, all that being what it is, I feel that *you* should read the Brief first and seek the Lord about what is next."

David received his words with a humble smile and nod of acknowledgment, though he said nothing. It remained quiet for several minutes.

At length David spoke.

"Funny," he said. "I was feeling something similar, but in the opposite direction—there is a level of intimacy and knowing between father and son that is impossible for anyone from the outside to fully penetrate. It may be true that I saw some things in your father's writings earlier than you did. But let's not forget the most obvious fact, which is that I am, I think, about a decade older than you. Simple age sometimes has much to do with spiritual readiness.

"At the same time, you are your father's son. You shared life with him with an intimacy I cannot imagine. In that sense, you do know his heart, Timothy. You have probably always known his heart more intimately than you realize. Those years, as you say of being prepared to understand his vision and message, those were yet years of knowing at a deep level. You were absorbing his spiritual character all your life. His being was infusing itself into you, preparing you for the later understanding to come.

"This is the process for people who have bad parents as well as good ones, such as you and I had. It is even true for orphans. God's lessons are as unique as are the parents he gives us. God has truth to reveal—individual, personal, perhaps mysterious and hidden truth—whether our parents be bad or good, whether our life experiences are painful or pleasant. Our life's journeys are meant to lead us to find the unique truths he has to reveal to each one of us."

David paused and thought a moment.

"All this is my way of saying that I have been feeling *you* are the one who should take the lead and read the Brief first. You know your father. I believe you know his heart. You stand in the logical spiritual progression. It is the way God works, from fathers to sons to grandsons."

"Thank you," nodded Timothy. "You are very kind. I know you speak truth, and I will do my best to appropriate what you say. But there are, as you say, spiritual sons and daughters, who often play equal if not more important roles in the transmission of God's truth through the ages. You and Jaylene are no less my father's heirs than I am—his true spiritual son and daughter."

Silence fell. It remained quiet for ten minutes. It was Jaylene who finally broke it.

"I said I would not vote about what comes next," she said. "However, assuming the woman's prerogative of being able to change her mind as often as she likes, I will now go back on that. I feel strongly about what I am about to say—which is that you should *both* read the Brief at the same time. He made two copies hoping that you would both be led to read them."

Timothy and David smiled.

"You have spoken wisdom, Mrs. Marshall," said David.

"I concur," nodded Timothy.

"Then I propose," said Jaylene, "that we heed Stirling's caution one more time against haste, and plan to meet again in a week. Between now and then we will all pray but not discuss it—pray for unanimous confirmation, but also pray, if we have not discovered God's Voice correctly, that the Lord will stay our hand and will speak a cautionary word to one of us that we should continue to wait. Both men nodded in agreement.

"You indeed speak wisdom Jaylene," said Timothy.

69

PATTERSON PARK

OCTOBER 2033

MIKE BARDOLF had done his homework. Who knew that the South American dart frog possessed the power to change history. It took some doing to get his hands on the stuff. With the help of the best hacker at UCLA, president of its Oraculus chapter Rod Aiken, he had become familiar with the shady workings of the dark web and its blackest of marketplaces. The vial came by special courier two weeks after his return to DC.

His trip to the West Coast had proved profitable on several fronts. He made some valuable connections in addition to Aiken and the journalism major Stewart who were sure to prove useful in the future.

For now, he could involve no one else. Once he learned how to navigate the dark web, not even Aiken knew the reason for his interest. Obviously, he needed help if he was to get close enough. But they didn't need to know why he was there. He'd arranged to be assigned as liaison to the presidential detail. Erin Parva wasn't overly curious. Palladium's people stuck together. Mike led her to believe he was on his father's business. That was enough for Parva.

While infiltrating the dark web, he had also initiated some untraceable chatter, sure to circulate and gradually filter up the pipeline into the ever-listening ears of the FBI, to the effect that a neo-Trumpite group was planning something. That should provide cover and distraction.

★ ★ ★

Court Masters arrived in Baltimore two days before the event, renewed what old acquaintances were left on the first, capped off by a delightful dinner with the man and woman who led him to the Lord when he was at the University of Maryland. He met the next day with Director Parva to coordinate the two local details from Baltimore and DC with her Secret Service contingent.

"We'll have the place pretty well manned up front," said Parva. "I want your officers blanketing the crowd, moving about, mixing everywhere front to back. I want people seeing uniforms wherever they look. I know it's cosmetic. Still, if any of your people spot anything, alert one of my men or women. There are reports of Trumpites making trouble. We can't be too careful. Those people are lunatics if not outright terrorists. I would love to bag a few of them and haul them up on charges of treason."

"We'll take care of the crowd, ma'am," said Masters. "You take care of the president."

Inwardly he was wishing it was Trump making an appearance rather than ACH. How ironic that he was here to protect the woman who thought so little of the country's roots that her first executive order had been to change the offensive racist name of the *White* House to the Presidential Manor. It was followed immediately by a similar order, for the same reasons, to paint the Washington Monument black from ground to peak, a change which would be accompanied by its new name, the Martin Luther King Monument. What would they do next, he thought, altogether get rid of the flag whose principles were already in tatters?

Yet a man like Trump, who had tried so hard to right the sinking American ship, was considered a lunatic, and those who still honored his memory were treated as domestic terrorists. It was now considered a "hate crime" to wear or use the name *Trump* in public, whether on cap, shirt, bumper sticker, poster, or placard. So far none of Trump's offspring had run for office, which might have created some interesting dynamics in the enforcement of what was called the Trump Domestic Terrorism Act. In ultra-liberal circles, the name Trump was synonymous with Hitler.

The next day arrived blustery and cold, a thick cloud cover threatening rain. But ACH was undeterred. Her open-limousine motorcade from the airport wove its way through the streets of Baltimore to cheering throngs and arrived at Patterson Park about noon. A podium with microphones was waiting for her in the center of a cordoned-off knoll in the center of the park's expansive lawn of several acres. Local and national camera crews were on hand. Every inch of the park was packed with the press of humanity.

The news media continually characterized the far right as dangerous, never failing to raise the specter of terrorism, bombs, and militia groups intent on anarchy—warnings which surfaced whenever a Democrat president appeared in public. Ironically, however, the only violent anarchist activity of the past twenty years—which could hardly be applied to the minor Capitol incident in January of 2021—came from leftist groups such as Antifa and BLM. Yet these facts were inconvenient truths for the media. As their teams went live on this day, their introductory comments focused heavily on the "unconfirmed reports" of neo-Trumpite factions said to have descended on Baltimore in large numbers with violent intentions.

The president's motorcade slowed as it approached the Park, inching its way through those crushing together behind rope barriers, and finally stopped. President Hunt stepped out, waving and beaming, obviously enjoying the adulation. She then began the two-hundred-yard walk through the eight-foot-wide roped pathway toward the knoll. The crowd continued in a frenzy, hands reaching wildly as she passed, while Erin Parva's men did their best to keep them back and prevent the makeshift rope fence from collapsing altogether.

70

THE BRIEF

AS THE Marshall-Gordon trio took their seats in the elder Marshall home a week after their prior discussion, at about two o'clock Pacific time, they had no idea of the events unfolding three thousand miles to the east, where President Hunt had just landed in Baltimore in preparation for the open-air event and her speech.

The mood of the three was serious but upbeat.

"I will begin," said Timothy, "by saying that I have felt no check whatever. Just the opposite. As the week has progressed, I felt confirmation after confirmation both that my original sense was correct, that the time has indeed come for us to read my father's Brief and ask the Spirit what is to come next, and also that Jaylene has truly spoken God's wisdom for you and me, David, to both read it."

"Exactly as it was for me," said Jaylene. "No doubts at all. I felt a solemnity that something truly significant is at hand. I believe God has entrusted us with a word to his people."

The two men pondered her words soberly and thoughtfully.

"Then a threefold cord is not easily broken," nodded David. "I too felt only confirmations—not necessarily that Stirling's message, whatever it is, is to be spread to a wider audience, at least not yet, but that the time has come for us to prayerfully read it and be attentive for what is to follow."

Timothy rose, walked across the floor and into his father's office. The two sealed packets had lain on his father's desk for the past six months. He returned to the sitting room carrying them. He handed one to David.

"I will go for a long walk," said Jaylene. "You two need to read free from distraction."

She rose and left the house.

Timothy and David looked at one another expectantly, then each slit opened the packets in their hands and removed the identical typed manuscript from inside.

As they began to read, an atmosphere of holiness descended upon them.

> *What follows are some general perspectives and outlooks, a worldview, and a spiritual orientation of what I call a Common Life—a term I have borrowed from the fourteenth century, as I will explain.*
>
> *Much of what I sense God's Spirit saying as the curtain closes on my life will not appear at first so revolutionary or controversial beyond what others have said at various times through the years. If given closer and prayerful attention, however, the expansive implications of these ideas—if followed to their logical and imperative conclusions, and put into practice by dedicated disciple-Christians—contain the power to shake and remake the body of Christ—to shake the church of man, and to remake Christ's true Church into a bride capable of fulfilling his final commission.*

As David read, he could hear Stirling's voice as if he were still seated in his favorite chair, as he had listened to him many times in this very room, speaking spontaneously out of his heart.

> *Most of what goes by the name of "Christianity" is not true Christianity. A true Christ-ian is a "follower of Christ," a disciple of Jesus. A disciple obeys his Master's teaching. Many call themselves "Christians" because they hold certain beliefs, not because they have dedicated their lives to obeying what Jesus taught. They are therefore not true Christians—followers*

and life-obeying disciples. They are "believers," and that may be a good thing. I am not sure belief in and of itself is a good thing, though it may be. But it is not the same thing as being a Christian—a disciple, a follower of Jesus.

There are indeed beliefs inherent in true biblical Christianity. For discipleship to flourish, it is imperative that these are true scriptural beliefs emerging out of the character of God and his eternal purposes, not doctrinally biased teachings originating in traditional theologies of man. Yet even such true belief does not comprise the substance, the sine qua non of discipleship Christianity. It is a necessary component of it, but not its lifeblood.

True biblical Christianity can only be lived by apprehending the foundational truth Jesus taught that the kingdom of God and the kingdom of man are intrinsically opposite in every way. One cannot maintain equal allegiance. There are no dual spiritual citizenships. It is possible for only one of the two kingdoms to rule as supreme in the core of man's soul and spirit.

One of Satan's great lies is that coexistence is possible between God's eternal objectives and man's methods. This can never be. The tiniest false priority of man will act as disserving leaven to God's purposes, and will ultimately, like the falsehoods of man always do, leaven the whole lump like a fatal cancer.

Though it accomplishes much good and has historically been an influence for noble objectives in the world, the organized so-called "church" of Christendom—from Amish, Baptist, and Catholic to Wesleyan, YWAM, and Zionism—is also at its root the world's Ally. By attempting to use the world's methods and systems, and by adopting the world's outlook and accepting its cultural trends, the organized church has also done much to prevent the kingdom of God being lived within the hearts of its members.

I consider the church a manmade institution, not necessarily initiated and given life by the Spirit of God, and thus *often unknowingly functioning in collusion with the kingdom of man and the world's ways and means.*

In contrast is the completely distinct Church—an invisible worldwide community of living stones being built into God's eternal temple, men and women, to the extent their circumstances make possible, living in the world but not of it, who have separated themselves from the world's priorities, its outlook, and its false measures of right, wrong, and truth, its culturally accepted lifestyles, a brotherhood not bound by time, place, organization, structure, doctrine, group activities, or times of worship, but by the common commitment to obey the commands of Jesus in the corners of the world where they live.

Building precept upon precept, Stirling continued to amplify the conviction which comprised the central message he felt God had given him, that a time was coming for the Church of the third millennium when it would be required to recognize the imperative of separation from the world and even separation from the lower-case church of man—in order that at last the intent of Jesus to further the objectives of his Father among men might be fulfilled.

A little over an hour later, just after 3:00 p.m., the manuscript laying on his lap, David leaned back in his chair and closed his eyes.

Five or six minutes after that, Timothy exhaled deeply, rose, and left the house. He returned ten minutes later with Jaylene, though neither had spoken since they met. They walked inside and sat. All three remained silent for several minutes.

At length David drew in a long breath and sighed. "I'm not sure what I was expecting," he said softly. "Something maybe even more controversial and forceful. Yet the implications, as he said at the beginning, are enough to rock Christendom at its foundations."

It was silent a moment. Timothy grew thoughtful.

"I found myself with two very different reactions as I read," he said. "On the one hand, I thought to myself, 'There's nothing so earth-shattering here. Why the secrecy? Why the warnings about not sharing it? I've been hearing all this for years. It's not so new or remarkable.'

"But then I thought what it would be like for one who had not been hearing my dad talk about these things all their life. Maybe for such a one it *would* be revolutionary, controversial—more than they were able to take in."

Timothy paused and a smile came over his face.

"I had the image of a supertanker unloading a full cargo of high truth to someone sitting in a rowboat who hadn't had the benefit of having his understanding of my father's perspectives built over the years one idea at a time. It would be like taking someone from middle school and throwing them into one of Jaylene's doctoral courses!"

Jaylene and David laughed lightly at Timothy's imagery.

"I see what you mean," said David. "I found myself also reading, in a sense, through two sets of eyes—my own, and through the eyes of one who had never heard any of it before. Such a one, hearing a completely foreign perspective on the Church, about end times, about what comprises true discipleship—he or she could easily be overwhelmed. It would be too much to take in.

"I have been accustomed to Stirling's outlook on spirituality for, what . . . sixty years? His Brief is the summary of his entire life. Your father's strength was his ability to digest and analyze a wide range of ideas, then clarify the themes of high truth and weave them into a cohesive vision of how God's people are to think and live. In so doing, he challenged the orthodoxy that has impeded the Church's growth for centuries. But it is just as you say—encountering those perspectives all at once at the summit, without benefit of the gradual hike up the slopes of Mt. Stirling, might well leave spiritual novices in confusion."

"Mt. Stirling—very funny, David!" laughed Jaylene. "Yet your imagery, too, like Tim's, highlights everything Stirling has said about being cautious in sharing what he has written."

"It is nothing short of my father's manifesto," added Timothy. "A manifesto of the centered Christlike life and his vision of the Church—his entire life's perspective encapsulated in fewer than a hundred pages."

"A remarkable document," added David seriously, "even though perhaps for us a confirmation of much we were already aware."

"So now what?" said Jaylene, looking back and forth between the two men.

"The next step, it seems to me," replied David, "would be for you to read your father-in-law's Brief."

"Then after that, obviously," added Timothy, "we pray for direction."

71

COLLAPSE

PRESIDENT ADRIANA Carmella Hunt stepped forward, took a sip from the small bottle of water in her hand, then set it on the podium. The grassy expanse in the middle of Patterson Park was an exposed site. But she wasn't worried. Her confidence in the public's adoration made the idea of potential danger so remote it never crossed her mind.

No one would harm *her*. Not even right-wing neo-Trumpites. The country loved its new president.

Midway back in the crowd, Court Masters's instincts kept him distracted as she began her speech. His eyes were constantly roving, looking for signs of trouble.

He wasn't interested in what the president said anyway. She had been spouting the same liberal talking points for a decade and a half, with now and then a few crazy ideas thrown in guaranteed to make college students love her and conservatives think she was nuts. Her politics were completely contrary to the New Testament, though his wife would disagree. Nor was it difficult to see through the façade of her character. But he would take a bullet for her. Whenever he put on the badge, it was his duty to protect even those who hated the police.

The thought of taking a bullet sent his hand unconsciously to his chest where he felt his service pistol beneath his coat.

There hadn't been a hint of protest. No posters, no demonstrations, no arrests. So far it was a love fest. Still he panned his surroundings. He had a queasy feeling, almost like watching a movie go into slow motion as the sound faded.

His eyes came to rest on the cadre of agents at the front of the crowd—stoic, unsmiling, like him searching the crowd for the telltale signs they were trained to look for. All except one. He seemed uncharacteristically fidgety, glancing every few seconds over his shoulder at the president.

Odd, he thought. He never saw the Secret Service looking directly *at* those they were assigned to protect. Their eyes were always scanning in the *opposite* direction where potential danger might originate.

Probably nothing, thought Masters.

The president paused and coughed lightly.

"Sorry, I seem—uh, *ahem*—to have a tickle—*ahem*—in my throat."

She reached for the water bottle again and took a longer swallow.

"That's better," she said.

She tried to resume, but again coughed—then tried to draw in a breath.

"I'm—I'm sorry—*ahem*—I just—I can't seem—"

She was clearly struggling. It was obviously more than just a tickle in the throat.

She clutched at the edge of the podium, her mouth moving but making no sound. She coughed, choking several more times.

Her knees wobbled momentarily. She grabbed the edges of the small lectern to steady herself.

Suddenly her knees buckled, and she collapsed. Still clutching the podium, her hands pulled it toward her—the pedestal and bank of microphones crashing down on top of her. Her muffled cry amid the clatter and banging was amplified with alarming reality over the loudspeakers.

Gasps and shrieks erupted from the crowd. A dozen agents rushed forward to encircle the president, now motionless on the grass. Within seconds the siren of an ambulance came screaming toward them. The crowd parted in panic like a human red sea.

The man Court Masters had observed a few moments earlier had faded into the crowd and was quickly forgotten in the pandemonium.

72

NEWS REPORT

JAYLENE MARSHALL'S cell phone rang.

"Mom . . . hi . . ." she heard when she answered. She hardly recognized her daughter's voice.

"Heather . . . what's wrong? You sound—"

"Mom, where are you?" interrupted Heather. "Are you near a TV?"

"Yes, I'm at your grandparents with David and your dad."

"Turn on the TV, Mom. Something's going on."

"What channel?"

"Any channel. Right now."

And with that, Heather was gone.

Jaylene rose from her chair, glancing at Timothy and David as she walked toward the television.

"That was Heather," she said. "She was . . . I don't know . . . I've never heard her like that. Her tone was . . . almost afraid."

Seconds later they all knew why. Jaylene returned to her chair, and the three sat silent as they watched.

☆ ☆ ☆

". . . still sketchy as reports come in," FNC anchor Denver Stone was saying. "President Hunt had just begun to speak at the outdoor venue in Baltimore's Patterson Park, when she began coughing and struggling for air. Less than a minute after the first sign of difficulty, she collapsed. The ambulance on the scene rushed her to Johns Hopkins hospital where her condition is unknown at this time. No statements have been released."

The day's events were then replayed from the landing of Air Force One at Thurgood Marshall Airport, following the motorcade through the city, the president's triumphant walk through the crowd, then the beginning of her speech, and finally her collapse.

A deathly pall settled over Baltimore, indeed over the entire country. Cameras sweeping the crowd at Patterson Park, so jubilant a short time before, recorded only an eerie silence. Not a soul had left.

☆ ☆ ☆

When Stone returned on air, a woman was standing beside him. "I have Secret Service Director Erin Parva with me," he said. "What can you tell us, Ms. Parva?"

"All we know at this time," she answered, "is that we suspect the bottled water the president was drinking prior to her fall. The three agents who were first at her side to pull the lectern off her and give CPR have experienced symptoms as well. They have also been taken to Johns Hopkins."

"You think it was something in the water?"

"That is our assumption at present."

"And your agents . . . you're saying it could have been absorbed by touch?"

"Dermal absorption appears possible."

"How lethal is it?"

"I would not want to speculate on that."

"How could something so dangerous get through the president's security?"

"That is unclear. We have no idea how long she had it. It may have come from Air Force One. It is hard to imagine it being introduced after they left the airport. My people handling the motorcade made no stops. We will of course review all available video. I must emphasize we know nothing for certain. The bottle has been rushed to the FBI lab here in the city and being examined with extreme care. The surrounding area where the water spilled has been sealed off. Until we know more, it is being treated as a crime scene."

"There are no suspects?"

"It is far too soon for that—though we are looking for the Trumpites who were at the Park. Our investigation will focus on them."

"Is there any word on the president's condition?"

"Not at this time."

☆ ☆ ☆

Another agent now approached the director. Parva stepped away and listened for fifteen or twenty seconds, nodding occasionally. Stone stepped closer, trying to listen. Parva held up her hand toward him. The two agents stepped a few more paces away.

After about twenty seconds, Parva returned to Stone.

"The results of the tox screen on the contents of the bottle have come back from the lab," she said. "A substance known as homobatrachotoxin has been identified in the water. It is a very rare and extremely powerful toxin, hard to obtain and prohibitively expensive."

"By toxin . . . are you saying there was *poison* in the president's water bottle?"

"That is correct. We are obviously checking for fingerprints and other clues."

"Knowing this, then—what will be done?" asked Stone. "How will the president be treated?"

Ms. Parva did not answer immediately. She glanced away briefly then back to Stone. "I'm afraid," she said slowly, "that there is no known antidote."

"What treatment, then, will the doctors—"

Stone paused and put a hand to his earpiece.

"Just a moment . . . I am being . . . an announcement is coming momentarily from the hospital. Stand by . . . we are going now to Presidential Press Secretary Amanda Warren outside John's Hopkins."

★ ★ ★

The television screen broke to the hospital. Amanda Warren had just walked through the emergency room doors and approached the assembled crowd of journalists and cameramen. It was twenty minutes after one o'clock. Her face was pale, her eyes red.

"I have a brief statement," she began in a halting voice, then wiped at her eyes. "I will take no questions. Everything will be answered in due course."

She drew in a shaky breath, then looked down and read from her handwritten notes.

"President Adriana Carmella Hunt was rushed unconscious to Johns Hopkins Hospital behind me at approximately twelve-seventeen local time," she said. "The admitting physicians suspected that she had ingested a powerful agent, which has now been identified as homobatrachotoxin. A team of physicians was unable to revive her. President Hunt was pronounced dead at 12:58 p.m. Eastern Standard Time."

Warren choked down a sob, turned, and walked hurriedly back through the hospital doors. For one of the few times in recent memory, the assembled crowd from the media was silent.

FNC coverage returned to Denver Stone. He listened briefly through his earpiece, then drew in a deep breath.

"I have just learned," he said, struggling to steady his voice as he looked into the camera, "that the announcement of the president's death was not made until family was contacted. Vice President Xavier Pérez, who was at an event in New York, was notified immediately. He is en route to Washington as we speak. Supreme Court Chief Justice Davis will be waiting at the Capitol building in approximately ninety minutes. There Mr. Pérez will be sworn in as the forty-ninth president of the United States."

★ ★ ★

THIS ENDS BOOK 1

Tribulation Cult Book 2 follows: *Birth of a Remnant*

CHARACTER LIST

THE MARSHALLS—THREE GENERATIONS

Stirling and Larke (Stevens)	1941–2032, 1942–2031
Woodrow (m. Cheryl Burns)	1973
Cateline (m. Clancy Watson)	1974
Graham (m. Lynn Davies)	1976
Jane (m. Wade Durant)	1978
Timothy (m. Jaylene Gray)	1980, 1983
Heather	2014

THE FORSTERS—THREE GENERATIONS

Robert and Laura (Clay)	1973, 1976
Janet (m. Collis Nason)	1998
Mark (m. Grace Thornton)	2000, 2001
Ginger	2028
Craig	2030
Gayle (m. David Dowling)	2005

THE GORDONS—TWO GENERATIONS

Pelham and Isobel (Hamilton)	1939–2014, 1945–2041
David	1971

THE RHODES FAMILY—THREE GENERATIONS

Harrison and Sandra (Nelson)	1975, 1977
Jefferson (m. Marcia Bergen)	2000
Bradon	2027
Melissa	2029

THE HUTCHINS FAMILY—TWO GENERATIONS

Truman and Eloise (Warton)	1972, 1973
Sawyer (m. Inga Daven)	1995
Ward (m. Deidra Lindberg)	1999
Linda (m. Cameron Trent)	2000

POLITICAL INDIVIDUALS

Viktor Domokos (1939–2035)

Akilah Samara (1993)

Slayton Bardolf (1949–2014)

Loring (1976)

Mike (2001)

Amy (2004)

Talon Roswell (1950–2043)

Storm (1983)

Anson (2010)

Adriana Carmella Hunt (1989)

Todd Stewart (2013)

About the Author

MICHAEL PHILLIPS was born (1946) and raised in the small northern California university town of Arcata. After a year at Lincoln University in Pennsylvania, Michael completed his higher education at Humboldt State University (now California State Polytechnic University), where he was a standout miler and half-miler, graduating in 1969 in physics, mathematics, and history. During his final year at Humboldt, he began a small bookstore in his college apartment. He and wife Judy, music major and harpist in the university symphony, were married in 1971, the same year they discovered the life-changing influences of C. S. Lewis and George  MacDonald. Moving to nearby Eureka, their One Way Book Shop grew rapidly. For the next thirty-five years, while carrying on their writing and harping pursuits, Michael and Judy's bookstore ministry was a fixture in the life of Humboldt County's Christian community.

MacDonald's profound influence in their lives, coupled with the realization that none of his books were in print and the Victorian author was in danger of being lost to posterity, prompted Michael, amid the busy life of a rapidly expanding business and homeschooling their three sons, to begin the ambitious task of editing and republishing

MacDonald's works. At the same time he began writing seriously in his own right, publishing several books in the 1970s.

Michael's efforts inaugurated a worldwide renaissance of interest in the forgotten nineteenth-century Scotsman. In the years since, Michael has been known as one whose skillful diligence helped rescue George MacDonald from obscurity. Throughout the following forty years, he has published over eighty studies and new editions of MacDonald's writings in diverse formats, and is recognized as a man possessing rare insight into MacDonald's heart and spiritual vision.

Paralleling his work with MacDonald, Michael's own author's reputation in Christian circles expanded quickly. He became one of the premier novelists of the Christian fiction boom, his books appearing on numerous CBA bestseller lists with an enthusiastic worldwide following.

In 2021 Michael and Judy celebrated their 50th anniversary. Michael continues to write as prolifically as ever. Judy continues the ministry of her harp music, teaching and as a therapeutic musician in several hospitals and medical facilities.

Recognized as one of the most versatile and prolific Christian writers of our time, Michael's wide-reaching corpus and the multiple genres of his work now encompass well over a hundred titles. For many years his books have demonstrated keen insight and uncommon wisdom to probe deeply into issues, relationships, and cultural trends. His writings are personal and challenging. He encourages readers to think in fresh ways about the world and themselves.

The impact of Michael's writing is perhaps best summed up by Paul Young, author of *The Shack*, who said, "When I read . . . Phillips, I walk away wanting to be more than I already am, more consistent and true, a more authentic human being."

A FEW NOTABLE TITLES BY MICHAEL PHILLIPS

FICTION

Rift in Time

Hidden in Time

The Secret of the Rose (4 volumes)

Secrets of the Shetlands (3 volumes)

American Dreams (3 volumes)

Angel Harp

Legend of the Celtic Stone

NON-FICTION

Endangered Virtues and the Coming Ideological War

George MacDonald, Scotland's Beloved Storyteller

George MacDonald, A Writer's Life

The Commands of the Prophets

The Commands of Jesus

The Commands of the Apostles

Make Me Like Jesus

The Eyewitness Bible (5 volumes)

INFORMATION AND BOOK AVAILABILITY CAN BE FOUND AT:

https://michaelphillipsbooks.com

https://fatheroftheinklings.com

447

Endnotes

1. Saul Alinsky (1909–1972), native of Chicago and graduate of the University of Chicago (in archaeology), who turned his attention to community organization and activism prior to World War II. Though never a direct target of McCarthyism, Alinsky was linked to communism, and was associated with other activist, fringe, and civil rights groups during the tumultuous 1960s. In the late sixties he endorsed the Black Power movement, stating, "We've always called it community power, and if the community is black, it's black power." He wrote two books, bookends to his career as an activist: *Reveille for Radicals* (1946), and *Rules for Radicals: A Pragmatic Primer* (1971), published the year prior to his death.

2. The term "groupthink" was first coined in the 1972 book by I. L. Janis, *Victims of Groupthink: A Psychological Study of Foreign-Policy Decisions and Fiascoes* (New York: Houghton Mifflin, 1972).

3. The term "political correctness" first appeared in Marxist-Leninist vocabulary following the Russian Revolution of 1917 to indicate undeviating loyalty to the policies and principles of the Communist Party—in other words, adhering to "the party line."

4. The Riemann hypothesis is an absurdly complicated theory (and of dubious significance, though mathematicians will certainly disagree) involving the sum of inverted sequences of numbers, the harmonic series, $(1 + +$ etc.), and their sums when the denominator is raised to different powers $(1 + +$ etc.), and when the fractions are combined in different groupings, and when prime numbers form the basis of various denominator sequences, all involving the question whether the ultimate sum of an infinite number of fractions converges or infinitely diverges depending on the power used in the denominator. If I understood it, I still could not explain it. First proposed as a "hypothesis" in 1859, it has never been proven, and many suspect Riemann's theory about the convergence and divergence of the fraction-sum to be unprovable. What is most interesting, however, is that the *most* significant query mankind can raise, the existence of God (probably unprovable) is mocked as a valid "hypothesis" in the scientific community, while mathematicians positively salivate to contemplate the (perhaps equally unprovable) completely *useless* Riemann hypothesis.

5. Stephen Jay Gould, "Dorothy, It's Really Oz," *Time*, August 23, 1999, 59, https://content.time.com/time/subscriber/article/0,33009,991791,00.html.

6. I had written much of this section between Timothy and Jaylene before I became familiar with the work of Christian physicist Dr. Sarah Salviander. It was a pleasant surprise to find our "theories" of Genesis in such close alignment. Obviously my sequence above is more fluid and not meant to be exact, so there are differences with what Salviander proposes. Timothy was not giving a scientific lecture but explaining his understanding of Genesis 1 in broad terms. Getting yet more specific, in her presentation, "The Six Days of Genesis," Dr. Salviander outlines her take on the sequence of events by comparing the Genesis account with the generally recognized view of modern science.

From Dr. Salviander:

Let's compare what Genesis and science say happen on each of the days.

https://image.slidesharecdn.com/sixdayspublic-160616035204/95/the-six-days-of-genesis-123-638.jpg?cb=1509496076

> *Day One: Genesis 1:1–5 The Bible says: God creates the universe; God separates light from dark. Science says: The big bang marks the creation of the universe; light breaks free as neutral atoms form; galaxies start to form.*

https://image.slidesharecdn.com/sixdayspublic-160616035204/95/the-six-days-of-genesis-124-638.jpg?cb=1509496076

> *Day Two: Genesis 1:6–8 The Bible says: The heavenly firmament forms. Science says: The disk of the Milky Way galaxy forms; the Sun, a disk star, forms.*

https://image.slidesharecdn.com/sixdayspublic-160616035204/95/the-six-days-of-genesis-125-638.jpg?cb=1509496076

> *Day Three: Genesis 1:9–13 The Bible says: Oceans and dry land appear; the first life, plants appear; Kabbalah holds that this is only the start of plant-life, which develops further during the following days. Science says: The Earth has cooled and liquid water appears 3.8 billion years ago followed almost immediately by the first forms of life; bacteria and photosynthetic algae.*

https://image.slidesharecdn.com/sixdayspublic-160616035204/95/the-six-days-of-genesis-126-638.jpg?cb=1509496076

> *Day Four: Genesis 1:14–19 The Bible says: The Sun, Moon, and stars become visible in heavens. Science says: Earth's atmosphere becomes transparent when photosynthesis produces an oxygen-rich atmosphere. Once Earth's atmosphere is transparent, the Sun, Moon, and other celestial objects are visible from the surface of the Earth.*

https://image.slidesharecdn.com/sixdayspublic-160616035204/95/the-six-days-of-genesis-127-638.jpg?cb=1509496076

> *Day 4 is often seen as a problem, because Genesis appears to claim that plants were growing before the Sun was made. However, Jewish scholarly tradition holds that the Sun was made on Day 2 with the other stars in the firmament, and provided light to the Earth's surface as soon as the Earth*

formed. In terms of the science, the Sun finally became fully visible from the Earth's surface on Day 4, along with other stars in the sky and the Moon, after the Great Oxidation Event (GOE) caused the Earth's atmosphere to become transparent.

https://image.slidesharecdn.com/sixdayspublic-160616035204/95/the-six-days-of-genesis-128-638.jpg?cb=1509496076

This eliminates the problem of plants growing on Earth before the Sun appears. The Sun is made before plants, but becomes apparent later.

https://image.slidesharecdn.com/sixdayspublic-160616035204/95/the-six-days-of-genesis-129-638.jpg?cb=1509496076

Day Five: Genesis 1:20–23 The Bible says: The first animal life swarms abundantly in waters; followed by reptiles and winged animals. Science says: The first multicellular animals suddenly appear, the waters swarm with animal life having the basic body plans of all future animals, and winged insects appear.

https://image.slidesharecdn.com/sixdayspublic-160616035204/95/the-six-days-of-genesis-130-638.jpg?cb=1509496076

Day Six: Genesis 1:24–31 The Bible says: The appearance of land animals; mammals; and humankind. Science says: A massive extinction destroys 90% of life. The land is repopulated by mammals; hominids appear, followed by humans.

https://image.slidesharecdn.com/sixdayspublic-160616035204/95/the-six-days-of-genesis-131-638.jpg?cb=1509496076

Day 6 is often confusing to readers who assume that "human" and "hominid" are synonymous. However, contrary to popular misconception, the Bible has no problem with the fossil records of early humankind. The ancient biblical commentators accepted the existence of hominids, who were physically identical to Adam and his sons but lacked one all-important feature: the human soul. These hominids possessed the animal spirit (nefesh in Hebrew) but not the human soul (neshama). The great biblical commentator, Maimonides, called these beings "mere animals in human shape and form."

https://image.slidesharecdn.com/sixdayspublic-160616035204/95/the-six-days-of-genesis-132-638.jpg?cb=1509496076

In the original Hebrew language, Genesis 2:7 says ". . . and the adam became to a living soul." Nahmanides argues that the grammatically superfluous "to" is an important clue: God chose a pre-existing hominid and endowed it with a neshama—"communicating spirit" in Hebrew—to make it fully human. This implies that humans are distinguished from the hominid animals by their ability to communicate spiritually with their Creator. In other words, it doesn't matter if human bodies are biologically related to those of cavemen or apes. The part of us that is in the image of God is the spiritual, not the physical.

https://image.slidesharecdn.com/sixdayspublic-160616035204/95/the-six-days-of-genesis-133-638.jpg?cb=1509496076

> *There is no problem with the biblical claim that Adam was the first human. He was. But the Bible also has no problem with pre-Adam hominids who existed many years before Adam.*

https://image.slidesharecdn.com/sixdayspublic-160616035204/95/the-six-days-of-genesis-136-638.jpg?cb=1509496076

> *As powerful as all this is, none of it proves God's existence. It does, however, show two important things. 1. It shows that the claim that science and the Bible are at odds is false. 2. It shows that Genesis is the most tremendous record of the natural history of the universe ever written.*

https://image.slidesharecdn.com/sixdayspublic-160616035204/95/the-six-days-of-genesis-139-638.jpg?cb=1509496076

> *Genesis 1 makes at least 26 scientifically testable statements about the origins of the universe and the emergence of life. All 26 are compatible with modern science and in the correct order. This amazing feat was accomplished 2,500 years before the dawn of modern science.*

https://image.slidesharecdn.com/sixdayspublic-160616035204/95/the-six-days-of-genesis-140-638.jpg?cb=1509496076

> *It has taken many centuries for science to catch up to the wisdom of the Bible. Science is still catching up. We may not currently understand the basis for everything in scripture, but the truth of Genesis should support our faith in the written word of God.*

From: https://www.slideshare.net/SarahSalviander/the-six-days-of-genesis-63120073.

I have also explored many other dating options, as well as the fascinating conundrum of "Adam" and "adam" and their relation (and dating possibilities) to the hominid family tree, in Volume 1 of my *Eyewitness Old Testament*.

7. Lee Strobel, author of *The Case for Christ* (Grand Rapids: Zondervan, 1998).

8. These quotes are out of sequence, though no less apt, with Jaylene's and Stirling's conversation, which came several years before the book. They are taken from Rod Dreher's *Live Not by Lies: A Manual for Christian Dissidents* (New York: Random House, Sentinel, 2021), pp. 40, 57 (in a quote by Sir Roger Scruton), and pp. 58, 14–15.

9. The term "Ally" was first used, to my knowledge, in Harold Bell Wright's novel *The Calling of Dan Matthews,* published in 1909 by Book Supply Company. Pastors throughout America were said to have been incensed by the book, in which Wright, himself a former pastor turned novelist, took the cliquishness of churches to task. Wright resigned from the pastorate after his first book was published in 1902, saying he had to do so to maintain his integrity.